The DISCARDED
Lighthorseman

Marjorie Jones

M PRESS

Jewel Imprint: Sapphire
Medallion Press, Inc.
Printed in USA

Dedication:

*For Keith, my hero, for inspiring not only
the words I write, but the life I live.*

10 9 8 7 6 5 4 3 2 1
First Edition

ACKNOWLEDGEMENTS:

Special appreciation to Australian-born authors Tracy Cooper-Posey and Liz Lapthorne for their tireless efforts describing their beautiful homeland to me,
and for moving the sheep.

Thanks also to those wonderful Australians who helped me get to know the Yowie and the Ironclad Hotel.

I want to send out a giant hug to all of my readers. Your letters and emails keep me going when the screen gets blury. Without you, I wouldn't have the strength to refocus. Thank you so very much!

And finally, thank you to my critique partners who spent so many tireless hours working with me on this project — listening to my ever present, "Crikey!" when something wasn't quite right. You're the best.

Prologue

Blue crouched on the tall column of rock. A fly buzzed near his eye in an annoying reminder that all creatures have their place. He refrained from swatting the insect away and allowed it to finish its inspection before it chose to pester some other creature.

The sun, low in the sky after a long, hard journey from morning, cut a path over rolling grasslands. As far as he could see, the earth was fertile and provided life for those who took it. Wide fields, cut here and there with fences, turned from bright green to a dusky bronze in the twilight. The scattered gum trees, starkly silhouetted in the sunset, stood like black sentries over the land—guarding, watching.

A scraping sound from behind him drew his attention and he turned.

In the distance, beyond the last of the grassy fields,

the desert burned red and auburn in the failing light. Sand shifted in the late summer wind and turned the eastern horizon into a blurry mass of black and gray. It was a full day's walk to the desert from Tower Rock, but a man on a horse could make that distance in only a couple of hours.

A tiny hand appeared over the edge of the precipice. Dale Winters climbed the side of the rock, his chubby legs covered in coarse, beige leggings to protect his white skin from the elements. A shirt the color of sunset protected his arms and shoulders. A cap of the same color covered his blond locks.

The whitefellas burned as red as the earth in the summer heat. It was good that the young boy's parents took such care so he did not suffer.

Satisfied Dale would not fall, Blue turned his attention back to the sun. He closed his eyes and waited for the inevitable questions that would come from the boy.

When the questions failed to materialize immediately, Blue cracked an eyelid. He spied on Dale as the boy tucked his legs beneath his bottom and squatted on the rock a foot or so away. The scent of soap and beef wafted on the evening breeze.

Dale squinted into the bright orange and yellow rays. He looked much like his mother, with bright blue eyes and wavy hair the same golden shade as new wheat. The boy may have inherited the color of his mother's eyes, but the curiosity that sparked in them, as well as the often determined set of his strong jaw, came from his father. Finally settled, he asked, "What are you looking at, Blue?"

"Nothing. At least, nothing out there."

"Why do you sit here like this every night?"

"I don't."

"Yes, you do. I watch you from my window." As if to prove the possibility, the child twisted and pointed toward the large house that sat a short distance from the rocky tower. "You sit here for the longest time. Every night, you do."

"I'm in the Dreaming."

Dale's eyes formed full moons in his unlined, pudgy face. "When you're awake? How do you dream if you're not sleeping?"

"It's not that kind of dreaming. The Dreaming is the place that holds all the answers. Out there. At the beginning of time."

"Like what?"

"Many things. Like why the eagle flies higher than the magpie."

Dale heaved a sigh.

Blue cracked the same eyelid and hid a smile. "You must learn patience, mate. Not all answers are yours to have. They are given when you are ready to listen and understand."

"What are you dreaming about now?"

A heavy weight settled on Blue's shoulders. He carried more than his share. The boy's question needed more than a simple answer. Should he tell Dale the whole truth, now? He was so young. He couldn't possibly understand.

But, then again, why would Blue see the dream before the boy was ready?

Not often did the spirits visit him without purpose. But they were ever cryptic in their messages.

He released a long breath and looked at Dale. Dale stared up at him with trust and love in the deep blue of his eyes. His bottom lip, still bruised and full from the fall he'd taken off his horse the day before, was tucked between his teeth.

Blue shifted his eyes to the pastures along what the whitefellas called the Coongan River. Mangrove trees dotted the shoreline and squat palms grew in majestic groups on the outside edges. Short, stubby trees dotted the open pastures where hundreds of sheep grazed in cloud-like bunches. A family of kangaroos raced over the field where Charles, one of the owners of Castle Winters, often camped rather than stay in the house.

"Look at the 'roos, Blue. Do you see them?" Dale jumped to his knees. "Look at them go!"

The huge, bouncing creatures turned as a unit and headed toward a grove of trees. A clump of sheep screamed and scattered from the intrusion. Short, black legs carried the sheep in one direction, while the kangaroos' powerful hind legs made short work of their travels.

Overhead, a bird of prey called on the dry wind. It was an eagle. A good sign. But deadly.

The kangaroos disappeared into a sparse forest of gnarled gum trees on the edge of the river. From there, they leapt over the shore and splashed through the low waters. Dale watched them, as he watched everything, with eyes older and wiser than they should be. His path would be difficult. Hardship would follow him on his journey to peace. How much of that could the four-year-old boy grasp? How much should wait until he grew into a strong, capable man? How much knowledge was too much?

When it grew obvious that the kangaroos had disappeared for the evening, Dale settled back into his crouch. Small fingers laced together until his tiny knuckles turned white. "Can I go to the dreaming place?"

"No, child. You cannot."

He seemed to think for a moment; his head tilted to one side as if he solved some immense riddle. "It's because I'm a whitefella, huh? Dad says that blackfellas can see the past and the future better'n anyone. Are you seeing the future, now? Or the past?"

A chuckle tickled the back of Blue's throat. Everything was simple to the boy.

Past? Or future?

Blue sobered. He saw neither, really. He saw only death. And life.

"Go find your mother. Ask her when Joel will arrive."

"Who's that?" Dale's face broke into a wide grin. "Is he a friend to play with? Paul lives too far away. I get bored."

"Yes. You can play with Joel. Go ask your mother."

Dale leapt to his feet and scurried over the tower's eastern edge. Once he cleared the edge, Blue returned his gaze to the setting sun. The boy would not find death from the tall, slippery, silt-covered rocks. He would not find it for a very long time, in a different place.

Chapter One

An explosion decapitated a sand dune twenty feet from Dale Winters' position behind the command tent, a few hundred yards south-west of the front line. He ducked and grimaced while he wiped the gritty sweat from his brow. His fingers itched and he ran them over his stubble-covered jaw. In a matter of hours, the battle would end.

One way or the other.

Joel, his younger brother by five years, approached from the east, where he and several of the younger, more exuberant of their number had mounted a rise to watch the battle for *Tel el Saba*.

His brother's horse was lathered in the late afternoon heat and its mouth frothed from lack of water. All of the horses showed the same signs of exhaustion and thirst. Their ribs undulated beneath dull coats of dust-covered, lifeless hair. Their hipbones protruded at stark angles.

They needed water and a few weeks of grazing to rebuild their strength. The noise of the distant battle, mixed with the apprehension of their riders, made the mounts nervous, as well. As if they, too, couldn't wait to enter the fray.

If the Desert Mounted Corps didn't capture Beersheba soon, they would be forced into another retreat. The previous battles had been fought closer to the sea, against the more heavily defended Eastern portions of the Gaza line.

But here on the outer most edges of the world where some modicum of civilization met the wasteland of the great desert, Beersheba had fewer defenses. The main enemy now was the heat and thirst that made their mouths feel like lamb's wool.

Just a few miles away, Beersheba lay in an oasis of victory and life. The only thing that stood between the regiments and water was the Turkish Ottoman Empire's southern boundary and the several hundred Turkish soldiers who guarded it.

"What's the word?" Joel threw himself off his horse and withdrew his canteen. He pressed the rim to his lips and drank. Another mortar round landed less than a hundred yards to their right and they both ducked. The motion came as a reflex. Not really fear. They were out of range of those big guns and safe enough behind General Chauvel's headquarters. But the blasts carried the fine desert sand to them on hot, dry winds. The tiny granules deposited on them, inside them. Even Dale's teeth tasted of silt.

Dale straightened. "We're still held in reserve. But I'd

wager we're put to it soon. We'll lose the sun in another few hours."

Joel screwed up his features as if he'd sucked on a lemon and turned his canteen upside-down. "Crikey, that's terrible."

Empty. Except for a few grains of sand that shifted in the wind as they escaped the metal container.

Dale's canteen had been empty for more than half a day.

"How the bloody hell did sand get in there?" Joel replaced the screw-top on his canteen, shoved it into his saddlebag and sighed. "We need to win those wells, brother. What do you say we ride on in there and take them?"

Dale frowned. His brother, always the adventurer, would do that very thing, given half a bloody chance. And, more than likely, get himself killed in the process. "Settle down. I'm sure we'll have our chance. Sooner or later."

Together, like they had been ever since Joel's birth twenty-one years ago, they made their way across the compound. They passed small groups of soldiers, all waiting in nervous anticipation for their turn to serve. Joel hated the fact their regiment had been held in reserve. He wanted to race into the battle and gain his place in history. A born hero.

But Dale appreciated the fact that the initial units in the fight would need their help. Fresh men, fresh horses. Fresh blood to pay for the water the colonial forces tried desperately to steal from the Turks. The wells of Beersheba had been written about in the Bible. They had been fought over for generations. But Dale didn't care about history. He only cared about this fight. And the fact that neither he, nor his horse, had felt moisture in their mouths for almost ten hours.

"Brother?"

Dale's head snapped up at the solemn tone in Joel's voice. "Yeah?"

"Let me ride up front when we go in."

"Oh, no. You ride in the back. Just like Gallipoli. That was the deal when I agreed to let you sign up for the regiments in the first place."

"C'mon, mate. I'm as good a rider as you. And I may have been underage when we joined up, but I've paid my dues and I'm of age now."

"Age for what? To get yourself killed? Do you have any idea what Charles would do to me if I came home alone? Sorry, kid. Not going to happen."

"Those bloody Turks can't hit the side of a barn with those guns. They aim like women."

"I've met a few women with pretty good aim." Dale glared at his little brother with his hands firmly placed on his hips. Sweat trickled down his back and his shirt stuck to his waist just above his belt.

Damn, it was hot. The last thing he needed was his brother whining like a schoolgirl.

Another blast punctuated his thoughts. "No, Joel. You stay with your unit."

"Attention!" a deep, harried voice boomed from the

command tent.

Dale turned toward the voice and drew his exhausted frame to attention. All around him, his fellows fell into hasty lines. His back ached, but he gritted the sand between his teeth and stared at the tent as it flapped in the brisk, dry wind.

General Grant, a man of advanced years with hard-won experience evident in his light eyes, appeared from within. War and the same hardships that plagued his men had drawn harsh lines in his sunken cheeks, but a spirit resided in the Regimental Commander that offered hope and pride to his men. At least, it offered them to Dale.

The old man's narrow, fastidious glare raked over his men, settled on Dale for more than a heartbeat and then continued down the line. He stepped forward, set his booted feet shoulder width apart and rested his fists on his narrow hips. "We're received our orders. It's up to us, men. It's up to you. The Fourth is to take the bloody town! Mount up!" The General executed a severe left face and disappeared around the tent.

For what seemed like a moment frozen in time, only the wind rushed through Dale's mind. A long, empty stretch of foreboding and fear filled the air until Joel released a jubilant cry and leapt back on his horse.

Dale shook his head and grumbled. "You live for this, don't you?"

"Of course I do. What else matters?"

"Wait here."

Joel offered a lazy salute. The look in his eyes spoke of defiance and trickery. Like the time he'd slipped a sand monitor in Dale's bed. Joel had been ten, and lucky to see eleven, but this wasn't a practical joke. This was a matter of life and death. "I mean it, Joel. You wait for me."

"Aye."

Dale hesitated as long as he could, then raced to the paddock, leapt on his horse and followed several of his mates out of the gate. When he returned to where he'd left Joel, his brother was gone.

Bloody hell.

Paul Campbell trotted his horse next to Dale's and frowned. "I just saw that bleedin' brother of yours taking up a position in the head of the charge."

"Damn that kid. Do we have time to get him out of there?"

Paul shook his head. "I don't think so. But we have time to catch up and ride alongside. If we hurry."

Dale kicked his mount into as fast a trot as he dared. His fellow lighthorsemen, in various stages of mounting, rushed to take up their places. The lines formed several hundred yards to the west. Confusion reigned over the soldiers. The horses took their emotional cues from their riders and stomped the dry earth with stiff, anxious strokes. Billows of dust obscured most of the line by the time Dale and Paul arrived. Any chance they had to find Joel in the melee vanished in the thick, opaque air.

With the first squadron already complete, Dale and

Paul had to find positions in the second wave of the attack. Dale ground his teeth over a silent curse.

If Joel survived, Dale would see to it he never pulled another stunt like that again. Always the dare-devil, Joel let his desire for glory cloud his judgment. His common sense. Of all the men in the line, Joel was either the bravest, the most insane, or the biggest idiot.

A rider shot past Dale and raised another thick cloud of damnable desert dust in his wake. "Pull your bayonets, men. Hold them high."

"What the devil for?" Paul placed his reins between his teeth and released his bayonet from its position on his rifle. Dale did the same as he nodded to the row of horsemen that stretched as far as he could see in either direction. What sunlight managed to cut through the dust reflected off dozens of bayonets. "We're to look like a true cavalry. We might be infantry, mate, but the Turks don't know that, now do they?"

"No, I suppose they don't."

Dale gripped his reins in one gloved hand and tucked his bayonet under his arm. Then he adjusted his haversacks and gained a firm seat in his light infantry saddle. He gripped the bayonet around the base and turned it in the sunlight. "You know, they could've just issued us swords to begin with and saved the bloody charade."

Paul grinned. "No, mate. The Brits carry swords because they aren't near so fearsome as we are. We don't need 'em."

"You sound like Joel." Dale shook his head. "Fearsome only gets you so far, Paul. Don't think for one moment that we're anywhere but in harm's way."

Paul sobered and turned his gaze toward the expanse of sand and abandoned fields that separated them from their target.

The plan was hasty. A full-scale cavalry charge with no cavalry in sight. Just a bunch of lighthorse regiment soldiers, accustomed to fighting on the ground, armed with .303 Lee Enfield rifles and no swords.

The back of his neck burned in the dry heat of the *San-ai*. Beersheba lay to the north-northwest, just to the right of a large, red sun that wriggled in the heat. No more than three miles or so distant, the Turks manned their trenches. Three miles at full charge. Outgunned. Out numbered. A suicide mission if he'd ever heard of one.

And Joel in the front of a doomed column.

"It seems as though you'll get your wish, little brother," Dale whispered, the sound lost in the stamping of restless horses. A hush fell over the line as everyone seemed to contemplate the same thing as Dale.

A swift, complete victory. Or death.

"Full charge!" The cry came on the wind, as if God Himself ordered the Lighthorse Regiments to seize the day.

Dale dug his spurs into his horse's ribs. Dust blew from every direction and enveloped the Fourth Light Horse Regiment in a jaundiced blanket of silt. In the space of a few seconds, the squadrons moved from a trot to a gallop.

The line spread wide, with a full five yards between each man the closer it came to the Turks' position. Large guns thundered in the distance, but the Australian horse artillery soon destroyed the enemy positions.

Everything around him faded behind the shroud of heavy dust, except the noise. Hooves thumped the earth like heavy sacks of wool thrown into the belly of a ship. Horses screamed as they fell. Men screamed as they died.

Joel. Where did his brother fall in the midst of it all? A blast to his right threw Dale's balance off for the barest of seconds. Still, it was enough to bring his attention to the issue at hand. Survival.

Paul still rode beside him, his distinctive profile beneath his felt slouch hat just visible through the dust.

Faster across three miles of the most barren, unfortunate land to ever grace the pages of the Bible, the Fourth rode toward the southern tip of the Turkish Ottoman Empire.

But more than that, they rode toward water. The only water within several days' ride. The life-giving water that would rejuvenate the Colonial forces and bloody well win the war in the Middle East.

After what seemed like hours, the enemy's line came into view. Hidden behind bulwarks and in trenches, the Turkish army stared wide-eyed into the faces of the Australian troops whose horses had crossed a blazing ocean of sand in what should have been an impossible task.

"Why aren't they shooting?" Paul glanced at Dale.

"They are. They bloody-well forgot to adjust their

sites." Which meant if Joel had survived the first few hundred feet of the charge, he would likely survive the attack! Dale released a victorious cry and pushed his mount into the air over a deep trench. On the other side, he leapt from the saddle and faced his opponent—a tall, barrel-chested Turk with long black mustaches that curled at the ends. Dale dropped his bayonet and leveled his rifle at the man's impressive stomach. "Don't move, mate. I don't really want to kill you, but I will if you choose it."

"Moony. You take."

Dale raised a brow. "Say again?"

The Turkish soldier reached into his loose-fitting, bright red strides and withdrew several notes and a few coins that appeared to be silver. He shoved them at Dale and smiled. "You no kill me."

Dale rolled his eyes. "And what the hell am I supposed to do with that, mate? Do you see any boozers around here? Put your money away."

When the man's forced smile didn't change, Dale shoved his hands away and forced him to his knees. Three of his comrades fell to the ground behind him and covered their heads.

Paul marched to Dale's side with two prisoners of his own. "I can't believe that actually worked. Can you? The Lighthorse Brigade just won the day." He shook his head. "Who would've thought?"

Dale laughed the kind of laugh that could only come from near exhaustion, fear, and adrenaline. "Joel, for one.

He's been waiting for this since we signed up and shipped out of Melbourne."

"Now that, I can believe."

Dale scanned the mass of confused prisoners and soldiers, some of whom still sat on their mounts while others guarded prisoners or tended to the wounded. He turned, glanced over the line to his other side then leveled a glare at Paul. "Have you seen him?"

Paul frowned and followed the direction Dale had searched. "No, mate."

"Take over here, will you?" Dale forced his right boot into the thin metal stirrup and threw his left leg over his heavily laden saddle. His horse skirted four exhausted soldiers and stamped the desert floor. Dale ran his hand over the animal's damp neck to settle him.

"Too right. But if you get to the wells before I do, don't bloody drink all the water."

Three hours later, the sun settled on the horizon. The hills around Beersheba reflected the oppressive heat and the failing light in a mystical blending of night and day. His throat burned and his tongue seemed several sizes too large. At least the sun would soon set and the intolerable heat and glare would go with it.

But then, he'd be unable to search for Joel in the dark. He quickened his pace.

The infantry had rounded up the last pockets of resistance and soldiers had formed small groups around smaller cook fires. In just a few hours, a crowded city had sprung to life amid rocky outcroppings, the bombed remains of ancient mud dwellings and abandoned Bedouin fields. The horses had been watered and soldiers drank their fill. Several members of the British Fifth Mounted Cavalry scooted in front of Dale's horse, their hair soaked and their uniforms clinging to their torsos after a visit to the wells. The Desert Mounted Corps celebrated its miraculous victory.

Except for Dale. Parched and heavily ridden with guilt, he continued his search. He'd visited the new command center, the hastily erected mess, the corrals and the aide stations. By the time he'd made a full circle of the new city, the preliminary medical personnel had erected their makeshift hospital. *Please, don't let him be in there.* With a knot in his stomach the size of Western Australia, he pointed his horse in the direction of the oversized tent, marked with a large red cross on the doors, sides, and roof. *Let him be alive.*

"Winters!" Bruno Saunders, a wide-shouldered Aussie with arms like an ape and the demeanor of a bull elephant, motioned to him from behind a first aid station.

"Aye, Lieutenant."

"Are you looking for Joel?"

Dale nodded and swallowed. Hard. "Have you seen him?"

"He's inside. Rather torn up. He took a nasty fall on the trench defenses, but still managed to come up with three prisoners. The lucky bloke. I think he'll make it."

Dale closed his eyes, gritted his teeth, and slid from his saddle. "Can I see him?"

"Aye. But the docs are pressed for space, so don't stay long."

Dale unwound his tethering spike from its position on the front of his saddle, shoved the point into the earth, and dropped his reins. Then he pushed the tent flap aside and stepped into what could only be the seventh ring of hell. Blood soaked the sand beneath his dusty boots and formed macabre mud. Someone had stacked several human limbs against the canvas wall like so much firewood. Screams echoed off the ceiling and harried field surgeons cursed over the din.

A surgeon wearing a bloody apron glared at him over what could only be his patient's intestines. "What do you want?"

Dale pulled off his hat and clutched it in both hands. "My brother. Winters."

"Like I know anyone by name." The medic all but rolled his eyes. "What company?"

"The Fourth."

The doctor's expression changed from annoyance to wide-eyed amazement in the course of a heartbeat. His eyes seemed to pinpoint Dale's rectangular regimental colour patch, light blue over dark separated on the diagonal, that identified him as a member of the Fourth Light Horse Regiment. Then he smiled. "Bloody amazing charge, mate. Well done. We've put all the charge casualties at the other end. The doors are bigger there, so it's a bit cooler. So far, only a dozen or so have come in."

"Thanks."

Dale weaved his way through the cots and bodies until he found George O'Malley. A blood-soaked bandage covered half of his face. His one visible eye twitched in restless sleep and he looked as if he barely breathed. No sense waking him. He'd earned his rest. Instead, Dale scanned the men in the nearby cots until his gaze fell on the one face he wanted to see. Instant relief, like torrents of water over a fall, filled his chest.

Joel lay on his back in the seventh bedstead along the far wall. Dale rushed to him and dropped to his knees. His brother opened his eyes and smiled. "About time you got here."

Dale laughed. "Were you worried about me?"

"Worried? No, of course not. I was hoping you'd find some water for me. I'm more than parched now, mate."

"I'll just bet you are." Dale glanced at his fingers where they gripped the rim of his hat. "What were you thinking? Riding in at the head of the charge? You should have been in the third squadron. We agreed."

Joel's eyes misted. He sniffed and then offered a wide smile. "It just felt right, Dale. Like I was supposed to be there. The blood thumping in my head. The hot wind in my face." He glanced down at the bandage that covered his left thigh. "It's only a scratch."

"It's a sight more than a scratch by the looks of it.

You're bloody lucky you didn't lose your leg. Or worse."

Joel's eyes grew dark in the dim light of dusk. "Stop treating me like a child. You don't have to protect me all the time."

A reply hovered on the edge of Dale's tongue. Of course he had to protect him. He'd been protecting Joel his whole life. If it weren't for Dale, Joel would have found his own demise any number of times.

But he spoke none of the defenses to his brother. Joel was right.

In the beginning, his task had proven difficult. Especially after their parents died in a flash flood that had almost taken Charles Castle away from him as well. But he'd been watching over Joel for so long, it now came as naturally as each breath. Even after Charles had been named their legal guardian by the territorial courts, Dale had taken it upon himself to make sure Joel stayed safe.

Maybe it was time to let go. Joel had proven his bravery, although Dale still likened it to idiocy, by placing himself at the front of the charge. Wasn't that worthy of manhood? Joel wasn't a boy anymore. He was twenty-two years old and a soldier in the lighthorse regiments. Three long, bloody years in the ANZACSs had done what Dale could never have done.

Those years had turned Joel into a man.

"I suppose you're right. But don't go thinking I won't be watching out for you. I made a promise to Mum and I intend to keep it."

"You made that promise when you were five."

Dale's voice seemed trapped in his throat. "A promise is a promise, mate."

"And there is nothing wrong with dying for something you believe in."

Dale swallowed over the lump that suddenly appeared in the back of his throat. Or maybe it had been there for so long he simply didn't notice it much anymore.

"I don't know, Joel. I rather like the idea of living to a ripe old age, marrying a good woman, and raising the best bloody sheep in Australia."

Joel scoffed. "Like that Rachel Macomber. That she-devil has her claws in you but good."

The somber mood lifted enough for Dale to force a smile. "That one? Not on your life. I mean, she's a fine girl, don't get me wrong, but she's not the one for me."

"Right then. Who is?"

"I haven't the foggiest. But I'll know her when I see her, I'll warrant."

"Not me. I'm staying in the service. I'm going to see the world. Conquer it. Then maybe I'll share it with some willing wench."

Paul appeared beside the short cot and knelt at Dale's side. "Good luck finding one who can stand to look at your sorry face for more than a day."

Joel smiled. "It's not my face that keeps them coming back."

"Now what the blazes have you gone and done to

yourself, mate?"

Joel made a mocking wince. "I had a frightening vision of that creature you bedded just after the Gallipoli campaign and lost my seat. If ever I'd need a reason to race headlong toward suicide again, she would be the one."

"Ah, so you say now, but I seem to recall you grumbled another tune when you slept alone that same night."

Joel grasped Dale's hand and winced. Dale hid a groan and swung his gaze over his brother's legs, bent at opposite angles. Blood seeped through the bandage on Joel's thigh.

From somewhere behind him, a medic appeared and lifted the thick gauze padding. Dale's stomach knotted at the raw, torn flesh of a gaping wound. Paul's breath sucked in with an audible gasp. From just above the knee to his groin, Joel's leg looked like he'd been chewed by one of the giant crocs that lived in the Coongan, back home. The medic swapped the old bandage for a new one, and then, without a word, moved to the next bedstead.

Dale forced a steady expression and fisted his hands to keep them from trembling. "Have they managed anything for the pain, little brother?"

"Aye. A bit. But it's rationed until the main medical units can get here. I'll be all right."

"Sure, you will. No worries." Dale's throat closed over the words. He'd seen men blown apart by the dozens, even hundreds, since the start of the war. He'd watched his comrades slaughtered in Romani, Magdhaba, Rafah, then later in the First and Second Battles of Gaza. Through three different regimental assignments, he'd managed to keep Joel safe—managed to keep them together so he could watch over him. Even when their last division had been divided earlier in the year and the new Fourth Light Horse Brigade had been formed in Cairo, he'd used his friendships with higher ranking officers to make sure he and his brother served together.

In all of that time, he'd learned a few things about battle wounds. And Joel's didn't look good.

"I'll be right as rain in a few weeks and just try to keep me out of it, mate. Can't wait to climb back on my horse and give those bastards another taste of the Fourth."

Dale tried to look at his brother as if he believed everything he'd just said.

No, brother. You'll never ride again.

The truth stung the back of Dale's throat. What would happen to Joel when he shipped home? Riding meant everything in the bush. If Joel couldn't ride, he couldn't work. If a man couldn't work, he withered away until he died. And what about Sally, Joel's buckskin mare? Joel loved that horse as much as Dale loved Jezebel, the best damn Whaler in all of Western Australia. How could Joel return to their home and know that he could never feel the wind on his cheeks or the powerful muscles of a mount between his thighs? He'd never jump another wash or climb another rocky slope searching for strays.

Their entire lives had been spent on horseback. That's why Dale had joined the Light Horse Regiments right after he'd graduated from the King's Academy. That's why Joel had joined as well.

Dale cursed himself now. War had broken out only a few months later and before he knew what happened, they'd been sent to Egypt to train in the heat and God-forsaken middle eastern desert.

And Joel had paid the ultimate price for Dale's stupidity. Dale's lack of judgment had cost Joel everything. His livelihood. And his ability to do something as simple as ride a horse or make love to a woman. He didn't know which one of those things Joel would miss more, but he suspected he'd miss his horse most.

The thought drove a wedge through Dale's heart. Joel and Dale had been closer to their mounts than any sheila. Women took more work. Women demanded more attention. But their horses had always been loyal and taken care of Dale and Joel as much as the brothers had taken care of them.

But not anymore. For Joel, those days were over. He'd go back to Western Australia, all right. He'd go back to the sheep station, to their sprawling home beneath Tower Rock. He'd go home a cripple.

"How about that water?" Joel's voice cracked as if he'd been thinking the same things that plagued Dale's weary, pain-filled conscience.

Dale nodded.

He'd promised his mother, on the day his brother had been born, he'd watch over Joel. He'd promised to never let anything happen to him. His heart seized in his chest. He couldn't swallow. "I'll be back in a few minutes. I'll storm the wells myself if I have to, but you'll have that drink in a blink." He forced a smile and gained his feet.

Joel's hand trembled and grasped Dale's wrist. "I love you, Dale."

"I love you, too, you rotten brat. Now let go so I can find a canteen to steal."

Dale exited the tent through the extra-wide portal. Paul spoke to Joel for another moment, then appeared next to Dale where he stood right outside the tent-flap. Unable to breathe.

Did Joel even realize that he'd likely as not never walk again? Did he understand that he'd never feel a horse, or a woman, between his legs? A chill rose on Dale's arms and the sting of tears burned his eyes. His brother. *Crippled.*

"Bad luck, mate." Paul clicked his teeth, clapped Dale on the back and urged him toward the center of the new headquarters in Beersheba.

"Yeah."

"But look at it this way. That there is a discharge if I've ever seen one. Little brother is headed home to a nice, safe sheep station in Western Australia where your friend Charles can take care of him proper-like."

"I should have stopped him."

"How? Can you tell me that much? I mean, if you think — Get down!" Paul pulled Dale to the ground behind a boulder a few yards from the tent. Confusion clouded his mind and his vision. A roar brought his attention to the sky. A German bomber banked and turned overhead, its wings a black outline against an orange sky. Dale's gaze traced behind the plane until he found a black oblong cylinder in horrific silhouette on the wavering, heat-twisted wind.

It seemed to hover, floating on the elements. Downward. Like a leaf, it balanced in the air as if it weighed nothing at all. Dale's mouth opened to scream. He leapt from behind the rock, but Paul pulled him down. "No!"

An explosion forced him back.

Fire.

Desiccating heat, enough to make even the great *Sanai* jealous, enveloped him with gnashing teeth and searing claws. Shrapnel flew in all directions, red hot and smoldering. A jagged piece caught him in the shoulder and propelled him to the ground several feet back.

He pushed himself to his feet and stumbled forward.

A giant hole, dotted with the splintered remains of equipment, cots, and men, gaped in front of him where the medical tent had been.

Chapter Two

Quiet, mysterious strains of music filled the *casbah*. Dale pulled on a handle of warm beer and wiped his mouth on his sleeve. Late afternoon sun poured though dusty windows that faced a busy market street. Behind him, the door stood open. Somewhere, two men argued and their hoarse, guttural voices rambled and squeaked in an unique Arabic rhythm. A motor car pulled in front of the window, its shining black paint screaming through the dingy glass.

An Egyptian woman, much older than himself, approached the table. Transparent scarves in an array of bright jewel-tones covered the lower half of her face, most of her hair and very little else. Wide hips gyrated back and forth in time to the orb and flute-produced song. Tiny cymbals on her fingers clapped like fire-crackers.

One of the musicians started to sing in a high-pitched, nasal voice that seemed to come from another century. That's what he loved about Cairo. Nothing changed. For centuries, this part of the world had remained the same.

Mysterious. Timeless.

Dale stared at the woman's navel, decorated with a ruby and marked with a sunburst tattoo. He made the image out clearly, despite her limber movements.

Proof he was far from drunk enough.

He pulled on his beer again, emptied the mug and slammed it on the table. The other patrons, an elderly Arab man and a group of young boys, stared at him. "Another."

The proprietor, Gahiji, circled the bar with a large clay pitcher in both hands. His long tunic flapped around his bare ankles as he made his way over the dirt floor on open-toed sandals. Gahiji filled Dale's mug and then scurried behind the bar.

The woman's fingers continued to work the cymbals. Her hips swung in a seductive pattern only a few inches from his face. He had to give her credit. She was determined. But even if Dale had been interested in what she offered, he no longer possessed the funds.

He would sleep alone tonight, when the alcohol seeped into his blood enough to make him forget. When the world ceased to turn and the pain stopped.

For a short while.

He emptied his mug in a single long, slow draft. This time, Gahiji appeared at his side and filled Dale's mug on his own.

"Mr. Winters. When you go back home?"

Dale ignored him. For months the thin reed of a man had been trying to make Dale sober up and return to Australia. But he had nothing to go home to. Joel was dead, blown to smithereens by a goddamned German bomb. Within a few weeks of that fateful October day, the ANZACS had seen fit to discharge Dale because of the wound to his shoulder. A few pieces of sizzling shrapnel to his right shoulder and the Australian government had turned him to the wolves.

The dancer's hips picked up speed. The music around him grew to a boisterous, steady cadence that made him think of all things improper. She'd removed the tiny disks from her fingers and now those same long, slender extremities moved over her costume's dangerously low waist line. Her belly rocked and swayed, her hips undulated and teased in an imitation of what she offered. Dale narrowed his gaze on her full breasts, concealed behind equally sheer fabrics in shades of ruby, amethyst, and gold. Then he slid his eyes to the long column of her neck, the strong, distinctive line of her jaw, both visible through her flimsy veil, and her heavily made up eyes. Black lines surrounded her almost-black orbs, adding an exotic, enticing allure to her otherwise plain features. A headband made from golden disks and imitation jewels crossed her forehead. She rested her hot, inviting gaze on him and crept closer on bare feet. If he bent his head forward even an inch he could taste the salt of her flesh.

Dale smiled through a drink-induced haze. "Go away."

At once, the prostitute's features fell into an irritated frown. She cursed him in Egyptian, made a rather unladylike gesture with one hand and stomped toward the bar.

Dale chuckled and finished his beer.

"Crikey, it's worse than I bloody thought."

Dale closed his eyes and leaned back in the rickety chair. The other chair at the small, round table scraped against the earth. When Dale opened his eyes, Paul had settled into it. He tapped twice on the table.

One tense moment later, Gahiji placed a mug of beer in front of Paul's elbows, resting on the edge of the table. Paul wasn't wearing his uniform. Surprising, considering the ANZACS hadn't given Paul the boot. Just him.

Instead, Paul sported a cream blazer over a beige shirt, opened at the neck, but decorated with mother-of-pearl button covers down the front. Dale leaned back in his chair and peered under the table. The crease in Paul's strides had been pressed by a cutlass-maker and threatened to slice anyone who deigned to touch it. Brown leather loafers tapped an anxious cadence on the dusty floor. Dale glanced back to his friend. "Aren't you just pretty?"

"You're a hard bloke to find, mate."

"That's because I didn't want to be found." Dale downed the last draft of his beer, set the empty mug on the table and rose. "Now, if you'll excuse me, I'll just get lost again."

"Where are you going?"

Dale glared into concerned blue eyes. They stared back at him from a clean-shaven face beneath short, neat hair that screamed military service. A reason for living.

Pride in himself and in Australia.

A curse formed on his lips, but he bit it back. He couldn't fault Paul for all of those things. "What does it matter?"

"It matters plenty."

Dale scoffed, leaned too far to the left, then overcorrected to the right and fell back into his chair. He laughed and pushed back the sting of his tears with his palms. "Why did you find me? How did you . . . Nevermind." He waved a hand over his empty mug. "I don't bloody care. Just leave. Forget you found me and let me be."

"You can't hide in Cairo forever. A bunch of us are shipping home next week. General Grant says your ticket home is still good and if I could find you, I could bring you with me. Now, I'm not leaving here without you."

"Rack off, mate. I'm fine where I am. I don't need you, I don't need the infantry and I don't need Joel." The lie tasted like lizard dung and he all but choked on it.

Paul growled and rubbed his hands over his face. "You don't mean that. You just need a week's worth of coffee and a cold bath. C'mon. We'll have you right as rain by morning."

"I don't need you."

"I know. I heard you. Now get off your arse and come back to my room. The boat sails on Thursday."

"What day is it?"

"Monday."

"Is it really?" Dale laughed. He hadn't known the day of the week in more months than he could recall. "Monday?"

"Aye. Up we go." Paul heaved Dale to his feet and

pointed him toward the door. Orange light tinted the sandstone floors and walls, casting eerie shadows over the dingy plaster and mosaic tiles. Another sunset.

Dale stumbled when he passed through the door. Even the dim twilight sent razors through his eyes and he squinted. Paul's hands steadied him and he allowed his friend to lead him to the black motor car. The convertible gleamed like a gem in the dusty street, boxy and proud on its spoked, rubber wheels. "Where did you get this? Did you lose your horse?"

"It belongs to a friend of my father's. We'll be staying with him for the next few days."

"A friend?"

"Aye. A sheik."

"You don't say?"

Paul opened the left side door and shoved Dale onto a hard bench seat. Then he circled the front of the machine, turned a crank several times, and the engine roared to life.

If only his heart could be started in such a fashion. Dale closed his eyes. He was a fool.

He hadn't had a heart for months.

⚔ 🐎 ⚔

The next morning, Dale woke in a strange room. He glanced to either side of a wide bed covered in silk and found it empty. His head pounded a cadence to wake the dead and his throat itched. He tried to sit up, succeeded on his fourth attempt, and swung his legs over the edge. He still wore his uniform pants and loose cashmere jersey, the only pieces of clothing he'd owned since the day he'd been booted out of the service, spent a king's ransom on any booze he could find, and suffered the painful humiliation of being robbed, beaten, and left for dead in a Cairo alley. If Gahiji hadn't found him, he shuddered to think what may have happened to him next.

Crikey, he needed a drink. Wherever he was, there had to be a bottle of something stronger than water in the room. Somewhere. He stood on shaky knees and headed for a cabinet beside the wide, sparkling windows.

The view offered a glimpse of a courtyard fit for a king and a gilded fountain that glistened in yellow and gold sunlight.

Paul crossed the tiled floor two stories below in his quick, familiar stride then disappeared beneath the window. A few seconds later, a knock sounded on the door.

Dale winced as the heavy rap split his head into several jagged pieces. "Rack off, mate."

The door opened and Paul sauntered into the room as if he owned it. For all Dale knew, Paul did own the huge mansion. He hadn't seen his friend in nearly a year.

"And a fine g'day to you, too."

Dale sneered.

"You'll find new clothes in the wardrobe, over there, and something to shave that fur off your face, over there, beside the wash basin. I've taken the liberty of finding a suitable barber for you, as well. He'll be here within the hour."

Dale growled.

"The ship leaves for Melbourne day after tomorrow. I expect you'll be clean enough by then—if we soak you in a tub for a few hours. Then we'll board a steamer to Port Hedland. Should be home in a few weeks."

"Why are you doing this?"

"Because you're my mate. And what kind of friend would I be if I allowed you to wallow in some filthy *casbah* when you have a perfectly good home waiting for you? You've had your year of mourning. It's time to start living again."

"What do you know of mourning?" Dale fisted his hands and turned toward the window. He may have little pride left, but he had enough. His eyes stung. He ran both hands through his long, unkempt hair and blinked away the pain.

"I lost him, too, you know."

"Aye." Dale's hands dropped to his sides.

"Only, I lost you as well." Paul raised an eyebrow. "I wrote to you, you know. And imagine my surprise when Charles wrote me back. That's how I knew you hadn't gone home. And when I traced you to Cairo, it took me another month to find you."

"Why? Why did you even look for me?"

"Oh, I don't know. Maybe it has something to do with the fact we grew up together and I've often thought of you like my brother. Or maybe I couldn't stand the thought of facing my mother with the news I'd left you behind in the wilds of Egypt. Or maybe, just maybe, because you'd do the same thing for me."

Dale scoffed. "You don't know anything."

"You're a drunk."

"I stand corrected. You do know something."

"Sadly, I know something else, as well. Charles is dead."

He spun to face Paul and searched his eyes for the lie. He couldn't find it. Not Charles, too.

"My father wrote to me two months ago. I'm afraid Charles contracted pneumonia this past winter and never recovered. He died in mid-July."

"What about the station?"

"I suppose that's the question, isn't it?" Paul leaned his backside against the bureau and crossed his arms. "His niece came from America when he first got sick a few months ago. She took over the place when he died. He left her his half, apparently. But what could she possibly know about running a station?"

"Niece? What niece?"

"Emily Castle. An American."

"Oh, yeah. I remember Charles saying something about her. Long time ago." He shrugged. "What do I care? If she wants the place, she can have it."

"Damnit, Dale!" Paul's face turned crimson. His friend crossed the floor in three long strides and gripped Dale's shoulders in his rough hands. "You have to care."

Dale shoved Paul's hands away. "About what? What's

left? You said it yourself. Charles is dead. Everybody's dead."

"You're not."

Paul couldn't have been more wrong if he'd said that the sky was purple and the sea bright red. Dale had been dead for months. He'd died in a field of *San-ai* sand when he failed to protect his brother; when he'd broken a simple promise to watch over him.

He'd made a vow that day. A vow he would keep in recompense for the vow he hadn't been able to. Dale couldn't go back to Australia. If Joel couldn't work the station, then neither could Dale. How could he ever do those same things they'd shared? Long rides in the bush? Roughing it in the red canyons? Setting their horses free in the range and swimming in the billibong? He couldn't do any of those things. Not anymore. He'd be better off never leaving Egypt.

Because he'd promised Joel that he'd never sit a horse again for as long as he lived.

🐎

Emily Castle had faced herds of crazed horses and droves of drunken men in her twenty-four years. She'd faced her own father on a drunken rampage and her mother's silly tantrums. Nothing had ever frightened her so much as this, however.

"Be a good boy and go play somewhere else." She bit the inside of her cheek when the tall, furry, and apparently angry animal just stared at her with deep, black eyes.

"Please, go away!"

Still nothing.

Oh, why did she even come to this forsaken place half way around the world from where she belonged? What had possessed her to think she could operate a sheep ranch . . . no, a sheep station . . . in the middle of Western Australia by herself? It would serve her right to die at the hands of a rogue kangaroo. It really would.

She shifted the bucket of grain from one hand to the other.

The grain. Maybe the kangaroo just wanted the grain? Did kangaroos eat grain? She cursed under her breath and lifted a handful of the golden kernels. Then she tossed them to the left, away from the direction she needed to go. The beast didn't even move. Not one flinch. He just glared at her as if she were . . .

Dinner.

Emily gulped. The giant rat was going to eat her.

"She is just looking at you, Miss Emily. That's all."

Emily's heart leapt into her throat at the unexpected voice. She spared a glance away from the vicious beast and found Blue walking toward her from the far side of the house. "Thank God you've come, Blue. Please make this . . . this . . . thing move so I can get out of here."

"I can only ask her."

Blue strolled across the dusty expanse of courtyard between the landscaped garden and the small corner where

Emily trembled with her back against the rough, plank wall. Trapped by a giant gray monster.

When he finally arrived, not as if he'd been in a hurry, either, he raised his arms and shooed the kangaroo toward the gap in the fence. It hesitated, bobbed its muscled torso twice, then finally bolted away.

So, this is what it feels like to forget to breathe. A long, relieved sigh found its way out of her lungs and into the hot morning air. "Thank you. I don't know what I would have done if you hadn't come along when you did." She wiped the moisture from her forehead with her shirtsleeve.

"No worries, Miss Emily. You would have been fine." Blue smiled and his bright white teeth made a remarkable contrast to his dark skin.

She still hadn't grown used to Blue, if she were to be completely honest. With black eyes, often misty, he seemed ancient; knowledgeable in a way that she'd never seen before. Long hair, not as coarse as she would have thought, fell to his shoulders in thick strands. He appeared to be somewhere between thirty and a hundred and thirty, with strong limbs but a slow walk that belied that strength. When he'd disappeared last week, she'd thought he'd be gone for months, but he came back. Like he always did. Just in the nick of time, too.

This time, he looked like he'd fallen into a mud puddle. Yellow mud caked his naked chest, shoulders, cheeks and hair. The whites of his eyes were shot through with red bolts of lightning, like he hadn't slept the entire week he'd been away.

Something about him struck her as wise. Powerful.

"So, where have you been?" Emily moved toward the barn to give Apache his daily portion of grain. She'd brought enough for Jezebel and Sally as well. Now that the weather turned warm, she needed to exercise all three of the horses more often. The rest of the stock, twenty burly Australian Stock Horses, or Whalers, grazed in the pasture, waiting for their herdsmen to claim them for the day's work.

Blue fell into step beside her. "Just a little walkabout."

"Well, I wish you'd tell me before you do that. I was half crazy with worry."

"There is no need."

"I'm sure that's true, but just the same . . ."

"Of course, Miss Emily."

"Oh, I'm sorry, Blue. It's not my place to keep track of your every move, is it? And you certainly don't have to answer to me. Though, I suppose I should be used to it by now. But I can't help it. I tend to worry about people. If you'll recall, that's what brought me here to begin with."

"Your uncle was a good man."

"Yes. I suppose he was. I only knew him through the letters I showed you. Other than the time right before he passed away. I wish I could have spent more time with him." Charles Castle had been her only family besides her mother and father. She'd known him her entire life through the long, descriptive letters they'd exchanged over the years. He'd told her all about Australia and the sheep ranch he'd started with his life-long friend, Andrew Winters. And about how they'd come into a large sum of money when they'd struck gold several years before Andrew had met and married his wife, Gayla. Emily's father had hated those letters and often cursed his brother for leaving America to find his way in this massive foreign land. He'd been equally upset with Emily when she'd made the decision to come here herself.

"And did you learn much about Dale Winters from your uncle's letters?" Blue canted his head and grinned.

A wide smile almost made her face hurt. "Yes. And Joel as well."

"He is coming home."

"Someday soon, I hope. I don't want to burden him with Uncle Charles's passing, but I can't keep it from them forever."

"He already knows."

"He does? But . . ."

"This place is full of danger and death, Miss Emily. The people here watch out for each other. They have to. The neighbors told Dale about your uncle."

Emily had been waiting for Dale to come home since before her uncle died three months ago. Of course, she'd wanted to meet the fabled hero of her dreams since long before then. A twinge of guilt slid over her spine; Dale had been as deliberate a reason for her journey to Australia as her uncle's illness.

Because of those magnificent letters. They'd spoken of long summer nights in the bush and a boy, only a year or two older than herself, who'd ridden like the wind, feared nothing, and even played with dragons. By the time Emily had reached the age when boys became something coveted instead of something shunned, she'd fallen in love with Dale Winters at least a hundred times.

Emily reached for the latch on the barn door, paused, and turned to face Blue.

The back door of the main house slammed and Ruth, Emily's companion and friend, rushed down the three wooden steps, her skirt lifted in one hand and a piece of folded paper in the other. "Miss Emily! Miss Emily!"

Ruth was a large girl, two years younger than Emily, with shimmering blue eyes and cheeks that always seemed rosy, no matter her mood or the weather. Today was no different. Although the impressive smile she wore added to her cheerful display. As well as the fact she all but skipped across the dusty red courtyard in her haste to reach the barn. "Miss Emily," she called again. "We've received a telegram. It's from Mr. Campbell and he says we should make our way to Port Hedland at once if we're to meet the ship!"

"What ship?" Emily dropped the bucket of grain, took the telegram and read the stilted words aloud. *"Dale, Paul to arrive P. H. noon one week. Stop. Please meet steamer on our behalf. Stop. Yours, P. Campbell."* A lump formed in the back of her throat and her voice cracked on the last words.

She blinked away several tears and wiped her eyes with the insides of her wrists.

"Miss Emily, are you well?" Ruth placed her hand on Emily's shoulder and squeezed. "I thought you'd be pleased with the news."

"Pleased isn't the right word for what I feel right now, Ruthie. I . . . I can't believe he's finally decided to come back."

She'd loved Dale for most of her life and now he would come home.

He'd finally decided to make the long journey back. Alone. How would he find the station? A lonely reminder of his losses? Or a comforting embrace from a life he once knew?

"I told you so." Blue picked up the bucket Emily had dropped and brushed past her into the barn.

Emily turned and hooked her arm through his. "Blue? Can I ask you something?"

"Of course."

"How did you *know* he's coming home? Is that where you've been? In Port Hedland? Did you hear something there?"

"No. I learned of it in the dreaming." Blue smiled, unhooked his arm from hers, and continued into the barn.

Emily's heart raced.

If there was one thing that impressed her from Charles's letters, it was the amazing Aborigine her uncle had called Blue. He'd claimed Blue knew things. Before she'd made the four-month journey from Arizona to Australia, she'd thought her uncle only said those things to entertain her. Now that she'd spent more than a few weeks in Blue's company, she believed the statements with all of her heart.

And he'd been right again. Dale Winters was coming home.

Chapter Three

A mass of screaming onlookers, family, and friends lined the pier at Port Hedland's main docking facility. Tired, happy men in smartly-tailored, sand-colored uniforms hurried down the long, narrow gangplanks leading from the decks of huge steamer ships and into the arms of their families. A group of older men in purple and green kilts played jolly tunes on their bag-pipes as young lovers embraced for the first time in months, or even years. Fathers held their children for the first time, mothers cried as they held fast to their sons. Old men preened as they slapped their sons on the back.

Emily stood in the front of the creaking buckboard wagon, while Ruth chose to remain seated to Emily's left, and strained to make out the faces of the soldiers that had already disembarked the massive steamer ships that lined the pier. Her stomach fluttered as if a swarm of butterflies had taken up residence, and her fingers trembled. Somewhere in that throng, Dale Winters had finally come home.

She swallowed, smoothed her black suit skirt over her thighs and clenched her fingers into the coarse material.

"Emily, your dress," Ruth chastised.

Emily glanced at her hands, still gripping the fabric, winced, and smoothed the material again. "Blue? Do you see him yet?"

"No, Miss Emily. Not yet."

"You're sure he's on *this* boat? There are so many boats arriving this week. You're sure it's this one?"

"Yes, ma'am."

"I mean, you're absolutely certain? You checked the manifest?"

"There is no need."

"Oh," she grumbled. "You should have checked it. What if he's not even here?"

Ruth stood and brushed several lingering wrinkles out of Emily's skirt. "I checked the manifest when we arrived last night. He is on this ship, I promise you."

Emily smiled at Ruth and gave her a quick hug. "What would I do without you?"

"I haven't the slightest idea." Ruth laughed and adjusted the wide brim of Emily's hat.

When she'd finished, Emily turned back toward the dock and scanned the crowd one more time. "Oh, where the devil is he?"

"Have patience, Miss Emily."

The waiting seemed the worst part of the past week. Because she had brought only her personal maid with her from America, she'd moved a few of the women who worked on the sheep station into the house to help her ready it for Dale's arrival. The *Jillaroos*, as they were called, were more than happy for their transfer indoors. Candice, it turned out, had a knack in the kitchen and Roberta, though she enjoyed working with the herdsmen, had been thankful for her new position as maid. The Castle-Winters house was one of the largest in the territory, built to the specifications of Andrew Winter's rather proper British wife. Instead of the long, low buildings that served as homes on most of the territory's sheep stations, Gayla Winter's home, with its wide porches, gables, and second floor rounded tower, would have looked quite appropriate on any street in Bristol.

Together, Emily and the other women had dusted, cleaned, and shined every surface in the sprawling ten-bedroom manor. When Emily had asked Charles about the size and expense of the house, he'd told her how his best friend had been able to deny his wife nothing. She'd wanted each of her children to have rooms of their own. Unfortunately, they'd filled only two of the rooms before she and her husband had been killed in a flash flood when Dale and his brother were children. Hopefully, Dale would see what care she'd taken with his mother's home and know just how much he'd been missed.

Rising on her toes, she craned her neck toward the crowd. "Do you see him yet?"

"No." Blue chuckled. "You are as impatient as Dale."

Emily reclaimed her seat in the front of the wagon and bit her lip. "He's impatient?"

"Aye. He always wants something before he should have it. When he was a little boy, he used to scare the lambs by running to catch them. But later, he learned to wait and approach them slowly, so they could learn about him. And he ever pushed himself to ride faster, jump higher, climb taller mountains. He and Jezebel grew up together and he was often hurt when he tried something that neither of them was ready for."

A wide smile formed on Emily's lips. "So. He was a daredevil, was he?"

"There he is." Ruth pointed into the massive, milling crowd.

Emily's breath caught in her throat. She doubted her heart beat and placed one hand on her throat to verify her pulse. "Where?"

Blue answered for her maid. "There. The tall one with no jacket. Do you see him?"

She stood and followed the direction Blue now indicated with one large, pointed finger. A man, head and shoulders above those around him, stood next to another man, not quite as tall. Wearing a loose, beige jersey and the distinctive felt slouch hat of the Australian forces, he looked both forbidding and tense. Was that him? Why wasn't he smiling like the hundreds of other returning soldiers? Why did he look as if he could turn a small child on a spit?

She swallowed again. That couldn't be Dale Winters. Her uncle's letters had described Dale as an honest, kind, watchful person with a bit of a wild side when it came to his recreational pursuits. As Blue had said, a daredevil. This man looked positively ferocious. Even if he did resemble the few photographs she'd seen of him around the house.

His brow formed a low, heavy line over pale eyes, a straight nose and full, rich lips. Lips that scowled at his companion.

Now, the companion looked something like what Charles had described, and he could be the man in the photographs she'd seen. Lord, she hoped so.

The happier of the two men must have noticed Blue. He smacked the first man on the chest and dashed toward the wagon.

Emily swayed on shaking legs. Steady. He's just a man. The reminder became a litany before the gentleman reached the wagon, tossed his bags in the back, and tilted his head at her. He threw a wink at Ruth and, with strong hands on his hips and a cocksure expression on his handsome features, he gazed at her for a moment. "You must be Emily."

She smiled at the sound of her name on his lips. She had yet to adjust to her name pronounced with an initial "I" instead of an "E".

Good grief. Where had her voice gone? She cleared her throat, found her voice somewhere in her stomach, and replied, "Yes. Emily Castle. It's nice to meet you finally,

Mr. Winters."

Ruth giggled.

The man scoffed. "No such luck." He pushed his hand toward her and she took it in an easy grip. "The name's Paul Campbell and I live about a half-day's ride further into the bush than you."

"My apologies Mr. Campbell. I thought—"

"No worries. But this here's the bloke you want." With a conspiratorial gleam in his eyes, Paul lowered his voice enough to make his words sound secretive, but not enough to keep Dale from hearing them. "He's in a foul temper, that one. Still cranky, I'd wager, about having to leave a perfectly good *casbah* in exchange for a shave and a ticket home."

Emily's gaze settled on Dale Winters as he moved across the last ten or so feet that still separated him from the wagon. His stride spoke of confidence and irritation, but managed to send heat from her limbs to her belly just the same. When he finally raised his head to look at her, his eyes narrowed even more and he frowned.

With effort, Emily moved her gaze off the handsome, rugged features and glanced at Paul. "*Casbah*?"

"Aye. *Casbah*. A boozer. You know, a pub?"

Ruth sucked in a breath. "You shouldn't talk of such things in front of a lady! Shame on you."

"Shame on me? Aye, but for far worse than that, I reckon." He winked again, and for a moment it seemed as if Ruth might sway right off the side of the wagon. Emily took her friend's arm and helped her alight on the bench before she succumbed to a serious case of the vapors. "It's fine, Ruth. We're not in America anymore, remember? Things are different here."

"It's barbaric!"

Paul laughed. "Been here a while, have ya?"

Emily returned her attention to Dale, who scratched the back of his neck and scowled.

So that's where he'd been for most of the past year. A *casbah*. Instead of coming home to see to his property and family, if he even considered her uncle to be a part of his family, he'd lost himself in some drinking establishment.

A rip of something akin to anger stiffened her spine. She stared at Dale again. "Oh, now I see why you didn't come back straight away."

"Do you really?" Dale's mouth set in a firm line.

"I believe so. You ran away from home."

A dangerous fire blazed in his eyes, but alongside that something else flickered. He turned away before she could make out exactly what she'd seen in the light shadows that hid inside those bottomless pools, and focused his attention on Blue.

"Welcome home, boy." Blue's eyes, often misted, shone with moisture and a hint of . . .

Sadness?

Emily frowned. No, it couldn't be sadness. The old man was simply overwhelmed Dale had finally come home.

"Thank you, Blue."

What was it about men that precluded a hug, even when the obvious course of action called for one? Emily sighed and waited for Dale to swing his gaze back to her. She smoothed the back of her chignon under the brim of her hat and folded her hands in front of her wide, black belt.

But Dale didn't acknowledge her presence again. He simply tossed his bags into the back of the wagon and climbed onto the seat.

Emily took a step back, and then another, and almost lost her balance when the wagon rocked and creaked under Dale's massive weight. His huge frame crowded her as if she weren't even there. How dare he? Why, Dale Winters was nothing more than a bully!

Her heart fell into her shoes and every girlish dream she'd ever had about the brave, tough, gentle Australian vanished in a puff of desert dust.

"Paul. If you want a ride as far as Castle Winters, I suggest you get your arse in the back of this wagon."

"Too right." Paul leapt in the back, helped Blue climb the rails, and settled the older man on a sack of flour. Then Paul reclined on another sack and nodded at Dale.

Ruth stood. "I think I'll ride in the back as well, if that's all right with you, Emily. There's precious little room in front now."

"Of course."

Paul assisted her maid into the back of the wagon and once he had settled her in a corner, Dale lifted the reins and slapped them down on the back of the single draft horse.

A Model T scooted away from the front of the dry goods store and forced Dale to pull hard on the reins. The horse dodged the lumbering automobile, but the wagon tilted and Emily swayed against Dale's arm and thigh. A shock of something that reminded her of lightning over the desert made her limbs tremble. The feeling, one she'd never experienced before, settled in her womb. Her cheeks heated.

"You know," Paul chimed from the rear, "I've been thinking about getting one of those motor cars. Did you see the ones parked in front of Grogg's boozer? Right fascinating, those."

Was he talking to Ruth, Emily, or Dale? Emily studied Dale's stern profile. *He* certainly wasn't going to answer. She shifted in her seat to face the passengers. "My father purchased a Ford several months before I left home. He rarely used it however, because it kept getting stuck."

"Aye. I can see where that could be a problem. We'll have to improve the roads. I'll give it some thought." Paul leaned his head back and shifted his hat to cover his eyes.

Blue offered Emily a wide smile, then closed his eyes.

Emily turned forward again.

Dale pushed them through the crowded streets until they reached the edge of town. Then he stepped up the their speed until they clipped along the road at a steady, even pace. The road met the De Grey River on their left and they followed it for several miles. The gentle waters meandered a lazy course behind irascible mangrove trees, gnarled gum trees, and a fairly wide expanse of white sand beach. Every so often, Emily caught a glimpse of the sun's reflection on the glassy surface. But her attention focused more on the quiet man at her side.

Every time she looked at him, her heart skipped a beat. Despite his surly demeanor, she found her hands fastened to the bench beside her knees to keep from sliding closer to him. He drew her like bees to apple blossoms. Her initial reaction to his missing year needled her conscience as well.

After all, his brother *had* died. Who was she to judge how he dealt with that grief? She'd never lost anyone, except Charles, and she'd only met him in person a few months before he died. She'd loved him, of course, but how could a relationship built on letters compare to two brothers? Two inseparable brothers, from what Blue and Charles had told her. Even Charles, on his death bed, had spoken only hopeful, love-strewn words about Dale. He'd asked her to be kind to him.

So much for living up to one's responsibilities to a dead man. She cringed. She'd been anything but kind, so far. But then, Dale had been rude and dismissive. Her shoulders went back another notch.

Still, she should apologize, shouldn't she? Offer the proverbial olive branch? In truth, she'd insulted him, not the other way around.

She stared straight ahead, took a deep breath, bit her cheek, and sighed. "I'm sorry."

Nothing. Not a single response.

No growl.

No scoff.

No grunt.

She waited another moment, then turned to face him. He sat forward with his elbows on his knees, the reins folded over large, weathered hands. "Did you hear me, Mr. Winters? I said that I'm sorry. About earlier. I didn't mean to insult you."

"Of course you did."

"No. I just . . . just . . ." What *had* she meant? A groan formed in her chest, but she swallowed it. "I simply made an observation."

He faced her with one eyebrow raised in an expression of disbelief. More than disbelief. He accused her with those blue-gray eyes.

And she deserved it.

"Oh, all right. I admit it. I have no excuse for my behavior and as I've already apologized, it seems to fall to you to either accept my apology or not." Emily folded her hands in her lap and squeezed them until her knuckles turned white.

A minute stretched into five or more before a half-hearted chuckle crossed the bench. "If you don't let go, your fingers are like to fall off."

She glared at him. His gaze moved to her hands and she followed the path he drew with his eyes. She released her fists and placed her palms on her thighs. Her hands tingled from lack of blood and they looked as if they belonged to someone else. Her womb tingled for a whole different reason.

"I suppose you're right," he continued, his back straightening as he changed his position on the bench. "It's up to me, and I choose to accept your apology. However, what I did or did not do after my discharge is my business, and my business alone. If we're going to work together for the time being, you'll need to remember that. If this is the last time we discuss the matter, we'll get along just fine."

"Why *didn't* you come home?" Emily cringed. Why in the world would she ask such a thing? Especially now. But she didn't take the words back. Instead, she clung to the heavy whisper of his breaths.

The silence deafened.

"I'll not discuss it. I had my reasons; now leave off."

Emily bit the inside of her lips to keep from speaking.

He'd had a home. People who loved him. Even the *Jackaroos* that worked the sheep station had missed him. Charles had loved him like his own son, and Dale had cast aside that love for nothing more than an escape at the bottom of a bottle.

If he wanted to be alone and dispassionate for the rest of his life, who was she to interfere? A whispered reminder sounded in the back of her mind, like a gentle song at first, but it built to a crescendo so loud she couldn't ignore it. Who was she to interfere?

She was the woman who loved him.

In fact, she'd loved him for so long, the thought of not loving him seemed wrong, somehow. A hole opened somewhere in the region of her chest, an emptiness that cried to be filled. Dale Winters seemed so much different from what her uncle had described. The man at her side was distant and cold. Had she been in love with someone who only existed in her girlish imagination? A phantom? Or did he live somewhere deep inside the sullen man at her side? Was there some remnant of the boy he used to be buried in his dark, injured soul? The tremble in her bones when his voice washed over her; the way his eyes seemed to find a window into her soul, just as she'd always known they would, told her there was. She simply had to find him.

✦ 🐎 ✦

Emily Castle had a way of looking at a man as if she would consume him, blood and bones, until there was nothing left but a wasted, spent casing. If she didn't stop washing her violet eyes over him, Dale would be hard pressed not to kiss her. Which surprised the hell out of him, considering he hadn't felt that particular desire in more months than he could remember.

She sat in turgid silence next to him. For hours, they'd traveled the long, dusty road to his former home, and not once since her attempt to apologize had she spoken a single word. He hadn't known women could stay quiet for so long. It must be killing her.

A grin threatened to crack his fierce composure.

He hadn't known what to expect when he arrived at Castle Winters. He sure as hell hadn't expected Charles's niece to be in Port Hedland to meet him. The three-day trip was long and hot. Most people avoided it at all costs, especially since the township of Marble Bar offered much of what the bushmen needed to survive in the harsh wilderness that was the Pilbara. And yet, she'd come for him personally when she could have sent any one of the *Jackaroos* in her place.

She had guts, that much was obvious.

And what she would look like hadn't even crossed his mind until Paul had pointed her out at the docks. She'd been standing on the wagon, her gray suit jacket and black skirt trimmed against her hips and breasts in tight relief. Her long, porcelain neck caught the morning light and reflected glorious brilliance to her sculpted cheeks and dark eyes, all but hidden beneath a wide-brimmed hat, complete with plush black ostrich feathers that would have made any regimental soldier proud to be an Australian.

Bright red lips had formed a straight line the moment before they parted on a sharp breath.

Stunning.

More than stunning, she presented a larger problem. For months, he had been content to let nothing past the wall around his heart. He felt nothing. He loved nothing.

Had Paul not nabbed him from Gahiji's, Dale would still be there. Feeling nothing. Loving nothing.

Instead, he sat next to the most adorable creature he'd

ever seen and every time he caught sight of her from the corner of his eye, his heart swelled right alongside his shaft.

Crikey, she was something else.

Paul's head shot into the space between Dale and Emily on the front bench. "Hey, mate! There's the old billibong. Slow down a bit."

"What for?"

"It's as good a place to spend the night as any."

"I want to get a few more miles behind us."

Ruth appeared beside Paul. "I'm ready to stop as well. I don't know how much more of this road I can stand."

A growl formed in Dale's throat and he swallowed against it. It was too early to stop for the night, but perhaps a few minutes to stretch their legs wasn't a terrible idea.

Emily pointed to a clearing between several gum trees. "That looks like a nice spot to pitch Uncle's tent."

"We're not spending the night here. We have about ten more miles before we reach the Coongan River. We'll stop there for the night." Still, he pulled the wagon next to the clearing and set the brake. "We'll eat something and then we're moving on."

"The women are tired, Dale. We've slept here before. No worries."

Dale ran a hand through his hair and replaced his hat as Paul leapt out of the wagon and helped Ruth to the ground. Emily sat still as a canyon wall beside him, her eyes like a branding iron on his cheek. "What?"

"Aren't you going to help me down?"

Crikey.

He dismounted from the wagon and took her hand. Shocks, like searing shrapnel, raced up his arm and straight to his gut. He dropped her hand as soon as she'd steadied herself, and hurried to the back of the wagon. This was the last thing he needed. Some sheila wreaking havoc in his mind and body when all he wanted to do was forget. Forget the war, forget the pain, and do his best to ignore the agony that would be his future.

For about the millionth time since he'd looked up to discover Paul had found him, he regretted his decision to come home.

"Let's go for a dip," Paul suggested as he helped pull several baskets from the rear of the wagon.

Emily gasped. "Do you mean swim?"

"Aye. Many's the day we wasted in that old pool. Me, Sorry-wuss over here, and Joel."

"We're not staying." Dale clenched his teeth until his jaw ached.

"Well, we're most certainly not swimming. But I agree with Paul. This seems a lovely spot to spend the night."

"No." Dale faced Emily and almost choked on the word. She'd removed her hat in deference to the shade. Thick swirls of her hair had escaped their sterile knot to frame her face with shimmering strands. Pink stained her cheeks, either from the heat or her flaring temper, he couldn't be sure. And her lips . . .

Full, moist, and made for kissing, those lips were. His

mouth watered and he swallowed hard while he struggled to remember what he'd been about to say.

"Why not?" Emily waved one tiny hand in front of her face to shoo an insect before she leveled a keen, questioning glare at him. "It's a delightful little pool."

"It's not as good a place to camp as it looks." He searched his mind for a less transparent excuse, but came up with nothing. There was only one valid reason not to camp here, and he wasn't about to share it with some prissy American he'd just met.

Emily tossed her hat onto the wagon's front bench, pulled out her parasol and opened it. Turning her back, she marched toward the water. "I'm staying right here, Mr. Winters. The only way you're getting my backside into that wagon again today is if you pick me up and put me there yourself." Her tone and the raised eyebrow she threw him over her shoulder held more than a little challenge.

Funny she should mention her backside, when that was exactly the part of her anatomy that had garnered his complete attention. He inclined his head as it swayed, back and forth, toward the river's edge.

Infernal woman. He snapped his attention back to the wagon.

"Do you remember the first time we camped here?" Paul jogged to his side, dragged the tent from the back of the wagon to let the massive canvas land with a dusty thud at Dale's feet. "We set the tent too close to the water—"

"That was a long time ago, mate. Leave it alone."

Stories of their childhood on the river were the last thing Dale wanted to hear. That's what made this particular billibong the least attractive. That's exactly why he didn't want to spend the night. The sooner they passed the *delightful little pool*, the better. Joel would never again swing into the water from the old rope they'd tied to a tree. He would never again feel the fresh water glide over his limbs, or dive to the bottom and collect whatever rocky treasures were imbedded in the sand.

A lump formed in his throat. Huge and overwhelming, it threatened to cut off his air supply. His eyes stung.

Of course, the only way to continue their journey included manhandling one Emily Castle back into the wagon—something he wasn't willing to do.

The last year really had turned him into a coward, hadn't it? He couldn't explain to Paul or anyone else why the thought of spending the night in this particular location made his stomach sour, and he couldn't invent a valid alternative. If he were a man, he'd suck up the wasted emotions and get on with it.

If he were a man.

With arms that weighed as much as the steamer ship that had carried him home, he lifted the canvas tent and tossed it on his shoulder. When he stood, Emily appeared in front of him, parasol in hand.

She bit her cheek in a manner that he'd already come to recognize. She wanted to say something, but either her pride or her good sense prevented it.

Just as well. He didn't want to hear her voice again. Not when he could barely focus on the task at hand— willing himself through the next few days' travel without kissing her mad.

✝ 🐎 ✝

A huge splash sounded from outside the tent Emily shared with Ruth. She poked her head through the door and squinted. Darkness hovered around the tent with only a sliver of moon to slice the velvety black of night. Still, it was enough to reveal Paul when his head surfaced in the middle of the river.

He shook his head and droplets of water flew off the ends of his hair, catching the moonlight like tiny pieces of silver. "You comin' in, or what?"

Emily followed the direction of Paul's question. On the edge of the beach, just in front of the water, Dale sat with one knee supporting his arm and his other leg stretched in front of him. He shook his head, apparently in response to Paul's question.

"You can't stop living forever, you know." Paul swam to the beach then strode from the water wearing nothing but his military issue long-Johns.

"Oh, my!" Ruth whispered. "You shouldn't be watching this, Miss Emily. You really shouldn't!"

"Shh. Neither should you, then. Now, be quiet."

Emily refocused her attention on Dale, who now lay

flat on his back as if he studied the stars.

"I haven't stopped living," he mumbled, his voice dark and coarse.

"Of course you have. All you do is eat, sleep, and drink. That's no way to live."

"It's a good way to die." Dale hoisted himself to a seated position with some effort, it seemed, picked up a bottle hidden behind his muscled thighs, and took a long pull from it. He swallowed with a grunt and shook his head. Raising the bottle in Paul's direction, like some kind of mock salutation, he laughed. "It's a damned good way to die."

Ruth sucked in a sharp breath. "Why, he's drunk!"

"Shhh." Emily tucked her head back inside the tent. "Yes, he is." She bit her lip and reclaimed the cot Paul had set up for her after they'd consumed the dried meat she'd packed for the trip. It creaked under her weight. It would be a rather long trip back to Marble Bar if Dale kept up this sort of behavior.

"What are we going to do with a drunk cluttering up the house, Miss Emily? Honestly, I thought we'd left that sort of thing behind when we moved here. He's no better than your pa."

"Don't say that!" Emily soothed her lip with the tip of her tongue. "Dale isn't a drunk, he just happens to be drunk at the moment. There's a vast difference. We'll simply have to keep him occupied when we get home; give him reasons to be productive each day. He doesn't really want to die, Ruthie. He doesn't want to hurt anymore, that's all."

"I suppose that's one way to look at it. But I still think it's going to be a mess."

"We're used to cleaning up messes, aren't we?" Her maid nodded as she lay down on the other cot. "Of course we are. The first thing is to survive the next few nights intact. There is little we can do about it now, except see to it that he stays alive. Then, when we arrive home we'll dispose of all the spirits we can find. Including Dale's personal supply."

✶ 🐎 ✶

Dale woke with a sledgehammer in his head. Worse, he had sand in his strides and the sun blasted him with rays that felt more like cauldrons of burning oil. A cool reprieve settled over his face and he cracked open his eyelids.

And immediately shut them again. Emily stood between him and the dawn and she looked more than angry. She looked positively furious. And ravishing, if he were to be completely honest. Just as she'd looked the past three mornings when she'd awakened him from troubled sleep.

"I know you're awake, Mr. Winters. Constant drunkenness is no excuse to be a lay-about. Up, up, up! We have quite a ways yet to travel today if we're going to make Castle Winters before nightfall."

The sound of her prim, black boots turning in the sand scratched in his ears. The fierce summer heat covered his face again and the backs of his eyelids turned red before he opened them, shaded the sun with one hand, and watched her storm toward the wagon.

Paul had already broken camp. Ruth sat in the back of the wagon while Paul leaned against the railing and winked in her direction. The maid blushed and turned her head to hide a smile behind one hand.

What rot!

He scanned the clearing for Blue, but who knew what medieval magic that old man was up to. He could have strolled half way to the station since moonrise.

"Get off your bleedin' arse, Dale!" Paul shouted. "We're ready to leave."

"I'm coming," he mumbled. When he gained his feet, his boots kicked an empty bottle of Russian Vodka, the clear glass sparking in the sunlight. The flash burned his eyes and turned his stomach. He must have been more than little rotten last night to fall asleep so close to the water's edge and away from the fire.

Croc bait. That's what he'd been last night. Bleedin' croc bait.

His stomach rolled and he shoved the sobering image aside. No such luck. Not for him.

No, he'd lived to see another day. And this day would bring him home.

To a big, empty house and a few thousand acres of life without Joel. Acres filled with guilt instead of sheep. Landscapes of aching reminders.

He climbed into the wagon and took the bench next to Emily, who perched in her seat like a minister's wife on Sunday morning. When she finally faced him, the scorn he'd seen in her eyes had disappeared. Worse, she gazed at him with pity in the glassy orbs. He'd rather have her contempt.

He waited for Paul to climb in the back of the wagon, turned to make sure everyone was settled, and then clicked his teeth. The horse jerked the wagon into motion with a jolt that sent Emily into his side.

His heart embraced the gentle contact, then crashed at her murmured apology when she scooted further away. He must present quite the picture this morning. Pity *and* revulsion.

They rode in silence for several hours, spoke very little over a hasty lunch just outside of Marble Bar, and when the rocky tower that marked the location of his mother's house rose above the horizon, Dale almost choked. How many times had he and Joel climbed those rocks? A hundred? A thousand? He'd honestly never expected to see the tower again and it made him more than a little uncomfortable.

How could anyone expect him to live here? Torture would be more pleasant. It would definitely be easier.

Just as they made the final turn toward the house, Dale's gaze settled on the lush, irrigated pastures his father had painstakingly created for the stock horses. More than a dozen Whalers either grazed on the long, sweet grass or raced along the fence lines. He found Jezebel in the center, her long black mane dancing on a warm breeze when she shook her head.

A buckskin mare nudged her with its muzzle. Sally. His brother's horse. Both animals had put on weight since he'd last seen them, probably from lack of exercise.

A wicked, shrieking cry carried to him on the wind and he frowned. Behind the grazing workhorses, he found a section of the pasture had been cut out and fenced in with a double row of barbed wire. Inside, a magnificent stallion reared and pawed at the sun. His glossy coat, blacker than night and an almost perfect match for Jezebel, glistened in the light. He looked like some great magical beast come to conquer.

He was tempted to ask about the stallion, but he didn't really need to. He could belong to only one person. Emily. He slid his gaze over her slight figure. How did a woman so small handle a horse so powerful?

Someone called his name and he dismissed the curious direction of his thoughts.

Instead, he drove the wagon into the courtyard where half-a-dozen *Jackaroos* had gathered. All of them old men, or young boys, stood in a knot. Their eyes scalded Dale with pity.

Dale pulled the reins and the horse jerked to a halt.

He stifled a sigh. Might as well get it over with.

"Welcome home."

"It's about time you showed up. Where've you been all this time?"

"It's good to see you again, mate. We were right

worried over you."

Voices from his past crowded around him, tugged at his shirtsleeves and strained his capacity to breathe. He responded to each of the men. Men who'd helped raise him after his parents' death. Men who'd watched over him when his guts overpowered his brains.

Except for one.

A fist seized his chest. Like Joel, Charles wasn't there.

Why the bloody hell was *he* there?

And then, like some kind of damned angel, Emily spoke. Her voice, like the petals of a desert rose, sung above the din. "Everyone, please give Mr. Winters some room. He's traveled quite far and I'm sure he would appreciate some time to adjust."

A few hearty claps on his back later, and the men dispursed. Even Blue wandered away from the wagon in search of something in the barn. Paul gathered their bags from the back of the wagon, tossed Dale's haversack to him, and made his way into the house. "If it's all right, I'll bed down here tonight and head home in the morning."

Dale stared at Emily with a wonder he hadn't realized he still possessed. Their eyes met. He'd witnessed desert storms in the bush that didn't match the current between them.

"I'm sorry. I hope I didn't speak out of turn, but you seemed a bit . . . overwhelmed."

"No worries."

"Is it all right with you if Mr. Campbell stays for the night?"

"Paul? Paul can sleep anywhere he pleases."

"All right then. I'll just have a room prepared for him."

She lifted her skirt, apparently out of habit since the hem rested more than a few inches off the ground, and turned toward the house. When she moved from the packed red earth of the stable yard into the softer, grass-covered garden, her dainty boot-covered ankles wobbled for just a moment before she gained her footing.

She moved like light across the garden. When she climbed the wooden steps to the porch, her hips swayed like treetops in a heavy wind. Then she was gone.

And Dale still stood in the middle of the stable yard like a boy in his first blush. He slung his haversack over his shoulder and wiped one hand over his jaw.

Get a hold of yourself, Winters.

No sense getting all riled up about a woman when he had no plans to stay long enough to do anything about it.

✦ 🐎 ✦

Emily gathered a handful of feed and threw it to the squawking chickens. To the west, the sun made its way behind the trees and sent rose-hued rays of light over the pastures where Henry Albert brought Jezebel and Sally into the stable for the night. Soft clouds moved across the horizon in shades of pink, lavender, and gray. On the opposite horizon, night loomed in a dark band dotted with the first stars.

Once she'd fed the chicks their ration, she tucked the bucket handle over her arm and made her way to the barn. A voice caught her attention at the door, however, and she stopped.

It was Dale's voice. Deep. Rich. Inherently masculine with its swaggering lilt. She strained, but couldn't make out the words. Only that whatever he said, his voice spoke of regret and inherent sadness.

She closed her eyes and leaned her head against the rough wood. So much pain resided inside the man, she couldn't begin to understand how badly he must feel about . . . simply everything.

Even coming home must have been a terrifying experience. No wonder he'd been so cool when he first came off the ship. But Paul had been right. Dale had to start living again at some point. No one could suffer through something like what he'd been through alone. Not if they hoped to come out of it with a measure of sanity, or perhaps even some happiness.

She pushed on the door and winced when the hinges squeaked. Dale spun in her direction and she smiled. "Sorry about that. I didn't mean to intrude."

He stood in front of Jezebel's stall and the large black Whaler nudged his hand. He scratched the horse's nose and shrugged. "No worries."

Inside the barn, Emily placed the feed bucket on a scarred work surface next to a rack that contained several metal tools and pieces of tack. "She's very beautiful."

"Jez? Aye. She is. Did you groom her?"

"Yes. I hope that was all right."

"Of course. Thank you."

He continued to rub the horse's muzzle, but never took his eyes off Emily. Heat flushed her cheeks and she crossed her arms over her breasts. "I've heard from several of the townsfolk that you are quite the rider, Mr. Winters."

"Once upon a time."

"Oh, come now. It wasn't that long ago, was it? You've been gone for a few years, but I'm sure, now that the war is all but over, that annual horse race I've heard about will come around again. Will you enter?"

"No." Dale turned to face the stall next to Jezebel's and kissed the air. The buckskin mare, Sally, whinnied and pushed her head into Dale's hand.

"Why not? You can't be terribly out of practice, after all. The Light Horse Brigade made quite a name for itself as far as exceptional horsemanship is concerned. Why, Charles and his friends were still talking about the charge at Beersheba when I arrived, and that was months and months later."

"I'm not interested, that's all." He patted Sally's muzzle and leaned his forehead against hers.

"But everyone has been expecting you to win again this year."

Dale shot a glare in her direction that had the presence of a thunderhead over the Grand Canyon.

"Oh, very well . . . I'll *leave off.*" She paused. She'd

add his racing wins to the list of topics he preferred not to discuss. "I'm thinking I might enter. Have you seen Apache?" Emily crossed to the first stall in the row and leaned on the edge of the door. Her black thoroughbred stallion stomped the ground and nickered. She reached into the pocket of her loose-fitting trousers and pulled out a cube of sugar. Apache's teeth clicked over her palm and the cube disappeared. "There you go, boy. A little treat."

"It's an awfully big horse for a little woman like you."

Dale stood so close that his heat seemed to envelope Emily's much smaller frame. When had he moved? The man walked like a cat. She swallowed against the flutter in her stomach.

"I've been riding since before I could walk, Mr. Winters. Much like yourself. I can handle Apache."

"How long have you been here?"

"Here?" She gulped. His breath heated the top of her head.

"In Australia."

"Oh. Um. I arrived in June. Uncle Charles hadn't written in quite a while, and when I telegraphed from Arizona one of the neighbors, Mrs. Macomber, was living here taking care of him. I booked passage the next morning and left home within the week."

"Just like that. You left everything you knew, everyone you loved, and moved to the other side of the world."

"Of course. I might never have met my uncle, but I'd come to love him very much over the years he wrote to me."

How would Dale react if he knew he was a large part of the reason she'd come? Or, if she told him how concerned Charles had been about him.

She swallowed against a sudden image of Dale's lips pressed against her own, their bodies entwined. She cleared the image as wholly improper and shook her mind's eye free. "He needed family around him. And you were . . . well, you weren't here."

Dale stood to his full height. "I'm sorry about that. If I'd known he was sick, I would have come home."

"Would you?"

"Aye."

It was on the tip of Emily's tongue to argue the point, but she bit back the words. The cold, defensive pain had returned to his voice. Then he whispered, "I'm very sorry about your uncle. He was a good man. A true friend."

"He loved you very much."

"Aye. He was like a father to us after our parents died. And I loved him like one."

"He loved Joel, too." Emily bit her cheek again. Dale didn't need to know that it was Joel's death that sent the burly sheep rancher to his sickbed. And he certainly didn't need to know that Dale's failure to return after his discharge had stolen what little life Charles had left.

"I know he did."

"I've heard so much about you boys. Charles wrote to me every week and, it seemed, the two of you had been through some new adventure."

Dale scoffed and slid his hand beneath Apache's jaw to scratch him.

"No, it's true. He was so proud when you used to win all those races. And how you always seemed to look after Joel. He called you Joel's guardian more than his brother."

"Some guardian."

Emily's heart sank for Dale. Did he blame himself for Joel's death? It was a war. One of the most famous battles of the Great War, in fact. How could he possibly blame himself for something over which he'd had no control?

The desire to ask him about that very thing fell beneath the weight of Dale's stare. His eyes told her she'd queried him enough for one evening. She bit her cheek and turned her eyes back to the horse. "I'm sorry about Joel. I would have liked very much to meet him."

A grunt. The shuffle of feet over the dirt floor. She turned to find Dale paused by the door. His hand rested on the latch. "I've already mentioned that I don't want to speak of what is past. Please don't do it again."

Chapter Four

Dale woke with a remnant of something bitter on his tongue and a hollow scream in his head. An explosion. Thick, yellow dust. *Blood*.

Sweat beaded on his brow and upper lip. He wiped it away with a trembling hand.

He hated that dream. But it was all he had left, so even the part of him that prayed it would never come back welcomed the memory.

He steadied his hands and wiped his cool, damp palms on the sheet. Then he threw the sheet aside, put on his strides and pulled a lightweight jersey over his head and shoulders.

The clock on his bedside table read half-past eight. The distant sounds of activity permeated the quiet of his room.

He glanced around the space he'd lived in since before he'd left for the Academy. No remnants of his childhood remained. They were stored in the attic. But a few reminders of his years at the King's Academy adorned the walls. Horsemanship trophies, a plaque he'd received in honor of his academic scores, silk ribbons from the various athletic events he'd entered and won. Running. Skulling. Polo.

Joel's room would look very much the same, if Dale had been man enough to look inside.

He needed to pack everything in Joel's room. He needed to do the same thing to his room. But not today. He heaved a weary sigh and went downstairs.

The landing at the bottom of the staircase had changed little since he'd left. The lace curtains hanging over the windows on either side of the massive front door hung a little lower and showed signs of wear. Four years was a long time, apparently, even to curtains.

But the entire house sparkled with care and a fresh coat of furniture wax. Even the hardwood floors reflected morning light from the windows.

A deep, masculine voice caught his attention. He frowned.

"You're going to marry me, Emily Castle, if I have to come here every damn day to convince you of it."

Gerald Brown? What the bloody hell was that whanker doing here? And what did he mean, Emily would marry him?

Dale strode through the hallway that led from the foyer to the kitchen and shoved open the swinging door. It crashed against the icebox. Gerald turned with a start and stared at Dale with a forced grin. "Winters? I heard you'd come back."

"What's this all about?"

"Nothing much. I've been explaining to your partner here how much she needs a husband. A sheila working alone in the bush is only asking for trouble. You know what I mean."

Emily's delicate hands balled into fists and her eyes blazed. Color rose high in her cheeks, turning them pink. If it were possible for daggers to shoot from a woman's eyes, they shot from hers. "I'll not marry you, Gerald. Not now. Not ever."

"Why would she marry you?"

"Because I have the most to offer her, of course."

Emily smiled over clenched teeth and stepped forward. "Gerald. While I'm flattered by your offer, and all of the similar offers you've tendered over the past few months, I have already explained. I am perfectly fine and have no wish to marry."

"If you had half a brain, you'd jump at the chance to double your half of the station."

"It doesn't work that way, Gerald. She owns the whole station, and so do I. There are no boundaries between our halves. So if you think you're going to double your own land by marrying her, you're mistaken."

"We'd be partners then. No harm there."

"I don't want a partner."

"What about the sheila?"

Emily's cheeks deepened to a rusty hue. Apparently, she didn't like being referred to as if she weren't in the room any more than he would. Her voice, steady and strong, echoed through the kitchen. "*The sheila* is fine without your help."

Gerald chuckled and shook his head. "You're alone and you're going to find more trouble than you know what to do with."

"That sounded like a threat."

Gerald stammered and backed away. "No, mate. Not a threat. Just an observation. She's alone here, now isn't she?"

"No, she's not. I'm here. And anyone who wants to get to her, has to get through me." A part of Dale's conscience reared its head at the possessiveness of the words. She didn't matter to him, so what the devil made him think he had the right to protect her? One look into Gerald's feral eyes gave him the answer. It wasn't his right to guard her, it was his responsibility to defend her against someone as base and reprehensible as Gerald Brown. A lower creature didn't exist in the whole of Oceania.

"Too right. So the two of you are going to have a go, then?" Gerald's mouth spread into a lecherous grin.

Dale's fist shot forward before he even knew his intention. It connected with Gerald's jaw and sent the younger man's head reeling backward. A second later, Gerald sat dazed on the floor.

"Get out of my house, Brown, and off my land. Don't come back here again."

Gerald stood slowly, as if he measured the possibility of another blow and his ability to defend against it, rubbing his jaw. The man's wild eyes never left Dale. "A sheila has no business running a sheep station and you know it, Winters. If she don't marry me, there's plenty of less promising blokes who'll press their suit as well."

"Let them try," he warned. "She won't be here long enough to make a difference. We're selling the land and the herd and we'll be gone before winter."

Gerald grinned. "Selling? Sure you are, mate. Your father would roll over in his grave if he heard that."

"My father's grave is not your concern. Now, rack off before I change my mind about sweeping the floor with your arse."

Gerald cursed, picked up his hat and vanished through the back door.

A hush fell over the kitchen. Dale took his time turning around, and when he did, he found exactly what he expected. Emily stared up at him with fewer, but still deadly, daggers shooting from her eyes. This time, they were aimed at him.

"You're selling? No, wait. You said *we're selling*."

"That's right." He forced his feet to move to the stove where he poured himself a cup of coffee. Coffee—he stifled a grunt. What he really wanted was a measure of Vodka. A large measure.

"And I suppose since I'm just a *sheila*, I have no say in the matter? Is that what you think?"

Dale set his mug down on the kitchen table, moved toward the tall cupboards on the far wall and tossed them open. Charles kept a stash of Irish Whiskey in the back.

"Something like that."

"I have news for you, Mr. Winters. I have no desire to sell the station and as you pointed out, you need me to agree. Honestly, I don't see why you'd want to, either."

"It's not your concern." He closed the cupboard door and opened the one to the left. Shoving aside various dry goods, he searched the interior. Where in hell had Charles hidden his bloody whiskey?

"It most certainly is my concern. I own a half interest in this place. My uncle Charles loved every acre of it, and he loved his life here. Including you. Why would you just throw all of that away?"

"I didn't throw it away. It died. The whole bleedin' place died, Emily. There's nothing here for me now. Hell, I didn't even want to come back."

"Then why did you?" Emily screamed and huffed her way through the swinging door.

Dale slammed the cupboard door and rubbed the back of his neck. He shouldn't follow her. He should just let her scream and pout until she realized she had little or no say in what he did with the land. But something drew him to her. Something made him follow her.

When he pushed open the door and traced her path down the wide hall, he found her pacing the worn Oriental rug in the parlor. Her fingers clasped in front of her belt. Her mouth worked as if she spoke, but whatever she said he couldn't hear.

His foot landed on a loose board and the squeak

sounded like an artillery round in the otherwise quiet room. She spun on him with the look of a lioness stalking her prey—all wild eyes and glossy fur.

"I don't pretend to know what you were running from all this past year, but you're not going to come home and start running all over again."

"I'm not?" His eyes left her just long enough to scan the sideboard for the level of spirits in his mother's imported crystal decanters. Each of the elaborately etched pieces sparkled empty. *Bloody hell.*

"No. You're not. This is my home now, and I'm not going to let you ruin it."

His attention snapped back to Emily, who studied him with a curious glint in her dark eyes. "Your home? Lady, you're on holidays as far as I'm concerned." When her mouth formed an "O" and her shoulders moved back several heated notches, he paused. "Listen, thanks for looking after the place and all that, but this was *my* home. I'm the only one left and I can do with it as I please."

"You're wrong. According to my uncle's Last Will and Testament, it's half mine. And I won't sell. To you or anyone else. So if you want to sell your half, fine, but I'm going to insist that you not sell it to Gerald." She squared her shoulders again. "Maybe Paul would like to buy it."

Dale paused. Paul? Did she want Paul to buy him out? For some reason he couldn't name, that thought made his heart race and his blood boil. "Paul has his own place." He paused. "Where is he, by the way?"

"He left about two hours ago for his father's station." Crimson lights played over her dark eyes. Her head titled backward just enough to make her look like a queen, and her fists shot to her hips. "He took one of the horses and promises to send it back with one of his father's *Jackaroos*. Stop changing the subject."

"All right. I'll help you pack."

"No."

"You'll pack alone, then? Cheers. How long will it take you?"

She stomped her foot. "No. I'm not leaving."

"Gerald's right, you know. When word gets out there's an unmarried woman living here, every man within a thousand miles will come to propose."

"It's already started and I don't care. I can take care of myself."

She could, too. Dale had seen bravery and honor in many forms during the war, and Emily Castle had both. She stood tall and straight and had more passion in her eyes than most of the men he'd served with.

"In fact," she continued. "I can take such good care of myself, *I'll* buy your half. I'll just buy you out and you can go on living in the bottom of some whiskey bottle. Go back to Egypt and do your best to forget everything this place, this land, once meant to you. Go right ahead and forget everything you fought for, everything Joel died for."

Dale couldn't have been more shocked if she'd taken his father's Remington shotgun from over the fireplace, aimed it at his chest and pulled the trigger.

He ignored the pain and, as a matter of self-defense against the agony, concentrated on her offer. Then he forced a laugh. "You? Buy my half and run this place on your own?"

"I'm glad you find the thought so amusing, but the truth is I'm perfectly capable of it. And I'm not alone. I have Blue and the others."

"Blue? That crazy old man? And what happens when he goes walkabout for a few months. And the others aren't going to work for a woman."

"They've been working for me for months without complaint. I've even helped them with the sheep on numerous occasions. I am an accomplished rider, after all."

"They've been working for me. I tell them I'm leaving, for good and ever this time, and they'll disappear."

Emily's expression fell into a thousand ashen pieces. In one moment, he wanted to push her as far away from his heart as he could, and the next, he wanted to hold her. Protect her—even if that meant protecting her from herself.

He swallowed. God in heaven, no. He would not be responsible for another person. Yet, that's exactly what she asked of him, even if she didn't know it. If he stayed on, at least until he convinced her to sell with him, he would be her guardian. Not legally. She looked to be of age and better, from the curve of her breasts to the span of her hips and the smooth lines of her neck, but in any realistic view he would stand between her and the wilds of the bush. Both man and beast.

Bloody hell.

He was going to do it. He had to. He owed that much to Charles, and more. But first, he was going to bloody well find something to drink before he could no longer control the ache in his gut. There had to be a bottle of something somewhere in this damned house! He stalked to the sideboard and threw open the narrow doors. Squatting, he shuffled his mother's china from one side to the other, the clink a vivid reminder of happier times. The memories only made him want to find Charles's stash that much more.

"What the devil are you looking for?" Emily snapped and then released a heavy sigh.

"Nothing that has anything to do with you."

"If you're looking for spirits, you won't find any."

He froze for a moment before he slowly gained his feet and faced her. One eyebrow raised in a smug expression that told him she'd known what he searched for all along. "And why, exactly, is that?"

"Because Ruth and I poured everything out," she squeaked. She'd tried to maintain her blustering, infuriating, and severe aplomb. But her voice had definitely squeaked.

Dale's bones suddenly reminded him of the gelatinous muck when rain fell on the red silt of the desert. He wanted to sit on the settee and bury his head in his hands and wish the world away. Instead, he nodded to Emily, who frowned with more pity than anger now, and brushed past her toward the stairs.

In a whisper that sounded very much like a plea, Emily said, "I don't want to sell, Dale. I love this place, and I know you love it, too."

Which was exactly why he had to leave. As soon as he possibly could.

✦ 🐎 ✦

The heavy barn door slid open on quiet hinges. Blue moved it back and forth a few times, then closed it behind him. "You oiled the door."

Dale didn't turn from the workbench where he adjusted the harness worn by the draft horse. "The hinge was loose, that's all."

"It's good to have you home."

"Thanks."

"The land missed you."

Dale released a loud breath; not quite a laugh. "How can the land miss someone?"

"You're a part of it. When you're not here, the trees notice."

"You're still talking in riddles, I see."

"They are not so much riddles as they are . . . observations."

"Yeah, well, observations don't do me any good."

"What will do you good, then?"

Dale dropped the rigging and cursed. He picked it up

again and pried open the buckle with a screwdriver. "What do you want, Blue?" he ground out between clenched teeth while he struggled with the rusted clasp.

"The question is not what I want. It's what you want."

"I want to be left alone." The buckle broke free.

"No one wants to be left alone."

"I do." Dale released the buckle and laid the thick leather band flat on the wooden surface.

"Sometimes, the gods know what we want more than we do."

"Your gods have no reign over me." He picked up a mallet and an awl, placed them over the leather and beat a new hole into the strap.

"The gods have reign over everyone." Blue positioned himself next to the work table, crossed his arms over his torso and leaned his elbows on the edge.

"If you say so." Dale punched another hole in the leather.

"Why do you make new holes in the strap?"

Dale's brow furrowed. "Because it's too big. The horse is a bag of bones. Miss Emily probably isn't feeding him enough."

"You make the strap fit the horse? Why not feed the horse more?"

Dale sighed. "Because that will take too long and I need to make a run into Marble Bar."

"So you make the world fit your needs."

"No, Blue. Not the world. Just the harness."

"Why can't you make the world fit? Aren't you strong

enough?"

Dale dropped his tools, crossed his arms and leaned one hip on the table. "What exactly are you trying to say?"

Blue shrugged. "I'm just curious."

"You're never 'just curious'. You're trying to teach me something, but I'm in no mood for your cryptic lessons."

"You're afraid to answer me. I understand."

Dale's face flushed. "I'm not afraid."

"Aye. It's nothing to be ashamed of. Fear teaches us caution. But we are the ones who must decide where the fear will lead us."

"What the devil is that supposed to mean?"

"Fear can lead us to hide from the world, or make it fit. It's our choice."

"Listen. All I want to do right now is fix this harness. If you don't mind, I'd like to get back to it."

"Who's stopping you?"

Dale growled in the same ferocious manner he'd employed as a child. Turbulent and strong. Blue didn't have to sense his young friend's patience ran thin; it was written in his eyes.

"Have you given much thought to your destiny?"

This time, Dale did laugh. A derisive chuckle that said he only humored the ramblings of an old man. "No. Can't say that I have."

"Every man has a destiny. We are never certain what our destiny is, but we must always look for the signs that show us the way to meet it. Have you watched for your signs?"

"If every man has a destiny, what was Joel's? He was only twenty-two years old. How can a man reach his destiny in so short a time? And what about a child who dies of a fever before he's out of his crib? What about that? No destiny there, mate."

"We are not to know another's destiny. We must concentrate on finding our own."

"Ah, mate. If we aren't supposed to muck around in other people's destiny, then why are you so concerned about mine?

"I'm special." He preened and offered Dale a toothy smile.

"You're babbling. Why don't you go bother Emily?"

Blue only continued to smile. The seeds had been planted and, with enough encouragement, they would grow. Dale had only to cultivate his own dreams to find the answers. He must fit the world to his own desires, just as he resized the harness to fit the horse. He must embrace the destiny he'd been given. "It's not so hard as you might think, finding the signs."

Blue pushed off the table and crossed to the door. He opened it and tested the hinges again. Dale studied him with a dim light in his eyes. Dim, but most definitely there.

"Thanks for fixing the door, Dale. That squeak liked to have driven me batty before long."

✳ 🐎 ✳

"You shouldn't have eavesdropped, Ruth." Emily curled with her pillow on the bed in her room. Ruth stood at the foot with her hands on her hips and a pious expression on her rounded features.

"Be that as it may, you were still rather harsh with him, weren't you?" She dropped her hands and circled the bed to stand beside Emily. "Besides, I didn't have to eavesdrop, really. The two of you screamed loud enough for the man on the moon to hear you." She sat on the edge of the bed and brushed a few loose strands of hair off Emily's forehead.

"I didn't mean to lose my temper, but he makes me so angry! How can he not love this place? How can he even consider selling it?"

"Have you thought, perhaps, that this house holds too many memories?"

"Of course I have. But they are all happy memories, aren't they? Well, except for his parents' passing. But he never mentioned selling the house, or not coming back to it, before the war. I'm sure my uncle would have said something if Dale had such thoughts."

"Maybe, maybe not."

"No, he would have. I know it." Emily pushed herself upright and leaned her back against the thick wooden headboard. "It's me. He doesn't want to stay here because of me."

"Posh. I don't believe that for a minute. Why, he knew you were here before he decided to come home, didn't he?

Yes, he did."

"True. But he didn't know me from Adam then. Now he knows me. And he hates me."

"Posh. I think the best thing for you to do now is to apologize to the poor man before he thinks you hate him as much as he hates himself."

"I could never hate him!"

"I know that and you know that. But he doesn't know that."

Emily chewed the inside of her cheek for a moment. "I've apologized more to that man than I ever have before in my life, you do realize."

With a chuckle that shook her ample breasts, Ruth replied, "Yes, I do. But then, passion comes in many forms and we can't always help the way some folks make us feel. Dale makes you feel like you must save him, no matter the cost."

"Can a person be saved from themselves?"

"Time will tell, Miss Emily. Only time will tell."

⚔ 🐎 ⚔

Dale stared at the closed door for a full minute before he shook his head and turned back to the work table. "Crazy old man."

What had he said about changing the world? A load of cod's wallop. That's what it was.

The door swung open again and cast a sharp line of

sunlight over the table. "Forget something, ya old bastard?"

"Um. No, I just thought I'd see if you were hungry."

Dale spun at the sound of Emily's voice. "Crikey. I thought you were Blue."

Her smile sent a fresh course of blood through every vein in his body, hot and throbbing. He sucked in a breath at the soft shadows of her face and the way her dark hair curled at her temples. "Do you always treat Blue with such respect?"

"Beg yours?"

Her brow wrinkled.

"I meant, I beg your pardon."

"You called him a rather nasty name, just then, since you thought I was he."

"Oh, that. No, not really."

She closed the door and crossed to her horse's stall. The stallion greeted her then nudged at her hand with his nose.

"He wants more sugar."

"Yes," she sighed, "but I'm afraid we haven't any. The market was out when we picked up supplies last week."

"I'm taking the wagon into town tomorrow. I'll see if they have any."

"But you only just arrived home. Surely, there isn't anything we need so badly that you must leave again so soon."

"It's a large station. We need supplies to mend the fences before winter and I have business to conduct. I don't see where how long I've been home has anything to do with it."

Emily leveled her gaze on him as if she searched him for an answer to some unknown question. A part of him wanted to find the answer for her, if he only knew the question. Apparently unable to find what she looked for, she asked, "You're not going to advertise the station for sale, are you?"

He hadn't thought of that. Over the course of the last few days, he hadn't given the sale much thought. He'd been too busy making repairs and inspecting the flock. Not that he could do a decent job of it. To properly inspect the flock or the fences, he needed a horse between his legs, not attached to a wagon.

Of course, if he were to be completely honest with himself, he'd been avoiding Emily. Something about her made him want to live again. The guilt that feeling caused cried out in sorrowful, hallow pain. Looking at her, even now, made his whole body ache and tremble.

He had no business wanting her. He had no business enjoying anything.

But to make the final move and sell the station, as much as he wanted to . . . no, he wasn't ready. Not yet.

"So, will you?"

"No. We need a few more supplies. That's all."

Emily's shoulders relaxed and she turned to face Apache again. "I'm glad."

"Why is staying here so important to you?"

Her shoulders stiffened again. "No reason. I like it here. It's something of my own."

"I see."

Dale lifted the harness from the table and made his way to the door. "If Candice has made something, I could eat."

"She did. She put on a stew this morning. It smells heavenly. How long will you be?"

"Not long."

Emily nodded and the dark curls framing her face bounced. "I'll let her know to expect you, then." She crossed to the door and reached for the latch at the same time as Dale.

His fingers brushed hers and heat that could be likened only to the wound in his shoulder scorched him. Like fire. But hotter.

He ripped his hand away before the burn could reach his heart.

He allowed her to open the door herself, doing his best to ignore the hurt expression that marred her delicate features. She stepped into the sunlight and dashed to the rear entrance of the house.

He'd seen something in her eyes. Something wonderful and sad at the same time. He stared at his hand where their fingers had met and the sudden, fierce shock remained, lingering now like the scent of rain after a storm. Nothing good could come of this, nothing good whatsoever. He'd been around long enough to know when a woman was attracted to him, and he knew himself well enough to know he'd welcome it, given half a bloody chance.

What the bloody hell was wrong with him? He didn't

want this. He didn't need to add a woman to the complex battery of guilt he already endured every time he opened his eyes. But if he didn't control himself, Emily would find her straight-laced, prideful and shapely arse a sure-fire target for seduction.

That was the last thing either of them needed. She needed, deserved someone who would be around in another month, and he sure as hell didn't need the guilt that would come from taking pleasure from a trusting, complicated . . .

Beautiful woman.

Aye. The sooner he took himself to Marble Bar and the longer he stayed away, the better. For them both.

Chapter Five

Emily ran across the dusty stable yard, up the thick wooden steps and into the house. Without so much as a glance at Candice, she dashed down the hall, up the stairs and into her room. The sting of tears behind her eyes made the journey seem longer than it should have, but once inside her room, with the door securely fastened, she threw herself on the bench beneath the window.

"What's the matter?"

Ruth's voice came from the corner by the wardrobe where she refolded the contents of a drawer. It startled her and Emily sucked in a breath.

"Didn't he accept your apology?" Her friend rushed to the window and knelt in front of her.

"I never had the chance to apologize. Oh, Ruthie . . . what have I gotten us into?"

"It can't be as bad as all that. What happened?"

"He can't even stand to touch me. He accidentally brushed my hand and you would have thought I carried the plague or something. He couldn't wait to get away from me." She wiped her eyes before the tears could flow and straightened her back. "I was right about why he wants to sell the ranch. It's because he can't stand the thought of sharing it with me, that's why." Was she so hideous that no man could ever want her?

No, she wouldn't think of that. Not today. Ruth handed her a small lace handkerchief and Emily blinked away the start of fresh tears and wiped her eyes with it.

"Do you know that my engagement to Rudolf Van Clement failed for one reason, and one reason alone? Because I loved someone else. As much I tried to belittle that reality, Rudy knew it to be true as much as he knew his own name."

"That wasn't meant to be, that's all. And to tell the truth, I never liked him much."

"Oh, Rudolf was a lovely man. You shouldn't say such things. He just wasn't the man I wanted to spend the rest of my life with. And I'm not exactly the catch of the county on any continent." Her inability to return his affection had caused the rift between them, then later, between their families. It had nothing to do with the fact that he never once tried to kiss her, or hold her. He never mentioned how beautiful she was. He never noticed when she wore a new gown or tea-dress. But it was her unrequited love for a hero in a simple series of letters that had given Rudolf the reason he'd needed to break off their relationship.

It hadn't been her . . . shortcomings.

"Stop that nonsense this minute!" Ruth sprang to her feet and tilted the oval, full length mirror in the corner so Emily could see her reflection. "Now look at how beautiful you are. There isn't a man in the world who wouldn't find you simply delightful."

Her eyes were swollen and just a hint of red encircled them. But otherwise, she looked . . . passable. Her dark hair, piled on top of her head in a fastidious Gibson knot, held a hint of auburn when the sun touched it just right. And her skin seemed healthy enough. Her waist, cinched from years of tight, immovable corsets, could easily be spanned by a man's hand.

"Fine. I'll admit I'm not some deformed monster. But if what you say is true, then tell me why Dale has failed to notice I'm even female? Except to tell me what a woman can and can not do, of course."

She made a face in the mirror and glanced out the window. Dale was in the process of fitting the harness on the draft horse. His shirt stretched tight over his back and the play of muscles beneath the fabric reflected the sun in undulating rhythm. When he finished, he urged the horse backward and attached it to the wagon.

"In fact, he's leaving in only a few moments for Marble Bar . . . where I imagine he'll lose himself in as much whiskey as a man can possibly drink."

"Then you'll have to go with him, won't you? To make sure he doesn't overindulge and harm himself in some way."

Emily turned slowly away from the window. "What

did you just say?"

"I merely suggested that you go with him to Marble Bar."

"I couldn't possibly go with him by myself. You'd have to come along as well."

"If you insist, of course, I'd be happy to."

Her lips curved into a smile. "Pack our things, Ruthie. We're going to town."

She dried her eyes a final time and raced down the stairs where she found Candice setting the table. The older woman glanced at Emily and smiled. "Will Mr. Winters be joining you for lunch?"

"Yes, he will, Candice. And then we'll be going to Marble Bar for supplies."

" 'We'?" Dale's voice caught Emily by surprise and she almost jumped out of her shoes.

With a hand on her heart to steady the erratic increase of her pulse, she faced him. Square shoulders. Confident stance. "I thought you might enjoy the company."

Dale removed his slouch hat and placed it on the sideboard. "No."

"But I need a few things and thought—"

"Make a list. I'll pick them up for you."

"I'd much prefer to select them myself."

"I don't know how long I'll be gone. You'll be needed here." He pulled the seat from the head of the table and squeezed his hulking frame into it.

Emily squinted her eyes at him, but he didn't look at her to see the damaging glare. "I'm not your child. I don't need your permission."

"It's my wagon. Unless you have another means to reach Marble Bar, you're staying right where you are. If you want your things, make a list."

Candice returned with a large pot of stew and ladled the fragrant mixture into wide-mouthed bowls. Emily slid into her chair, directly to Dale's right, and lifted her spoon. Let him think he'd won. No harm would come from it. But after lunch, when she appeared at the side of the wagon with her portmanteau, he would have no choice.

Emily spent the next few minutes consuming her stew in silence. Every so often, her gaze landed on the handsome man at her side, but he concentrated on his own meal to the degree that he never once lifted his eyes. It was almost as if he deliberately ignored her. Instead of the usual disheartening flare in her chest, however, she grew more determined with each bite of salted beef. When she finished her stew, she folded the linen napkin and laid it beside her bowl.

"It shouldn't take me more than a few minutes to gather my things."

"What?" Dale's head snapped up.

"For the trip? I'll only need a moment."

"You're not going!"

"Yes, I am!"

Dale rose to his full height and moved away from the table. After a moment, his expression hardened and the pulse in his jaw jumped in an erratic rhythm. It looked as if he actually ground his teeth. "I'm going alone. Can't you understand that? I just . . ." He didn't finish his sentence, choosing instead to snatch his hat from the sideboard and exit into the kitchen.

Emily followed him, but stopped short on the back porch when she saw him climb into the wagon and slap the reins on the horse's back.

Her blood heated her limbs and she fisted her hands. Very well, then. If he was so *bloody* determined she should stay behind, then a list he would most certainly receive.

"Candice!" she called back into the house. When the maid arrived, she continued, "Bring me a piece of paper and something to write with, please."

Candice hurried into the house while Emily raced to the side of the wagon. Dale pulled on the reins and brought it to a creaking halt.

"You've forgotten my list."

He emitted a low growl.

Before she could comment, Candice arrived with the requested items. Emily scratched a few entries, folded the paper and handed it to Dale. He tucked it into his shirt pocket. "Is that all?"

"You aren't going to read it?"

"I'll read it. Eventually."

Ooh! The man was positively infuriating. "Very well." Emily forced a satisfied grin, then turned to walk back into the house. When he arrived at the dry good store and read that list, he'd wish he hadn't been so stubborn!

"Listen." The gentle tone in Dale's voice sent a shiver of wanting up her spine. She hid a tremble and spun to face him. "I'm sorry about before. But three hours on a hard seat, each way, with the sun baking you every minute . . . I just don't see why you should have to go through that. You'll be much more comfortable here."

Her heart all but melted. He only thought of her comfort? Her mouth grew moist and she swallowed against a sudden wave of guilt.

"I'm perfectly capable of picking up a bag of sugar," he continued in the same whisper; deep, sensual. "I'll be back in a day or so."

Dale whistled to the horse while Emily's entire frame seemed to melt into the earth. The wagon lurched and had traveled several feet across the stable yard before Emily managed to move an inch. "Wait!"

Dale's shoulders tensed and he pulled the wagon to a stop again. "What?"

"I've changed my mind. I don't need anything, really. I'll take that list and—"

"Don't be silly. I'll get your things for you. I really don't mind."

Just then, a loud roar sounded over Emily's head. She raised her eyes to a magnificent blue sky to find an airplane waggling its wings just over the barn. "Good Lord . . . what in the world?"

"It's an airplane. Haven't you ever seen one?" Dale dismounted the wagon and pushed his hat backward. "The question is, who in the world?"

"Of course I've seen an airplane. What I meant was, what is it doing here?"

The plane roared and banked overhead for a moment then dropped lower before it disappeared behind the house. Emily and Dale hurried to the front steps and stood on the porch as the plane glided in for a rather bumpy landing not a stone's throw from the garden.

The pilot threw them a jaunty wave and removed his headgear and goggles.

"Paul?" Emily gasped. "Isn't that your friend, Paul?"

"Aye. What's he gotten into now?"

It mattered very little what he'd gotten into, so long as it delayed Dale's trip to Marble Bar long enough for her to get her list back.

🌟 🦓 🌟

Inexplicable fury made Dale's chest swell. What the bloody hell did Paul mean—*he wants to court and eventually marry Emily?*

"So, do you think I impressed her enough, mate? I mean, I figure the competition will be plenty fierce, so when my oldies told me they picked this monster up at a surplus sale last month, I spent four whole days learning how she worked. Just to sweep on in here and steal her heart away."

Dale's vision blurred and reddened against the bright

yellow paint of the airplane. He closed his eyes for only a second, then opened them and glared at Paul with all of the restraint he could muster. "I'm sure you blew her bleedin' stockings off."

Paul's eyebrows waggled and Dale immediately regretted his choice of words.

He cleared his throat and amended his previous statement. "I don't think it's such a good idea."

"Why not? She's available. I'm available. I'm thinking we could make a right nice team. Not to mention it would make you and me partners and owners of the largest spread in the territory."

"No."

"Wait a second . . . you mean to tell me that you and—"

"No! What I mean is, Gerald Brown was here a few days ago and she was rather voiced in her opinion that she wants no part of a better half. That's all. If you want to end up with her, you'll need to take it slow-like."

"Humph. You think so?"

Dale could only nod.

What the hell was he doing? Why did he give a rat's tail-feathers if Paul and every other man in the Pilbara came to woo the little minx? She was nothing to him.

Except the only reason he'd bothered to get out of bed for the past week.

A groan born of frustration echoed in his brain. Paul said something, but the screams in Dale's head drowned out the words. "What was that, mate?"

"You looked like you were headed out. Is this a bad time for a visit?"

"No worries. I was going to head into Marble Bar, but I'm in no hurry. How long, exactly, were you planning to hang around?"

"A day or two, if that's all right. I've got a bloke from Queensland flying in to Port Hedland to show me a few tricks with this lovely piece of modern mechanical genius."

A day? or two?

"You go on and I'll hang about and watch the place for you."

"I wouldn't hear of it." Dale slapped Paul on the back and gave his opposite shoulder a squeeze. "I don't have to head to the big smoke for at least another few days."

A soft voice came from behind him. "But I thought you needed to get moving right away?"

He spun to face Emily and his heart leapt into his throat. "No sweat. My mate has come all this way, by air no less, what would it look like if I left now?"

Emily's lips pursed into a half grin. "Well then, why don't the two of you go for a nice long ride?"

"Sounds good to me. I've been in the air so much lately, I haven't been in a saddle for a week or better."

"I have work to do." Dale cringed as the words flew out of his mouth.

"What work? You were just about to leave a few minutes ago." Emily's left eyebrow rose a fraction of an inch.

"Well, if I'm not going to town, then I'll need to

unhitch the wagon, put the horse away."

"That won't take long. I'll saddle Jez for you and I'll take Sally."

"I don't want to go for a ride. Didn't you get enough saddle sores in the infantry? Crikey." Dale tossed his slouch hat to the back of his head, wiped the sweat from his forehead and replaced the hat.

"Sure. We don't have to go for a ride."

"It was only a suggestion. You've been so busy around here lately, you haven't had a single minute to enjoy yourself." Emily's wounded voice cut him like a dull knife.

Busy? He hadn't been busy. He'd been making work, creating whatever small task he could to avoid her soft whispers and the scent of lavender which seemed to follow Emily from room to room. Anything to look as if he had some purpose for living besides the need to share a moment of her time. Anything to avoid his own conscience. "Is there any lemonade?"

Emily nodded and those curls bobbed again; begged to wrap around his fingers.

"I'm right parched," Paul spouted.

Dale frowned. He'd actually forgotten Paul was there. Emily took Paul by the arm and led him to the porch. Dale followed a few paces behind, an ache in his heart that rivaled the bloody moon.

When he reached the porch and took a seat in the rocking chair next to Paul, Emily excused herself to get the drinks.

"Do you remember the time you, me, and Joel roughed it at Python Pool when my oldies caught me with that sheila in the loft?" Paul stretched his legs and crossed his ankles.

"Aye."

"I was just thinking about that, I don't know why."

"Because you're not ready to settle down yet." Dale offered the solution so naturally, he almost believed it himself.

"I don't know. But all you have to do is say the word, and I'll back off Miss Emily."

Dale shifted in his chair. "Why would I say anything?"

"Because I can read you like a bloody book, mate, and you've got it bad."

Dale forced an ironic snort. "You don't know me as well as you think you do."

"If you say so." But the grin etched on Paul's features spoke the lie for him.

Emily emerged from the front door with a tray between outstretched hands. A pitcher of lemonade and three glasses balanced on the thin tray, then wobbled when her heel caught on a loose board. Dale leapt from his chair and gripped the tray before it tipped. The pitcher fell over and splashed the sweet liquid down the front of his shirt. "Crikey!"

He took the tray, set it on a small table between the two chairs and wiped the front of his shirt with both hands. The gesture did little to remedy the situation, however, and he gave up, shaking lemonade off the tips of his fingers.

Emily stared, open-mouthed. Her full, red lips formed a perfect circle before she covered them with her hands.

"Oh, Dale. I'm so sorry."

Dale's brow narrowed. Was she laughing?

There was no mistaking the guffaw that came from Paul's end of the porch. Dale glared at him, but his friend laughed that much harder.

He turned his gaze back to Emily and his heart skipped a beat or two at the light that danced in her eyes. He'd happily play the fool to keep that sparkle from ever leaving her expression.

"Aren't you going to say anything?" she asked, a giggle perched somewhere in her throat.

"Aye. I'm going to change my shirt."

🐕

The first part of *Mission: Recovery* had gone just as she'd planned. Now she needed to get his shirt away from him, under the pretense of laundering it, of course. Emily chewed the inside of her cheek as Dale strolled to the front door and disappeared into the house.

She smiled at Paul. "If you'll excuse me, please. I'm just going to see that Dale is all right."

Paul grinned. "You do that."

Heat flushed her cheeks and she spun toward the door. "I'll send Candice out with more lemonade," she called over her shoulder as she dashed into the foyer.

Tempted to take the stairs two at a time, her narrow skirt forced her to proceed more slowly. She reached the landing just as Dale passed through his bedroom door.

"Dale?"

"Yeah?"

"I really am sorry. I didn't mean to spill the pitcher." All right, so that was a lie. But a necessary one. And it's not as if she'd poured boiling oil on him. She cringed anyway.

"No worries."

"If you give me the shirt, I'll wash it for you." She took a step closer to his room. The door stood open, not quite all the way, but enough that his shadow fell across the floor in front of the gap. She took yet another step. The shadow removed its shirt and hung it over a chair.

"It's fine, really. Accidents happen."

"But I feel terrible."

"Come again?"

She cleared her throat. "I said, 'I feel terrible'," another step, "about it." Another step.

Emily stood just outside his door. His room, one of the only rooms she'd never been inside, seemed to fit him. What she could see of it did, anyway. The scent of leather and a hint of pine drifted from the masculine space. The foot of his wide bed, covered in a folded, thick green comforter, peeked from around the corner. The posters, made from a dark, rich wood and polished to a lustrous shine, rose to almost scrape the ceiling.

Another step.

Then she saw him. Dale's back faced her in sinewy detail. He stood in front of his wardrobe and shifted numerous shirts aside as if he looked for one in particular. Every time his right arm slid a hanger across the thin bar, the muscles in his back rippled and tucked in on themselves.

Her gaze followed the path of his spine until it rested on the waistband of his trousers, low on his narrow hips. A thin white line of flesh contrasted with the golden, sun-kissed bronze of his back, shoulders, and arms.

A flush warmed her whole body, from her face to her toes, and everything in between. Even her breasts clenched at her first image of true male perfection.

He found the shirt he looked for, yanked it from its hanger and turned around.

His front was — she swallowed — even better than his back.

Thick muscles defined the wall of his chest and formed little rectangles on his stomach and lower still, until they, too, disappeared into the low waistband. Stunned by the trail her eyes had taken it upon themselves to blaze over his figure, she forced them upward to his neck and shoulders.

She gasped. A large scar with jagged edges marred his right shoulder. He'd been wounded in the war. She had been aware of that. She'd even been aware that the injury had been severe enough to warrant his discharge, but . . .

The pain he must have endured brought the thick, burning sensation of tears to her throat and eyes.

He glanced at his shoulder before he turned those amazing blue eyes on her and shrugged. "It looks worse than it was."

"I find that hard to believe." Emily swallowed. "I'm sorry."

Dale advanced. One step, then another, his boots muffled by the thick rug covering most of the polished wooden floor.

Within the span of a breath, he stood a few inches from the doorway. The sweet lemon scent mixed with the heavy afternoon air and brought images of picnics and lovers to her mind's eye.

"Look at it. It's not as bad as it first seems."

He forced her gaze to his shoulder and her fingers itched to trace his flesh, to offer some sort of comfort. "What happened?"

"War happened."

His finger caught her chin and urged her face upward. The touch sparked and sent rivers of flame to her womb. Her breath hitched.

"You should go home."

Of all the things she might have expected him to say in that moment, those words were the last. "Go home?"

"Back to America. There really is nothing for you here."

Somewhere, deep inside the shock of blue in his eyes, the lie lived. She only needed to show it to him. "I don't know exactly why you've chosen to cut everyone out of your heart, Dale. But there is room for more than pain, if you'll just accept it."

Dale's face inched toward hers. He moistened his lips, leaving a shining, damp shimmer on them. His chest rose and fell as if he struggled for the very air he breathed.

Emily's pulse quickened in anticipation of his kiss. To feel those full lips pressed against her own, to experience the heat of his humid breath on her cheek . . . Her eyes fluttered closed. Her pulse raced.

Dale's hand trembled, then dropped.

No. Don't leave. Emily's eyes swung open just as Dale shifted backward one, two, then a third step. The icy sensation of loss permeated the cleft of her chin, where his finger had rested, then spread throughout her entire body. By the time she focused on his retreating form, he stood beside the chair, several arms' lengths away.

Chapter Six

Emily's eyes misted. Even from several feet away, with her gaze cast downward to his shirt, her large, violet orbs glistened. Dale had been so tempted to taste her lips that everything else had ceased to exist. The guilt that had been his constant companion vanished and it made his skin feel as if it belonged to a stranger.

He hadn't had a drink since the day they'd arrived at Castle Winters. Still, when he looked at Emily, when she slid next to him with her full breasts, narrow waist, and that damnable scent of lavender, his vision blurred and his head spun as if he were drunk. But the intoxication he found in Emily was different, more intense. It was a full, rich drunk that consumed him more than liquor ever could.

And it was far more dangerous.

When he was drunk, nothing mattered. But this new, bewildering fog that seemed to settle over him whenever she came near posed an even greater threat than what he'd faced in Gaza. Bullets. Bombs. Mines. Even the deadly thirst of the *San-ai* seemed a minute danger when compared to what Emily did to him. What she made him feel.

Crikey, he didn't want to feel anything.

Not for her. Not for anyone.

"I'll have this back to you soon," she whispered. Her voice cracked and sent a rivet through his heart.

"No worries."

She nodded and her lips parted as if she would speak. Then she pressed them together and retreated down the hall. Her footsteps echoed on the stairs.

Dale ran a hand through his hair, scrubbed the back of his head with stiff fingers and paced to the door.

He never should have come home. He'd been a fool for letting Paul talk him into it. In Egypt, he had ceased to exist. Little, if anything, had tempted him there. But here, surrounded by memories and faced with the overwhelming temptation to let his heart heal? He closed his eyes and threw his head against the doorjamb. The pain in his forehead dulled the pain in his soul, but only for a moment.

He pushed himself away from the door. After he donned a new shirt, he made his way back to the front porch where Paul awaited him with his boots propped on the railing. "It's about time, mate. I thought maybe you got lost."

"Have you seen Emily?"

"Not since she went after you. She was supposed to bring more lemonade."

"I'm sure she'll be along shortly."

"So, have you managed to keep busy since we've been back? Now that you're in charge of the place, and all?"

"Aye."

"But not riding?"

Dale frowned and glanced at Paul who looked like someone who knew more than he should. "No. Not riding. I haven't had time. Why?"

"It just struck me as odd when Emily mentioned you hadn't taken Jezebel out since you got home."

"I have a sheep station to run."

"Which usually requires a fair amount of time in the saddle."

"Usually."

"What do you say we mount up and inspect the herd for a bit. It shouldn't take long, then we can—"

Dale swore under his breath and stomped off the porch. Paul's voice trailed behind him for a moment, then his friend caught up to him in the garden. A few paces later, Dale stopped by the wagon and pulled on the harness bindings.

Paul worked the buckles loose on the far side. "When we're finished here, we can take the horses for a run by the river. It'll do us all good to spend a bit of time in the bush."

"No, thanks."

"All right then, we'll exercise them in the paddock and—"

"Crikey, Paul! Can't you take a hint? I'm not going riding today, tomorrow, or any other bleedin' day. Now, rack off!"

"Why the bloody hell not? Is there some earth-shattering reason why you won't ride?"

"It's none of your bloody business!" Dale carried the harness to the stable, kicked open the door and moved inside. Paul followed with the reins and hung them on the appropriate peg. After Dale stowed the harness and remaining tack, he moved to the front of Jezebel's stall. Her wide, black eyes stared at him as if she begged for his attention. If he didn't know better, he'd believe she smiled when he came near. He raised one hand and she nuzzled it, then her full lips brushed his palm and tried to ingest his fingers. He curled them and used his knuckles to rub the velvety top of her muzzle.

Was there a reason he wouldn't ride? Of course there was a reason. There was a reason for damn near everything in the world. There were reasons and there were answers. Except the one answer he needed. Why?

Why had Joel not survived that day? Why had Joel died when Dale survived? Why had Dale made that vow to his mother so many years ago, and why did he feel the need to honor it so many years later?

He'd been unable to keep that promise to his mother. He'd sworn that nothing would ever happen to Joel, that no matter where they were they'd be together and Dale would protect him.

But Dale stood in the stable, his horse's hot breath warming his hand, while Joel lay in a sandy grave on the other side of the earth. Alone in the dark.

How could he be forgiven for letting that happen? And how in blazes was he supposed to go on living with himself? Every morning he forced his eyes open, forced himself to walk like some ghost through the day.

Guilt made for a bitter companion. It sucked at his soul like a goanna after an eagle's eggs until only a shell remained—cracked and splintered from the onslaught.

In all of the months since he'd lost Joel, he'd found only one thing to lessen the pain. Rather, one person. A black-haired, dark-eyed pain in his arse who made him want to live again. And it wasn't Jezebel.

If only he could allow himself the pleasure of feeling something again. But every time he wanted Emily, every time his body grew hard at the mere thought of her in his arms, the guilt came back. Ten fold. A hundred.

The door opened and light spilled into the shadowed recesses of the barn. Dale leaned on a warped railing.

"Well? You want to tell me what the devil is going on?"

Dale stiffened his spine. "Nothing's going on. I'm fine."

"The hell you are. You've been killing yourself for almost a year, mate."

"I said it's none of your business."

"Bloody hell." Paul shoved away from the stall and kicked the bottom board. "It is my business. You're the closest thing I've ever had to a brother and I'm not going to let you do this to yourself."

"Do what?"

"Suffer. Punish yourself for something you had no control over."

"A promise is a promise."

"No. All promises are not the same. You made a vow to your mother when you were five years old."

"And I renewed it every day."

"You're cracked. You know that? Bleedin' cracked."

"Why? Because I keep my word? No matter what? Because I feel responsible for the people I love?"

Paul paced several steps away, ran a hand through his hair and sighed. "You don't have to take on the whole world, you know. You've paid your dues."

"Joel paid the dues. He's the one who died."

"Exactly. He's the one who died. Not you."

Dale stifled a groan, cleared his throat and ground his teeth against the burn of tears. God, he was so weak. Everything he had to live for died in that goddamned desert. How could he expect Paul to understand?

His friend, the man who'd pulled him back from the edge, approached him and laid one heavy hand on his shoulder. "You didn't die. And you don't have to shovel yourself into some corner because of it."

"I made a promise."

"A child's promise, twenty-some-odd years ago when you couldn't even lace your own boots. Let it go."

"Not that promise." Dale straightened.

"What in bloody hell are you talking about now?"

Dale cleared his throat and wiped a hand over his lips.

If anyone knew what he'd done, they'd understand more clearly. He couldn't tell anyone that particular secret. Half of it had died with Joel and the other half would die with him. But he could give Paul a portion of the truth, and maybe that would convince him to rack off and leave him the hell alone. "I promised Joel that if he couldn't be here, if he couldn't enjoy the life we had together, that I wouldn't either." Dale rubbed the back of his hand over his lips to still the tremble. "I'll never sit another horse as long as I live, Paul. Don't ask me to."

"You *are* cracked."

Dale snapped his gaze to his friend's face, expecting cynicism. Prepared to defend his decision, his commitment to his brother's memory with his fists if he needed to. What he found in Paul's expression startled him.

Compassion. Trust. Maybe even . . . love?

He couldn't stand it and turned his back to Paul. "I can't *just let it go*. It's my fault."

"It's not your fault. And I don't believe for one minute that Joel would believe it, either. You don't have to punish yourself like this."

"Aye. I do."

⚜ 🐑 ⚜

The list was gone. Emily searched each of the shirt pockets again. Her fingers shook as she delved for the fourth time, into the large breast pocket where Dale had placed the folded notepaper.

Empty.

She had to find that list. If Dale read it, she would never be able to face him again. She shook the shirt twice then craned her neck toward the floor. *Please, let it be on the floor.*

She swallowed her panic and folded the sticky garment over her forearm. He must have taken the list out in his room. She tossed the shirt into a wicker basket that contained several other items in need of a scrubbing, and dashed back upstairs.

Dale's door was closed. She bit her lip. Was it trespassing if the item she sought belonged to her? Realistically, the list was hers. She had every right to retrieve it. On the other hand, a closed door *was* a closed door. The space wasn't hers to invade.

She simply had to get that list back.

For roughly the tenth time in the last ten minutes, Emily cursed herself. She really needed to control her temper and impulsive reactions.

Dale was in the barn. She'd watched him and Paul from the mud-room window. They'd unhitched the wagon and taken the tack inside. The question was, would they be there long enough for her to search Dale's room?

No, she wasn't going to search his room, exactly. She was only going to step inside to see if the list sat on his bureau, or perhaps had fallen on the floor. Right? No harm in that.

Pride could be a terrible enemy. At that moment, it rested in Emily's soul like an albatross. Heavy. Impatient. It breathed on her neck in short, tempered gasps. She wiped her palms on her trousers.

Then she opened the door and stepped into Dale's private bedroom. She inhaled the deep, masculine perfume that surrounded her. Leather. Spices. The rich aroma that defined the space as his. Her heart ached and guilt battled with her pride.

Just find the list.

She glanced at the tables on either side of the wide, four-poster bed. Then shifted her gaze to the desk and the bureau. Nothing. She squatted and looked under the bed by the wardrobe. Still no list.

Damn.

The front door opened, then closed downstairs. Footsteps came up the stairs. Heavy, masculine, slow bootsteps.

Emily sucked in her breath and dashed out of the room. She stood in front of her own door and placed her hand on the brass knob just as Dale reached the landing.

He stopped when he saw her and offered a nod. "You coming back down?"

"Yes. I just wanted to gather a few more things for the wash." She swallowed.

A dim light sparked somewhere in the depths of his eyes. It called to her in a voice that strained to be free for more than a moment before it flickered and died. He cast his gaze to the floor, turned and went back downstairs. Her breath caught somewhere near her heart and she stared after him for what was probably too long.

Then she shook her head to clear it of all too improper images of Dale's naked back, dashed into her room and pulled her spare trousers from the wardrobe. Perfectly clean and neatly folded trousers. She whined as she crumpled them, tucked them under her arm and followed Dale's path to the main floor.

After a slight detour to the mud-room to deposit the garment that made good her lie, and the kitchen for a new tray of lemonade, she ventured back to the porch.

She found Paul leaning against a pillar, his back straight and his arms folded over his chest. A few scanning glances around the yard yielded Dale, leaning against the high fence that surrounded the paddock.

He cut an imposing frame. His shirt stretched taut over the muscles in his back. The memory of those sinewy muscles beneath the smooth, golden surface brought heat to her cheeks. When the glasses on the tray chimed against one another, she forced her eyes away, placed the shaking tray on the short table next to Paul and claimed a chair for herself.

As if she had no control over them, however, her eyes slid in Dale's direction once more. "He seems lonely, doesn't he?"

Paul glanced over his shoulder. "Aye. He's not the same man he used to be."

"Is it because of the war?"

Paul nodded, pushed free of the pillar, and took a glass of lemonade.

"It's more than that, though, isn't it?"

"It's not my place to say, Em. You'll have to ask him."

Ask him? He barely tolerated her and his moods shifted by the ticks of a clock. Should she ask him about something so painful and personal as the war, which he'd already made perfectly clear he wished not to discuss, she might as well pack her portmanteau and book passage back to America. She would have no chance to prove her love to him. No chance to earn his love in return.

No. Whatever demons ate at his soul, Dale would have to confess them of his own free will.

Her gaze caressed his back again. Dale pushed off the fence and whistled to Jezebel. The black raised her head and meandered in the direction of Dale's outstretched hand. She nuzzled it before sliding next to the fence and laying her large, oblong head on Dale's shoulder.

The animal loved Dale. Anyone with a pair of eyes could see it. What had Blue said? Dale and Jezebel grew up together? The mare was as much a part of Dale as his legs. Why would he torture himself, and her, by ignoring the majestic black's one desire? To carry her rider over the soft grass pastures like the wind over the sea.

Jezebel stomped one of her forelegs and jerked away from the fence. She seemed aloof and refused to turn back to Dale. He whistled again, but this time Jezebel ignored him and moved back into her stall. Apache neighed from his paddock on the far side of the pasture.

Dale's head hung low for a moment. Then, as if his shoulders alone bore some invisible burden, he left the fence and turned back to the porch.

Emily's heart leapt into her throat. He was so devilishly handsome. Her fingers itched to brush the soft, wheat-colored strands away from his face. To expose the full beauty behind those brilliantly translucent eyes and trace the line of his firm, square jaw. She fisted her hands in her lap.

Paul swallowed a mouthful of lemonade then yelled, "That horse wants to be ridden, mate."

Dale seemed to ignore the comment, at least until he reached the porch. "Leave off."

Paul shrugged, turned to Emily and poured his large frame into a chair with panther-like grace. "About ten or so years ago now, this blighter right here won the territorial horse race by better than a half a day. He and Jezebel were the fastest pair in all of the Pilbara, and I'd bet my own mum that they still are."

Emily smiled. "I don't think I'd take that bet. You've never seen Apache run, have you?" She clicked her teeth and shook her head. "He beat every horse for a hundred miles around back home."

Dale grunted and stared into the pasture as if he hadn't heard her at all. For a moment she thought he hadn't until he looked at her with those light eyes, filled with misty memories. "I won't be entering Jez in any races, so I guess we'll never know whose mount's faster, will we?" He stared right through her, pinned her heart with one solid glare until it beat against the backrest of her rocking chair. "So Paul, you'll be staying over a couple of days, then, mate? Good. I need someone to help me pin down the roof on the barn. Wind keeps kicking it up."

Paul leaned back and crossed his legs. "Where's all the *Jackaroos*? Oh, that's right. They'd be out tending the flock. Since you won't go out there and check on them yourself. You might have to climb on a horse."

✶ 🐎 ✶

Dale tamped down the urge to place his fist dead-center in Paul's face. Lord knew, the cocky son-of-a-bitch deserved it, but Dale couldn't bring himself to do it. Instead, he forced his hands open and ran both of them through his hair before he climbed down the creaking wooden steps.

Jez approached the fence again, her head turned to one side as she stamped the earth with her front hoof, and glared at him with one huge, black eye. She blinked but never looked away, as if to say she understood his pain and would do her best to guide him through to the other side. He reached the fence for the second time in less than ten minutes and leaned against the planks. Jez nudged his shoulder.

"Easy, girl."

She whinnied. Right in his ear.

Somewhere behind him, Paul laughed. Dale didn't turn around to see his best friend flirt and tease Emily. He could live to a ripe old age, never see the like, and be pleased as a magpie in a billabong about it. Instead, he scratched Jez's ear when she rubbed her neck against the fence.

"You like that, do you? Aye, you like it when I scratch you just so. Ah, if only things had worked out differently. But you understand, don't you, girl? You don't mind a bit. You'll get all fat and sassy, and that sits just fine with you."

She tossed her head and backed away from the fence. A scream cut the still, afternoon air and she reared. Dale jumped away and frowned. Jezebel slammed back to the ground and spun in a blur of black hide and flying mane. She ran to the far edge of the paddock, spun and ran back to him. Without so much as a falter, she turned to the south and raced along the fence line. She flagged her tail and the long, shining strands danced in her wake. Her mane shimmered in the light when she tossed her head. Faster and ever faster she ran. Thick muscles bunched and released beneath her glossy coat. Dale's breath caught in his lungs. His fingers itched to hold a pair of reins.

About halfway around the fence line, Sally and a half-dozen others joined in the impromptu race. Sally, smaller than the other mounts, ran on the inside at a disadvantage. Still, she kept up with the racers, running close to Jezebel.

The larger horses pushed against each other as if they urged one another to run that much faster, that much harder. When the herd passed Dale's position on the fence, a cool blast of air offered a welcomed chill.

More than chilling him, it was like ice water in winter.

Jezebel hadn't died that day in the desert, either. Neither had Sally. They ran and played as if nothing had changed. As if the world kept turning. As if he still breathed.

But he didn't breathe. Not really. Not anymore. And if Jezebel wanted to run, if she wanted a rider on her back, she'd have to do it with someone else.

✤ 🐎 ✤

Long, black shadows drew stark lines across the paddock, stable yard, and garden. Emily hugged herself and leaned against the porch railing as the sun crept behind the trees and finally disappeared in a flash of orange, pink, and azure. A band of violet sky made way for bright, twinkling stars that reminded her of home.

She'd searched everywhere she could think of for the hasty list she'd written for Dale. She'd even ventured into his bedroom a second time. Nothing. There was only one place she hadn't looked. The only place he could have hidden the note and the only place she couldn't look. At least, not until he went to bed. He must have shoved it into a trouser pocket.

Once he fell asleep, she could sneak into his room and search his pockets. It had to be there. She had to find it before he read it.

An eagle cried as if offering her encouragement, and she smiled.

How could Dale not want to spend the rest of his life here? As a child, she'd wished on every first star she'd ever seen that somehow, someway, someday she would live in Australia. Not just Australia, but on the Castle Winters Station. She would work side by side with her uncle and the two wild boys she'd grown to love. One more than the other.

When her father lost his daily battle against the demon whiskey, Emily would often pretend she was already here. With Apache's strong back beneath her, she'd ride high into the rocky cliffs by her family's ranch for days at a time. Lost in the realm of dreams. Now, here she was. And nothing was as she'd imagined.

A twinge of something sour tickled the back of her throat. Of course, her uncle and Joel were gone. Dale had failed to fall in love with her the moment they'd met. But he did call to her with soft eyes and a pride that encompassed everything he touched. It didn't matter that her plans hadn't worked out *exactly* as she'd imagined. It only mattered that Dale was home. She simply had to find a way to make him stay.

Earlier that afternoon, she'd seen something in his normally smoky blue eyes she hadn't seen before. A spark. It might have been anger, or it might have been something less hostile; she hadn't been able to judge because it had disappeared as quickly as it had appeared. But she'd seen it just the same. It had come when Paul had mentioned riding.

She rubbed the evening chill from her arms and glanced at the paddock.

The horses meandered through the pasture, clipping the grass as they went. Had Dale mentioned something to Paul? Something that might explain why he so desperately wanted to sell the station? Something that could explain why he'd run for so many months and why Paul had been forced to all but drag him home?

She glanced in the direction of the cumbersome, yellow contraption with its wings, one set stacked above the other, that filled most of the side yard. Paul slipped out of the second of two holes in the top of the main body and climbed to the ground.

A loud, sudden whistle captured her attention, and she started. Jezebel must have heard it, too. Her head, perched elegantly atop her thickly muscled neck, faced the stable. She snorted, pricked her ears in the same direction and shuffled toward her stall. A moment later, Sally followed her.

Emily crept down the steps, across the garden and into the open door of the stable.

Dale spent an awfully great amount of time in the stable. For someone so adamant about not riding, anyway. He stood at Jezabel's stall, his forearms and hands flat against the top of the door, his chin on the backs of his hands. His hair, disarrayed as if he'd just run his hands through it, caught the shadows and held firm. Even the planes of his profile seemed to play with the light, giving him the appearance of someone much younger than his years.

Or maybe it was Jezebel herself who did it? When he looked at his horse, the pain in his expression seemed to slip away. For a moment, at least, before the stern set of his jaw or the narrow crease above his brow returned. It was obvious he loved the animal, that he missed her as much as she missed him.

Emily cleared her throat.

Apparently surprised, Dale shot up from the stall door and frowned.

"I'm sorry. I didn't mean to disturb you." It was a lie. The almost imperceptible flutter in one of his eyebrows said he knew she lied. But she smiled and stepped into the stable. "I seem to do it a lot, don't I?"

"Can I help you?" He crossed in front of her and faced the scarred work bench against the far wall. His back pulled against his cotton shirt as if he tinkered with something on the table. A few clicks and pops confirmed it.

"I thought we could go for a little ride. It's a beautiful night."

"Not enough light."

"Back home, I used to ride at night all the time. I loved to go down to the riverfront and sit by the bank. Just me, Apache, and the Joshua trees."

"The Pilbara isn't Arizona. If you venture down to the billibong at night, by yourself, there's a good chance you won't come back."

"Arizona isn't exactly a summer garden, either."

"Do you have King Browns there?"

"Pardon?"

"Brown snakes? Do you have them in your *Arizona*?" He glanced over his shoulder and his gaze roamed over her face for the barest second before he turned back to his work.

"We have Diamond Back Rattlers."

"Those are the little brown and grey buggers that shake their tales at you to scare you off?"

She nodded and stepped toward the soft lull of his voice. Of course he couldn't see her nod, so she answered, "Yes. They rattle to let you know they're there and to leave them alone. One is wise to respect them."

"The King Brown doesn't warn you. He doesn't care if you leave him alone because he knows he can take you down in a fight. If you come on him at night, in the dark, and he bites you, you're a gonner and that's no lie." He tsked. "No joy in that."

"I thought all snakes tended to run away from humans, really." She leaned against the table and picked up an awl. "Isn't that true?"

"What happens when a rattlesnake bites you? Have you ever seen anyone snakebit?"

She nodded again. "A little girl who lived in town, oh . . . it must be ten years ago, now . . . she was bitten on her hand. Screamed and screamed, the poor thing. The doctor was able to save her life, but not her hand, I'm afraid."

"I see. So she felt the bite?"

"Yes. Of course she did. She cried right away. Thank goodness, it was during a church picnic and everyone in town, including Doctor Taylor, was there. She'd come on the snake in the shade of a few trees. Her father was with her, but wasn't able to grab her before she tried to pick it up."

Dale set down the odd device he'd been adjusting and leveled a calm stare into her eyes. Warmth clouded her mind like a soft mist from a lake. He had such beautiful, warm eyes.

"When the King Brown bites you, you don't feel it. It's that sharp and that quick. You get a headache, you get sick to your stomach, and then you die. You're dead before you even know you've *been* snakebit. I wouldn't advise you taking any midnight rides on your own."

Emily swallowed and stared into the swirling blue orbs until his words echoed into the warm night air. She put down the awl and leaned on her elbows. "All the more reason for you to come with me."

He huffed and tossed himself away from the workbench. "I already told you. It's too dark."

"How about in the morning?"

"No."

"Why not?"

"Because I said so."

"That's childish."

"And you're whining."

She scoffed. "I am *not* whining. I never whine. I haven't whined since I was . . . eleven years old."

He pulled a pitchfork from its hook on the wall and snorted. "You may think you haven't whined, but you're whining."

She stomped her foot. "Then go riding with me!"

"Why is this so important to you?" He lifted a forkful of straw and tossed it into an empty stall.

Like a bullet aimed at her heart, a thought burst into her consciousness. Had Dale been injured more severely than he'd let on? Was there some medical reason he could no longer ride? "It's not important. It's just . . . an idea. Something to take your mind off things."

Another forkful of straw joined the first; he stabbed the earth floor with the tines and leaned into the handle. "And why do I need to take my mind off things?"

"Because you're . . ." *Sad.* "Because you're always working so hard. You should learn to relax."

"You need to find someone to mother, you know that?"

Mother? "I'm not trying to mother you."

"Could've fooled me. Listen," he groaned as he resumed pitching straw into the stall, "I don't need anyone taking care of me, but that Paul Campbell . . . now, he's another sort altogether. You could mother him all you like and he'd love you for it."

"I am not mothering you. Or anybody else."

"Then you might want to think about marrying him. That's why he's here."

Emily almost choked on her tongue. "Pardon me?"

"He fancies you. Thinks he might be just the right bloke to take your mind off your worries."

"I don't have any worries."

"Sure you do. You have Gerald and any number of others chasing you like a goanna on an egg. You could do worse than Paul."

"I don't need a husband. And when I decide I want one, I'll do the picking. If that's all right with you."

He shrugged. But he didn't look at her.

She already missed the mysterious tingle that churned in her belly when he cast even a simple glance in her direction. Something about him made her think of fresh butter on warm bread and the gentle call of the crickets just after sunset. Like a sweet illness from which she never wanted to recover. "Someday, I'll marry."

He turned and she cringed. Had she spoken aloud?

Someday, I'll marry you.

Chapter Seven

She thought he might never fall asleep. For hours, it seemed, Emily had sat up in her bed waiting for Dale's room to fall into silence. Each time she believed him asleep, something in his room would shift. The chair would creak as if he'd sat in it. Or it would scrape against the floor. His door would open and close a few minutes later. His footsteps would disappear down the stairs only to arrive back on the landing after only a few minutes.

She glanced at the gilded anniversary clock. The glow of her lamp reflected off the glass and the gears, spinning silently inside, dancing in the light. Twenty-five minutes past two in the morning. Dale's room had been as quiet as a tomb for thirty minutes.

She tossed the coverlet away and swung her legs off the bed. She shoved her feet into her slippers, then toed them off. The soles might shuffle on the wood floors. A deep breath, a silent prayer, and she left the relative safety of her room and entered the hall. Neutral ground . . .

Emily peered down the darkened hall. No light came from beneath Dale's door to her left. No light came from the servants' quarters at the far end, or the guestroom on the opposite side of hers, where Paul slept.

Good.

With everyone asleep, she could sneak into Dale's room, find the list in his trousers, and be back in her own bed with no one the wiser.

She crept down the hall—cringed when her foot landed on a loose board—and held her breath. Finally, she grasped the cold doorknob, twisted, and pushed.

It didn't open. Had he locked it? She tried again, a soft click sounded like a gunshot, and the door released.

A sigh forced her eyes closed in another prayer. This one of thanks for small miracles.

Inside his room she pushed the door closed, but made certain it didn't latch. She squinted into the darkness. The moon had passed and very little light shone through the open windows, but if she were careful . . . "Ouch!"

Both of her hands flew to her mouth and she stared at the huge form sprawled across the center of the bed. A tear escaped the corner of her eye and her foot throbbed and burned. She forced herself to examine the floor beside the bed. She'd kicked a crate of something, but the words on the side failed to pierce the darkness. Who would leave a box in the middle of the floor? A person could hurt themselves!

She steadied her breath and, careful not to collide with anything else that might be lying about in careless abandon, made her way to the wardrobe. Slowly, deliberately, as if the slightest wrong move would give up the ghost, Emily unlatched the wardrobe door and opened it.

"What are you doing here?"

She closed her eyes and rested her forehead on the edge of the door, still gripped in her hands as if she were some thief in the night. Of course that's exactly what she was, wasn't she? Her heart burst with guilt, and she turned.

Dale had rolled onto his back and flung one arm across his forehead. Eyes closed. Long lashes captured what little light came through the window. His chest moved in an easy rhythm. She narrowed her gaze and studied the relaxed lines of his jaw.

He was still asleep, thank heavens.

His head shook. "I don't want you here. I told you that. Rack off."

Gone was the gentle set of his features. His eyebrows came together in a scowl and his lips curled in a grimace. He tossed his head twice, then rolled to his side.

A nightmare. About the war, more than likely. Such wickedness could only led to nightmares the likes of which she would never know. She took a single step toward the bed before she caught herself.

Would she soothe him? In the middle of the night, in her nightgown? What if he woke up? How could she explain her presence in his room?

"No!" One of Dale's long, muscled legs kicked as he thrashed to his other side.

Emily rushed to the bedside and placed the flat of her hand to Dale's cheek. His flesh, clammy even in the temperate midnight air, was rough with almost a day's growth of beard. His eyes flew open and something exploded in the dark, sea-blue depths. Something angry. Something . . . frightening.

She pulled her hand away, but he caught her wrist in a firm, not-ungentle grip. "Why did you come here?"

"I . . . Please, let me go."

"You should have stayed home with Charles. I can't take care of you. Go home."

"Dale, please, let go."

His eyes grew dim again. The lids fell closed and he reclined on his pillow. His hand, warm and strong, released her wrist. It was as if he'd never spoken. As if he hadn't looked directly at her. She doubted he'd seen her, anyway.

She retreated two steps, rubbing her wrist. She should have known better. It wasn't her place to console him.

The dream seemed to have passed. At least, he hadn't spoken again. So she turned to the wardrobe, gathered his trousers and searched the pockets. Any moment she would find the list, take it back to her room and burn it in the oil-lamp.

Five empty pockets later, the trousers dangled from her fingers as she stared at them. Her reflection in the mirror caught her attention for some reason, and she snapped her mouth shut. Where in blazes was that stupid list?

✦ 🐎 ✦

A song hung in the air. The melody was familiar but the words came from so far away, Dale couldn't make them out. The voice, pure and full, embraced him. Drew him awake, away from the dreams.

He opened his eyes to the stark, unyielding light of another day. Another day stolen from Joel. Another day through which he would walk as if he deserved it.

The song drifted in his open window again. Whoever sang the notes had a strong voice, and curiosity bade him discover the source. The words grew clearer until he made out the ridiculous lyrics. Something about bubbles fading and dying. He rose and glanced out of the window.

Directly beneath him, as naked as she pleased, Emily sat in the old copper tub. Bubbles, the inspiration for her little concert no doubt, filled the tub. Her hair caught the light, piled atop her head in a mass of wild curls. No knot. Just piled there as if she hadn't bothered to brush the impossibly long strands.

His fingers curled. He rested them on the sill to keep them from trembling.

She shouldn't be bathing in the middle of the garden. Especially with Paul staying over. What if he wandered into the rear of the house? What if he happened on her before she finished her bath? Did she put something in her bath water to make every inch of her body and every strand of her hair carry that damnable lavender perfume?

He swallowed hard and forced himself away from the window.

All manner of fantasies spun through his mind, and his limbs, until the heady desire they wrought took up sordid residence in his strides. His body ached.

Whose wouldn't?

A man sees a naked woman first thing in the morning and a physical reaction is only natural. It had nothing to do with the wild dreams he'd had last night. Nothing in the least. Just because, for the first time since . . . for the first time in over a year, he'd dreamt of something other than killing his own brother didn't mean it had anything to with Emily.

Of course, he had dreamt of Joel as well. But instead of the constant barrage of bloodied and battered images of his dead brother, he'd been granted a reprieve. He'd dreamt of the time before the war, when Joel's incredible lust for life had brought Dale joy along with the incessant desire to protect him. Soon, the nightmare had returned, however. But it was different. Emily had been there. She'd soothed his aching heart; made his flesh burn with desire. Or she'd tried to. In the end, she'd begged him to let her go. Begged him not to touch her.

And he'd spent the rest of the night in limbo, in that place where one floated between heaven and hell, sleep and waking.

Until her voice had called to him.

He turned back to the window and trampled the urge

to peek outside again. He pulled a shirt from the wardrobe, donned it, gathered his hat and his boots and went downstairs. He'd leave for Marble Bar as soon as he could harness the horse and hitch the wagon. If the only way to get that woman out of his system for a least a day and a night was to leave, then he'd leave. Simple.

She'd say he was running away.

His conscience twinged. He wasn't running away. He was protecting her. Protecting himself. Always protecting.

With a huff, he threw on his hat and sat on the chaise in the parlor. Within only a few moments and with an economy of movement born of seven years in the regiments, he had pulled on his boots, buttoned his shirt, tucked it into his strides and headed out the front door.

To the stable. Harness the horse. Hitch the wagon. Escape.

"G'day, boss," Henry Albert called from the roof of the stable. A tall aborigine with long, light hair and a huge, ready smile, Henry Albert had been working on Castle Winters for as long as Dale could remember. "Betcha feel good sleepin' like that. Miss Emily says I should fix the roof for you, seeing as how you didn't sleep much last night."

"What?"

"Miss Emily. She says we should let you catch up on your rest. Said you didn't sleep."

"I'm fine. Thanks for fixing the roof though, mate." He swung open the stable door. "I'll be gone for a day or so and you doing that chore gets me on the road that much sooner. Do me a favor and pass the word to the others. If they need anything, Paul is here. He can help."

"I imagine we'll be fine. Emily managed a fine station before you came home."

Dale froze in mid-stride. His hand clenched the door handle and he gritted his teeth. *Emily had managed a fine station*, he mimicked to himself. He'd just bet she had. She could probably manage ten stations, or a hundred.

Well, she wasn't going to manage him. He grabbed the nearest harness, threw it over his shoulder and snatched the reins off their hook on the wall.

Jezebel whinnied and Apache answered her with a snort and a loud blow. Sally lifted her head and shook her mane. They wanted attention, but he had none to give. Not today. Not when his sanity depended on getting the hell out of there.

He threw the reins around the draft horse's neck and led him to the stable yard. There, he made short work of the harness and led the hulking beast to the wagon.

"Going somewhere?"

Damn!

Dale glanced over his shoulder. Emily stood at the horse's head, stroking his muzzle. Wet tendrils framed her face even though she'd let her hair down. The mass of curls framed her from her head to her hips. Made her skin glow like alabaster in the morning light. He looked away. He had to. He had to concentrate on something else or he'd be done for.

He grit his teeth as he pulled the straps on the hitch. "Marble Bar."

"Oh, I thought you'd put that off until Paul left."

"Changed my mind."

"I can see that."

"Good."

"Fine."

"Fine what?"

"Fine. Run away. I can't stop you."

"Bugger off, lady. I don't need you telling me what for. Not now. Not ever."

"Of course you don't. You know as well as I do that you're running away."

He finished attaching the hitch, straightened to his full height and glared at her. As much as anyone could glare at something so beautiful. He shook his head to clear the erotic image of her in the bathtub. "What exactly is it you think I'm running from?"

"Oh, any number of things."

"Such as?"

"The past. Or the future. Memories."

Dale snorted, but inside his bones melted at her insight. "I'm not running away from anything. We need supplies."

"Oh, I don't need anything. Not really. I just picked up supplies when we collected you from the docks. Really, there isn't any reason to go into town."

"Sugar."

"Pardon?"

"Sugar. We're out of sugar."

"We can live without sugar for a while longer, I think."

"I'm going. And that's that."

Fire flashed in her eyes a moment before sweeping concern replaced the flame. She bit the inside of her cheek in that way she had that sent a tremor straight to his loins, spun, and fled into the house.

In her wake, a breeze caught her scent and wrapped him in it like a blanket. Lavender.

Damn.

Lavender and bubbles. Two of the three things he needed least in his life.

The third had raven hair and the deepest eyes he'd ever seen.

He sure as hell didn't need her. How the bloody hell did she know so much, anyway? Of course, she didn't know everything. She'd forgotten herself. She'd neglected to mention he ran straight away from her.

He climbed into the wagon and urged the horse forward, out of the stable yard, and onto the road to Marble Bar. He glanced at his feet and found a folded piece of notepaper.

Emily's list. He'd almost forgotten about that.

He picked it up and shoved it in his shirt pocket. Obviously, she needed something. He'd buy the items on her list and make nice when he came home. In the meantime, he could pretend he didn't care about her.

⚹ 🐎 ⚹

By the time the wagon lumbered onto Marble Bar's General Street, Dale's mood had deteriorated in equal proportions to the emptiness of his stomach. Three and a half hours over bumpy roads in searing heat had left him looking for someplace to find a bit of cold meat and colder beer. He smacked the reins on the horse's rump and it sped to a reluctant trot, over the bridge at Sandy Creek and then Dale turned onto Francis before stopping in front of the dry goods store.

The town hadn't changed much since he'd left. A group of school children dashed in and out of the few buildings along the wide, dirt street. Two women strolled out of the dry goods store and he tipped his hat to them. They smiled and moved toward their automobile, parked on the street like a beacon to the future. He left his lists with Old Man Bartholomew and walked across the street to the Ironclad Hotel.

Another group of five boys who looked about ten years old swamped him when they left the store. How many times had he and Joel done that very thing? On the long trips to Marble Bar as children, he and Joel would clamber from the wagon, pennies in hand, and race to Bart's for as much candy as they could carry. His heart skipped more than one beat as the boys disappeared into the store he'd just left.

Crikey, he needed a drink.

A buckboard rumbled past and he stared after it. A young couple sat in the back. They looked at each other as if they knew something no one else in the world knew. A secret.

The Ironclad's taps beckoned and he hurried across the street. Covered in iron sheeting, the single story rooming and drinking establishment hadn't changed either. The wide, ground-level porch offered welcomed shade to passers-by beneath a pitched-roof entry. Old Man Kincaid sat in the same rocking chair he'd occupied the last time Dale had seen him, before the war.

An American miner, the slender man with an unruly mop of silver hair straggling from beneath a wide-brimmed cowboy hat, was an almost permanent fixture at the hotel. When he wasn't wandering into the Great Sandy Desert in search of the elusive vein of gold he insisted he'd find someday, he lived here. But every so often, he'd pack up his burro, Lucy-Jean, and disappear into the bush for a few weeks—searching for what he called *the mother load*.

Apparently, he hadn't struck it rich quite yet.

Kincaid's eyes opened, and he smiled. "Little Dale Winters? Is that you? While, as I live and breathe." He struggled to his feet and waddled across the creaking planks. "When did you get home?"

"Not too long ago, Mr. Kincaid. How've you been?"

"Hangin' in there, son. Hangin' in there. We've missed you around here."

A twinge of pride tickled the back of Dale's neck.

He rubbed it away with one hand and forced a smile. "Thanks."

"That Gerald Brown took a might too much advantage of the fact he was the toughest kid in town for a while. But now that you're back, I'm sure all that's gonna change, right?"

A frown replaced Dale's smile. "What do you mean?"

"Oh, just the same cowardly bullshit he always pulled. Only nobody here was strong enough to stop him. All the good men were off fighting, like you and your brother."

Dale swallowed. "I imagine he'll settle down now that we're home. Don't you worry about a thing."

The old man's eyes seemed to mist for a moment and he stared into the street. "I sure wish I couldha' gone with you boys. Given them Germans a run, I would've, back in my younger days."

"I'm sure you would have. You want a drink?" Dale opened the door to the pub and clapped Old Man Kincaid on the shoulder. "I'm buying."

"No . . . no, that's mighty nice of you. I think I'll just sit out here a spell longer."

Kincaid shuffled back to his rocking chair and eased himself into it. His hand landed on the chain of his pocket watch and he withdrew the timepiece. Clicking it open, he gazed at the face. A heavy sigh escaped his feeble chest.

Poor old chap.

The public room was dark and it took a minute for his vision to adjust. Shadows filled the corners and the same old piano covered most of the back wall. The floorboards still squeaked. The mirror over the bar still captured the light from the front windows in an eerie, half-lighted reflection that did little to brighten the room.

"Well, look who finally decided to pay us a visit, mates!" Tim Lancaster, a permanent fixture behind the bar, rounded the end of his fortress and met Dale halfway across the floor. "It's good to see you, boy."

"It's good to be home." The lie tasted sour.

Dale accepted the clasp of several tendered hands, even managed a smile or two before he settled at the bar with a tall, cool beer and plate of beef tips and gravy.

"It's on the house, Dale. Your money's no good here. Told your mate the same thing when he stopped in. You and Paul are heroes as far as we're concerned."

"Thanks."

"You be needin' a room, too?"

"Aye. Just for the night."

"I'll have my sister fix one up for you." Tim leaned on his elbows and lowered his head. His eyes grew dark, and he frowned.

Here it comes. He swallowed a draft of beer and set the mug back on the bar.

"Listen. We're all tore up about Joel. He was a decent bloke and we all liked him."

"Thanks."

Please. Not another word.

"He used to come in here every time he came to town,

back just after you left for school. I used to have to run him out with a broom!" Tim chuckled and the light came back into his eyes. The light that said it was okay to remember. It was expected that those who were lost would be thought of with a certain joy.

Must be nice to be able to remember someone without guilt. Without that gnawing, grinding, speculating knife twisting in his back. "Sounds like Joel, right enough."

"And Charles, too. You know, he and I were pretty good mates there toward the end."

"Yeah. I know. I reckon just about everybody loved Joel and Charles." Too bad they were gone and only he remained. Who could love him after what he'd done? Abandoned the man who'd been like a father to him and signed his own brother's death warrant.

Tim clapped him on the shoulder and slid down the bar into the back, apparently to arrange for Dale's room.

Dale stared at the steaming plate of food. His stomach roiled, but not from hunger.

Maybe he shouldn't have come here, after all. Too many memories. Like the time he and Joel had snuck in the back door and run off with two bottles of the cheapest, most foul-tasting rot-gut whiskey man had ever made. They'd managed to drink one half of the first bottle before they'd been so ill they hadn't given a kangaroo's arse if they were caught or not. They'd assumed they would be dead by morning anyway, but they'd both wanted to see their mother one more time before they met their maker.

A smile threatened to bend one side of his mouth and he rubbed it away with the palm of his hand.

That had been six months before their parents died.

Bloody hell.

Could he not even have a drink without something wicked and painful attacking him? This was why he hadn't wanted to come home.

He shoved the plate away, swallowed the last of his beer and stood. He wasn't as hungry as he'd thought, apparently. "Give me a bottle of scotch, will ya, Tim?"

Tim handed him an unopened bottle and a room key. Dale tossed a few coins on the counter. His stomach knotted on itself and he turned around.

Gerald Brown sauntered through the door with two of his thugs in tow. When their eyes met, Gerald stopped and rocked back on his heels. "If it ain't my old pal, Dale. Didn't think to see you in town so soon. The little woman harder to deal with than you thought?" He laughed and slid into a chair behind a round, scarred table.

Dale resisted the urge to respond. What did it matter? Gerald was a horse's arse and always would be. Nothing he said would change that.

"That's right, boys. Winters here has come home to that sheila we've all heard tell about. Seen her myself, I have, and she's a right pretty one. The kind to keep a man warm on cold nights."

Dale pivoted on his heel and glared at Gerald. Rage shook him to the center of his being. Hot. Violent. It rocked him like a storm at sea filled with untamed passion and certain death on the outer fringes, held in check by a single dam made from exhaustion and remorse. The dam was cracking.

"What's the matter with you? Don't think for a second we don't know what goes on out there. Tell me something. Is she as hot between the sheets as she is between her legs?"

The dam broke.

A year's worth of enraged guilt poured out of Dale's heart and into his arms until it curled his hands into tight fists. He grabbed Gerald from behind the table and lifted him against the back wall. "You've had this coming for a long time, mate. Can't thank you enough for letting me be here to deliver it."

He dropped Gerald to his feet and planted his fist alongside the shorter man's jaw. Gerald fell in a heap. Dale dove on top of him, his fists making contact over and over again with Gerald's face. One of Gerald's cohorts wrapped Dale in a bear hug, but Dale whipped his head backward until it came into contact with the man's nose. A sickening crunch echoed in the tavern. Chairs skidded and creaked on the wood floors as those closest to Dale and Gerald hurried out of the way.

"Get up, you son-of-a-bitch. On your feet!" Dale found Gerald's lapels and hauled him up. "You make me sick, you know that? You treat people like they're dirt. What did Emily ever do to you, except turn you down?

And you make her sound like some kind of whore."

Gerald mumbled something, but the only thing that came out of his mouth was a bit of blood and spittle. Dale dropped him again, gathered his hat from the floor and reclaimed his bottle of scotch.

When he left the boozer, he made a sharp left and stalked to his room. He planned to drink the entire thing. Alone. Where nobody could judge him. Where nobody could blame him.

✦ 🐎 ✦

Emily wandered through the parlor, a dust rag in one hand and a canister of bee's wax in the other. Just like her home in Arizona, the Western Australian desert made dusting a daily chore. She'd rather be exercising the horses, but Dale was due home sometime today. She'd helped Ruth finish the laundry earlier in the morning, and been more than disheartened that her foolish list hadn't miraculously appeared in the soiled clothes.

Since then, she'd helped scrub the kitchen floors, swept the front porch, and polished every piece of wood in the house. It was a lovely house, full of rich, dark wood, with high ceilings and a comfortable atmosphere that made it feel like a home. Even though no family had lived here since before the war.

Still, the essence of memories clung to the floral wallpaper like someone else's dreams. She'd practically grown up here through her uncle's letters. The draperies that adorned the front windows had been a gift from Dale's father to his mother around the time of Dale's tenth birthday. The shining, mahogany sideboard that displayed Dale's mother's dishes had come from America around the turn of the century, just four or five years before Mr. and Mrs. Winters had been killed in a flash flood. Every piece of wood, molding, every rug and each tooled column had been lovingly imported from Mrs. Winters' native Bristol.

How many memories had Dale wished to forget when fate had so cruelly stolen his parents? Had he retreated into himself then, too? If he had, Uncle Charles had never mentioned it.

Emily stopped her inspection in front of a tall bookcase filled with leather-bound classics. She set her cleaning supplies on the rim of the third shelf and examined the volumes. One book stood out among the rest and Emily pulled it free. The butter-soft cover caressed her fingertips and the binding creaked as she opened it, as if it hadn't been handled in a great many years.

It was collection of photographs. She carried it to the sofa and rested it in her lap. Images from the past filled page after page. The first page was a wedding photo dated 1886. Dale's mother seemed so young compared to her much older husband, and despite their stern expressions their eyes held a certain happiness that even the old camera had captured with ease. Toward the middle of the book, she found pictures of other family members and even one of Charles, taken years before age and the elements had taken their hold. She touched his face and recognized herself in the shape of his jaw and set of his mouth. He had been a proud man. Capable and strong. But in the end, he had been so lonely his strength hadn't been enough. She sniffled. At least he hadn't died alone.

She turned the page and found a picture of two small boys. The younger of the two, maybe two years old, had a bruise over his left eye, light hair to his shoulders and wore a white dress-like garment made from linen trimmed with lace. The older boy had a mischievous glint in his eyes that had since changed to regret and remorse. Still, she would have recognized Dale anywhere, at any time or age. Dale had been an adorable child, with long lashes and a strong build. What would his sons look like?

Footsteps pulled her attention away from the photographs just as Paul slid into the armchair next to the sofa. "What have you got there?"

"Photographs. These boys here," she turned the book so Paul could see the images, "that's Dale and Joel, isn't it?"

Paul smiled and his eyes lit like huge stars. "Too right. Where did you find this? I've never seen these pictures before."

"Just there, on the bookshelf. Did you know the boys then?"

"Aye. That bruise, there. I gave it to him, if I remember right. We'd been swimming in the river, in that billibong where we camped that day we came home, and Joel didn't give me enough time to get out of the way before he swung in on the rope. He landed straight on top of me and jammed his eye right into my skull. Crikey, that hurt." He laughed.

"You loved him very much, didn't you?"

"Everyone did. He was a laugh a minute and had more guts than any two men alive."

"And what about Dale? You've been friends all this time, too?"

"Since we were just little tykes, bitin' ankles all over Western Australia." Paul winked and rested his elbows on his knees. "But enough about the brothers. What made you decide to come to Australia, a little girl like you?"

"I'm not so little. And this place isn't so much different from my home. Red earth. Brilliant scenery. We raise cattle there, and horses of course, but livestock is livestock as far as I'm concerned. My uncle needed me, so I came." She shrugged and turned to the last page in the book.

The picture gripped her heart. Dale sat atop a beautiful mount. His chin held high, a slouch hat with a monstrous ostrich feather on his head and wearing the pristine, adventurous uniform of the Light Horse Regiments, he looked like he had been born for service. A true hero.

He hadn't looked at the camera, rather at something far beyond the lens. It was almost as if he were looking beyond himself, toward whatever the world had in store for him. He sat on a large, dark-colored horse. Probably a sorrel, though it was impossible to tell from the photograph. Both man and horse were stern—majestic—in their bearing. This was the man her uncle had described in his letters. This was the boy who had stolen her heart. Her breath caught and she traced her finger over the stark planes of Dale's face.

Everything her uncle had told her about Dale indicated a special bond between the young boy turned soldier and his horse. The townspeople in Marble Bar had raved about their champion rider the moment they'd learned she would live at Castle Winters. This photograph proved he'd been born to ride.

So, perhaps a part of him *had* died with his brother that day. Otherwise, how could he live without that amazing feeling of a running horse beneath him? The gentle rocking of a horse in a full-out run over the grassy hills and red desert. Floating, as if the horse and rider would arise at any moment and gallop through the stars.

To anyone raised among the magnificent animals, the feelings were addictive. The first time Emily had galloped her mother's gelding through the rough, high desert that surrounded their home, she'd known she would spend her life on horseback. She'd been only eight years old then, but the sensation never grew old or boring. Even now, her legs itched to grip the saddle and give Apache his head.

How could a man like Dale Winters give that up?

"Emily?" Paul's voice broke through the silt-covered haze of memory.

She snapped her head in his direction. "Pardon?"

He glanced at the photograph and she followed the

invisible line cast by his gaze. Her fingers were still touching Dale's face.

He looked at her again and the burn in his eyes singed her cheeks. He cleared his throat. "You care for Dale, don't you?"

Emily swallowed the lump that suddenly filled her throat.

"Did Dale tell you I'd come here to court you?"

She started. "No. Well, not in so many words."

"I did. I changed my mind after I saw Dale's reaction. Of course, he told me to do whatever I liked, that it made no difference to him. But I knew better. Dale never could cover up how he felt. No matter what, he always wore his heart on his sleeve. Hell, he's doing it now." He paused as if something heavy had stolen his train of thought. Finally, he smiled. "Now that I see you in a clearer light . . . Well, let's just say I know my place and when to make my exit."

"I'm sorry, Paul."

"No worries." He gained his feet. "I was just thinking about the future, you know? Women are scarce around these parts. The one's worth marrying, anyway. It's not like I'm madly in love with you or anything." He winked.

The kind gesture made Emily laugh. No, he wasn't in love with her. That much was obvious. Why, he flirted more with Ruthie than anyone. "You said Dale responded to you in a certain way?"

"Like a mongoose in a viper pit. Ready to kick some-ones arse, but outnumbered and outgunned."

"Really?"

"Don't break my heart again, Miss Emily. Tell me I'm being honorable for good cause and I'll bugger off where I came from. You love him, aye?"

Emily set the open album on the low table and stood. "With all of my heart, Paul. I've loved him since I was a little girl, dreaming of a far away land that only existed in letters from an uncle I'd never met."

"And that's the real reason you came, isn't it?"

She nodded. "I came when I heard of Charles's illness, of course, but I would have come anyway. Eventually."

"I'm glad you came now. Dale's in a dark place and I don't know how he'll come out alive without someone warm to come back to. If I had to lose out on the most beautiful woman in Oz, I can't think of a better bloke to lose her to."

Chapter Eight

"It's time to wake up, Mr. Winters."

Fog. Foghorns. Rolling waves. Someone pounding on his door.

"My mum says you have to get up now. She says she won't hold your breakfast any longer."

Dale clasped one hand on either side of his head and forced his eyes open. The room he'd rented at the Iron-clad Hotel stopped spinning. He wasn't caught in a stormy sea and the only foghorn to penetrate the ache in his head came from an astounding, mind-altering hangover.

Crikey. What had he done last night?

"Mr. Winters!" The impatient, high-pitched voice must belong to one of the seven children who'd barraged him with questions about the war last night. "You have to get up if you want anything to eat."

"I'm up!" He cleared his throat. "I'm up. Tell your mum thanks but I won't need any breakfast." Hurried footsteps trailed away from his door.

His stomach turned a summersault. *No, mate. No brekkie this morning.*

How had he lived like this for a whole year?

The answer came to him with another turn of his stomach. Simple. He'd stayed rotten the entire time. Stay rotten and the horrors of the next morning never come about. The horrors stayed away right along with guilt and grief. And loss.

He pulled on his strides and glanced out the small bedroom's only window. Already the sun perched on the rooftops across the street. He squinted, shaded his eyes with one hand and pulled the shade with the other.

A year ago, he would have crawled back into the bed, covered his head with the blanket and slept the day away. Hell, he would have done that four months ago if Paul hadn't found him. The thought of doing it now seemed foreign, as if the behavior had belonged to someone else.

Too bad.

But it had nothing to with Emily.

He frowned and sat on the edge of the bed. Of course it had nothing to do with her. Why would he even think that? He pulled on his left boot and stamped his heel on the floor to adjust the fit.

Just because Emily smiled like an angel and fought like the devil didn't mean he was falling for her. He pulled on his right boot. Stamped the floor again.

He wanted her gone. Out of his life, right? She never should have come to Australia to begin with. Not that she didn't fit in. No, she had adjusted to living on the station quite well, in fact. But it wasn't her place and the sooner she realized that, the sooner he could be rid of her.

His heart squeezed.

He put on his shirt, gathered his meager belongings and went downstairs. Mrs. Bullock stirred a pot of something on the stove. Four of her seven children cleaned around her. A sturdy woman in her early fifties, or thereabout, Madeleine Bullock was a woman made for the Pilbara. Tough. Determined. Thick. She had what it took to survive. She'd been tending guests at the Ironclad ever since her husband died, the same year Dale had left the Pilbara. His bones ached. Twelve years and what did he have to show for it? Not a bloody thing.

"Ah, there you are, Dale. We missed you at brekkie."

"I'm not hungry."

She snorted. "You mean you've got the horrors and you couldn't stomach it this morning. Well, that's all right. Everybody deserves it every now and again. I just hope you got it out of your system. The last thing young Miss Emily needs is to take care of the likes of you if you're going to be a burden. You'd be served to remember that."

What was that supposed to mean?

"She doesn't take care of me. She just . . . lives there. That's all."

"Now, don't you go getting all snakey on me." She shook the spoon at him as if it were an extention of her finger. A few drops of stew landed on the immaculate tiles.

"Be a darl, Katie Lynn, and wipe that up for mummy. As I was saying, Dale. You have a look about you just like the late Mr. Bullock had when he courted me, God rest his soul. Oh, those were some times." Her wrinkled face glowed for a moment, as if caught somewhere in a distant dream, before she frowned and seemed to shake off whatever it had been. For just that short span of moments, she'd been beautiful, young.

"You've got it wrong."

"Doubtful. I'm never wrong about these things. You have the look of a man in love who doesn't want to be. I'd wager a year's rent on it."

"I only met the woman ten days ago. How in the bloody hell . . . pardon," he added when five pairs of eyes fastened on him. "I think you're imagining things that aren't there, love, that's all."

"Could be. But I'll stand by my words. Now, will you have a lunch packed before you head out? You'll be hungry before long."

"Thanks. I'm going to collect my things from the market and I'll swing back around before I leave town."

Dale hurried across the street and held open the door of the General Store while Old Man Kincaid meandered through.

"Thank you, son. Seems these old bones move slower every year."

"Maybe you should head back to the big smoke so some nice old gal can take care of you?" Dale smiled while he closed the door.

"Me? In the city?" scoffed Kincaid. "Never again. Did I ever tell you about the time I struck the mother load in Californey? It was in 1853 in the Northern Californey Territory. Purtiest vein any man had ever seen, it was, and my cut made me a wealthy man. The richest man in town, that was me . . ." His moist eyes, clouded with age, shimmered.

"Yeah, old man. You've told me."

Kincaid turned away, his shoulders folded as if he carried a younger man's share of the weight and limped to a bench. "Her name was Caroline . . ."

"Old Man Kincaid is still making up those crazy stories, as you can see." Bart smiled a greeting and pulled Dale's list from his vest pocket. "Now, I think I got everything you need on this first list. Sugar. Flour. Grain. Fourteen four-by-four-by-twelve posts. Building up the fences, are you? I suppose it's about that time, though the fences Miss Emily added for that stud of hers should still be in good shape. But this other list, well, I'll have to order a few things in from Port Hedland, I think."

"Fine, go right ahead. I'll be back in a few weeks to collect them." Dale shrugged. "That's not really my list, anyway."

Bart laughed. "I didn't think it was. It must belong to the missus."

The missus? "She's not the *missus*, but aye, that's Emily's list."

"Her things are just there, at the end of the counter."

Dale moved to the side and lifted the first item in the stack. Soft fabric slid between his fingers. He took the waistband in both hands and held up the garment.

Lady's drawers. Not just any lady's. Emily's. An image of her, dressed in the knee-length undergarments and— his hand shifted to the next item while he groaned—the matching, sleeveless chemise burned into his mind's eyes. Soft hair flowing over her shoulders. Alabaster skin hidden, but still tempting, beneath the all-but sheer fabric.

"Here's the last of it," Bart called from the opposite end of the counter. He brought a pair of white suspenders and laid them on top of the drawers.

"She asked for suspenders?" He raised a brow.

"These are a lady's suspenders." Bart grinned and shook his head. "That's what I have to send away for. Your lady-friend wanted two of these, but this here is my last one."

Dale picked up what appeared to be a very long set of suspenders. Emily wasn't nearly tall enough to use these. And they were defective. "There's something wrong with these. The hooks have been put in the wrong places."

Bart shook his head and put yet another contraption on the stack of Emily's things. Dale handed the suspenders back to Bart and picked up the box.

From somewhere behind him, feminine giggles floated through the shop. He turned to find Mrs. Kelly, a stern matron with a reputation for tongue wagging, standing not four feet behind him. Her two youngest daughters, Bridgett and Mary, attempted to hide their faces behind their hands while their mother glared at him as if he'd recently murdered a small child. The older of the two girls, Bridgett, blushed until he thought her cheeks might burst into flames. He nodded and turned his attention back to the box. In large, bolded typeface, the product description ran the length of the side of the box.

FEMININE BANDAGES FOR USE WITH THE MRS. SMITH'S UNIVERSAL BANDAGE SUSPENDERS—QUEEN CITY SUSPENDER COMPANY
No. 179 Main Street, Cincinnati, Ohio

Dale closed his eyes and gritted his teeth. Feminine products. For when her . . . for when she . . . He tossed the box on the counter and squared his shoulders. "Apparently, those suspenders are just fine, Bart. If you'll package these items separately and have them loaded into the wagon, I'd be much obliged."

Three hours lay between Marble Bar and the Castle Winters Station.

He planned to make it home in two.

✦ 🐎 ✦

The wagon swayed over the rutted road. The bright, hot sun of early summer beat like a smith's hammer on Dale's back and sweat pooled beneath his light chambray shirt. He'd pushed the horse too hard and lather collected around the harness. He'd slowed his pace more than an hour earlier, but he'd managed to make the trip home in just over two hours.

Home.

Castle Winters wasn't his home anymore. He didn't belong there anymore than he belonged in Australia. Or in Cairo. Hell, he didn't belong anywhere. He should have died in the desert with his brother. Rather, he should have died instead of his brother. He had no business carrying on with his life as if nothing had happened.

The day Joel had been born had been warm. The sun had shone high in the western sky. He remembered as if it were yesterday. Sitting on Tower Rock with Blue. The old wiseman had told him stories to pass the hours. Dreaming stories from before the beginning of time. It seemed fitting, even to a five-year-old boy with no knowledge of such things, to hear those tales at the same time his brother had come into the world.

After more hours than any boy could be expected to endure, his father had rushed from the front of the house into the stable yard and waved at them. Dale had been the first off the rock. He'd descended the tower with no fear, no concept of the danger hidden in the slick, silt-covered outcroppings and sandstone. When he'd reached the bottom, he'd run to his father.

Andrew Winters had had tears in his eyes. Dale had never seen his father cry before and never witnessed it after. "You have a brother," he'd whispered in a voice that sounded on the verge of breaking. "Joel."

"Can I see him, Papa?"

"Aye. But you must be gentle. We'll give him a few weeks before we make a man out of him, I reckon."

He'd rushed into the house as quickly as his tiny legs could carry him. Through the foyer, up the long stairs and into his parents' bedroom. His mother had lain in her bed, her hair a tangled mess. But she'd looked more beautiful in that moment than he'd ever seen her before, with color high in her cheeks and a smile that would have put the Virgin to shame. "Come and see your new brother, Dale."

Dale had pulled himself onto the foot of the tall bed, covered in pristine linens. That's when he'd seen Joel for the first time. Swaddled in a blue blanket, only his pink cheeks and nose peeked from the folds. "He's tiny, Mummy. Is he going to live?"

"Of course he is. All babe's are small when they're born."

"Sometimes the lambs don't live very long."

"Aye. But Joel isn't a lamb. He's a baby and he is as healthy and whole as any. You have nothing to fear."

Dale had looked into his mother's eyes. Inside the deep brown depths he'd recognized trust and love, even then. She'd trusted him to take care of Joel. "I'll keep him safe, Mummy. Every day, for good and ever, I'll make sure nothing happens to him."

"What a brave boy you are. Will you stand guard, then?"

He'd nodded. "I promise."

The wagon's rear wheel slipped into a rut and snapped Dale's attention back to the road. He blinked away the sting of tears and adjusted his hat. In the distance, Castle Winters rose on the horizon. He'd be back at the station in less than a half-hour. Back to the source of his ill-conceived notions of heroism and glory.

Everything had been simple then. For years, he'd been true to his word. He'd never let Joel out of his sight. From the time Joel could walk, Dale had been there to catch him. Even after their parents' deaths, especially then, he'd made certain Joel was safe. Right up until the day Joel had shown up in Melbourne.

A light streak caught his attention and he shot his gaze to the right.

Sally raced beside the wagon with Emily forward in the saddle, urging her to greater speed. "Welcome back, Dale!"

"What the hell do you think you're doing?"

"Riding, and you?"

"Stop the horse. Now!" He pulled on the reins and applied the brake.

Emily's brow furrowed, but she brought Sally to a skidding halt beside the road. Both horse and rider were breathless from the exertion of what appeared to have been a long, tiring exercise. Emily's hair fell past her shoulders in a riot of curls and knots. It looked as if she'd worn it swept away from her face and neck at some point and it had fallen free as she rode. Her cheeks held more than a hint of rosy color and her eyes danced in the afternoon sunlight.

That wasn't the only thing that danced. His heart all but waltzed in his chest despite the fact he was furious with her—or maybe because of it. She wore a pair of snug strides, obviously cut for a woman the way they clung to the curve of her hips and thighs and left nothing to his imagination. Well, perhaps a few things remained hidden. Like what she would taste like if he were to find himself in a position to sample her many charms. Or how she would feel wrapped around him, their bodies slicked with sweat in the oppressive heat of lovemaking in the heavy Australian air. She was the most beautiful creature he'd ever had the misfortune to meet. His body hardened.

"What's wrong?"

He licked his lips and abandoned the course of his thoughts. He had more important issues at hand. Like why the bloody hell Emily rode with his *Jackaroos* like some common station hand. "That is my brother's horse."

"Yes. It is."

"Who said you could ride her?"

"I didn't know I needed permission. The horses need the exercise and the hands don't seem to mind when I help them, so I thought—"

"You thought wrong. Nobody rides that horse but Joel."

She frowned and stared at him as if he'd sprouted a third eye in the middle of his forehead. Even then, she was stunning.

"The horses deserve to be cared for. That means a fair amount of exercise before they're so fat and lazy they aren't good for anything."

"They don't need to be good for anything. Consider

them retired."

"That's cruel and you know it!" She dismounted and led Sally to the wagon.

With eyes that shot fire, she stared up at him with one hand shading her face from the afternoon glare.

Something told Dale to stay in the wagon, but he ignored the nagging voice and leapt to the ground in front of her. "I don't care if it's cruel or not. Nobody rides these horses."

"The horses didn't die, Dale. It's not fair for you to treat them as if they did."

"Give me the reins and get in the wagon."

"No." Emily stepped to Sally's left side and raised one tiny, booted foot to the stirrup. The fabric of her strides molded to her hips, exposing the gentle curves, sending his treacherous loins into spasm. Damn.

Dale's gaze fastened to the image with more desire than he would have liked, and he forced his eyes to the grim, determined line of her chin. Her lips pursed in the same expression she wore when she scrubbed the laundry in the rear garden, or when she studied a recipe from one of his mother's old cookbooks.

Unstoppable. Unwavering. And positively enchanting.

He swallowed and stalked to her. "Do not mount that animal, Emily. I mean it."

"Try to stop me. I've been raising horses my entire life. Ignore them and they waste away, they suffer, and they're as good as dead. Now, get out of my way and let me mount."

Before Dale even realized what he was doing, he grasped her shoulder and spun her to face him. Her boot shot out of the stirrup and for just the barest of seconds, she leaned into him. The rounded tip of one breast grazed his chest and he winced.

He'd never known anyone so soft and so tough. Like lace and steel.

Worse, she was intelligent and knew full well she was right. Of course the horses needed the exercise. He couldn't do it, so why shouldn't she? At least the horses would be doing what they loved instead of growing fat in the pastures with little or no outlet for their massive energies.

Emily glared at him from beneath her thick, black lashes. The tiny strands curled into impossible arches, black as pitch, and they looked as soft as a newborn chick's feathers. When she blinked, they grazed her full cheeks and his heart grew jealous that he'd never touched her there. Just below her eyes where the flesh was as soft as down.

Her lips parted and her breath mingled with his own. When had he moved so close to her that his chest crowded her? Her glare softened and the warm surrender he found in them called to him.

Barely an inch separated their lips. He could already taste hers, sweet as candy and delicate as rose petals. His head moved closer, closer and closer still until her breath became his own.

Sally blew, stamped, and raised her head.

What the hell was he doing?

He didn't deserve anyone like her. He should spend the rest of his life alone. He'd promised Joel, the day they'd buried him the sparse remains of a ruined Bedouin field, he would never know the happiness that should have been Joel's. He would miss Joel, love Joel and mourn Joel for the rest of his life. If he succumbed to the restful peace promised in Emily's heated gaze, misery would be banished to the furthest corner of his soul.

One look toward the bliss of contentment with a good woman felt more like a kick in the gut. By a mule. A kick in the guts by mule who wore steel boots and had the face of an angel.

✶ 🐎 ✶

Blue crouched on the pinnacle of Tower Rock. An eagle banked on a current, soaring above the station as if it kept silent vigil against unwanted forces. Or maybe it only hunted for snakes and rabbits.

Far below Blue's perch, Dale and Emily exchanged heated words. Blue sighed and the sound was lost in the wind.

Emily was good for Dale. On more than one occasion, she'd made him think of things he would rather ignore. Left to himself, he would fester like the wound left in the wake of a dragon's bite. But Emily treated him, even if she didn't know it.

She made him feel. Made him look deeper into himself

than he'd ever wanted to.

It was good for a man to see more clearly into his own soul on occasion. He usually found a part of himself he didn't like, and only when that part was realized could it be changed.

Dale had been too hard on himself the whole of his life. From the moment of his birth, he had possessed an old soul. He believed he should already know the answers, and when questions arose he couldn't answer, he panicked. It had always been so.

Blue scratched his head then rubbed the palm of his hand over his jaw. The day had grown warm since he'd climbed the rock with night's retreating shadows. He'd met morning on the tower's flat surface and waited.

Waited for the sun to reach its zenith. Waited for Dale to make the final bend in the road that would lead him back to Castle Winters. Waited for Emily to exercise the horses.

Waited for Dale to admit his feelings and claim Emily's heart.

The younger man and woman stood in stark defiance of one another. Still, they argued. Dale, ever impatient retreated when he should have advanced. The spell had been broken.

Blue frowned and gained his feet.

He would have to wait a bit longer, it would seem.

✳ 🐴 ✳

Dale whipped the horse to a trot and followed the winding drive to the stable yard where three of the *Jackaroos* met him. He jumped off the wagon just as Emily raced toward the pasture fence.

She leaned low over Sally's neck and raised her rounded backside off the saddle. Dale's blood ran cold. She didn't plan to jump the fence. She *couldn't* be that foolish.

Sally gathered herself and the solid muscles of her hindquarters rippled in glossy relief. Lathered from a hard ride, the animal blew audibly before she soared over the fence. Masterful. Magical. As if she could fly.

How many times had he and Joel done that very thing?

That was different. They were boys. Full of piss and misguided immortality. Emily had no business putting herself at risk. Something told him to chase her down and scold her. Shake some sense into her bleedin', cracked skull. But he didn't trust himself. He didn't trust himself not to kiss her, not to hold her. Not to fall into some trap of feminine comfort.

He followed her with his gaze as she crossed the pasture and gradually circled Sally to bring her to a walk.

Emily's cheeks burned as if she'd spent a week in the sun. Her eyes glistened. Despite their argument, a smile parted her full lips.

Exhilarated.

Just like he'd been when he used to take Jez on an overland race or . . .

Enough.

He didn't deserve the hint of love promised in Emily's eyes, and he sure as hell wouldn't break the last promise he'd ever made.

Emily could exercise the horses. They had little need of him.

He rubbed one hand over his chest in the region of his heart.

"These things belong to Emily, I think."

Dale focused his attention on Thomas, who held Emily's package in his large, black hands.

Dale took it, but his attention drifted back to the pasture. Emily had dismounted and led Sally toward the outside door of her stall, where Henry Albert met her and took the reins.

An eagle called overhead and she glanced to the heavens. Her hair, loose and curled over her strong shoulders, shone in the light. A butterfly flitted around her head, but she didn't seem to notice. Sally nudged her forward with her muzzle and Emily frowned.

When she glanced at Dale, her eyes narrowed.

Even furious, she was beautiful.

Dale shook his head.

What was the matter with him? Standing about like a boy in his first blush over a woman who shouldn't even be in Australia?

He glanced away, turned a smart about-face and went into the house. Setting her personal items on the kitchen table when he passed, he paced into the living room.

He'd thought a day away from her would lessen the impact of those violet eyes. Or the sweet scent that followed her around as if it were hers alone.

He breathed that scent now. Lavender.

But not just lavender. It was a mixture of lavender and Emily. A mixture of lavender, Emily, and his own sweet desire.

She'd been in this room recently. He closed his eyes and despite his conscious decision to the contrary, allowed the unique blend to encompass him. No harm could come from just a minute or two of indulgence.

The front door slammed and heavy footfalls creaked over the hardwood floor.

The last thing he wanted now was company. Dale opened his eyes and spun to leave the room.

Too late.

Blue blocked the exit to the foyer stairs. Covered in red silt from his bare feet to the long, thick strands of his light hair, he smiled. "You're back."

"You don't say?" He shoved his hands in his pockets.

"Paul left this morning. His friend with the other flying machine came and they flew away together."

"Thanks for the information."

"What are you doing here all by yourself?"

"Can't a person take a few minutes in his own bloody house?" Dale lifted his chin and folded his hands over his chest.

"You were looking at the family pictures?" Blue pointed

to the table in front of the sofa.

His mother's photograph book rested in the center of the table, laid open like a gaping wound, to an image of himself and Joel. The old photo, taken a lifetime ago, contained a likeness of Joel in a lacy dress. Dale's likeness wore short pants and a tailored jacket. He couldn't have been more than seven years old. But he remembered that day.

They'd been in Sydney for an extended vacation to visit his mother's parents, who had sailed from England. His grandmother had insisted on the photograph and the prissy get-ups. At home, he and Joel would have been covered in mud, rolling about the pastures fighting against some invented enemy with imaginary pistols. They often played at cowboys and Indians as if they were rangers from western America or some other such nonsense based on the stories Charles had told them too many times to count.

Blue clapped him on the back. "Those were happy times."

That trip to Sydney had been the only taste he'd had of what his mother had given up when she'd married his father.

Dale tore his gaze from the picture and stared into Blue's misty eyes. "That was a long time ago."

"Not so long. You should find more happy times."

Dale laughed. "Where? You point out the rock under which they hide and I'll bloody well dig them up."

"You shouldn't run away from the past. You can't, even if you try."

Blue's eyes had always seemed like a window not into

his soul, but into the soul of whomever he set his gaze upon. Dale's spine tingled and the hair on the back of his neck jumped from parade rest to full attention. "Don't look at me like that. You don't know half as much as you think you do."

"I don't?"

"No. You don't. You think I'll find happiness here? Wrong. I'm selling out. You hear me? I don't care if I never see this place again."

"Running." Blue shook his head. "You used to be stronger than that."

Dale shrugged and his gaze moved back to the picture. He closed his eyes and turned his back on Blue. "I used to be a lot of things."

"Where will you run to this time that your pain won't follow?"

Dale cringed. Even in the pits of his own lascivious drunkenness he'd still felt the pain. He'd easily lied to himself; told himself he'd numbed the pain for a whole year. But it hadn't been true then and it wasn't true now. His heart knew it, even if his head didn't.

There was only one place that held solace. One escape that called to him with soft whispers of contentment. And he needn't leave to find it. But he didn't want it. He sure as hell didn't deserve it.

He had no other choice. "Just leave it alone. I'm selling the station and there isn't a damn thing you or that . . . woman . . . can do about it."

A sudden intake of breath forced him to turn toward the hall. Emily stood with her full, red-tinted lips parted and wounded eyes rounded into saucers. Her jaw snapped closed and her glare turned to full-on, spitting-fire brilliance. "I thought, just maybe, you'd changed your mind about this foolishness. I can see I was wrong."

"I've given it a great deal of thought and there just isn't any other way. It's for the best."

"The best for whom? For you? So you can pretend you've always been a perfect idiot? Fine then. If this is what you want, what you need to live with yourself, then sell the whole damnable place. It's obvious you're not man enough to take care of it properly."

He could have taken such a barb from just about anyone besides her. But coming from Emily, the words cut like a dull knife straight through to his heart. Still, he wouldn't be swayed. "Give me one good reason why I shouldn't sell."

He ran a hand through his hair and faced the fireplace. Where had that come from? He didn't want a reason to stay. He didn't need her to give him one. He already had a very good reason. Too good, in fact. Given half a chance, he might find himself in love with . . .

"I can't think of a single one."

Emily's hurried bootsteps climbed the stairs with ferocious clarity. A moment later, her bedroom door slammed shut with a vehemence that made the walls of his heart shudder.

Blue snorted.

"What? You have something to say, so just bloody say it!"

"Have you thought, perhaps, that you were spared for some greater purpose?"

An impatient sigh hovered on the edge of his lungs, but he reined it in. "What purpose?"

"Ah, my boy. That you must discover for yourself."

⚡ 🐎 ⚡

Emily threw her portmanteau onto her bed and tossed it open.

"Oh, no. What has you all in a flutter now?" Ruthie followed Emily into her bedroom and opened the wardrobe doors.

"That . . . that . . . man!" Emily unlatched the main compartment in the oversized trunk she'd purchased especially for her sea voyage to Australia less than a year ago. "Dale Winters is nothing more than a brute. A bully who has to have his own way, no matter what anyone else might think. Ha! If you asked him, he'd probably say he's the only one who ever thinks about anything! The rest of us are too addle-brained to think for ourselves so Mr.-High-and-mighty Dale Winters will do all our thinking for us." And she, for one, wanted nothing to do with this place. And she wanted nothing to do with him.

Emily ignored the fact that her heart broke even as she

balled a white tea-dress and stuffed it in the case. She had come to Australia with naïve dreams. Ridiculous dreams of a boy who lived in a series of letters.

She laughed through tears threatening to unleash a crying jag she'd sooner avoid. No sense crying over something she'd never had. She'd never had the slightest chance to prove herself to Dale. To show him how much worth he still possessed. The war had changed him, obviously. He barely resembled the man in the photographs, much less the spirited and defiant boy described in her uncle's letters.

For all she knew, her uncle had elaborated his descriptions to play into the fantasies of the niece he'd never met. That was probably it. The boy she'd fallen in love with had never even existed.

Somehow, that made her heart wrench all the more.

"Would you mind telling me where we're going, at least?" Ruth tossed a few more items into the trunk then returned to the wardrobe.

"We've overstayed our welcome, I think." Emily pulled her undergarments from the top drawer of her dresser and dumped them in a heap in the portmanteau. "We're going home to America. Mrs. Durnell offered me a position in her training program in Louisville, if you'll remember, and I may just take her up on it."

"And if the position has been filled? What then?"

"I can find a position with one of the other stables in Kentucky like I'd planned before Uncle fell ill." Before she'd made the foolish mistake of coming to Australia to search of what she'd believed to be her heart's true desire.

She was, after all, a full-grown woman in a modern age and she could make whatever decisions she liked. Her inheritance grated her the freedom to go anywhere. She didn't need Dale or her parents telling her what to do.

But wasn't that exactly what she was allowing to happen? Dale wanted to sell his half of the station. He wanted to run away from his own emotions. Wasn't that what she was doing? Running away? Wasn't she allowing his decisions to affect her life? *Her* decisions?

She picked up a handkerchief and blew her nose.

No. It wasn't the same thing. She was simply granting Dale enough rope to hang himself. She'd given enough of herself to the station, the horses, and the man. He'd cast aside her offers of friendship and partnership and made it perfectly clear that she wasn't wanted here.

Why should she force herself on him?

She wasn't running away. She wasn't.

"What are you doing?" Dale's voice boomed from the doorway.

With her hand to her racing heart, Emily spun to face him. "A closed door generally means the occupant expects her privacy."

"I knocked. You didn't answer."

"I repeat, the door was closed. Go away."

How those words stung her. She never wanted to tell him, of all people, to go. She wanted to hold him close and soothe the worried lines from his brow. But she couldn't do that if he wouldn't let her, could she? And nothing in his eyes, in the squared set of his shoulders, indicated he would welcome her attentions in the slightest. The pieces of her heart shattered all the more.

She turned her back to him before a fresh set of tears defied her will to keep them in check.

"Ruth, if you'll excuse us, please. I'd like to have a word with Emily alone."

"It's not proper—"

Dale cut off Ruth's objections with a single glare and Emily watched in stunned horror as her maid fled the room.

"Wh . . . what do you think you're doing?" *Coward.*

"I didn't mean for you to leave. This is as much your home as it is mine."

"No, it isn't. I don't belong here. You've made a point of proving that fact for quite long enough. I am many things, Dale, but I'm not dense."

"I'm sorry I yelled." Dale's voice was strained. Tight. As if the words choked him. "Don't leave."

"You don't want me here. That much a child could see. Don't let something as foolish as honor convince you otherwise." She closed the traveling case and snapped the brass latches.

The floorboards creaked behind her. "You can train the horses as much as you like. I won't stand in the way. I . . ."

Only Emily's heavy breaths filled the room. "What?"

She turned to find him less than an arm's distance

away. If she wanted to, she could touch him. Her fingers curled. Oh, how she wanted to.

He gazed into her eyes and something changed in the depths of his own. They grew softer. More tolerant. As if he'd come to some conclusion. He licked his full bottom lip and pinned that intense stare further through her wavering defenses.

He was so handsome. But it wasn't just the firm line of his jaw, or the width of his muscled shoulders that attracted her. It was the man inside. The wounded soldier who needed a reason to come alive again. She wanted to be that reason, no matter how much her mind tried to convince her otherwise. In truth, she needed him as much as he needed her. Even if he didn't know it.

"The horses have grown accustomed to you." His whisper reached out with warm, accepting fingers. "And, if I had to admit it, I suppose you've niched out a place for yourself. I don't know what it is exactly. You're a nuisance more often than not, and you don't listen. To anyone." He paused and his shoulders squared as if the words he spoke threatened to steal what soul he still possessed. "I was too harsh on you about the horses, and for that I apologize."

"Apologies are unnecessary. Jezebel and Sally are yours. I should have gained your permission before taking them out."

"No. You've been right all along. They needed the exercise. I suppose I should have thought of that before. . ." He frowned and his gaze slid to the side, as if he were trapped in some memory—another time, another place.

"Before what?" Emily approached him, tempted to brush his cheek and erase the studious frown that marred otherwise perfect features. Instead, she locked her fingers at her waist and waited.

Dale smiled, but the expression seemed more forced than natural. "Nothing." He cleared his throat and the smile grew wider, more genuine. "Your . . . things . . . are downstairs, by the by. They had to order something in from Port Hedland, but everything else is on the table in the kitchen."

"Oh!" Emily's cheeks burned.

"Would you like me to fetch them? I can bring everything to you, for your trip." He nodded to the portmanteau.

Emily found his suggestion and reference to her baggage a convenient reason to turn her back on him. Only to find a rather delicate piece of intimate apparel hung from between the two sides of her luggage.

She spun a quick circle and placed herself directly in front of the partially visible chemise. "No. No, that's quite all right. I can collect them. Er . . . you had the list with you then?"

"Obviously. Remind me never to anger you in public." He grinned again.

"Of course. Well, I suppose if you feel I add some kind of a benefit to the station, I can stay a bit longer. But you must promise me you will not sell the property or the stock. Who knows? If the dividends from this year's shearing are worthwhile, I may purchase your half as my own."

He frowned and seemed to find something rather interesting to study on the floor. "Agreed."

"Dale?"

No response. It was as if he'd wandered into some other part of himself. A part no one save himself could see.

"Dale? Look at me." Emily gave in to the temptation to soothe his harried features. She took his rough, unshaven cheek in her palm and directed his gaze to meet hers. "Is it so terrible, really? Coming home?"

He pulled away. "Bloody hell." He ran a hand through his hair and paced to the window. "I never wanted to come back here. Did you know that?"

"I suspected. When you didn't come home at the end of your enlistment, Charles said Australia would be lucky to see the likes of you again."

"Charles said that?"

"Yes. You must know he loved you ever so much." Emily skirted the foot of the bed to stand next to him. She followed his gaze to the pasture where Jezebel and Sally grazed together in a thick patch of grass. Apache was in his corral pacing the fence line and impatiently tossing his head.

Dale scoffed. "Aye. He was like a father to me, and I was like the ungrateful son he never had."

"That's not true. You were like a son to him, but I doubt very much if he thought of you as ungrateful. He said that you were too sad to come home. He seemed to understand and accept it."

"Sad? Aye. But there was also the guilt."

"What would you feel guilty about? You should be proud of your service. It's not your fault you were wounded before the end of the war."

"There's more to it than that, Emily." He pinned her with a pain-filled stare. "I killed him. I killed my own brother. How in the name of God am I supposed to live with that for the rest of my life?"

She frowned. "You didn't kill him. What are you talking about?"

Dale's jaw quivered and a tiny muscle along his jaw pulsed. He turned away and ran a hand through his hair before he let his fingers settle on the back of his neck and squeezed the obviously tense muscles. After a moment, he lifted his head and faced her again. "If I hadn't joined the ANZACS, he wouldn't have either. He always followed my lead, from the time we were boys. I set the example and he followed, no matter what. I should have talked him out of it. If I'd done that, he wouldn't have been killed."

"Is that what you think? Is that why you've been trying to destroy yourself all this time?"

He nodded and stared out the window. "Not very good at it, am I? I'm still here."

"You mustn't talk like that." Emily tugged his shoulder until he faced her. The sadness had returned to his eyes, like a pool of regret fed by a spring of self-loathing. "Dale Winters, you are an amazing man. You must not blame yourself for a tragedy of war. It was Joel's choice to go and we should remember him with pride, not sorrow."

"I can't." He pulled away and took several steps back. "I live and he doesn't. I can breathe, smell, taste and lo . . . live. And he is buried in some God-forsaken spit of sand I'll never see again. How can I enjoy even the simplest parts of my life without seeing his face? Without feeling his arms around me?"

"Don't you see? His memory is a blessing, not a curse. Let it embrace you." She paused. "Is this why you've refused to ride Jezebel?"

"How can I do something he loved so much when I'm the one who took it from him? I promised. I'll never ride again."

She studied the sad lines that surrounded his frown. He honestly believed Joel would hold him to such a promise. "I see."

"Do you?"

"I think so. You wanted to punish yourself. But now, as you've grown and come to understand that your life didn't end that day, you're having problems with it."

"Lady, most days, I have problems getting out of bed."

"But you do get out of bed. You see? You haven't completely lost the will to carry on. You must harness what inklings of that desire to survive you possess and use them. Let them grow."

"I can't." He seemed to realize he'd bared his soul and a shield fell over his expression.

"You can! You can be sure Joel would find your sacrifice honorable and more than a little daft. Do you think he wants you to spend the rest of your life suffering? Lost in some swamping river of discontent? Of course not. He wants you to be free. And happy."

"What if there is no happiness out there?"

"I refuse to believe that. Happiness is a state of mind, available to anyone with a heart. And you do still have a heart, Dale, even if you can't find it at the moment."

She'd stepped closer to him before she even realized it. Staring into his sullen expression, eyes danced with each other and their breath mingled. For a moment, she believed he would retreat, but he didn't. His gaze touched her like a tangible caress. First her eyes, her hair, and then, finally, her lips.

Her mouth grew dry as the desert and her pulse increased until she thought her heart might burst. In her belly, something clenched and teased. If only she could read his thoughts. Then she'd possess the knowledge to help him.

All she wanted to do was love him.

Large, strong hands took possession of her shoulders in a touch so light she couldn't be sure it was real. And then his mouth descended to hers. Tentative at first, the kiss grew with a will and power born of something pure and elemental. His grip on her shoulders increased until her entire body rested against his. His hands moved over her back with possessive force and sinewy muscles played beneath her breasts.

Everywhere he touched her came alive. Her nerves danced and her lungs failed.

His lips were soft and he urged her to open her mouth with the tip of his velvety tongue. She complied as if she'd been born to kiss him. When his tongue swept over hers, she thought her knees might buckle, but his strength consumed her even as his mouth claimed her.

This was the reason she'd come to Australia. This was her only reason. To love Dale Winters and earn his love in return.

Chapter Nine

Dale's body throbbed and hardened with a will of its own. At least, that's what he told himself as he lost his way through the pure light and intense power of Emily's kiss. She tasted sweet, like honey and moonlight. Her body molded to his and he relished it—embraced her as if he had the right. In her arms, like this, in the mysterious blending of their hearts, he somehow set aside the pain that had eaten his soul raw.

Her innocence confused him, made him want to devour and protect at the same time. With strength born of primitive and basic desire, he pushed away any thought of honor or pride. He'd been in pain for so long, the prospect of even a few moments of peace drew him deeper into Emily's offered comfort.

Not that he deserved it.

He'd lost the right to peace or comfort months ago on the very day his brother had died. Because of him. If Emily knew the truth about why Joel had been in Palestine . . .

She would feel differently and scorn his kiss rather than return it. She would loathe his touch as much as he hated himself.

But she didn't know and her tempting lips moved against his in a slow, steady rhythm that decried his attempts to reason. Where was his compass? His determination to pay his debt to his brother? He had no right to enjoy her soft breasts pressing against his chest. He didn't deserve to breathe her sweet breath into his burning lungs.

Pull away. Save Emily from the despair of your company and the curse of your love.

No. His conscience could go to bloody hell. He wouldn't let her go.

She murmured against his lips and the vibration shot like a boomerang to the hollow of his chest, where his heart should have been, before it ricocheted out of his body and back into hers.

He fought against his principles, against the nagging honor that his father and Charles had always drilled into his mind with a miner's sledge. Damn them for that. Damn them all.

Emily's delicate hands shifted on his shoulders before her fingers teased the curls at the nape of his neck. The soft touch sent a river of fire to the pit of his stomach.

He could spend the rest of his life in her arms.

But she deserved so much better than him.

Heart racing and lungs aflame, he broke away from the vortex she'd created around him. He stumbled to the door before catching one hand on the jamb. "I'm sorry." His voice rang hoarse. Shallow.

"Beg your pardon?"

He knew that voice. That was Emily's *I'm-rather-disappointed-in-you-at-the-moment* voice. He glanced over his shoulder and stifled a groan.

The God who had created a woman so beautiful either had a heart full of love for mankind, or one bent on Dale's complete and utter destruction. Pink the same shade as a desert wildflower tinted her cheeks. Her lips were swollen, full and red. But her eyes damaged him more than anything. Not only were they sparkling and obviously earnest, they held a confusion he couldn't begin to quiet.

So innocent.

How would she react if he told her what the town's people were saying? Or, more to the point, what Gerald Brown had said in the Ironclad Hotel? More than likely, she'd take Brown down with a single glare. He almost smiled. He'd like to see that.

But, in the meantime, her reputation suffered. Because of him. And because of her determination to see the station through whatever problems he'd managed to bring home with him.

But the fact remained.

Despite her insistence to the contrary, someday she'd need to marry. She'd want to marry. What man would have her after she'd lived with him for an indefinite period of time?

Not that she seemed to care about that. But Dale did. What breath remained in his lungs seized. For the first time in a year, he cared about something. It suddenly mattered to him what effect his desire might have on Emily.

But the longer she stared at him with that innocent and all-too-wicked gleam in her eye, the greater the chance of her not going to her marriage bed the least bit innocent.

"Why are you looking at me like that?" Her bottom lip quivered.

He licked his lips and the sweet honeyed taste lingered. His body swelled and throbbed in time with the roiling in his stomach. Why did he look at her like . . . what? Like he could devour her? Like he would take her? Here? Now? Right there on the bed at her back? Crikey, he was in trouble.

He'd been fighting it since the minute he first laid his bloody eyes on her at the docks. Tall. Proud. Obstinate. Glorious.

If he failed to take greater care in the future, he'd lose this fight. And both of them would suffer the consequences. She'd be ruined. And he'd have yet another broken vow to answer for when he faced his Maker.

He gained his full height and willed his rioting body to obey his chilling commands. "I shouldn't have done that."

She smiled. His knees buckled and any moment he'd fall to the floor in a great heap of wasted man. He could barely stand and she *smiled*. As if she were in complete control of herself. It wasn't only her lips that curved into a wicked grin. Her entire face lit up, her eyes exploded in a thousand tiny beams of chaste desire and the color in her cheeks deepened. It irritated and amazed him, all at the same time.

The silken muscles of her neck contracted when she swallowed. "You have nothing to apologize for."

His tongue ached to follow the undulations of her throat to see where they might lead beneath her starched, white collar. He opened the door. "You have my word. If you stay, I'll not take advantage of you again."

Emily's shoulders moved back a notch and her chin rose. The color in her cheeks flamed a deeper red and she cleared her throat. Worse, the remnants of her smile disappeared beneath the stern line of her full mouth. "Very well."

"You'll stay?"

"Of course. But I will have free reign with the horses. Agreed?"

"Agreed."

With a stride that would make a general proud, she marched to the door and ushered him into the hall. "If you will excuse me, I'd like to unpa—"

The front door opened and what sounded like a herd of elephants crashed into the foyer. A great, booming voice carried up the stairs. "Is anyone home?"

"Who the devil is that?" Emily pushed around him, hurried to the landing and disappeared down the stairs.

Dale inhaled deeply and then followed.

Matthew Macomber stood at the foot of the steps

surrounded by full skirts, chatting, preoccupied women, and one freckled little girl. Always a broad man with more than his share of gray in his hair and beard, Matt carried a rotund waist that had once been lean and muscled and a disposition better suited to a clerk than one of the most successful station owners in Western Australia.

Matt's wife, Carole, stood beside him in a green and white striped dress. Her matching hat, which covered a shock of bright red hair, had been tied with a massive bow beneath her chin. She smiled at her husband, with an adoring gleam in her moist blue eyes.

Next to Carole were her daughters and their heavy trunks, filled no doubt, with a month's worth of necessities. Lizzy, the youngest, looked like her mother. She'd been in nappies when he'd last laid eyes on the child. Susan, whose rounded form took after her father, pulled at the collar of her dress and complained she couldn't breathe.

Rachel Macomber glanced up the stairs and her mouth turned into a wide, genuine smile that broke his heart into a thousand pieces.

⚒ 🐎 ⚒

Emily reached the landing with as much of her composure intact as she could manage. Her body still hummed with the shocking power of Dale's kiss. Her heart ached at his apology and obvious regret.

What had she done wrong? What was it about her

that was so damned impossible to love? Tears burned the backs of her eyes, but she blinked them away and offered what she hoped was a welcoming smile and not a forced grimace to the family in Dale's foyer.

She offered her hand to Matthew and he took it in a firm, warm grip. "Matt. I hadn't expected you until next week." She leaned forward and he placed a fatherly kiss on her cheek. She turned to Matt's wife and daughters. "It's wonderful to see you all again so soon. How long can you stay?"

Carole Macomber smiled. "I'm afraid we'll be forced to impose for several days this time, dear. We've broken an axle on the wagon and Matt has hopes Dale will be able to help him repair it."

"Of course. You're welcome to stay as long as you like." She turned to Rachel, the eldest, and offered a smile. But Rachel seemed oblivious and stared with a shining light in her blue eyes at a point over Emily's shoulder.

Emily turned and followed Rachel's gaze up the stairs. Dale descended with one hand on the banister as if he might tumble down the steps and into the other woman's arms.

When he reached the bottom step, he stopped and glanced at the floor before his eyes captured Rachel's with obvious familiarity. Too much familiarity. He looked at her as if he *knew* her.

Rachel bit her bottom lip and threw herself into his arms. As if she belonged there. As if she'd been there many times before.

"I was so terribly worried about you, Dale. The whole time you were away, I prayed for your safe return. And now, God be praised, you're finally here."

"It's true," piped Lizzy, the smallest of the Macomber girls. "She talks about you all the time. It's more than bothersome." She stuck out her tongue.

Carole laughed and ruffled her daughter's bonnet. "Hush, now. It hasn't been so terrible. We all worried for you, Dale. It's good you've come home at last."

Dale finally raised his head and stared at Rachel. The sensual knowledge in his eyes wounded Emily to the very core of her being. Her chest grew so tight she feared she'd forgotten to breathe and forced air into her lungs.

Silence overtook the small foyer. Someone should say something. Anything to break the spell that joined Rachel and Dale like a band of steel.

Rachel slid a step away from Dale and placed her palm on his right cheek. She rose to the tips of her expensive kid-leather boots and looked as if she might actually kiss him.

"Well, it's very nice for you all to come and visit." Emily took Carole Macomber's arm, placed it through her own and all but dragged the poor woman through the foyer. In the process, she bumped into Rachel and sent her two full steps away from Dale. "Oh, I'm terribly sorry, Rachel. I'm so clumsy at times I just don't know what to do. Why, just a few days ago, I spilled an entire pitcher of lemonade all over Dale, just out there, on the porch. Why don't we all come into the parlor and rest? You must be tired from your trip." She took Rachel's arm and propelled her to the chair beside the fireplace. "Please, rest here and I'll put on a kettle for tea."

The entire Macomber family followed and sat in the parlor. Dale came last, as if he'd rather be anywhere but there. Stark lines etched the corners of his eyes, but the weathered flesh did nothing to detract from his strong, virile presence. He leaned against the wall with one shoulder and shoved both hands into his pockets. His gaze drifted from the floor to Rachel and back to the floor again. As if he couldn't bear to look at the willowy, beautiful girl he'd obviously known for quite some time.

Had they been lovers?

Emily almost choked on her tongue. She raced to the kitchen and braced her hands on the butcher's block. What had happened in the last few minutes? If the day kept up this brutal pace, she'd be lucky if the world didn't explode before supper.

Her bones still shook from Dale's kiss. Her lips still swelled from his gentle and passionate attentions, yet only a moment ago he'd embraced Rachel as if she were the most precious being he'd ever known.

Her father's words from a lifetime ago came back with haunting clarity. *What man will ever want you? You're just like your mother.*

She closed her eyes until the brutal echo drifted back into the closed recesses of memory. A fire blazed in the pit of her stomach and she drew strength from it. She was nothing like her mother, who expected the world given to her on a golden platter. And she wasn't like her father either, a bitter, sorrowful drunk who'd spent a lifetime building a future for his family only to see it rot in the bottom of a whiskey bottle.

She'd inherited an adventurer's spirit and ferocious determination from her uncle, and both had served her well. Until now. Her fingers trembled and she stilled them against her lips. She'd come to Australia with such grand expectations. And now they were gone. Systematically destroyed as if they'd never existed.

Dale had never belonged to her. Not really. And surely not this Dale. The boy who had wrestled dragons had lived only in Charles's letters. The sooner she realized that, the better off everyone would be. Especially her.

A soft sob inched its way up her throat but, with great effort, she beat it back.

So be it. She released the edge of the block and pulled the iron kettle from its place on the stove. If Dale had something special with Rachel, who was she to interfere? She had no claim to him. No rights to his love even if she had loved him since before she knew what love was. The reasoning bounced from one corner of her heart to the other with painful, hollow remorse.

For most of her life, she'd been in love with a dream. A fairy tale. A lie.

"Are you all right, Miss Emily?" Candice closed the back door with the heel of her boot and placed a basket of folded linens on the floor.

Emily spun toward the sink and worked the hand-pump. "Of course. Why do you ask?" Like a million tears, a steady stream of water poured from the pump.

"You don't seem yourself."

"I'm fine, I assure you." She must gain control of herself. It wouldn't do to let on to the others how deeply Dale's feelings for Rachel had affected her. She had lived without love for the past twenty-four years, she could very well live without it the rest of her life. Couldn't she?

Heat pooled behind her eyes and closed her throat with thick, weighted coals. "Will you put on the water for tea, Candice? I'm suddenly not feeling very well."

It was a lie, but she didn't care. She didn't even care if Candice knew the lie for what it was—a feeble attempt to persuade her heart to remain whole and fast. No matter how strong she'd pretended she was a moment ago, her heart spoke only the truth. She loved Dale more with each passing day. She ached for him, for his loss, and for the guilt that rode herd over his every breath.

She had no choice but to help him through the months to come. God willing, she'd share as many years as she could with him. Loving him.

She closed her eyes and placed a hand over her swirling belly. How could she do any of it with the knowledge that he could never give her a heart he couldn't even find?

✶ 🐎 ✶

Constant female chatter surrounded Dale. He leaned against the wall and pretended to listen. Rachel and her sister might have been discussing the relative normalcy of a man with four heads and he wouldn't have known. It all sounded like a flock of bleating sheep as far as he was concerned.

Matt had certainly picked the perfect time to arrive, however. Had he not barged into the foyer when he did, Dale might have acted on the desire that still waged a brutal war in his soul.

He might have kissed Emily again, despite his promises. And more.

And why not? He wasn't any good at keeping promises. Why should his word to Emily be any different? At least with a houseful of guests, he would be less likely to be alone with her. Less likely to force himself on her again.

The parlor door swung open and Emily glided into the room. Dark, damp tendrils surrounded her paler than normal complexion as if she'd thrown water on her cheeks. Was she ill? The thought disturbed him more than it should have and he tamped down the urge to comfort her.

Still, his gut wrenched when she attempted to set the tray on the table and the teacups rattled in her trembling hands.

"Are you quite well, dear?" Carole steadied the tray and helped Emily place it in the center of the table.

"Quite," she replied.

She lied. He knew her well enough to know something bothered her. He sensed it in the flutter of his belly and the thick tension that flowed from her every pore.

He pushed himself off the wall and his feet carried him to her of their own volition. He'd almost reached her when Rachel stepped into his path.

"Dale, I know it's been a long while since we've seen each other, but I have to say again how happy I am to know you're well and whole. You can't begin to imagine the suffering I've endured these past years."

He raised a brow. Suffering? What in God's name could Rachel Macomber know of suffering? She'd taken to her bed for a full week once when she'd twisted her ankle on an uneven patch of ground. Yet, her words carried a modicum of sincerity and her insipid green eyes stared up at him with a hint of moisture. Stifling his impatience, he replied, "I'm sure it's been terrible for you."

Rachel blinked and glanced at him with a coy expression. "Yes, it has been, but you're home now and we can begin where we left off before that ridiculous war."

Matt cleared his throat and took a cup of tea from his wife. "Rachel, dearest, won't you please sit down and leave the poor bloke alone. He's been through enough without having your unhappiness on his conscience."

"I'm not unhappy, Father. I'm positively joyous. My Dale has come home to me. How could I be anything but elated?"

Her Dale?

The words seemed foreign, as if she spoke of someone else. Maybe she did. The man Rachel had known more than four years earlier didn't exist anymore. He'd vanished in the heat of a desert sun more than a continent away. But she had no way of knowing that. To Rachel, he was still the carefree boy who had introduced her to moonlight and the excitement of impassioned summer nights.

At least, he was if the sparkle in her eyes meant anything.

Another mark against him come judgment day.

He glanced at Emily who'd seated herself on the edge of his mother's settee. Her lips pursed in a grim line and she stared into her cup as if something of great importance swam about in her tea.

"Things will be normal again," Rachel continued as she slipped her wrist around his elbow.

Her warm flesh only reminded him of Emily's heated touch. His gut tightened and the wicked claws of shame scraped his back. Had he not joined the regiments after he'd graduated from the King's Academy, he would have returned to Marble Bar, married Rachel and settled into the role of husband without a second thought. Any wild streak he'd possessed in his youth would have played out in the normal cycle of things.

But he hadn't come home. At least, not for good and ever. He'd spent one enthusiastic season in Rachel's arms, though never her bed, and then he'd joined the regiments after his final year at the Academy. He'd taken on the world with the same exuberance he'd done everything else. He'd been alive and whole.

So had Joel. In his first year at the King's Academy, his

brother had excelled in all of the same athletics and academics Dale had previously mastered. But Joel had done all of it better than Dale. He'd broken every record Dale had set within months. Long-distance running, skulling, football.

And horsemanship.

Dale sucked in a breath that tasted of guilt and shame. If only time could turn backward. If only he hadn't fallen into the deliberate rhythm of life in military service as if he'd been born to it. He might have left the regiments at the end of his first enlistment and Joel never would have died.

He should have thought the matter through. He'd been an adult and he should have done the responsible thing. He should have ignored his brother's insane ideas of glory and patriotism and sent him home on the next bloody train.

The walls of the parlor seemed to close around him. Instead of the smooth, hardwood planks of his mother's house, the sucking, heated sand of the *San-ai* pulled at him, tried to drown him. His throat dried and he swallowed to moisten it, but the grit of sand scratched and burned the raw passage.

"Dale? Are you listening to me?" Rachel leaned her breasts into his arm.

"What? I'm sorry. What did you say?" He coughed, but his thirst still burned.

"I asked if you've entered this year's race."

He gritted his teeth and forced a smile. "No, love. Not this year."

"Crikey, Rachel. I've told you a hundred times before now. Let the boy alone. You've whined so consistently over the past few years, you've failed to consider what Dale has been through. I imagine his experiences during the war are a sight more difficult to bear than your lack of finery. Now, rack off and leave the man be."

"Nonsense." Rachel stomped her foot and placed her hands on her thin hips. "Dale is a strong as they come, Father, and while a lesser man might have been cracked by a little war, he is quite well. Tell them, Dale. Tell them how nothing as trivial as a war could bother the likes of you."

If only it were so. If only he wasn't weak and the war could have rolled off his back like so much rainwater. But he *was* weak and it had affected him, the man he he'd been—the man he was now—far too much. Facing that reality in the eyes of Rachel Macomber only confirmed it. He stared at her and her brows creased.

Emily set her cup and saucer on the table. "Rachel, while I'm sure you suffered a great deal during the war, as we all did, Dale was there. He fought a horrid enemy in both the elements and the Turks and has more than earned his right to a period of adjustment." Her voice cracked and she gained her feet with a slight tremor. She circled the table, approached the foyer and paused. With one hand on the wall, as if the house itself held her up, she turned. "I'm sure you're all very tired. I'll have Ruth show you to your rooms."

And then she was gone.

He glanced at Rachel's wide eyes and the slack surprise of her narrow jaw. Whatever emotion he might have felt for her in the past, it had died that day at Beersheba. He'd thought he'd lost the ability to feel anything expect pain and guilt that day, but all that had changed when he'd come home. Oh, the pain was still there, tearing his soul into sagging shreds. And the guilt still filled him with tangible, wretched regret. But there was more. Something he didn't want to acknowledge.

There was hope.

He'd never have to pretend with Emily. She understood his sorrow, his guilt—even if she didn't know why—and the unnamed horror that had followed him for more than year. And she cared. She wanted him to overcome the torment that was every bit a part of him as his hands.

"I'm sorry, Rachel, but I think you may have misjudged me." He nodded to Matt and Carole and followed the path Emily had taken out of the house.

⁂

How could she have been so foolish? Emily hurried to the stable and slammed the door behind her. She inhaled the pungent aroma of horses and hay as she reached for Apache's bridle on the hook beside his stall. The thoroughbred raised his head at the sound of the jingling tack. A good, bruising ride overland would clear her head of such nonsense.

The lie sounded good, at least.

From in her heart, however, a river of molten regret flowed into her soul. She threw open the door and approached her horse with a practiced, steady hand. As angry as she was, she'd rather not add physical injuries to the emotional scars she already possessed. When Apache balked at her first attempt to slip the bit into his mouth, she forced a deep breath.

Not once since their first meeting months ago had Rachel Macomber said anything about her feelings for Dale. Of course, she and the whisper-thin girl hadn't formed a close bond, but the little twit could have said something. Anything. Instead, she'd spoken of her wedding for hours on end whenever the Macombers had come for a visit.

Her wedding?

Emily gripped the reins until the leather cut into her hands. Rachel had said she would marry as soon as her fiancé came home from the war, but she'd never mentioned his name. It had always been simply her fiancé. Could she have meant Dale?

"Of course, she meant Dale. Any fool can see how much she adores him." Her voice cracked and Apache nudged her. She sniffled and dried her eyes with the palms of her hands. "Everything is fine, Apache. Perfectly fine."

Emily stepped back, pulled her saddle blanket off the short wall dividing Apache's stall from several empty stalls, and placed it on Apache's back. Within a few short moments she'd saddled him and led him into his paddock.

A small voice called from behind her, "Here, Apache. Come here, boy."

She turned to find young Lizzy sitting atop the fence with one tiny leg on either side. Her red curls danced in a soft breeze and she pulled the strands away to tuck them behind her ear. "Mum and Dad said I could come see the horses, Emily. May I?"

Emily smiled in spite of herself and nodded. "Of course. Come."

Lizzy leaped off the fence and dashed toward her. "This is Apache."

"Very good, Lizzy. You remembered." With hands that still shook, she lifted Lizzy beneath her arms. "Up you go."

Once she'd settled Lizzy in the saddle, the little girl reached for the reins. "Thanks. May I ride him all the way to the other side?"

"Yes, but you mustn't go into the main pasture where the mares are. And keep him at a trot. He's much too fast for you if you let him have his head."

"I'll be good."

"I'm sure you will."

Lizzy kicked Apache's sides and he trotted across the smaller pasture. Lizzy's curls bounced despite the heat and Emily leaned against the fence railing to keep a close eye on the pair. How many times had she dreamed of her own children doing this very thing? In this very place?

She'd been a fool too many times over to count. Coming all the way from her home in America to capture the love of a man unwilling to spare even an ounce of his heart. Or perhaps he loved another. Was it possible he'd loved Rachel all along?

Something told her such a thing was more than unlikely. While far more beautiful than Emily, Rachel lacked a certain quality that a man like Dale would require in the woman he chose. Gumption.

Not to mention, Dale hadn't so much as spoken Rachel's name in the entire time he'd been home. Not once.

And then there was the kiss.

A knot formed in the back of her throat and her skin heated as if touched with an iron. Why the devil had he kissed her if he was engaged to marry Rachel Macomber? Had he simply forgotten? He might have if he never loved her. Or Rachel may have built Dale up in her mind over the past few years. She'd been little more than a girl when Dale had left for the regiments.

Either way, it mattered very little to her own predicament. She should have left Castle Winters when she'd had the chance. It seemed the only means to protect her heart from inevitable ache.

Footsteps crunched over the rough earth behind her. She glanced over her shoulder and swallowed as Dale made his way toward the fence. His shoulders swayed atop his long stride and his hat threw a dark shadow over his face. As if even the sun conspired to hide his feelings behind a rough mask.

She turned back to the pasture just as Lizzy and Apache passed the far corner of the field. "Are the guests settled in?"

Dale leaned his forearms on the highest rail and bowed his head. "Yeah."

"And Rachel? She's making herself at home?" At home. Emily's spine stiffened. In all of her childhood fantasies, which is all they would ever be, she'd never imagined she'd share the Castle Winters estate with another woman. This was *her* home. For better or worse.

"I suppose."

"Good."

Stilted silence tapped only by the distant rush of the Coongan River spanned what might have been miles between herself and Dale. He was close enough to touch but, as always, he drifted on some other plane.

Well, maybe not always. Earlier, in her room, he'd let down the curtain around his heart. She'd seen past the barrier and straight into his soul. Tortured and filled with guilt he shouldn't feel, it had reached out to her for comfort. He wanted to give himself the freedom to live, he just didn't know it yet. If Emily had even the slightest chance of breaking down the wall, once and for all, she'd have to help him see beyond the war, the guilt, and his own limitations.

She could do that. But she could only do it if she allowed herself to sacrifice her heart. What if he never loved her in return?

"Dale? Rachel is under the impression the two of you are to be married. Did you know that?"

His boots scraped on the hard, dry ground. "Yes."

Emily gathered whatever strength she could find from the pit of her stomach and turned to face him. Shoulders squared, her hands fisted, she prayed for courage. "Do you love her?"

His head snapped up as if he'd been stung. Bright eyes hidden in shadow narrowed and he licked his lips. "Yes."

Chapter Ten

An eagle soared overhead. Its cry echoed from one side of Emily's hollow chest to the other. At some point she would have to admit to herself that her dreams were nothing more than childish wishes. Fantasies born to failure in the cold, cruel light of day. Or the searing heat of day, as the case may be.

It had never dawned on her to ask Charles if Dale had been spoken for. It had never dawned on her to even suggest to Charles that she had feelings for Dale. After all, she'd never even met the man. She'd neglected to relate her feelings to the Macombers during their frequent visits even though Rachel had spouted off endlessly about her soldier and how proud she would be to be his wife.

Half the men in Australia were soldiers. She could have meant anyone.

But she'd meant Dale. It was plain now, spread out like the drifting clouds for all to see.

But less than an hour ago, he'd held her in his arms

as if she meant something to him, too. He'd kissed her damn near senseless and even now her fingers tingled from the sinewy muscles over which they'd roamed. A shudder crept through her womb, squeezed it like a vice and slipped away in a puff of smoke.

Finally, she forced a nod. "You love her. She's a fine girl. Woman," she amended.

"I should rephrase that. I thought I loved her. Once, a long time ago."

She studied the dark lines beneath the brim of his hat. He scowled, bent over and picked up a stone, which he promptly threw to the far side of the pasture. "I used to come home during holidays and spend the summers riding and getting into as much trouble as I could without killing myself. We both did, Joel and I. Eventually, that trouble included women. The only girls close enough to my own age to take notice of were Rachel and her sister." He shrugged. "Her sister was a bit on the young side for me, so when it came to romance, that left Rachel. We used to swim in the river, or I'd squire her around Marble Bar to a dance or wedding. That is, when Joel, Paul, and I weren't climbing some mountain or racing hellbent across the desert on horseback."

Taming dragons.

Emily's stomach fluttered. Heat that had nothing to do with a broiling midday sun steamed the back of her neck. What business had she to be jealous? An ocean and several continents had separated her from Dale during the time he'd courted Rachel. And even if he did so now, she had no claim to him. Still, she had to force herself to breathe. One breath after another, until she focused her attention back to his words. "And you fell in love."

"No, I don't think I did. I mean, sure, I've known her my whole life and I suppose everyone, including her parents and Charles assumed we'd get married someday. But I had other plans. I was going to see the world and answer to nobody. So I joined the regiments." A sardonic half-grin curled his lips, exposing one charming dimple. "So much for not answering to anyone."

Despite the crashing beat of her heart, she chuckled. His eyes had actually twinkled for a moment at his own jest. "I imagine you had a bit of trouble following orders, didn't you?"

"Too right," he laughed. "But I eventually settled in and just before Paul and I shipped out to Cairo, Joel came by the barracks. To say his farewells, or so I thought."

"It's only natural."

Dale snorted. "My barracks was on the other side of the country. He'd saved his spending cash for weeks for the train ticket so Charles wouldn't find out he'd come. He had something entirely different on that shady little mind of his. That's when he told me he was leaving school to join up."

He picked up another rock and tossed it farther across the field. "I'd bloody well filled his mind so full of romantic rubbage about the military in the letters I'd posted to him, he couldn't help but feel like he was missing out on something. He should have stayed at the academy."

"He would have enlisted whether you gave your blessing or not. You couldn't stop him. At the very least, he would have enlisted when the war broke out."

"Right. But then he'd have been in a different unit. He wouldn't have been in Beersheba when the bombs fell, would he?" His voice cracked.

"You can't stand there and tell me you believe he would have been in any less danger. Only he would have been alone. He might not have survived, but the last face he saw wouldn't have been yours."

Dale coughed and Emily suspected he only did so to cover what might have been tears clogging his throat. "I don't know why I'm telling you all this. You must be sick of me by now."

"No." She could never grow tired of his voice, or the strong, virile presence that surrounded him like a cloak. "But you really shouldn't beat yourself up about it. It wasn't your fault. Think about the good times you had together. Think about all of the wonderful adventures the two of you created. Right here, on this very station."

"I can't." He straightened his back. "God knows it hurts too bloody much."

"Of course you can. Do you remember the time you, Paul, and Joel took your horses on Joel's first overnight camping trip? Joel must have been something like . . . ten or so, I'd think. You and Paul made him sit awake most of the night watching for the Yowie monster. And then, once he fell asleep, you crept outside the tent and stood between the canyon wall and the fire so your shadow was huge." Emily raised both hands over her head and formed claws with her fingers. "Then you screamed like a banshee."

Dale canted his head, squinting one eye as if he studied her. "I remember it, sure enough. But how the hell do you know about that?" He wasn't upset, or at least he didn't appear to be. No, curiosity formed that deep furrow on his forehead, just below his hat.

She lowered her arms and tucked them at her waist. "Uncle Charles wrote to me about it. I was just a little girl then, but I remember I laughed so hard I thought my stomach would never stop hurting."

"Charles wrote to you about me?"

"Mm-hmm. All the time. I think I received no less than a letter a week for almost twenty years. When the letters stopped, that's when I came here."

The eagle swooped low over the treetops and called when it landed on the roof of the stable. Dale stared at it for a few moments as if memorizing every feather. "That was a long time ago, as well."

"Not so long. Truly, I think if you gave yourself permission, you could learn to see those times for the happiness they really are."

"No. And that goes for any bloody marriage with Rachel. I've changed since the last time anyone here knew me. I don't belong anymore."

Emily opened her mouth to respond, but a strangled cry cut off her words of comfort. She spun toward the pasture in time to witness Lizzy's fall from Apache's back.

"Lizzy!" She dashed toward the still form, but no matter how she willed speed into her limbs she seemed to gain no ground.

From the corner of her eye, she caught a blurred shape. An instant later, Dale raced past her. He reached Lizzy in what seemed like only seconds and threw himself to his knees. By the time Emily caught up to him, he cradled the tiny child's head in his lap. "She's not breathing."

Nothing in her life had prepared her for the utter helplessness that cascaded over the pasture as Dale pulled Lizzy's tiny form against his chest. Red strands shone in the sun like fire and settled against her freckled, pale cheek. Dale shook her but she made no sound, no cry.

"Dear God. Is she . . . ?"

"No. Her heart's racing like a whirlwind, but she's hit her head. What the hell happened?"

"I don't know. I wasn't watching." She should have been, but she wasn't. Lizzy would pay the price. Shivers of remorse threatened to envelop her in a cocoon of guilt.

"We've got to get her back to the house. Mount up. You can carry her back on Apache."

Emily turned to her horse, but the huge black backed away with a loud snort. "Come on, boy. There's nothing wrong with you." She took a step and Apache leapt to the side. "Easy, now. Easy."

"Here, take Lizzy." Dale stood and Emily opened her arms.

Emily's heart broke into a thousand shards when Dale handed her the tiny bundle. "Oh, Lizzy. Please wake up. You must wake up." She lifted her gaze to Dale. "What are you doing?"

"I'm catching your bloody horse."

With steady steps, he crept forward. He inclined his head and Apache stared back at him with huge, black eyes. Then the horse's head tilted to one side, as if he somehow understood what Dale wanted; what Dale needed from him. A moment later, Dale led the stallion back to Emily. Dale took Lizzy from her before she climbed into the saddle. Once she'd placed each foot into its stirrup, Dale passed Lizzy to her and she galloped across the pasture.

✝ 🐫 ✝

Dale pushed his limbs past any level of endurance he'd thought he still possessed. The air, hot and oppressive, burned his lungs and his gut clenched. Blood pounded in his temples and a cramp stole through his right side. He ignored the pain and forced one foot in front of the other.

In the distance, Emily reached the fence and called for help. Blue and Henry Albert ran to her, took Lizzy and rushed the little girl into the house. Emily looked back at Dale as if she would wait.

"Go. Go inside!" His voice, labored and breathless,

carried over the narrowing distance and Emily slipped through the fence and followed Blue through the front door.

By the time he reached the house, the parlor was full of Lizzy's family, the household staff, Blue, and Emily. He shoved his way through the mass then fell to his knees beside the setee, where a pale, but blessedly awake, Lizzy lay on her back.

Emily held one of Lizzy's small hands in her own and kissed the backs with her tears. "She only woke up a minute ago, Dale. I was so frightened."

Dale brushed Lizzy's damp, red curls off her forehead. "Can you hear me?"

Lizzy nodded. Dale lifted one finger in front of her face. "I want you to look right here, at my finger. Can you follow it for me, with just your eyes?"

She nodded again, but this time she winced.

"Don't move your head, just your eyes."

Lizzy did as he asked and her bright blue orbs followed his finger as he moved it back and forth. "Now, I want you to hold onto my fingers with both hands and squeeze the daylights out of them. Can you do that?"

She took his fingers in her pudgy hands and squeezed. When she applied the same tense pressure to both, he offered a reassuring smile. Then he pulled his fingers free and placed a kiss on her forehead. Finally, he stood and looked at her parents.

Carole wrung her hands in her apron and Matt's

narrowed brow formed a deep ridge above his large nose. Both of them had lost the color from their faces and stood pale as ghosts. "Relax. I think she'll be all right. More likely than not she'll be a touch groggy the next day or so. She shouldn't be allowed to sleep for the next few hours, then we'll have to wake her every few hours just to be safe. She's got a lump on her head and had the wind knocked out of her, but she'll be fine."

A soft hand landed on his shoulder and he turned to its source. Emily stared up at him with wonder and a certain longing in her eyes he'd never seen before. "How did you know what to do? I mean, how to examine her like that?"

"I was in the ANZACS, remember? More than a few blokes have bumped their heads. A mate of mine, early on, fell off a moving train, if you can believe that, and knocked himself cold. The doc showed me what to look for. No worries."

She smiled. "Thank heavens you were here."

Suddenly, the room seemed more crowded than it had a moment before. It seemed as if all eyes were cast upon him, judging him for his failures. He'd known what to do to help Lizzy. Why hadn't he been there for his own brother? He couldn't speak even if he'd tried. Heat crept into the back of his throat, clogging it with remorse, so he managed a nod and made his way back to the stable yard.

Outside, he closed his eyes and lifted his face to the sun. The world seemed still and quiet except for Apache's hooves on the fertile earth while he pranced from one end of his corral to the other, and the call of an eagle some-where overhead.

Henry Albert came out of the stable, and Dale opened his eyes, pushing away the sun's comforting touch. The blackfella approached Apache with care, and gathered the dangling reins. "I'll walk him a bit before I brush him and bed him down." He paused and then turned. "The girl? She'll be all right, mate?"

"Yeah, she'll be fine. Thanks," Dale answered. Lizzy *would* be fine. Something told him that. But what troubled him more was the uncanny, familiar rush that had fed his veins when he'd coaxed Apache. He hadn't experienced that particular emotion in a long time. He missed it.

Almost as much as he missed Joel.

"Will you hold him while I go for a brush?" Henry Albert handed him the lead.

While Henry Albert disappeared into the barn, the echo of Lizzy's strangled cry assailed him through the stagnant air like chimes in the sky. He shouldn't have distracted Emily from her charge. If he'd gone to the barn like he'd planned, instead of allowing himself to be drawn to her, she could have kept a closer eye on Apache. She would have seen Lizzy lose control of the horse and gone to her aid. Before Lizzy had been hurt.

Dale ran his hand over the sleek race horse's damp flanks as he approached his head. Apache nudged him and blew a snort.

"It's not your fault, boy." His words earned him another

friendly nudge.

The front door slammed and Dale turned to the sound. Emily hugged her narrow waist, descended the steps and slowly crossed the garden. "She's talking up a storm, thank heavens."

Relief washed over him.

Emily reached the gate and rested her forearms on the top railing with her chin on the back of her hands. "Why did you leave?"

He shrugged.

"It *was* a bit crowded. Carole took Lizzy to bed and insists she stay there for at least three days. It seems we'll have houseguests for a bit longer than we thought."

"No worries."

"You were amazing in there."

Amazing? Seconds counted and, because of a promise, he'd been unable to carry Lizzy himself—what kind of fool was he? "You were amazing, not me."

Emily laughed.

"What's so funny?"

"Oh, I suppose it's not funny in the least. But the way you deny your love for these animals . . . it's obvious you have a connection with them that I'd love to understand, but you still pretend you can live as if you don't."

He frowned. No, it wasn't funny. "You don't know what you're talking about."

"Sure, I do. My family has raised horses for forty years. Apache's sire competed in the Kentucky Derby three years ago, and damn near won. I've been around them my whole life, but I don't understand them. I can't read them or speak to them."

"No one can speak to a horse, love."

"You can. I saw you. Out there, in the pasture. Apache wanted nothing to do with anyone. He was agitated, yet you walked right up to him with a few soft words and that look you get in your eyes."

"Horses know when something's wrong. That's all. He sensed he was needed."

"I couldn't approach him and I've raised him from a colt."

"You were too tense."

"I suppose. But I think you wanted to ride him back with Lizzy. I think you've wanted to ride since you got here."

"I already told you. I can't." Why couldn't anyone understand that? What was so bloody important about the damned horses that Paul and Emily couldn't accept the fact he wasn't going to ride again. Not for himself, and bloody well not for either of them.

Apache bumped him with his muzzle and sent him a half-step to his left.

"Suit yourself. But I think your doing yourself, and Joel, a disservice."

🐎

Emily pulled Dale's shirt out of the wringer and, with a flick of her wrists, snapped it flat. She fastened it to the clothesline with two pins and wiped her reddened hands on her apron. Only three more pieces left and her afternoon chores would be complete. She'd waited until the sun had passed overhead to begin the laundering in order to avoid the furnace that was the rear garden most of the day. Even with the sun well past its zenith and night crawling from its slumber into a massive red sky, the temperature bordered on that of an oven. Thank goodness she'd spent the brutal heat of the day with Lizzy, reading to her from an old collection of nursery rhymes she'd found in one of the unused bedrooms.

Was it only yesterday that Lizzy had seemed on the brink of death? It was hard to believe with the way she complained about staying in bed. But her mother had insisted, and it *was* for her own good. Emily would finish her laundry and read to Lizzy for a while before bed, as well.

Someday, would she be lucky enough to have a daughter just as sweet and kind and young Lizzy? Would she have light hair and crystalline eyes? A sigh threatened to escape but she stifled it to avoid any prying questions from Ruth who stood only a few feet away, feeding the chickens.

She gathered another of Dale's shirts and dunked it into the washbasin.

"Don't you look fetching this evening, Miss Emily?"

Emily froze in mid-scrub and closed her eyes. "What are *you* doing here?" She dried her hands and turned to face Gerald with both hands on her hips. As he approached her, he wiped the sweat from his eyes with a dingy handkerchief.

"I thought I'd give you one more chance to change your mind."

"About what, exactly?" But she already knew. A shudder tickled her spine. Marriage to the slimy little man literally made her stomach turn. She placed the flat of her hand on her waist to still the motion.

"Why, about marrying me, of course. We should do it before Dale has a chance to sell this place out from under us."

"For the last time, I'm not going to marry you."

He stopped so close to her that the unmistakable odor of unwashed man assaulted her. She tried to back up, but her bottom crashed into the table she'd set up to do her washing. Gerald immediately moved forward to close the tiny space she'd created with the effort. He leaned forward and grasped the table on either side of her.

She stifled a gag.

Trapped.

"You know, the whole town knows about you."

"Please leave, Mr. Brown. I'm warning you."

"Did you hear me, Emily? The whole town is talking about you and Dale. About what goes on out here at night. I'm just about the only man in the Pilbara still willing to take you on." His putrid breath matched the filth of his words.

"I don't know what you're talking about. Leave me be!" She pushed against his chest, but he didn't budge.

Not so much as an inch.

Instead, he canted his head to study the curves of her face memorizing each and every line. Then he licked his lips, his head descending as if he meant to . . .

Kiss her?

She gathered her strength and hoped the fury feeding her blood would add to it. She pushed again, but this time she didn't stop until she'd managed to create an opening to her left where his hand lifted from the table. With knees that all but knocked together beneath her skirt, she escaped.

"Don't you go running off, love."

"How dare you come here, to my home, and repeat such vile rumors? Rumors, I might add, that have no foundation whatsoever."

"Come now. You can't expect me to believe that. You and Dale, living out here by yourselves. Hot, sweaty nights with nothing to do but—"

In a blur of swinging limbs and curses, Dale tackled Gerald to the ground. Emily jumped backward, pulled her old work skirt out of the way and found herself wrapped in Ruth's trembling embrace.

"Are you quite well, Miss Emily? Oh, I ran for Mr. Dale just as fast as I could!"

Looking more like some fabled Norse god than a man, Dale rose up and pulled Gerald to his feet by his shirtfront. The setting sun cast ruddy shadows over the gentle, glistening curves and rock-hard muscles of his back. Tempting blond locks brushed the tops of his shoulders. Fierce control emanated from pores that radiated heat, passion and fury. "I told you once already, Brown. Stay off of my property."

"You mean stay *away* from your property, don't you, mate?" Gerald nodded to Emily and she cringed.

"You bloody bastard," Dale retorted as he leveled an even, lip-splitting fist into Gerald's mouth.

Gerald swung back and within a second or two both men sported bloody lips and Gerald's left eye had begun to swell closed.

The back door swung open and Matthew flew down the steps. With his massive arms and superior weight, he wedged a gap between Dale and Gerald. "Hold off now, boys. Enough of this madness. What goes on here?"

Gerald stumbled several paces away from Dale and fell to one knee.

Dale stood like some ancient warrior with his wide shoulders set back, his chin raised at a defiant angle and his fists, like hammers, at his sides. "No worries, Matt. Brown was just leaving."

"Bloody hell, I was. I have every right to press my suit here. Emily is fair game."

"The hell she is. You don't want her, you want my station. I'm telling you for the last time, you can't have it and you can't have her!"

Matthew eyed Gerald as if to warn him to keep his distance before he circled behind Dale and approached Emily with a grin. "Has Gerald been courting you?"

"He's been trying to, but I want no part of him.

Honestly. I wish he would just go away."

Matt turned to Gerald. "She wants no part of you. Why don't you rack off and leave the lady be?"

Dale snorted. "Because he wants my station more than he wants her."

Emily didn't know if she should be offended or pleased with Dale's attempts to rescue her from Gerald's unwanted attentions, but the warmth in her heart rivaled that of the sun. Even so, his words meant more than that. For the first time since he'd been home, he spoke like he *wanted* the station.

"How about a race, then? Settle the whole matter."

"What?" Emily and Dale recited together.

"You want him to leave you alone, right? Seems to me he has a right to press his attentions on Emily if he chooses to make an arse out of himself. Why not let him race for the right to do so without losing what remains of his face the next time he pays a call."

"But I don't want him to press his attentions. I want him to leave me alone."

"Too right. If he loses the race, he'll leave you in peace."

Gerald's lips curled over his blood-stained teeth. "Sounds good to me."

"What do you say?" Matthew folded his arms over his chest.

Dale's shoulders moved back a notch. A muscle in his jaw ticked and his chest heaved either from exertion or emotion, Emily couldn't be certain which.

She stepped around the table and positioned herself between Dale and Gerald. "All right. I'll do it."

Matthew laughed. "Not you, Emily. I meant—"

She raised a hand to cut off his words. "I know what you meant. But this is my problem and I'll settle it."

Gerald crept closer, but maintained a safe distance as if he feared getting too close to Dale's fist. "What do you say we make the pot a little sweeter, then? If you win, I'll bloody well leave you be. But if I win, I get your half of the station. By marriage."

Dale rushed forward, but Emily pressed her back against him. Steamy tendrils of fire seemed to leap from everywhere her body pressed against his and her stomach clenched. "No, Dale. It's all right."

"What the bloody hell do you mean it's all right? It's not all right. You can't agree to this . . . this . . . farce!"

Farce? Maybe. But she'd been racing horses since she could keep her seat in a saddle. She couldn't possibly lose to some sheepherder who barely stayed sober long enough to roll over and scratch himself. "Not only *can* I agree to it, but I do." To Gerald, she continued, "Unless, of course, you're afraid of being beaten by a . . . *sheila*." She forced herself to offer her right hand to Gerald, who stared at it as if it were a snake.

Finally, a grin turned the corners of his mouth and he grasped it. "One month from now. One month, and you're mine."

✦ 🐎 ✦

"Are you out of your bleedin' skull, woman?" Dale slammed the bedroom door and stalked into Emily's room as if he had some kind of right to be there. As if he weren't intruding on her privacy. Again.

He stopped short in the center of the floor. Emily sat in front of his mother's vanity and rubbed lotion onto her hands. Her hair, normally bound in a tight knot at the top of her neck, flowed down her back with gentle, curved waves that caught the light from the oil lamp on the dresser. She frowned, spun on the silk-covered, cushioned bench until she half-faced him, and leveled a glare in his direction. She looked exotic and powerful. Intimidating and feminine.

Beautiful.

"Pardon me?"

"You heard me. You're bleedin' cracked, that's what you are. Do you have any idea what you've just committed yourself to? I don't know how things like this are played out in the great American West, but out here you're expected to live up to your end of a wager."

"The same is expected where I come from." She turned her back on him and picked up a silver-handled brush. With hands that looked soft as rose petals, she pulled it though her hair as if he weren't even standing there. Would her hair feel like silk on his lonely flesh? Would her body fit his? What would she do if he kissed her again?

He swallowed and ran a hand through his hair. The room grew hotter and the soft breeze shifting through the open widow did nothing to cool it.

"I suppose you'd have preferred it had I remained silent?"

"You can't win."

She laughed. "Of course I can. I've been racing Apache, and his sire, since I was eleven years old. I once rode at Churchill Downs, did you know that? And would have competed in the final race had Colonel Winn not discovered I was a girl." Her voice fell and she cleared her throat. "But it doesn't matter. I can't imagine any horse in Australia matching Apache for speed."

"You think you'll race Apache against Gerald and his gray Whaler of his?"

She nodded and when she smiled, her face glowed like a sunset over Chinaman's Pool. "And when we win, I'll be rid of Gerald Brown once and for all."

"Bleedin' cracked." He stomped in her direction until the heady lavender scent of her hand lotion erupted in a flowery haze around him. "Apache won't last half the distance. You're not *Running for the Roses* here. The race you just agreed to is an endurance run. Over terrain that resembles riding on the moon and taking the sun with you. You'll have to ride Jezebel and then I doubt you could even finish."

Emily slammed the brush on the vanity and leapt to her feet. She was so close, the tips of her breasts almost brushed his chest and his heart constricted until he couldn't breathe. He backed away, but immediately missed the warm embrace.

"What do you mean, I won't finish?"

"You're a woman. Trust me. I've run these races my whole life. They're brutal and, if you don't know what you're doing, they can be deadly."

A hint of color stained her cheeks a second before she paled. Still, she attempted to cover her obvious fear with typical bravado. "I can do it."

Something told him she probably could. But worse, she shouldn't have to. He should have declined the challenge and taken the blow to his pride like a man. Instead, like a coward, he'd allowed her to stand up for him. The steely glint in her flashing violet eyes told him she would die before she'd back down. No matter how slim her chances for victory were.

"You'll have to work with Jezebel every day. She's out of shape."

"You don't have to tell me that."

"And you'll have to train overland, in the desert."

"Of course."

"It's dangerous. More than you can know."

"I lived in a desert in America, if you'll remember. In fact, the countryside here is remarkably similar. But, you could train with me, teach me, if you're that concerned."

His gut clenched into a twisted knot. "You know I can't," he whispered.

A tender expression pulled the fire from her eyes and she approached him with the grace of a cat. "I know." Her voice whispered over his flesh like a wildfire.

"That's why you spoke out, isn't it? Because you wanted to spare me the humiliation."

She nodded.

"Damn." It had been so long since he'd let anyone into his heart, past the thick wall of his soul. It was different with Emily than it had been before he'd lost any of the courage he'd once possessed. Before, Charles and Joel had provided all of the love he'd thought he'd ever need. When he lost Joel, he lost that part of himself willing to accept love from anyone. Even Charles.

The way Emily's dark gaze settled on his face reminded him of that side of himself that might still live, buried deep. The same side of him that had reached out to Apache yesterday in the pasture. The side he thought he'd killed.

"What's wrong, Dale? You look like you've seen a ghost."

He wanted to laugh. A ghost? She really could read his mind, couldn't she? Yes, he'd seen a ghost, all right. His own ghost. "Nothing's wrong. Everything's wrong." His feet slid across the rug of their own accord. "Everything's right."

She cocked her head and her breath hitched.

"I promised myself I wouldn't do this."

"Do what?"

"Kiss you again."

She swallowed and the muscles in her neck glistened in the lamplight just as her unbound hair had. Shadows played over the curves of her face and her eyes deepened like a starless night. "Kiss me?"

"I promised *you* I wouldn't do it."

"Yes, you did." She didn't back away. She didn't even blink.

"I'm not very good at keeping promises."

Chapter Eleven

Emily's womb tightened in silent anticipation. "I suppose some promises *are* meant to be broken."

All of the desire she'd hoped for raged a battle in Dale's eyes. If only he could relinquish the wounds of the last year to the past where they belonged, his gaze might hold promises of a new life. Promises he *could* keep. Instead, he warred within himself, it seemed, as the light blue of his eyes turned a smoky gray. Like storm clouds before a drought-lifting rain.

Her throat closed and she swallowed against the sudden lump. When his large, rough hands clasped her shoulders in a not-so-gentle grip, she thought he might abandon his weakness. That he might break down the wall around his heart.

A whimper formed in her throat and she tilted her face against one of his hands. Rough, dry knuckles teased her cheek.

She should be ashamed of herself, allowing him to

remain in her room while she wore nothing save a sleeping gown of sheer linen. But she wanted him to know she was a woman. More, she wanted him to know he was a man. Proud, strong, and as capable as he'd always been. The war hadn't stolen that from him—at least, not yet.

Dale's other hand traced a ticklish path from her shoulder to her throat. The gentle touch left a trail of fire over her collarbone to land in the hollow of her throat like an inferno of lust. Something molten pooled at the juncture of her thighs and she shifted her weight.

Then both of his hands held her face in a warm cradle and his gaze washed over her features as if he searched for something he couldn't quite grasp. Wherever his heady gaze fell, she flushed and the power of it sent torrid longing straight to her womb. Her breasts contracted beneath the thin shield her gown offered. Sweet torment came from the touch of his stare and the weight of his insistent fingers.

"To hell with it." His voice sounded different, as if he couldn't control the stricture of his own throat. He bent his knees, bent his head and brought her to his lips with gentle pressure.

He tasted of lemonade and the honey-cakes they'd had for dinner. Sweet and masculine. His hands roamed over her back, bringing her closer to his chest. When he gained his full height, he brought her with him so she stood on the tips of her toes. But really, she floated on a cloud of passion. He could take her anywhere, do whatever he wished and she would only beg for more. Instinct told her his possession would know no earthly bounds if he would but take her to his will.

Before she even realized they'd moved, her back met the solid force of a wall. His body pressed her against the surface, strong and unyielding as the pulsing thrust of his hips, the beat of his heart against her breasts.

Such wicked delight and agony at once, she feared her own breath might disturb whatever power had formed this moment for them. But she must have breathed because the rich aroma of man and leather only teased her tingling senses all the more.

Such craving dwelt behind his kiss, he must be capable of life. He must have something of his old self still buried beneath the gruff shell he'd become since Joel's death.

A flash of blazing desire pulled at her core as Dale rocked his hips again. His body, hard with wanting, filled her mind with erotic and temptingly sinful images. Only his mouth and his body touched her. He pressed his hands flat against the wall on either side of her head, as if he held himself steady against a tempest.

With a hungry growl, he tore his mouth from hers. She moaned at the frigid loss until his lips found the bend between her neck and shoulder. When his tongue darted out to taste her there, she thought her whole body might come undone. It was as if her limbs no longer responded to her mind, as if her mind somehow belonged to someone else. So little was her control over the riot of her pulse, she simply leaned against the wall and delighted in the earthy, basic, and altogether new paradise found beneath Dale's masterful attention.

When he lifted his head to rest his forehead against hers, the world spun to a stop. He seemed more than a little exerted for his efforts, his chest rising and falling against her own. "Why did you stop?"

He smiled and a glimpse of light sparkled in the blue depths of his eyes. "If I don't leave now, then I'm afraid we'll put truth to the rumors Gerald spoke of."

"I don't care."

"Ah, but I do." He backed away, but never took his eyes off of her face. "I'm afraid I care a great deal."

What did he mean? Did he admit he cared for her, or only that he cared for the untruth of the reputation-marring rumors Gerald had started in Marble Bar and the neighboring community? As much as she wanted to know the answer, she couldn't bring herself to ask. For the moment, she could pretend he loved her as much as she had always loved him.

At least he'd found a light somewhere within himself, for it shone around him like the glow of a bush fire. She'd have to be happy enough with that, for the moment.

"You should go to bed now. You'll have to start working with Jezebel in the morning."

"Of course." But the last thing she wanted was to spend even one more night alone in the ornate canopied bed that took up half of her room. If he would stay with her, if he loved her, she could sleep instead of lying awake as she had so many nights since he'd come home.

But it seemed too much to hope for. He was slowly learning to live again. It would have to be enough.

For now.

✕ 🐎 ✕

If one thing could be said about Western Australia in the summer, it would be a comparison between Dale's homeland and the fires of hell. Sweat poured down his neck and back, drenched his shirt, the waistband of his strides, and dripped off his chin. He straightened his back, wincing from the ache in his muscles, and wiped a cloth over his face.

He'd been working on the sunnyside of Tower Rock all afternoon and the glowing orb had finally dipped toward the western sky. In another hour or so, the rock formation would throw a welcomed shadow over the area of fence Dale repaired.

The fences weren't badly damaged and probably would have survived the winter months intact, but it served as a convenient excuse to be away from the house. If he'd been able to ride, he would have camped out with the *Jacka-roos* who tended the flocks, but short of that, he'd make damned sure he stayed busy around the station. At least until after supper, when the household settled in a quiet rhythm and his presence would be missed.

He didn't know exactly who he avoided, but between

Rachel and her utter refusal to believe he harbored no romantic feelings for her, and Emily, with her beautiful features and a soul that pulled at him like a bloody magnet, he needed to keep his distance.

Last night, he'd been tempted to take Emily right up against the wall. Her gown posed little barrier and the soft, dark shadow between her legs had him hard with wanting. But she deserved better than he could ever give her. She deserved to be loved by the man she chose, and he had no love to give.

"There you are. I've been looking for you all morning." Matt approached on horseback and pulled Sally to a halt beside the buckboard wagon that held Dale's supplies. "Crikey, what time did you leave the house?"

Dale hammered the last nail into place on the top railing and shrugged. "Before sunup. There's work to be done."

"Sure there is. Nothing wrong with good, hard work. But the women were worried you wouldn't eat and sent me to bring you this." When his friend climbed out of the saddle, he opened the leather bags over the horse's flanks and withdrew a bundle wrapped in brown paper. It was on Dale's tongue to ask which of the women fretted over him, but he wasn't entirely sure he wanted to know. If it was Rachel, it only added to his guilt for leading her on before the war had changed everything. And if Emily had prepared the picnic lunch . . . That didn't bear thinking on. He'd begun to sense the depths of her feelings for him when she'd returned his kiss. The last thing he needed was something — or someone — to add to his already stony guilt.

"It's chicken, I think. Left over from last night, I'd wager."

Dale's stomach rumbled. He climbed over the fence and settled on the back of his buckboard. "Hand it over."

The chicken tasted better than it had last night. Emily's mother's recipe, from what she'd explained over dinner. Beautiful, erotically formed, and a good cook. He'd be crazy to part ways with her, but in the end, that's all he could do. She deserved a whole man, not a half of one who barely had the strength to breathe most of the time. Still, it was obvious now who'd sent the meal. The chicken suddenly tasted less than appetizing.

"It's good to see you, Dale. If I haven't said it already."

"You have." He cast a sideways glance in Matt's direction. The beefy man carried enough muscle to break Dale into pieces of broken bone, yet he fidgeted with the buttons on his shirt like a five-year-old child at church. "What's on your mind, Matt?"

"Oh, nothing much. I guess I'm just a little concerned about you. You had us all worried when you didn't come home after your discharge."

Dale tore off a piece of chicken and frowned as he chewed. Finally, he swallowed and wiped his mouth on his sleeve. "I wasn't ready."

"Figured as much. But then, when is anyone ready to face war?"

"I handled the war, no worries. I'm no bloody coward."

At least, he hadn't been when he'd left Australia. Australia had sure as hell received a coward when he'd returned.

"I'm not saying that. I'm just saying that sometimes things happen in war that we can't control, no matter how much we'd like to."

"What's your point?"

"It's not your fault Joel didn't make it home."

"What the hell are you talking about, Matt?" Was he so transparent these days? Did he walk around with a bleeding sign on his back that read, *"Pity me. I'm a failure?"*

"I just know how close the two of you were growing up, that's all. And I know you always thought of yourself as Joel's guardian. But you weren't then and you weren't in the regiments, either. People die in war. People change, the world changes. There is little that you, or anyone else, can do about that."

Dale leapt off the wagon and picked up his hammer. "I don't really need any lessons about what I can or cannot control, if you don't mind. Everything is just fine."

"Sure it is. That's why you stayed rotten for a whole damn year instead of coming home like you should have. Because everything is fine."

"Leave off, Matt. I've got nothing to say."

Dale was halfway back to the fence before Matt's voice cut him off. "You know, if things never changed you'd be married to my daughter by now, raising a passel of children and past miserable—instead of eyeing Charles Castle's niece like she was first prize at the fair."

✦ 🐎 ✦

Dale climbed the stairs with limbs more achy and tired than he'd experienced in far too long. It felt good to work hard, work up a sweat and accomplish something. He'd avoided real work for so long, he had surprised himself when he even remembered how to rebuild a simple fence.

But Matt's observations had surprised him even more. If an old bastard like Matt had noticed the way Dale's gaze fell on Emily more often than not, who else had noticed?

Rachel appeared at the top of the stairs with a stern set to her jaw and what could only be fire and ice in her eyes. "You're a mess. I suppose you'd like a bath, wouldn't you?"

He stopped in midstride with one hand on the banister and the other fisting the rim of his hat. "It would be nice."

"Well, I'm not fetching it for you."

"I didn't expect you would, Chelly."

"Don't call me that. No one has called me that in years. Not since I was a little girl."

"I used to call you that, before I left." He climbed the rest of the steps and stood over her on the landing.

"I know."

"You're upset with me, aren't you?"

Her pink lips tilted on one side. "I suppose I should be. And I've tried to be angry with you ever since we arrived and I realized you don't lov—"

"It wasn't meant to be. That's all. It was a long time ago."

"I realize that now. It's for the best, I'm sure. You've changed."

She had no idea how much. "So have you."

"Not really. I've grown up, is all. And I think it just wouldn't have worked out between us. It's not as if I haven't had other suitors, you know."

"Oh, I can understand that. A pretty girl like you."

She licked her lips and stared at him for what seemed like a full minute before she glanced away. "I'm glad we have that settled and you're handling this so well."

He stifled a chuckle. "I'll survive. In time," he added.

"Very well. In that case, I'll tell Candice you'd like the tub brought up and filled."

"Thanks, Rachel."

She swayed down the stairs with a light jump in her step. She seemed almost as relieved as he was. At least he didn't have to contend with a scorned woman. Still, he'd be sure to check his sheets before he crawled into bed for the remainder of her visit. A man couldn't be too careful. Who knew what kind of creature an angry woman might slip between his sheets. He couldn't help the smile that parted his lips as he shook his head.

A soft voice carried through the hall and drew his attention to one of the guestrooms. He crept over the oriental runner until he poised outside the door and made out Emily's soft inflections as she read aloud from a book.

His heart ached at the sound and he couldn't stop himself from peering through the thin crack formed by the slightly opened door. Lizzy sat propped up in the oversized bed, surrounded by light linen bedclothes in a color just off of white. She studied the doll in her lap and every so often glanced at Emily, who occupied a chair beside the bed.

Emily read from a collection of Mother Goose Nursery Rhymes. The thick, fully illustrated volume had belonged to his mother and the sight of it almost choked him. How many times had his mother read him those pages? How many times had he read them to Joel? But instead of the normal swell of regret, pain, and self-contempt that came from such a vision, his chest filled with wanting. Suddenly, instead of an ache, his heart swelled with desire.

No. Not desire.

Want. Pure and elemental. He wanted Emily. Needed her like a drug. And he wanted the picture he studied in the bedroom. Emily reading to their child. Emily mothering their child. Emily loving them both with her entire being.

He wanted her to have all of the happiness she deserved, and more. He scowled. There was no place for him that picture. No place for him in her happiness. Were he the man in such a family, happiness would be seldom found and more often non-existent.

He backed up and the floor creaked under his weight. Emily stopped reading. Lizzy's head sprang up until she stared at the door. "Is that you, Dale?"

Damn. He'd hoped to get away unnoticed. Instead,

he pushed open the door and leaned on the jamb. "Yes, it's me you little ankle-biter. How are you feeling?"

"Oh, much better, but Mummy won't let me out of bed yet."

"Listen to your mum. She's knows what's best. You scared us half to death yesterday."

"But I'm fine now."

Emily closed the book and laid it on the table beside the bed. "Of course you are, but you still have a quite the lump on your head and you must get your rest."

When she faced Dale, his entire body coiled like a spring. How did she do that? With just a simple glance, she wound him like a great clock to be released at her choosing. "You look a fright, Dale. Is there a single fence on the property you haven't rebuilt today?"

"I suppose I did my fair share, for once."

"Let me prepare a bath for you," she offered as she tried to slide past him into the hall.

Even in his current state of filth, her freshness over-powered him. Nearly brought him to his knees. "It's done. You should stay here, visit more with Lizzy before supper."

"If you're sure you're settled . . ."

Settled? He'd never been more unsettled in his life.

✴ 🐎 ✴

Wind rushed past Emily's ears. Jezebel stormed over the uneven ground that surrounded the Castle Winters Station as if she'd been born to it. Of course, this was the kind of riding she had been used to before Dale left for his military service. She was far more accustomed to the heat and the terrain than Emily.

Still, there was something wild and beautiful about the majestic desert that drew her in and made her want to be a part of the wild landscape. Not terribly different than the bright deserts of her Arizona home, Australia still held an aura all its own. The oppressive heat and red earth formed a vision of untamed dreams and endless possibilities.

A blending of rolling dunes covered with sturdy vegetation, long flat expanses of desert and rocky canyons, the Great Sandy Desert was deceptively alive. It breathed all around her in the wind and rocks. More than that, it surged through her as strongly as her pulse.

Jezebel rounded a jagged outcropping and Tower Rock came into view, its steep sides rising out of the earth like a sentinel. Just beyond the tower, the irrigated fields of Castle Winters beckoned with promises of cool water drawn straight from the well for Emily, and sweet, lush grass for Jezebel.

But more than refreshments and a well-earned rest for them both, Castle Winters promised more of Dale Winters.

No matter what she had to do, she'd made the decision to stay in Australia for as long as she could. Hopefully, that would mean spending the rest of her life with Dale. When he'd kissed her again last night, her whole body had come alive.

And Dale could deny it all he liked, but he had come alive as well. Even if it had been for only a few moments. She'd experienced too much passion to believe he didn't care about her, at least a little. If he cared about her a little, she found reason to hope he would care more. Perhaps, someday, he might even grow to love her.

Tower Rock loomed closer and a few minutes of hard riding brought her back to the stable yard where she finally slowed Jezebel. She trotted the horse in a wide circle before bringing her to a full stop and leaping out of the saddle.

On legs that felt more like jam than flesh and bone, she led Jezebel to the corral, opened the gate and walked her inside. It took Henry Albert only a moment to strip the saddle and bridle from the lathered animal and hand them to her before he took Jezebel out to the pasture to cool. Satisfied Jezebel would be fine, Emily carried the tack into the stable.

Dale stood at Apache's stall and fed the massive black a cube of sugar.

"Oh, Dale, we had the most exhilarating run. Australia is simply divine."

He wiped his hands on his pants and leaned against the stall, one booted foot crossed in front of the other. His damp shirt clung to every muscled curve of his chest and arms like a second skin. Her stomach clenched at the thought of those arms around her again. Heat that had little to do with the soaring temperatures of early summer flamed in her cheeks.

"Glad to hear it. I thought you'd be away longer, though. It's been less than four hours."

"I didn't want to work her too hard her first time out." Emily hung the tack on the appropriate hooks and joined Dale in front of Apache's stall. "But she did very well, I think."

A cloud formed over Dale's expression and he frowned. "She's a good mount, that one."

Emily rested her hand on Dale's forearm and applied what she hoped was the gentle pressure of reassurance. "You miss it, don't you? You miss taking her out into the desert and losing yourself."

He cleared his throat and shrugged off her hand. "You can't understand, Emily. Not really."

"What's not to understand? You're punishing yourself for something that you had no control over. It's insane, really. You need to move past this."

"I'm trying." He offered a hint of a smile and brushed a lock of hair off her cheek. "Thanks to you."

"Me?"

"I hadn't thought I could ever feel again. Hell, I didn't want to feel anything. And then I come home to find you here. Bullying me into finding a tiny part of my heart still beating."

She cast a glance to the dusty floor and smiled.

"You're beautiful when you blush. All rosy and warm."

His voice thrummed in her mind like the strains of a gentle song. Emily raised her gaze to his and he pulled her to his chest in an embrace that spoke of more than mere affection. "I don't know where any of this will lead, Emily, but I thank God every day that you're here. Mostly, because I don't deserve it."

"Deserve what?"

"You." He kissed the top of her head. "I don't deserve you."

"You deserve more than you give yourself credit for. And I still think you are bound by no promises made to Joel when you obviously couldn't think straight."

"I failed him once. I can't fail him again."

"You won't fail him by living your life as he would have lived. You know you want to. I can see it in your eyes when you look at Jez or Sally. Or even Apache. You love horses and they love you. Why deny yourself the right to enjoy them?"

"Because I promised."

✦ 🐎 ✦

"But, I don't want to leave. We only just got here!" Lizzy tossed a strawberry curl off her forehead and stamped one foot.

Susan took her sister's hand and encouraged her to move toward the loaded wagon. "We'll be back soon enough. And you'll have so much fun in Port Hedland, you won't want to leave there, either."

"But I want to stay with Emily."

"You can't."

"Why not?"

"Because it's time to leave, that's why."

"Why?"

Dale caught himself smiling and shook his head. He knelt in front of Lizzy and scratched his chin, smooth for the first time in several days. "I tell you what, Lizzy. If you don't drive your sisters mad on the way to town, as soon as you get back, I'll let you ride Sally for as long as you like."

Bright, round eyes studied him with a glossy sheen of skepticism mixed with contemplation. Behind the glass-like orbs, her mind skimmed his offer until finally she smiled. "Do you promise?"

"Aye. It's a promise."

"All right then. I'll go. But I don't reckon I'll like it." She marched past him with such force, tiny clouds of beige dust formed around her boots.

"Thank you, Dale," Susan whispered before she climbed into the back of her father's buckboard.

Matt clambered down the front steps with his wife and Rachel.

Dale waited for Emily to appear behind them, but only disappointment followed. He frowned. "Where's Emily?"

"She said her farewells in the house. Something about laundry and feeding the chickens." Matt huffed as he pulled a white handkerchief from the front pocket of his suit jacket and dabbed it across his forehead. "It's going to be bloody hot again today, mate. Lay off those fences or you'll work yourself into an early grave."

"You just worry about getting you and yours to town without cracking that other wheel, old man."

"Too right. Up you go, ladies." Matt helped his wife onto the front bench of the buckboard leaving Dale to help Rachel.

Just as she took his hand, a terrifying scream shattered the still morning. It came from behind the house and boomeranged off the stable before ripping through his ears like a gunshot. *Emily!*

He launched past Rachel and raced around the corner of the house. Then he skidded to a halt just before he reached the edging stones that enclosed a measure of grass, still sparkling with morning dew. Emily stood with her back pressed against a large white sheet that hung from the clothesline. Her face was a mask of terror, her eyes bulging from their sockets in shock and panic. In one hand, she clutched a tin bucket. The other had formed into a tight ball as if she would pound on anything that moved.

Unfortunately for her, the only thing that moved was seven foot grey kangaroo that had apparently taken a liking to her.

"Shoo!" Emily spat and slid a step to her right, unclenching her fist to wave the beast away as if it were a fly.

The kangaroo, obviously enthralled with the frightened human, nodded to her left.

Emily backed away, but the heavy, damp sheet impeded

her to the point she could go no farther without turning her back on her nemesis. From the expression on her face, she wasn't willing to do that.

"Go away, you oversized rat!"

Dale chuckled and drew the attention of both woman and beast. "Trust me, Em. The best move for you right now is stand perfectly still. You don't want to get her too upset."

"I don't want to upset her at all. I just want her to leave. I'd thought she'd gone for good the last time."

Behind him, the Macombers gathered to watch the spectacle. Rachel slid beside him and folded her arms. "You don't reckon she'll hurt her, do you?"

"No. Not that 'roo. Don't you recognize her?"

Emily pivoted to her left, but the curious marsupial followed on powerful hind legs, using her thick tail to maintain her balance. "I would greatly appreciate one of you scaring this *thing* out of my way."

Rachel laughed. "Why, it can't be her, can it? It's been years."

"Oh, it's her. Do you see the scar running along her back? Just there . . ." he pointed to a long, uneven ridge of fur, ". . . along her spine."

"Well, what do you know about that? It *is* her."

"Will someone please call this thing away?" Emily's frightened tone had the effect of a mortar shell on Dale's amusement.

"Martha, love. Leave the nice lady alone, will you?"

The kangaroo turned in a lumbering half-circle. When

she saw Dale, she coiled up like a spring and lunged at him. Apparently thinking better of it, she pulled herself short of the rocky stable-yard and hovered like a thick-trunked tree whose top-most branches swayed in the breeze.

Emily didn't move for what seemed like forever, then finally crept in an arc around the garden until she stood on the dusty earth beside Dale. "That *creature* has a name?"

"Of course she does. This is Joel's pet 'roo."

"Pet?" Emily sounded like he might expect if he'd told her Father Christmas had taken up permanent residency in the attic.

"I haven't seen her in years. I mean, even before the war. The last we laid eyes on her, she was about half this size. I wonder what brought her home?" Dale stared into Martha's black eyes and found himself tempted to match the gentle rhythm of her swaying shoulders.

Emily snorted, "I haven't the foggiest idea. She hasn't been around in a while. The last time *I* saw her was before you came home."

Dale severed the invisible line between himself and the kangaroo's curious eyes. "She's been here before?"

Emily nodded. "Four times. And each time, she manages to trap me somewhere. It's as if she's playing a game."

"No, she's just getting to know you. When she takes a whack at your head, then you'll know she likes you."

"I'd just as soon avoid that, if you don't mind."

Rachel stepped closer to Martha and held out her hand. "Come here, baby girl. Do you remember me?"

Martha's head inched forward until she sniffed Rachel's hand, then backed away and licked her muscled forearms.

"Well, she must have come home for a reason, right? Is she hurt?" Emily, somewhat over her fear if the color in her cheeks were any indication, ran her eyes over Martha's coat. "I don't see any obvious wounds. Are you sure that's an old scar on her back?"

"Aye. I'm sure. Joel found her when she wasn't any bigger than a small ewe. She'd been caught up in a fence Charles had strung a few days before, ironically to keep the 'roos out of the pasture. She was torn up pretty badly and Charles didn't think she'd survive the night. Neither did I, if you want to know the truth. But not Joel. Joel was convinced he could save her with all of the enthusiasm of a ten-year-old boy." Dale's heart leapt into his throat and tried to strangled him. "He was right."

"Oh, I remember now. Charles wrote to me about it. He never mentioned it again and I just assumed she'd died or something. Why would she come back now?"

Lizzy dashed between Dale and Emily, tangled slightly in Emily's outdated skirt and ran across the lawn. She bent over, resting her tiny hands on her knees, apparently eager to approach the 'roo, but knowing better than to try. Martha followed her with shimmering black eyes and a creased brow, but Lizzy had given it a wide enough berth that it didn't spook. "Look! It's a baby!"

Dale squinted in the direction Lizzy stared. A tiny nose poked from behind the low hedge that separated the garden from the pasture. A snout followed the nose until, finally, an entire miniature kangaroo slid from behind the curtain of leaves.

Martha spun and hopped to her joey. Dale opened his mouth to shout a warning to Lizzy, but having lived her entire young life in the bush, she'd already started to back away to give the powerful animal plenty of room.

When she hurried back to Dale and Emily, she wore a huge smile that spoke of wonder and adoration. "Can you see it? It's so lovely. I want one, too."

Dale ruffled her curls. "I don't think Martha would appreciate you taking her baby away. I'm sure she's just passing through and she won't be here very long."

"And we must be going anyway, if we want to reach Marble Bar by this afternoon. Come along," called Carole from the buckboard.

As if Martha understood him, she gathered her joey and disappeared around the far side of the house. Lizzy followed and, after a moment, returned with a frown. "She's gone."

"She's free, Liz. She'll come back someday." Dale rubbed the crown of Lizzy's head and the girl sighed.

After a renewed round of farewells, Matt and his family bounced over the drive with the ever present chatter of their youngest member keeping them company.

They were lucky, no doubt about that. Matt was luckiest of them all. A wonderful wife, charming daughters. No unanswered questions or debts to repay. Hell, even

Martha, a kangaroo who should've died more than fifteen years ago, had managed to renew life and move toward something more profound than herself.

A whispered breeze brought cooling air to his temples and he cocked his head. A voice in the wind caught his attention. "Life goes on."

He looked up and found Blue atop Tower Rock, squatting toward the sun.

Chapter Twelve

"Do you like picnics?"

Emily raised her eyes from a worn copy of *Pride and Prejudice* at the rich tenor of Dale's voice. She slid her reading spectacles down her nose so she could focus on his face. He leaned against the doorjamb in that way he had that made him look relaxed and caged at the same time. A lock of hair fell over his forehead in a pin curl that gave him a rakish charm and one side of his mouth lifted in a half-grin.

The image made her heart pound, but with conscious effort, she answered, "I don't know a woman who doesn't. Why?"

He'd shaved this morning, but his smooth cheeks only reminded her of the scratch of his whiskers when he'd kissed her that night in her room. Her stomach muscles convulsed in a flurry of tiny wings.

"Ruth and Candice have packed a lunch and I thought you might like to visit the Pool with me."

Dale looked so incredibly roguish as his eyes roamed her face, Emily couldn't stop her smile from widening. Heat flushed her cheeks and, if she wasn't mistaken, a bit of color appeared on Dale's cheeks as well. "I'd love to."

A few minutes later, she sat on the rough front bench of the wagon with Dale at the reins, a huge basket of food and two bottles of wine in the back. They traveled north along the Coongon River for several miles before Dale turned the wagon off the road and into a low, flat area dotted with dull green desert brush and topped with jagged outcroppings. He pulled the horses to a stop and set the brake before jumping to the ground with the grace of a cat. "Here we are."

Emily shielded the sun from her eyes with one hand and admired the marbleized rock that towered overhead. "Where's here?"

"Well, I reckon I should've said we're almost there. We'll have to walk for a bit. But it's worth it if the place hasn't changed too much. That," he added, pointing to a huge rock covered in deep, colorful striations, "is the marble bar."

He helped her alight from the wagon, grabbed the picnic basket in one large hand and guided her to a path around the edge of the glassy water with the other.

"It's beautiful. But, you still haven't told me where we're going." Emily sidestepped a jagged stone in the narrow path. In the center of the pool, the huge rock Dale had indicated towered like a great castle wall, a sentinel against the elements and a keeper of time. The slick surface was striated with varying shades of red, orange, black, green and white and it stood dozens of feet high.

"Not too much further."

"I don't mind. It's a beautiful walk, isn't it? What is that massive rock made of? Is it really made of marble?"

"No, it's jasper. But you're not the first to make that mistake. That's how Marble Bar got it's name."

Just as the words left his mouth, they turned along the bank and arrived at the edge of a wide pool that stretched in front of Emily like one of the desert springs she'd visited as a child. Only this spring was a part of the river system and the water teemed and spun in misleadingly lazy currents. Large black boulders, smoothed through eons of weather and time, jutted into the pool in a haphazard and twisting design.

Beyond the pool, the desert stretched for miles upon miles. Red sand and the muted green of the desert flora ran toward the horizon where they met the Great Sandy Desert. A huge, brilliantly blue sky shone overhead, quilted with the occasional fluffy, white cloud.

The very center of the pool, deceptively still, reflected the jasper rock in vivid detail, as if the surface were made of a mirror. "It's beautiful," she whispered.

"I thought you'd like it. This place is called Chinaman's Pool. A few years ago, back during the gold rush, the Chinese grew vegetables here along the bank and sold them to the diggers."

"I think Charles may have mentioned something about that. Your mother used to make him eat them."

"That's right. She used to say it was the only good thing to come out of a relatively small gold rush. She hated the thought that this area would become some great center of commerce or something. She was never so happy as when the miners left the sparse diggings here and moved farther away from town."

"Oh, I see," Emily laughed. "She had her riches from your father's gold mining days and preferred to enjoy the wealth in peace."

A smile cut Dale's face and his eyes sparkled. "Too right. Though, Dad always said there was more gold around here. He wanted to look for it, but never got the chance."

The words died on a whisper as Dale seemed to caress her with his eyes. At least, that's what it felt like—as if he touched her. The way he looked at her, as if she were some delectable treat, made her heart dance. Her mouth went suddenly dry and she wet her lips. "Why did you bring me here?"

He took several long steps to the edge of the pool and set the basket on a boulder. His back rippled beneath his shirt as if something had touched him and he stared across the water. "I don't know, exactly. I just wanted to see what it would be like."

"What *what* would be like?" She followed him to the edge of the water but decided against asking him to look at her. Something in the distance had caught his attention, and she suspected it had nothing to do with the exceptional view. It was as if he were looking into himself instead of at the world.

"Living." He cocked that half-smile and shrugged as if he were ashamed. "I used to come here with Joel. I hadn't planned to come here again, ever, until I met you."

Silence, broken only by the distant call of a dozen or more birds, crept between them. What did he mean? Her heart, guarded but determined in her quest to love him, threatened to leap out of her chest. She crept toward him and turned her ankle on a loose rock.

Dale's hands, strong yet so amazingly tender, gripped her arms until she steadied herself. "Careful, love. If you want to go swimming, I'd suggest we take off our clothes first."

For the first time since she'd met him, a wicked gleam appeared in his eyes. It tickled her in parts of her body she hadn't known she possessed. Mischievous and cunning, the spark reminded her of the little boy in her letters.

Still, the feral gleam made her blush and she turned toward the basket. "What did you pack for lunch?"

"Nothing terribly special. C'mon this way. There's a nice, flat rock over here where we can eat."

She followed him around a slight bend along the pool's edge until they came to a raised boulder beside a narrow beach. The sun highlighted the rocks in shades of pink, red, and gold and afternoon light mingled with the colorful rock behind them to cast a magical glow over the water. Together, they laid out the blanket on the coarse sand and Emily knelt in front of the basket. "Back home, I used to go on picnics with some of the families after church services on Sundays. By the time I was twelve, I'd become quite the master at climbing the rock walls around Apache Point."

"Apache Point?"

Emily set a plate in front of Dale's reclined torso and bit her lip. That lock of hair on his forehead begged her to move it aside, but she made a fist and returned her attention to the basket. "That's where we spent most of our time. In the late afternoon, the rocks provided enough shade for the grown-ups and we children would spend the rest of the day getting lost in the narrow canyons."

"Sounds like me and Joel." Dale bit into a piece of chicken and wiped his chin with the back of his hand. "We crawled all over this desert, growing up. The two of us and Paul, of course. We were practically inseparable."

"I know." With luncheon served, Emily rested on her backside and spread her skirt around her legs.

Dale eyed her as if trying to read her mind. Apparently satisfied with what he'd found, he glanced down at his plate again and selected a large, red grape. He popped it in his mouth and smiled. "What else did Charles tell you in those letters of his?"

"Oh, nothing much. He once told me you fought a dragon. He often made up stories, I think, to entertain his young American niece."

"No. Actually, that was true." He laughed.

Emily rolled her eyes and scoffed. "There are no such things as dragons." She threw one of her own grapes at him; he caught it and tossed it into his mouth. Her eyes fell on his lips and her stomach clenched.

"Sure there are. In fact, there are probably a few of them sunning on the rocks around this very pool right now. We'd only have to go look for them."

"Dragons? You mean to tell me huge, medieval reptiles with giant wings who breathe fire and eat virgins can be found right here in Western Australia? My goodness, the anthropologists will be so pleased."

Dale laughed. His eyes danced and for the first time in the weeks he'd been home, happiness enveloped him with a genuine glow.

"Too right. You've got me there. No, those aren't the kind of dragons Charles was talking about. But there are lizards the size of small horses in this part of the country. And if they bite you, you'll wish they'd breathed fire on you instead."

Emily rolled her eyes. "I should have known. I didn't believe him when he told me the desert was full of wild camels, either."

"It is, though. Hundreds of thousands of them. The original settlers used them instead of pack horses because of the climate. When the train came through, they turned the camels loose and well . . . let's just say some things come naturally."

Emily felt herself blush.

Dale chuckled and tossed another grape into the air only to catch it in his mouth.

Two months ago he had seemed so damaged she hadn't thought he'd ever come alive again. But lately, light had returned to his eyes and he seemed to carry less of a burden. Had she been a part of that change? Had her love offered the comfort he needed to cast aside his demons?

She hoped so. Perhaps his invitation to this picnic was some sort of indication he cared for her. Even a little. Or perhaps he was only being nice. She stifled a sigh.

When he finished his meal he sat up, returned the plate to the basket and withdrew a bottle of wine. A moment later, he handed her a glass and filled one for himself.

She took it and raised it between them. "To new beginnings."

🦒

Dale frowned.

Was that what this was? A new beginning? Guilt slid over his spine.

It had been a lifetime since he'd hiked in this country. Joel's lifetime. But the voice in the wind had been so convincing, so real, he couldn't ignore it. It might have come from Blue, or God, or even Emily herself. He hadn't known if it had been real but it seemed to call to him even now in the rush of the wind and the sunlight on the black water.

He shouldn't feel guilty for spending a pleasant afternoon with a beautiful woman, but he did. What right did he have to a new beginning?

None.

A part of him regretted bringing Emily here.

This was one of the places where he, Paul, and Joel used to camp in the summers. Most of the time they'd hang their food high in the trees to prevent the crocs from finding it, stretch hammocks from tree to tree and laze away the hours. Sometimes, they'd swim naked in the billibong, other times they'd hunt for lizards in the rocky crevices. They'd catch fish with their bare hands just to let them go and catch them all over again.

Everything had been so simple then. Wake up. Fill the hours with hard work and harder play. Go to bed.

Tiny reflections of light bounced off the water to play in Emily's eyes, shimmer in her hair, and highlight her rounded curves—barely hidden behind her skirt. Her waist had been made for a man's hands and he calculated the span of his hand across her naked belly. The image made him hard and flurries thrilled his stomach.

Between them rested the remains of their feast and a bottle of wine. He wanted to brush all of it aside and take Emily in his arms. And never let her go.

"To new beginnings," he repeated.

He almost believed it. But there was the guilt. The black sackcloth of his own failings still canopied his heart. At least enough to make the toast seem somehow . . .

wrong.

"Did I say something inappropriate?" Emily lowered her glass and stared into the amber liquid.

He pushed himself upright, set his glass on the blanket and stood. How could she understand? How could he make her understand that he wanted her more than he wanted his own life. But he couldn't have her. She deserved better. And he sure as hell didn't deserve someone like her.

Emily approached and rested her hand on his shoulder. "Dale? What's the matter?"

Her touch sent a flame straight into his soul. Not his heart. Not even to his shaft, although he still wanted her— needed to let himself go inside of her. No, her touch meant more than that. It was a redeemer of sins and a comforter of pain. In the simple gesture, the minute human contact, he longed to trust her. Trust himself. He wanted it. Nothing could prevent him from turning to her, gathering her in his arms and tasting her sweet lips, the salt of her flesh.

No, she reached deep into the most basic part of his soul, where he was naked and vulnerable. "No, you didn't say anything wrong. I just don't know if I can live up to it, that's all."

"I want to help you, Dale. Can't you see that?"

He gritted his teeth and made fists with his hands. Then he turned to look into her eyes. "You shouldn't." A bolt of lightning shot from her dark orbs and singed him.

She dropped her hand and took a step back. "I refuse

to believe that. You have nothing to feel guilty about. Do you think that you're the only man in the history of the world to lose someone? At least you had Joel for a while. You loved him and he loved you. The same with your parents. You may have lost them young, but the time you spent together has been ingrained in the man you've become. And Charles. Charles instilled appreciated in you for life, for horses, for the station. He taught you how to work and how to love. You have so much to be thankful for. You do all of them a disservice when you toss those gifts aside and wallow in your own self-pity."

She was even more beautiful when the sun competed with the fire in her eyes. Still, she couldn't understand him. The sooner she realized that the better. "You don't know what you're talking about."

"Yes, I do. I have never had any of those things, Dale. It makes me so . . . so . . . angry that you would throw all of it away. My mother spent her entire life regretting the fact I'd been born and my father was too drunk to even notice. The only family I had who acted like they cared one tiny little bit for me was an uncle who lived on the other side of the world. If it hadn't been for my father's love of horses, I don't know what would have happened to me. I spent my entire life living for two things, and two things alone. Racing horses and . . ."

She bit her lip until the edges turned white. A tear glimmered in the corner of her eye, shimmering in the slanted, afternoon sunlight. "And what, Emily?" He stepped closer.

"Nothing. We should go home now."

"Answer me. And what?"

A silent sob wracked her shoulders. "You."

Something powerful surged through him. "Me?"

"Those letters made me fall in love with a boy I'd never met. For all I knew, you weren't even real. Charles could have invented you, but I didn't care. You had everything I'd ever wanted. Love. Family. I wanted to be a part of that. That's why I came here," she whimpered. "Silly, wasn't it? I thought I could make a difference here, but I can't."

"You have made a difference, Emily. Without you, I'd still be dead."

Trembling fingers that seemed to belong to someone else ran along the edge of her cheek. She was too soft for the harsh Australian wilderness, but at the same time she possessed the drive and ambition a woman needed to survive here. Was that part of the attraction that captured his soul and refused to release it?

The tips of his fingers tingled when he ran them into the loose strands of her hair beside her temple. Soft as silk, the strands curled around his fingers. He drew her closer and her eyes widened. "You give me a reason to breathe."

"Dale?"

"Emily." He couldn't have stopped himself if he'd wanted to. With all of the pain and desire he possessed, he pulled her against him. He shouldn't kiss her again. He shouldn't have brought her here where no one could see them, no one could protect her from him. His body throbbed with a wanting deeper than any need he'd ever known.

Her eyes fluttered closed and he kissed her anyway.

She tasted of wine and long, slow sunsets. He traced the line of her lips with his tongue and she opened for him. Her tongue darted and played with his, sending rivulets of warmth over his flesh and a sword of fire straight to his loins. He could take her now. He could lose himself inside her and never leave. He wouldn't have to face his guilt or his shortcomings if he could only accept the warmth and compassion that resided within her.

For a few moments, she was the only thing in this life that mattered. The world swirled and then disappeared behind a misty sunset, only to renew in the bright flash of dawn. Her arms snaked around his back and the gentle stroke of her fingertips elicited a quiet groan. Finally, he lifted his face and inhaled a long, sweet breath of wine and woman. Emily's swollen lips curved into a smile. A tinge of pink stained her cheeks.

"To new beginnings," he whispered.

"To new beginnings."

"I feel like swimming." That wasn't true. He felt like he could climb a mountain, capture an eagle and soar to the heavens. Swimming would have to do.

"Swimming? You can't be serious."

✳ 🐐 ✳

Emily's eyes felt like they would burst from her skull when Dale stepped back and stripped his shirt over his head. "Wh . . . what are you doing?" She covered her eyes and turned her back on him. Heat fanned her cheeks even as she was tempted to peek behind her.

"I'm going to swim. I thought that was rather obvious."

"But you can't. I mean . . . it's not decent."

His answer came in the form of a loud splash. She jerked her attention to the water. Dale was nowhere to be seen until his head popped from the shifting surface several yards from shore. He shook it as if to clear the water from his eyes. His hair, disheveled, looked almost black. Then he disappeared beneath the surface again, and when he reappeared, his hair slicked back against his head. "You should come in."

"No. I'd rather not."

"There's nothing to be afraid of. The crocs won't come out to eat for another few hours."

Crocs? As in crocodiles? She hadn't even considered that particular danger. She shook her head. "No, thank you."

Instead, she sat down on the blanket to watch. Dale swam away from her, his strong arms cutting the water as if it weren't there. When he reached the center, he dove downward and exposed his legs and his . . .

Oh, dear. Quickly, Emily scanned the bank and found not only Dale's shirt, stockings, and boots, but his strides and his union suit as well. Of course, he wasn't wearing his union suit. When he'd surfaced that first time, he'd been bare-chested. Apparently, he was bare-everything-else, as well.

Twin flames heated her cheeks, but her eyes traveled back to the water. To Dale. He was too far away to make out clearly. Part of her, most of her, in fact, was disappointed. She strained her eyes to no avail.

And then he faced her, treading water in the center of the pool. The sun reflected off his wet shoulders but did nothing to mask the golden hue of his naked flesh. He stayed there for less than a minute before he stroked in her direction. Even strength seemed to propel him forward until he came into clearer view. She sucked in a breath as sinewy muscle slid beneath glistening, bronzed flesh.

Emily had spent many hours around men. Most of them smaller than herself, but well made just the same. And then there were the wranglers who frequented Apache Point, Arizona. Large men with well-muscled frames. None of them compared with Dale. He seemed to embody male perfection in a way few men could.

The closer he came to the shore, the wider his smile grew. Until he stopped, several feet from the bank. "You might want to turn around."

"What?" Her throat scratched and she cleared it. "What?"

"Suit yourself." He gained his feet, exposing his entire body, from mid-calf.

"Oh!" Emily's throat closed completely, her face flamed and she turned her head. One hand covered her eyes. "Have you no shame?"

"None." His voice came from only inches away. "Don't look. I'm dressing now."

She'd never been so close to a naked man before. She'd never seen a man's . . . parts. But the image of Dale's body had been seared in her mind. Beauty and perfection mingled in her blood, begging her to look again.

She shifted her head and raised her hand, allowing just enough light past her fingers.

Dale leveled his gaze on her. "You're peeking." He laughed.

"I most certainly am not." Of course she was. Embarrassment turned her bones to mud at having been caught. "Are you dressed yet?"

"Aye. You can look now."

Damn.

🐎

Dale put the last repacked basket and blanket into the back of the wagon before he helped Emily into her seat. She took her place on the bench and sat ramrod straight, her hands folded in her lap like a matron in church on Sunday. When he asked if she was comfortable, she only nodded, the remnants of a blush still staining her slender neck.

He hurried to the opposite side of the wagon, climbed into his seat and took up the reins. With a click of his tongue and a slight twist of the long leather straps, he pointed the horse toward Marble Bar.

Emily twisted and looked behind them in the direction of the station. "Aren't we going home?"

"Aye. But we're taking the scenic route. We're so close to town, it makes sense to pick up the rest of your items."

"Oh," she sucked in a breath. "There is that, isn't there?"

He laughed. What was it about Emily that made him, forced him to be happy?

"That was mean of me, wasn't it? Deliberately trying to embarrass you. I don't know what came over me."

"For a woman with a high opinion of herself, you blush rather easily, did you know that?"

"I don't have a high opinion of myself." She shifted her shoulders back a notch and stared directly ahead again.

"Sure you do. But that's not a bad thing. For instance, if you were possessed of less confidence, you might not have come all the way to Australia by yourself."

"But I'm not by myself, am I?"

"I don't count Ruth. She isn't much of a chaperone." He winked.

"She's not really my chaperone. She's my friend. But I wasn't talking about Ruth, anyway. I was talking about you." She glanced at her hands and twisted her fingers in a loose thread on her skirt.

Now what the hell was he supposed to say to that? The truth of the matter was that she did have him—at least a part of him. If he had to admit it, he found himself completely taken in by her wit, determination, and charm. Of course, if he had the sense God gave a wombat, he'd run away as fast as he could. She played with parts of his heart he'd long tried to ignore.

If he were smart, he'd yank back the shattered pieces and leave Miss Emily Castle to her own devices. But the honor that Charles and his father had instilled in him from the moment of his birth wouldn't allow him to do that. Not when a bloody shark like Gerald Brown had set his beady, black eyes on her.

She had no idea what manner of animal she'd agreed to play with. The way she'd looked at Dale with utter amazement when he'd spoken of the giant lizards he'd wrangled as a child told him she had been enthralled with the story as much now as she had been all those years ago. If she believed those to be dangerous, she had truly underestimated Brown. He made the venomous creatures of the Bush look like house pets. A greater abuser of women and debaucher of innocents had yet to be born.

If she lost the race, he would expect payment. In full. And that meant he'd want Emily, with or without the benefit of marriage. The law would be on their side of the unenforceable wager, but that wouldn't mean much to Brown. And the law was less than scarce in the far-reaching corners of the Pilbara. One only had to remember the bushranger Ned Kelly to know that much.

In order to gain what he believed was rightfully his, Brown would probably be willing to steal Emily in the middle of the night. Dale couldn't let that happen.

The town of Marble Bar came into view and he turned the wagon onto the Hillside Road. He followed the road until it widened, intersected General Street and retraced his earlier route—hell, the only route—to the General Store.

He set the brake and leaned his elbows on his knees.

Emily stared at him. "Aren't you coming in with me?"

"No, I think I'll pass."

She smiled and the radiance that surrounded her face melted something deep inside of him. What it was, he couldn't be sure. But he liked it and that irritated him worse than sand in his boots. Would he ever find a place where he could live in peace? Would the needle of guilt that pricked his battered conscience ever leave him? The fact he looked forward to a time when that might be possible only made matters worse.

He shifted his gaze to the horse's arse. Hell, he could be looking in a mirror. "I've already paid for the . . . items . . . so you'll only need to pick them up."

"Fine. I'll only be a minute." Emily shimmied off the wagon, the flow of her dress exposing each curve from her hips to her breasts. Even from the corner of his eye, she drew him in like a siren.

When she disappeared into the store, he ran a hand over his face and stared at the huge expanse of blue sky. "Why? Why would you send her to me now?"

"Who're you talking to, mate?"

Dale spun his head in the direction of Paul's voice. "Nobody. What are you doing here?"

Paul and Old Man Kincaid each carried a haversack over their shoulder and a crate in their hands. Paul obviously carried the heaviest items, although Kincaid struggled to maintain his grip and refused to ask for help.

"I just flew in from Port Hedland with a few supplies for the Ironclad and since I was heading this way, I picked up the post as well. What are you doing sitting here all by your lonesome?"

"Waiting for Emily."

The General Store's door clattered open and Emily sashayed toward the wagon—empty handed.

"They didn't have your packages yet?"

"Of course they did."

Behind her, Blake Huntington stumbled over the threshold on legs far too long for anyone who wasn't part toad and almost lost his grip on her neatly packaged purchases.

"I picked up a few other things as well." Emily tossed the young man a ravishing smile. "You can put everything in the back of the wagon, Blake. Thank you so much for your help."

After Blake settled the two large boxes and a bag of sugar in the back of the wagon, Emily withdrew a silver coin from her purse and handed it to him.

"I couldn't possibly, ma'am. Always a pleasure when you come to town." He nodded and scurried back inside like a giant spider, all long legs and arms.

Paul released a low whistle. "Got yourself a bit more competition, I'd say. He's a looker, that one."

A moment later, Joshua MacKendrick and Lincoln Howell, two of his fellow diggers from the Fourth, passed in a motor car. Both men turned their heads when they drove by, their eyes fastened on Emily's shapely figure by the side of the road. Joshua's ruggedly handsome face spread into a wide grin.

A smoky black force settled in the back of Dale's chest. He grunted and reached across the seat to pull Emily onto the bench. Once she settled herself into a stiflingly rigid posture, he tossed a wave to Paul and slapped the reins on the horse's back.

What the hell was the matter with him? What did he care if every man in the territory found Emily as beautiful and desirable as he did? He wasn't jealous. He liked Emily, right enough, but that was all. She couldn't mean anything to him. Ever.

The wagon jolted over a hole in the street and lunged forward. As if by instinct, Emily grabbed his arm to steady herself. Only this time, she didn't let go and slide to the far side of the bench like she had the first day he'd met her. This time, she scooted closer and tucked her arm into the crook of his elbow.

Against the will of his conscience, he found he enjoyed the contact to spite himself. He liked the way the townspeople looked at them as he made his way back to General Street and over the Sandy Creek bridge. Every man, woman, and child they passed seemed to inspect them as if they were some rare oddity. A few cast knowing smiles in their direction and at least one old digger tipped his hat with a wink.

A devious thought registered. *Good.* The more people in Marble Bar who assumed Emily belonged to him, the better. Let Gerald Brown try to take her away now and the entire territory would hunt him down like a rabid dingo and hang him from the nearest gum tree.

And Dale would be at he head of the pack.

✳ 🐎 ✳

Emily stepped out of the copper tub and wrapped herself in a large cotton towel. A soft current shifted the sheer curtain over her open bedroom window. After a long afternoon in the desert, the breeze comforted her still-damp skin.

And what an afternoon it had been. She smiled when the remembered sensations of Dale's kiss washed over her—at the perfection of his bronzed body against the shimmering water. She really should be ashamed of herself, but she simply couldn't manage it.

Even the scars that had caused him such intense physical pain were beautiful because they were a part of him. The imperfections made him perfect. They made him Dale.

She closed the window and wrapped a second towel around her hair before she dropped the first from her torso and donned her sleeping gown. The evening air made her shiver despite the heat when she sat on the bench in front of her vanity.

When she gazed into the glass, her reflection mocked her. Her nose was too long and narrow and her eyes were set too far back in her head. Her forehead was too large. Her lips too thin. What could someone as beautiful as Dale possibly see in her? She sighed. At least in her mind, she could have pretended she was beautiful enough for him. She ran one hand over her throat. Even her neck was too thin.

"Can I come in?" Dale's voice startled her and she spun on the bench. He stood in the doorway, his dressing gown in a deep, rich red accentuating the width of his shoulders. His hands were hidden in the silken pockets, but their size and strength weren't easily masked. The robe however, covered him with modest folds—only his lower legs and ankles extended beneath the shining silk. Black slippers encased his feet.

"Of course," she replied, her voice a husky whisper. "Come in. Is something wrong?"

"No. Yes." He sauntered into the room a few steps, looked around as if he wasn't sure what he should do with himself, then settled for leaning against her bedpost. "I want you to call off the race."

"You know I can't do that." She pulled her robe closer over her breasts and stood. Remnants of the evening's breeze wafted through the window and kissed her bare legs. "Please, don't ask me to."

"I *am* asking. We'll get word to Gerald and call the whole thing off. It's ridiculous."

"It is not ridiculous. It's a legitimate wager."

"Legitimate? I don't think so, Emily. The stakes are far too severe. And it can't even be enforced. If you lose, you lose half our land, period. The . . . other wager . . . isn't even relevant."

"Of course it is."

A grimace settled on his mouth and pulled his full lips into a frown. "You're not going to marry Gerald Brown."

"I'm well aware of that fact. Because I'm going to win the race."

"Damn it, Emily. Be reasonable." Dale grunted and ran one hand through blond strands of hair, which called to her fingers with exotic whispers. "You don't have to do this."

"I have only a few things in this world which belong to me, Dale." She squared her shoulders against the hint of regression begging her to concede to his demands. "I have Apache. I have my share of this station, and I have my pride. That's it. That's everything I've ever had, really. I can't give up any of them without a fight. If I withdraw from this race, this wager, I'll be seen as a coward. I can't let that happen."

"Nobody is going to think you're a coward."

"I will. You have to understand. I've never given up on anything or anyone in my life. I'm not about to start now."

He sighed and pushed himself off the bedpost. His eyes pierced her with an elemental possession. A command and a yearning followed. Then his mouth formed a half-grin and he released a huff that could only mean frustration and acquiescence. The set of his shoulders told her he wasn't used to the latter and he didn't like it. "You *are* stubborn, aren't you."

It wasn't a question and Dale's voice held no judgment, no sanction. He pulled his hands from his pockets and crossed the Persian rug in a single stride. Heat transferred from his body to hers and wrapped her in a tangible embrace. She locked her knees to prevent herself from falling into that warmth. When she found her voice, somewhere in her stomach, she said, "I suppose, I am."

One of his hands lifted in a slow arc and he pulled the towel from her hair. The damp locks, cold despite the day's lingering heat, fell to her shoulders and down her back. She shivered.

"Beautiful."

"What?" She swallowed the end of the word as her throat closed around it.

"Your hair is the same color as maple syrup. Did you know that?"

She didn't. She would be more inclined to liken it to dirty wash-water. But somehow, when Dale saw beauty in her, she wanted to believe it. Needed to believe him.

"Sit down," he breathed.

She did as he bid, not because he asked her to, but because she doubted she could stand much longer on knees that had turned to freshly jarred jam. He turned her to face the mirror, then lifted the brush from the vanity and pulled it through her hair. Only herself and Dale's massive, silk-covered abdomen filled the mirror. She missed his face, but the heady sensation of his hands in her hair and the bristles of the brush on her scalp held her mesmerized. It took only a few strokes before her hair lay in smooth layers around her face and longer strands down her back. The moisture seeped through her robe and chilled her back.

"You should wear it down more often."

"It gets in my way. Besides, it would be unseemly."

He chuckled. "Since when do you care what is, or is not, unseemly?"

Heat stole over her cheeks.

"You leave your home and move to a foreign country thousands of miles away. You insist upon working out of doors with the horses instead of pursuing more ladylike endeavors, and you live here, with me. Alone. I'd say leaving your hair down on occasion would be the least of your faults." He stepped away and her flesh grew cold—bereft of even the slightest warmth.

Still, Emily's heart froze at his words. So, he did find her lacking after all. She stared at the polished wood of the vanity and schooled her features into a complacent expression. The same one she used when her father chastised her for her shortcomings. Like being born female.

"What's wrong?"

She slipped from the bench and folded her arms over her chest. "Nothing. I'm just tired."

"You want me to leave?" He made no move to go. In fact, he shifted his weight and planted his feet as if he owned not only the floor upon which he stood, but the world in which it existed.

Her bottom lip trembled and she caught it between her teeth. *Did* she want him to leave? Her heart screamed that she didn't. She wanted him to hold her. She wanted the flurries in her stomach to cease their constant spinning. And she wanted to taste him again. But she didn't want him to leave. Never that.

"You want me to stay." Disbelief filled his voice even as his shoulders hitched back a notch in some primeval triumph.

Did he not understand how desirable he was? Did he have no idea how her sun and moon turned on him alone?

Yes, she wanted him to stay. She nodded.

"Good."

He shifted again and the front of his robe fell open, revealing sinewy muscles beneath sun-kissed skin. The muscles bunched as if he held them at bay and they wanted a release she couldn't name.

That wasn't true. Her own body pulsed for the same release. Her breath caught in her throat—waited for what he might do next. Advance or retreat. Silence surrounded her and somewhere in the quiet, his heart pulsed beside hers. She could feel it. To her complete astonishment, he wanted her. Every part of her that was woman knew it, from her joints to her soul. Something powerful and predatory roamed in her blood and begged her to end the game.

But like a stalked animal, another part of her enjoyed

the thick, heavy air that hovered just above her head, like a promise of rain on the longest, driest day of summer.

And then he was there. So close she had to tilt her head back to look into the clouded passion of his eyes. He looked through her. Past the wall he'd erected around his heart, past the terror of his recent past and the torture of his distant past. There was only her, and the thought made her knees weak.

"You make me question everything, Emily." His voice poured over her like melted chocolate. "I don't know if that's good or bad, and right now I don't care."

"It's a good thing. Questioning oneself. Isn't it?"

His head drifted lower, like a feather caught in a breeze over which he had no control. His eyes continued to bore through her until hers closed. And then his lips found hers. Gentle at first, it took only an instant before he deepened the caress. Those hands, so powerful and capable, took her shoulders in an embrace that spoke of relentless control at the same time his thumbs stroked her collarbone. Tiny rivulets of molten want devoured her.

His tongue begged entrance to her mouth and she obliged with an involuntary moan. He delved inside—ravishing, tasting.

Treasuring.

Never before in her life had she felt so desired. Even the kisses they'd shared before had lacked one thing. His compliance.

He'd always held something back, some piece of himself that he'd been unwilling to reveal. But now, there was no question about whether he acted on instinct or against his better judgment. He let himself flow into her. As his hands roamed from her shoulders to her back and pulled her against the granite wall of his chest, she knew he craved her as much as she had always coveted him.

He bent his knees, lowering himself until his face came even with hers. Then he broke the kiss with a breath that seemed to fill his soul instead of his lungs. When his lips found her neck in a tender suckle that sent fire straight to her womb, she shuddered and wound her fingers through the curls at his nape. Even those silken strands caressed her where they touched and her fingers tingled.

He trailed moist heat over her throat then slid the thin fabric of her dressing gown off her shoulder with his teeth. He nipped her sensitive flesh and her knees finally buckled.

But she didn't fall. Something about the way he held her, the way he paid such loving attention to her, insinuated he would never allow her to fall. He bore her weight the same way he'd born his own for so many lonely months—alone.

The more he touched her—with his hands, with his mouth—the higher the flames burned in the base of her desire. He broke away and stood to his full height. She had to see him, had to look into his eyes and know that he wasn't sorry, that nothing would make him hold back again.

Chapter Thirteen

Dale hovered on the brink of regret, but he pushed aside whatever warnings his conscience brayed. Instead he drank in Emily's pliant, all-but-naked form. Her dressing gown was made of a thin silk that clung to every curve. Her breasts. Her hips. The slight mound of her belly. From the moment he'd walked into her room, he'd known he would have her.

Tonight. This very minute.

Nothing else mattered. Not Joel. Not the fact that she deserved so much better than him.

Blood raced through his body with a will and power of its own. His body grew rigid with desire and there was no turning back. Staring into her dark eyes, he prayed she wouldn't turn away.

One of her tiny hands lifted to stroke his cheek. There was something powerful in the soft flesh that grazed the harsh plane of his jaw and soothed the day's growth of his beard. He caught her hand and placed a kiss on her palm.

Her eyelids fluttered and then closed. As if by some unknown, inherent knowledge, her lips tilted upward with unspoken invitation.

That was all it took. He dropped her wrist, pulled her against him again and kissed her mouth with weeks of pent-up desire. She tasted of freedom—a way clear of his self-imposed prison, even if it were only for this one night.

One night where nothing mattered except the two of them. He could lose himself inside of her and no longer suffer the agonizing torment that was his real existence. And he would do it, no matter the cost to either of them. He knew that as surely as he knew he would take his next breath. He deepened the kiss, tasting every soft, intimate part of her mouth.

On legs that shook beneath hot, moist desire, he lifted her off the floor, carried her to the bed and followed her down to the soft, welcoming surface. His hands found her full, soft breast. She fit his palm so perfectly, it seemed she'd been made for him.

No! She didn't belong to him and she never would. She was his only this once. But still, he couldn't stop himself. He should, but he just couldn't bring himself to push away. When she arched her back and pressed the hardened peak of her breast against his palm, he grasped her like a lifeline. Only she could save him and in that moment, he wanted her to.

With a groan he'd never heard himself release before, he pulled away from her mouth and trailed his lips over her jaw until he found the hollow of her throat. Her pulse beat a wicked charge beneath his tongue. Passion spiraled in his stomach like a desert wind, twisting his insides. Each breath came with a sharp reminder that he had no right to be there.

But he didn't care. He wanted—no, he needed—Emily. He needed to feel like a real man, just this once. Needed to remember what it was like to be whole and sound in body, mind, and spirit. Something elemental in the way her breath touched his flesh and the rapacious grip of her fingers on his shoulders told him only she could bring that to him.

He caught the tip of one of her breasts in his lips and suckled. She strained against the thin material of her sinfully provocative dressing gown and he pulled the lacy fabric away with his teeth before he resumed his attentions on her now bare breast. Somewhere in the distance, drums beat out a staccato in the night. Or was that her heart? Or his?

He couldn't be sure.

All he knew was he wanted more of her. He wanted to mark every part of her as his own.

She moaned and shoved at his robe. She wanted this as much as he did, of that he was certain. The knowledge fired him, charged him with the most basic powers of a desert storm—all crashing thunder and bright sparks of light. Swirling desire.

He forced himself to break contact with her long enough to shuck his robe and kneel at the edge of the bed.

Her legs, smooth and pale—like cream—beckoned for his hands, his mouth. He drew her gown over her knees and kissed each tender mound. Her back arched and her legs trembled. As he continued to lift her dress, he parted her thighs, trailing kisses over the soft, inner flesh. When he found her center, his body quickened with anticipation and lust.

Greed.

"Dear God, what are you doing to me?" Emily panted, her breaths coming hard and uneven.

He lifted his head and relished the vision of her body, barely concealed beneath her tangled gown—her breasts, turgid and full; her lips parted; her eyes dancing wildly in the amber glow of the oil lamp.

"Should I stop?" He smiled. He couldn't even if she asked it of him.

"No!" Her head fell back and she arched again, urging the most intimate part of her toward his waiting lips.

He took her again, tasting, exploring, until her hips bucked and she found rapture in his touch.

Hunger burned his soul and he slid his chest over her belly, her breasts until he could capture her lips with his own. She drank from him, pulling and suckling as if she were some wild beast who'd gone too long without a meal.

Her legs wrapped around his waist and she pulled him closer. With frenzied abandon, she rocked her hips against his. Something told him she acted on instinct alone. The pure innocence of the primitive dance, the basic desire that poured out of her, called to him. Made him want her even more.

Perhaps it was the ancient, fundamental need for man to conquer something, anything, that drove him forward. Or maybe it was the lack of erotic pleasure born of his self-imposed sentence. It didn't matter.

He gripped her wrists and held them firm to the bed as he stared into her dusky eyes. She stilled and searched his gaze with her own. And with one quick, hard thrust he entered her. The barrier of her innocence broke with barely a whimper from her swollen lips. He gave her a moment to adjust to his weight, his size—gave himself a moment to grit his teeth and regain control of the riotous thunder that claimed his entire body.

When Emily shifted beneath him, telling him in that ancient language that she wanted more, he tested her with a slight teasing of his hips. She matched his movements and pulled him toward her with her legs. With her heart.

He obliged. Lust warred with his conscience, but still he made love to her. His eyes never left her face while he enjoyed the passion playing over her expression. Her breathing grew tormented again, her legs tightened over his hips, and then she pulsed around him. Her neck arched back and a cry of gratification and glory left her throat. He caught it with his lips and matched her release with his own.

He collapsed against her, his heart pounding like a sledgehammer on a rail spike. Even now, as the earth rushed toward him in his descent from the heavens, she fit him as if she had been made for him. Every curve, every plane, matched his. Every breath, slowly returning to normal, mimicked his. Even the slight brush of her fingers through his hair left him thunderstruck with the rightness of it all. She belonged to him now.

He frowned.

Rightness? Belonging?

What the hell was he thinking? He willed his body to move, but it didn't. *Get up and leave her, now.*

Instead, he rolled to the side, urged her head toward the pillows, laid beside her and brought the comforter over them. She curled into his side in that damned perfect fit and released a contented sigh.

She was the most beautiful thing in the world. Precious. Rare.

But he could never love her. He could never love anyone. Not anymore.

🐎

Something tickled Dale's nose and he brought one hand to his face to rub away the irritation. When he did, his fingers tangled in a mass of soft curls that held a distinct scent of lavender. He cracked open one eye and glanced beside him. Emily lay curled like a newborn kitten at his side, the steady beat of her heart against his ribs and rhythmic sweetness of her breath an indication she still slept.

Regret swept over his spine but competed with the stinging reminders of the passion they'd shared the night before. More times than he could count, she'd come apart in his arms—and he'd let her—encouraged her with his hands, his lips, and his body. Even after their rapturous first loving, when he'd assumed she would sleep like the dead for the rest of the night, she'd come alive again. Stroking and teasing him to full, glorious wakefulness. He closed his eyes and gritted his teeth when his shaft came to life at the memory.

As if she could somehow sense his arousal, even in sleep, she curled closer against him. Her hand wound through the curls on his chest and settled over his awakened nipple. Her nail stroked him there and he winced.

"You like that, do you?"

He groaned. "You're awake, sweet. I thought you were still sleeping."

"I've been listening to you breathe."

He chuckled. "Tired of that already, are you?"

"Mm-hmm." She ran her nail over his nipple again and he caught her fingers in a gentle grip.

"You keep that up and we won't be leaving this bed anytime soon."

"Sounds fine to me. The sun isn't even up yet." Emily stole her hand away, turned to her stomach and propped herself on her elbows. Her eyes shimmered with the same wanton hunger she'd exhibited last night. But it was more than that.

Somewhere, deep inside the violet storm, a more profound emotion called to him. A part of him wanted her to love him, if that's what the emotion was. He wanted to spend the rest of his life figuring it out, but he couldn't. That part of him had begun to die when he lost his parents. The rest of it passed away that day in the desert. He wasn't capable of giving her what she really needed.

He could make her call his name in the night. He could lose himself in the precious few hours they shared in each other's arms. But that was all he could give her. Didn't that make him some sort of bloody arse? It sure as hell didn't make him honorable, or trustworthy, or anything else a woman like Emily deserved.

A decent man would have walked out of her bedroom and never looked back. He'd never had any trouble finding a willing bed partner when he'd wanted one, so what made him think he could simply take what he wanted from Emily and leave her behind like some discarded old shoe? But that was exactly what he had to do. For her own good.

"My goodness, we're having heavy thoughts this morning."

He snapped his gaze in her direction again. "Pardon?"

"If you scowl any deeper, I doubt the lines in your forehead will ever disappear. What are you thinking about?"

"Nothing."

"Nothing? As in, you're not thinking about last night? You're not brooding over what one might perceive as an injustice?"

Damnation, the woman could read minds, too? He sighed. No, she couldn't read his mind, but anyone with a brain could read his mood.

Emily raised herself on her hands, pulled her knees beneath her belly and placed a gentle, chaste kiss on his lips. The absolute tenderness in the gesture marked his soul with a gaping wound.

His loins tightened and he shifted his weight on the mattress. "You're quite the tempting one, aren't you?"

"I'm doing my best, actually. Is it working?"

He nodded.

No matter how shamefully or callously he'd treated her last night, he couldn't bring himself to regret making love to her. Not really. Certainly, the part of him that wanted to be better than he was had its doubts, but the rest of him—most especially the part between his legs—couldn't regret a single thrill, thrust, or moment of mind-numbing pleasure. And from the look in her eyes, she didn't either.

It was good enough for him.

He urged her forward with his hands and his gaze and she followed his unspoken suggestion. With a wicked gleam in her eyes and her bottom lip sucked between her teeth in an impish expression of curiosity and lust, she straddled him. He entered her at her discretion, her control. Within moments, she'd maneuvered herself to a panting, bucking, obviously intense, moist, heated and oh-so-uncontrolled explosive ecstasy. He grasped her hips and thrust forward until he gave himself this one last, inexcusable instant of craven lust.

She fell to her side of the bed, her chest bare and exquisite, her lips swollen from a thousand of his kisses. He steadied the thrilling beat of his heart as he watched her drift back to sleep; placated, exhausted, and well loved.

A needle of doubt pierced his soul. He didn't love her. He couldn't possibly love her. She was a grown woman capable of understanding that. Neither of them were young or foolish.

Right?

Still, guilt scratched at his soul. He scowled and gently climbed out of the bed, gathered his robe from the floor and put it on. He should be taken into the desert, shot, and left for the bloody goanna.

Dale peered first one direction down the hallway, then the other. Empty. Good. The last thing Emily needed was for the staff to whisper behind her back. Enough of the citizens in and around Marble Bar were doing that already.

Thanks to Gerald Brown.

Of course, he had only himself to blame for the fact those rumors had become truth.

Dale hurried across the hall and shut himself in his room. Tiny fingers of shame crawled up his spine as he glared at his unmade bed. What had he done? He closed his eyes and leaned against the door. All through the long, passionate night he'd warred with the possibility Emily might, in fact, love him, like she so fervently believed she did. Would that be so bad, really? What was so terrible about having a woman's soft caress after a long, hard day? But not just any woman. Emily. It wasn't so long ago that he would have leapt at the possibility of spending the rest of his life in her company.

But that was before. There wasn't anything left in his heart that might allow him such simple pleasures. Even if he were capable of returning those feelings, he didn't deserve it.

A harsh sigh formed on his lips and he released it with tangible resolve. The damage had been done. A part of him knew he would take her again should the opportunity arise, even as his conscience balked.

He opened his eyes, approached the foot of his bed and started to remove his robe.

Dale stood, frozen to the floor as if his feet had been nailed in place, and stared at his pillow. A stone, smaller than the palm of his hand, rested beside a pair of silver spurs. He hadn't worn those particular spurs since before he'd left for school.

He closed his eyes long enough to take a deep, steadying breath. Then he opened them, crossed to the bed, and reached for the spurs. Before he touched them, his fingers curled into a tight fist. When he forced his hand to relax, he picked up the stone instead.

Gray, with a smooth, almost polished, surface, the rock reflected the small amount of ambient dawn cast through the lace curtains over his window. He flipped it over and found an engraving.

Four wavy lines stretched across the length of the oblong stone. He carried it to the window, turned it to the light and squinted. Where had he seen it before? It seemed more than a little familiar.

It was obviously Aboriginal, so it must belong to Blue.

He glanced back at his spurs. The old man was trying to tell him something.

Again.

The spurs were easy enough to understand. Blue wanted him to ride. He winced as he strode to the bed and lay down on his side, the rock still clenched in his fingers.

If only it were as easy as putting on an old pair of spurs, saddling up Jezebel and racing into the desert. But it wasn't that easy. That was the whole basis for a vow, wasn't it? If it were easy to live up to, there would be little point in making one in the first place.

But he hadn't known it would be so hard to go on with his life, in general.

"You're awake."

Dale lifted his gaze toward the door where Blue stood with his hands crossed over his chest.

"Yeah, I'm awake." He held up the stone so Blue could see that he'd found it. "You've been up to your usual mysterious games, I see."

"Not so mysterious. It's the rainbow serpent you hold in your hand. The mother of us all."

"Your mother, mate. Not mine."

"She is the one who created everything. The rivers,

the trees—even the stone that holds her image right now."

"Right. So why give her to me?"

"After the Rainbow Serpent traveled the land, leaving behind the rocks, the grass, the canyons, and the whole shape of the world, she grew tired and retreated into the earth. From that place, she called to all the peoples to come out of hiding within the trees, the rivers, and the rocks. The tribes came in answer to her call and became our Ancestors. They lived in this great land until they had born their children, and then they returned to their hiding places."

Dale shifted his weight on the bed and glanced at the rock. "Go on."

"The Rainbow Serpent has always been my personal totem. I have carried that rock with me since I was a little boy and I lived with my grandfather's people. When I feel alone, or frightened, I remember the Rainbow Serpent and how lonely she must have felt when she, alone, lived in this great and massive land."

"You used to carry this with you when I was young. I remember now. I've seen it before."

Blue nodded and finally entered the room, as if he'd been waiting for an invitation. "Yeah. I showed it to you once, many years ago, before Joel came to us."

Dale pulled his brows together. "I'm afraid I don't remember that."

"You were still a very small boy in those days. But that doesn't matter. You may have it now. Perhaps it can help you."

"I doubt that."

"The Serpent calls to you. I can read it in your eyes when you look at the distant desert. You should listen to what she says."

"What? What does she say, Blue? You know bloody well I can't hear her. You told me that yourself. Whitefellas can't go to the dreamtime."

"I said that you couldn't go."

"Then what, exactly, am I supposed to hear?"

"Just listen with your heart, and you'll hear her calling you."

Dale hefted himself off the bed and stomped to the window. Outside, the world renewed itself. The sun peeked over the edge of the world and turned the distant desert into a blaze of red and gold. High above the horizon, the stars blinked out, one at a time, until only deep-blue velvet remained where black had ruled over the night.

Every day the same miracle repeated itself. Every morning, he was faced with another chance to live his life as if he hadn't died that day. "She's not calling me."

"She is."

He turned away from the window and tossed the rock to Blue. With the agility of a feral cat, the older man snatched it from the air and turned it in his long, black fingers. "It's time to come out of hiding, Dale. You've punished yourself enough."

"As if that were possible," Dale replied with a shrug. "Your snake is looking for somebody else."

"You have already made progress. With the woman."

Blue must've surmised where he'd spent the night when he brought his unwelcome musings and dropped them on Dale's pillow. "You're mistaken."

"I don't believe so. You love her."

Love? Not hardly.

He may have succumbed to basic lust. He might even harbor a deeper, emotional yearning for Emily. But there was a grand difference between lust and love. And an even further divide between either of those and choosing to live again.

That was something he could never do. That, and loving Emily.

A bright beam of sunlight filtered through the lace sheers on Emily's window, tracing a path from the edge of her bed to her shoulder and finally into her eyes. She squeezed them tighter, rolled to her left and tossed her arm over Dale's side of the bed.

When her fingers me only cold, empty space, she opened her eyes, raised onto one elbow and frowned. His pillow still bore an impression of his head and the sheets held a hint of his spicy scent. She inhaled and fell back against her pillow.

Parts of her body she hadn't even known she owned tingled with the memory of his rhythmic caresses. Her breasts ached from his attentions and her womb clenched with remembered tremors.

She'd never known how intoxicating making love could be. Of course, she'd never made love to anyone before Dale, so how could she have known? But she had friends who'd married and the stories they'd told her bore no resemblance to what she and Dale had shared, hour upon hour, through the long, dark night.

"Emily?" Ruth's voice came from the hall, just outside Emily's door. "Are you awake?"

On the edge of panic, she scanned the bedroom for any evidence of Dale's visit. She tossed the linens over the opposite side of the bed, recently vacated by her new lover, and pulled the extra pillow behind her back. One deep, lung-stretching breath, then she swallowed the lump in her throat and called for Ruth to enter.

"Oh, my." Ruth set Emily's breakfast tray on the foot of the bed. "Somebody was spinning last night, wasn't she? What a mess you've made."

Emily's gaze raced over the bed again. It did look a fright. The sheets were tangled beneath the coverlet, and the coverlet lay askew of its proper lines. Even the afghan that usually rested on the foot of the bed had fallen off some time during the night. "I . . . I wasn't feeling well, that's all. I'm much better now."

"Good. You've got some nice, warmed porridge there and a bit of toast, with fresh juice to wash it all down."

"Juice?"

"Aye. Paul arrived just this morning with fresh oranges straight from Sydney. It seems he's been flying that machine of his all over creation the last weeks."

"I see. Well, then. I suppose I should at least enjoy the benefits." Emily sipped the fresh-squeezed orange juice and made a face as the sweet liquid tickled the back of her throat and stabbed her jaw.

"Will you be riding today?"

"Of course. In fact, I don't really have time for breakfast, now that I think about it. I should have been working with Jezebel hours ago. I can't believe I slept so late."

She drank the rest of the juice, pushed the bed-tray to her knees and pulled her legs from beneath the coverlet. She couldn't have consumed any of the breakfast Candice had prepared, anyway. Her stomach was still too much of a giant, passion-filled knot to digest anything of real substance.

She pulled on her riding habit while Ruth made the bed and straightened Emily's vanity table. When Emily's eyes fell on the bench, a million tiny wings fluttered in her belly. A smile crept across her lips regardless of her attempts to assuage the giddiness bubbling in her chest. That's where it had begun. Right there on that bench. Innocent. Innocuous.

Yet the simple act of Dale's hands on her hair, the brush stroking through the stands, had led to wondrous, unchecked sensation. She really should be ashamed. But she wasn't.

How could she regret even one minute in his arms? It

was what she'd been born for.

With a light skip in her step, she hurried to the stable yard. With any luck, she might see Dale for a few minutes before she took Jezebel for their morning run.

She searched the stable yard, followed the fences with her eyes and then ducked into the barn. Nothing. The buckboard was still situated next to the barn, so he couldn't have gone far.

She walked down the corridor in the center of the barn until she stopped in front of Jezebel's stall.

Her shining black head dropped over the gate and nudged Emily's chest with her muzzle.

"Good morning, Jez. Have you seen your master today?"

"She has," Dale answered from the doorway.

"Oh!" Emily jumped and dropped her hands from the horse's muzzle. "I didn't see you there."

"I stepped out."

Suddenly, as if realizing that last night she'd been writhing naked in his arms, Emily's cheeks flamed. She had no earthly idea how to behave. Her eyes settled on his mouth. Those soft, full lips had taken her to such heights of passion only hours ago, she wanted nothing more than to trace them with the tips of her fingers—just to reassure herself they were real.

"Are you all right?" He sauntered over the dirt floor as if they were in some elegant ballroom. "Are you sore?"

Sore? Heavens, yes, she was sore. Her entire body screamed from overused muscles and begged for more of what caused the stress. "I'm fine," she giggled.

"I left because I didn't want Ruth to discover us together."

"Good thinking."

"Listen, about last night—"

She hummed, sliding closer and laying a hand on his thickly muscled chest. He took her wrist in his hand, refusing to let her touch him.

She frowned. "Dale? What's wrong?"

His face paled and he dropped her hand. Retreating, he ran his fingers through his hair before folding his arms. "I shouldn't have misled you."

So, that was it. Emily's heart fell like a stone tossed into a well. She blinked back a tear while acid burned her throat. "I see."

"Do you?"

"I . . . I know you didn't mean any of the things you said. I'm not a child."

"What things? Do you mean when I said you were beautiful? I meant every word."

The muscles in Emily's back flickered and she squared her shoulders.

"I was going to say that I probably shouldn't have taken advantage of you like I did, but I can't bring myself to regret it. A part of me wants to apologize and the other part wants to throw you into that haystack in the corner and have my way with you."

She spun to face him. She had to see his expression and know if what he said was the truth, or if he was simply carrying tales to make her feel less shameful. Only, she didn't feel shameful. She wanted the same things he did.

When he looked into her eyes with the fiery passion of the previous night, her heart imploded with the sheer weight of it. "You don't need to apologize for anything."

"I should."

"Don't. I'm a woman full grown and my own person. I could have stopped it."

He raised an eyebrow as if he doubted her words and she forced a laugh.

"I could have. Honestly."

"You should have saved yourself for someone more worthy than a broken-down old soldier with more scars on his mind than his body."

"No, Dale. I saved myself for you."

He frowned then cleared his throat as if he wasn't quite sure what he should say. Setting his slouch hat on the back of his head, he whispered, "You shouldn't have done that Emily. I don't have anything to give you."

✦ 🐎 ✦

Emily pushed Jezebel faster over the uneven, rock strewn desert floor. The wind roared in her ears. Jezebel's hooves pounded the earth like cannon-shot and still she couldn't block out the sound of Dale's voice in the back of her mind. No matter how fast she rode, no matter how far, Dale's nullifying statement ate at her stomach like acid.

After spending the night loving him, she had thought she'd made some progress. He'd taken her on a romantic interlude, shared a piece of his past with her. And he'd made love to her—over and over again. Yet it had all been a lie. He didn't care any more for her this morning than he had the day he'd arrived at Port Hedland, a shadow of the man he'd been.

Nonsense. How could she possibly know what kind of man he'd been before the war? Did she honestly believe she could know someone based on second-hand accounts of his exploits in a series of letters written for a child? What utter and complete … nonsense.

But it didn't feel like nonsense. It felt real and honest and tangible. She *had* known him. She couldn't have fallen in love with someone who didn't even exist! And if the boy in those letters was real, if the man her uncle had described as recently as eighteen months ago was real . . . Well, he had to live in the remains of Dale Winters, somewhere. She only had to find him.

She'd tried everything she could think of. She'd been patient and kind. She'd given him the space she believed he needed to sort out his desires. Last night, as he'd rained kisses over her flesh and ignited molten fire in her veins, she'd thought he'd succeeded. But apparently not. He still blamed himself—still withheld his heart in some warped sense of honor and sacrifice.

Jezebel leapt over a dry riverbed and Emily almost lost her balance, correcting her posture at the last moment before she fell. In front of her, tall rock walls cast long black shadows that stretched into the distance. The sun played over the red earth in a threatening dance. She pulled on the reins and brought the heaving, lathered animal to a halt in the shade of a monstrous cliff.

How could she have been so careless? Even if she turned back to the station immediately, it would be well past dark when she arrived.

How could she face him? How could she ride back to the station and look Dale Winters in the eyes, as if nothing had happened? Was it possible for her to live with him, day in and day out, and not love him? It seemed her only choice, now that he'd declared, point blank, that he could never love her. She had every right to be furious. She should be furious.

But she wasn't angry nearly so much as she was embarrassed and . . .

She didn't know what else. Just embarrassed. She'd thrown herself at him.

How insane that had been! One couldn't force another to feel something they didn't. Even she knew that. She could hardly march up to him, stand her ground and tell him to love her.

She sniffed. Utterly ridiculous. Crying over a man who shouldn't mean anything to her, but did. She was as hopeless as she'd ever been. Hopelessly romantic. Hopelessly in love. And hopelessly doomed.

She'd run her race and then return to America to pick

up the pieces she'd left behind. She could raise her horses—maybe even move to Kentucky and breed the finest racing stock America had ever seen. Who needed love or the complications of taking care of a man? Not her. No sir-ee.

She had an aunt in Natchez. Perhaps she could move to Mississippi and help her aunt with her mercantile. She could move to New York City and find a suitable position as a governess. Yes, there were plenty of things she could do that didn't include tormenting herself or Dale.

Anything was better than facing him every day knowing he would never love her.

She urged Jezebel forward and walked for several paces before quickening the horse's gait to a trot, then a gallop.

The sky bled along the horizon—brilliant red streaked with fingers of gold and hints of pink. On any other night, the view would have stolen her breath and embraced her in the majesty that was the Pilbara. But tonight, it only reminded her of the dangers lurking in the encroaching darkness.

She leaned forward in the saddle and gave Jezebel her head. She should have known better than to begin the endurance training so late in the day. She pushed Jezebel faster. The last thing she needed was to be caught in the desert, or even the pasture lands, at night with wild, rabid kangaroos.

Despite her best efforts, the sun had vanished, taking with it all traces of light, by the time she pulled an exhausted, lathered Jezebel to a skidding stop in front of the stable. A full moon cast silvery light over the stable yard and long shadows formed eerie designs on the earth. Emily dismounted, pulled the reins over Jezebel's head and led her to the barn.

"Put her in the pasture."

Dale's resonant command seemed to come from nowhere. Emily braced a hand over her heart and spun a quick circle to face him, half-hidden in the barn's black shadow. "You scared me to death! Don't do that!"

"You can't put her away in her condition." He stomped in Emily's direction with a hint of fury evident in what little she could see of his eyes. "I shouldn't have to tell you that."

"Of course," she half-shouted. "I was just taking her inside to put away the tack."

He scoffed, lashed out with one massive hand and snatched the reins out of her fingers.

For the first time in her life, Emily believed blood could actually boil. "Just what do you think you're doing?" She snatched the reins back. "I can damn well see to my own horse."

"She's *my* horse!"

What in the name of God's green apples had gotten into him? The set of his shoulders, the tilt of his head, and the white knuckled fists at his sides all screamed his wrath. Something terrible had happened while she'd been out riding in the desert. Something or someone had turned him from his normal slow, self-directed animosity to a passionate tempest in just a few hours.

His eyes closed for more than a breath and when he opened them he seemed to have more control over himself. But whatever it was seethed beneath the surface like a desert storm, just waiting for the right gust of wind to set it free. While she tied Jezebel to a hitching post, she shivered. In an attempt to ignore the impact he still had on her, she concentrated on loosening the cinch.

Dale, however, moved Emily to one side and finished taking off Jezebel's saddle himself. "Do you have any idea what nightmares have been spinning around in my head for the past five hours?" He spoke through clenched teeth, as if the very words wounded him.

Nightmares? "What?"

"You bloody well heard me. I've been waiting out here since before nightfall. Do you have any idea what dangers there are in the Pilbara at night? You could have ridden into a ravine, or been attacked by a dingo. What if Jezebel had broken a leg and you couldn't get home? What then? You might have been killed."

"Oh, don't be so dramatic. I'm fine. The horse is fine. Besides, what do you care?" Emily snatched the saddle and blanket from Dale, and stormed to the barn.

"Where are you going?"

"I'm going to put my things away, if you must know."

"Don't you walk away from me!"

She toed open the barn door, and marched inside.

"I'm not through talking to you, yet." Dale caught the

door with one massive hand and held tightly.

"Oh, yes, you are. I have nothing to say."

"I've got plenty to say and I'm damn well going to say it."

A ferocious glint sparkled in his eyes. The set of his shoulders, proud and feral, made her step back a pace when he entered the barn. He passed in front of her and in spite of her rising temper her stomach clenched at the scent of leather so uniquely a mixture of man and Dale. She closed her eyes against remembered ecstasy. The sound of a striking flint came to her ears and she forced the passionate images out of her mind. When she opened her eyes again he stood with his massive back to her, the glow of a lamp outlining him in golden light. Even with his head hanging low, he looked powerful. Commanding.

Unfortunately, she couldn't enjoy the image long. Almost at once, he turned to face her with a scowl. "Why did you come here?"

"Excuse me?" She put the saddle blanket on the rack by the stalls.

"Why . . . did you come here?" A muscle in his jaw jumped. "Was it because of Charles' letters? Because of me?" He stormed to the work table, snatched a curry comb and brush from the rough surface and held them in iron-like grips.

"You know it was."

"The boy who lives in those letters is dead. And I'm not talking about Joel."

"He's not dead!" she screamed. "*You* are not dead!"

Dale took two long strides and the barn seemed to shrink behind the sultry sway of his shoulders, as if space itself couldn't compete with the man. He stopped only inches from her, forcing her head back. She looked up, into his glorious face, and her eyes fixed on the muscle in his jaw as it jumped. "He is dead, Emily, and the sooner you understand that, the better."

"But you're here, Dale, don't you understand *that*? You're alive and whole. You were one of the lucky ones."

"Lucky?" He turned away.

Emily followed him. He wasn't getting away from her again. The anger holding him now was different than the bitter disposition he'd cloaked himself in. This was a bare, raw fury than seethed and churned with the same fire he'd displayed last night making love to her. Emotion seemed to spill from his pores.

"Yes, lucky. You're not buried in a desert thousands of miles from home. You're not confined to one of those chairs with wheels on it, nor do you limp about with one leg and a crutch. You have the ability to live the rest of your life with joy and warmth, surrounded by the people and places you love. You survived, Dale!"

He spun to face her, a mask of brilliant fury disguising his handsome features. "No, I didn't! My heart is like a rock in my chest and a day doesn't pass when I don't wish I could rip it out. You look at me with the innocent eyes of a child in her first crush and I die all over again." He left the barn, kicking open the door and letting it ricochet against the outer wall.

Forced to trail after him again, Emily cursed under her breath. "But why? Why can't you just let yourself feel, Dale? You started to, yesterday. At the pool. I saw it in your eyes, damn you. You *laughed*! Joel wouldn't want you to punish yourself like this. He would want you to find happiness."

As if the fight were too much for him, Dale rested the brush against Jezebel's withers and lowered his head. "I'll never be happy, Emily. You should go back to the States, forget about me. Forget about Australia and Charles's letters. Just go."

She stiffened her spine and folded her hands in front of her waist. "No. I've made my home here now and no one can make me leave." The words surprised her. Hadn't she considered leaving only a few hours earlier? Hadn't she all but given up on him? Something basic and pure made her want to stay as surely as if she'd been rooted to the very ground on which she stood. "Not even you."

"Don't you understand? You're only making things worse! Blasted woman!" He tightened his grip on the brush.

"I make things worse? How? How, exactly, do I make things worse?"

"Crikey!" He groaned, turning to face her. Raising his face in the yellow light streaming from the open barn door, he whispered, "Because I can never bloody love you."

Chapter Fourteen

"Why?" Emily screamed with such force her throat ached. "Why can't you love me? Why won't you let yourself feel *anything*?"

"Bloody hell!"

Emily followed Dale to the pasture fence. When he stopped, he put his hands on his hips and stared at the stars.

"Answer me, Dale Andrew Winters. Stop running away!"

"You wouldn't understand."

"How do you know unless you tell me?" She wanted to approach him, but his body was tensed and he would more than likely run farther away. So she anchored herself to the earth and waited. Waited for him to say something. Anything.

"Have you ever killed anyone?"

"No," she whispered, afraid that even her answer might scare him away again.

"Then you couldn't possibly understand." He shrugged.

"You were a soldier, Dale. There is no sin in anything

you've done."

He laughed but the sound was stale, stagnant. "No sin? You think I'm talking about the bloody Turks? Or the Germans?"

She ventured a step closer.

"I'm not. I did my duty to my country and, yes, I killed more than a few of the enemy, but so did everyone else. I'm not the least bit concerned about that."

"Then what is it? You're right, I don't understand." Another step.

"I killed my own brother."

"No, you didn't. He joined the ANZACS of his own free will. You must understand that."

"It's not that simple. God, if only it were."

Emily took one last step and if she dared, she could touch the strongly planed muscles beneath his shirt. She fisted her hand. "What is it that has you so torn inside? Please tell me. I can't help you if you don't tell me."

He glanced over his shoulder and his eyes were misted with unshed tears. "He was only sixteen years old."

"What?"

"When he came to me in Melbourne. When he left school and came to me with his dreams of glory and honor. He was sixteen bloody years old."

"But how—"

"He had all the papers with him. Special enlistment papers that required the signature of his legal guardian in order to join the military. So he could be just like me.

Because he always wanted to be just like me." Dale leaned against the fence railing as if the weight of his own body was too much to sustain. "And because I liked it, because I reveled in the damned idol-worship he'd thrust on me since we were children, I did it."

"What did you do?"

"I forged Charles's name on the documents and let a boy join a man's infantry." He growled and his voice bore the guilt and pain he'd suffered for so many long, lonely months. "I signed my own brother's death warrant."

For several heartbeats, Emily's soul wept for a man so torn, he couldn't see his own future. "That doesn't mean you killed him, Dale. Don't you see? He wanted to be there."

"He didn't know any better."

"Of course he did. He may have been a young man, but he was still a man."

"Cod's wallop. He was a child. A child I'd sworn to protect, and I failed him. I failed my mother and I failed him and I'll fail you."

Something very close to terror filled his voice then. It cracked like thunder and when he looked at her, his eyes sparked with bolts of lightning that singed her to her very core. "I don't believe that."

"I don't care. I died that day in the desert. There isn't anything you or anyone else can do about that. I thought you could, but . . . In the end, I made a vow. I promised Joel that if he couldn't live out his life, neither would I. And I won't. I have nothing to share with you, Emily.

Don't you understand? Every time I look at you I remember what I did and why I don't deserve a life here, with you. I see you with Jezebel and my heart cracks open all over again because I swore to my brother, on his grave, that I would never leave him behind. That I would never ride without him, or love without him. No matter what, Emily, no matter how badly I want to, I can never love you."

❊ 🐎 ❊

Dale's stomach knotted in a fist as Emily's bottom lip quivered a moment before she ran away from the barn and disappeared into the night. He ignored the tempest in his gut and approached Jezebel.

Maybe now he'd made his point. Maybe now Emily would leave the station and him in peace. No, not peace. It was the peace he found in her arms that scared him. If he allowed himself to love her, he'd forget about Joel and the debt he owed. He couldn't let that happen.

The problem was that it had already started. He'd already let himself slip into her compassionate eyes more than once. He only wished he'd stopped himself before he'd made love to her. The thought of turning away from the sweet love found inside of her, the love that she cast to him like a rope to a drowning man, tortured him like nothing else ever had.

What did that say about him? That he'd miss her more than he missed Joel? He couldn't win. If she stayed and he allowed himself to succumb to her enchantment, he abandoned Joel's memory as if his brother hadn't mattered. If he cast her aside, forced her out of his heart and soul, he'd hurt the only women he had ever considered loving and relegate his brother's memory to second place.

"It's not a race, my son."

Dale started at the sound of Blue's deep, resonating voice. "What?" Quickly, he retrieved the brush and rubbed down his horse.

"There is no contest here. You can love them both."

"What, you read minds now, mate?"

The old Aborigine laughed and tucked a thick strand of hair behind his ear. "Don't have to read minds to know what troubles you. It's plain to see for anyone who looks for it."

"I just can't do it. I tried. You know I did. But every time I look at her, and my heart sings, I remember Joel that day at Beersheba. He was so young, so full of life—and himself. He wanted to conquer the world. Crikey, you know I believe he would have. How can I push him aside and go on like I have the bleedin' right?"

"It's not our decision which way the world spins. You can't make it go backward any more than you can make it go forward. Life has a way of pointing us in the direction we're supposed to go. You have to follow the path you're shown." Blue shrugged and walked toward the house.

"Where are you going?"

"I'm following my own path. To the kitchen for

Candice's chocolate cake."

Crazy old man.

Dale opened the pasture gate and led Jezebel into the field where he walked her along the fence. When she'd cooled enough, he removed her lead and ushered her to the center of the pasture. "Go on, girl. Go get some of that sweet grass."

She stared at him with huge, black eyes, her ears perked forward, and she canted her massive head. If Dale didn't know better, he would have thought she looked sad. But that was cracked. *Horses don't get sad.*

"Go on. Get!" He shooed the beast away and she reluctantly trotted toward her pasture-mates. Dale should've returned to the house, but he leaned against the fence rail instead, his eyes focused on the small band of magnificent animals grazing in the moonlight.

Even with the serenity that enveloped him like a mother's arms, it took more than a few minutes for the tick in his jaw to settle—another reason he waited outside longer than he needed to. If he went directly to the house, he doubted he could trust himself not to seek Emily out, and who knew where that might lead. With any luck, be it bad or otherwise, he had a feeling he'd end up in her bed again. No bigger mistake in the world, that.

A soft breeze blew over the Coongan River and brought a slight relief to the day's oppressive heat. He focused on the darkened shapes of the horses as they took turns nibbling the pasture grass and nipping each other's shoulders.

322 🐾 *Marjorie Jones*

The night was so calm, the running water on the far side of the pasture echoed like a waterfall. A far cry from a few hours earlier.

For what had seemed like endless hours, he'd paced from the barn to the porch, from the rear of the house then back to the barn. He'd watched the sun sink lower and lower in the sky, watched the world turn from brightness to a muted sunset and finally into a black void.

And still Emily hadn't returned. He should have stopped her when she'd headed out. But he'd been angry with himself. And he'd been angry with her. How could she look at him with so much trust and love in those dark, angelic eyes? Didn't she understand that there was nothing left of him to save? When she looked at him his entire body reacted, his heart filled with something he couldn't recognize and beat an erratic pulse that made him want so much more than he should ever have.

Emily did that to him. With nothing more than a glance. It infuriated that part of him that needed to keep his promise to Joel.

That afternoon, Emily had turned her eyes to him and he'd been a goner. It had taken every ounce of strength he possessed not to give in to the hope. But what he hoped for was saved for people who didn't kill their little brothers.

Men who killed their brothers didn't get to enjoy their lives like nothing had happened. They didn't get to fall in love.

Not that he could help it much. He was falling so

hard, he doubted his heart would survive the sudden stop when the end came. She occupied his thoughts from morning until night. Even his dreams, when he wasn't battling nightmares, held softly woven images of Emily. So, when she hadn't come home by nightfall, he'd paced and worried, and paced some more.

Until, at last, she'd ridden into the stable yard and it had been as if his heart had exploded. Physical pain had gripped him with squeezing fists. Pain that came from knowing, if he would only let himself, he could love her forever. He'd pushed the feelings aside. It didn't matter. *He didn't matter.* What mattered was that she was alive.

And then, of course, he'd come down on her like a tidal wave, crashing in and destroying everything in its path.

He shouldn't have taken his lack of control out on her. Ultimately, he'd been right to worry. He would have worried about anyone in that situation and she'd had no business returning to the station in the dead of night. She had no business making him insane with little more than a glance or a word. She had no business needling his heart with hopes and dreams better left buried.

And he sure had no business loving her.

✦ 🐎 ✦

Emily raced through the house and made for her bedroom. The sooner she climbed into the soft folds of her bed and hid herself away from the horrors of the past few minutes, the better. Her blood boiled at the thought. Is that what she'd become? A frail shadow of herself who would run and hide when events didn't go her way? She stifled a cry and hurried even faster. So what? So what if she wanted nothing more than to wash the day's heat from her skin and hide in the dark? She had every right.

He could never love her. Even if he did love her, he would never admit it to himself or allow himself to enjoy it. Or share it with her. Yet, she'd been truthful when she said she'd made her life here. She wasn't going anywhere. If Dale Winters didn't want to be with her, then *he* could leave!

Blue appeared out of the blackened shadows of the hallway leading from the parlor to the kitchen. His deep black eyes sparkled in the light of several oil lamps and his black skin reflected the golden light. "Is something wrong, Emily?"

It wasn't really a question. Something in his eyes told her he knew exactly what she was feeling, what was happening between her and Dale. Rather, what wasn't happening. Still, she shook her head in adamant denial. "Everything is fine."

"Don't fear."

She frowned. "Pardon?"

"Everything will be fine at the end of it all. There is peace on the other side." Blue turned around and sauntered down the hall in that slow manner that defined him as a man who worried over nothing. The house could be aflame and he would escape at the same pace.

It didn't matter. She had no time for Blue's fortunes. With a sudden weight on her shoulders like a black, sackcloth shawl, she climbed the stairs.

"There you are!"

Emily snapped her attention to the upper landing. Paul stood with his arms folded over his chest and glared at her as if she were a rebellious child. Fabulous. Another man who failed to notice she was a full-grown woman perfectly capable of taking care of herself. "Don't you look at me like that, Paul Campbell. I'm in no mood to answer to you for anything."

"Did you know the whole territory has heard of the race next week? Bookmakers as far away as Perth have taken wagers on the bloody thing. Are you cracked, woman?"

Emily climbed the last five steps and stood with one hand on the railing and the other on her hip. "Out of my way."

"Not until you tell me what the hell is going on."

"It's none of your concern."

"The hell it isn't. If it affects my mate, it is my business. He's been through enough."

"Dale? He has nothing to do with it."

"Of course he does. Call the bloody thing off."

"I can't do that and you know it."

"Cod's wallup. You just won't show up, that's all."

"Then I forfeit. Is that what you want?"

"It's not enforceable."

"It's a question of honor."

"Get over it. You can't race."

"Get out of my way." Emily shoved against Paul's chest and he backed up several paces. From the solid wall of muscle she'd encountered, it was obvious he moved only because he chose to, which made Emily's temperature, already several degrees above normal, rise even higher. "Oh!"

She stormed into her room and slammed the door.

"Emily?" Ruth almost dropped the bucket she carried but managed to steady her grip. She hurriedly poured the contents into the shining copper tub, set the bucket on the floor and rushed to Emily's side. "Is something wrong? You look all a fluster!"

"Oh, I'm quite well, thank you. It's everyone else in this house who's out of their minds. At least, the men." Pacing to the far side of the bed, Emily removed her riding coat and tossed it over the rocking chair. Then she turned and paced to the door, her hands in fisted knots.

"I was afraid Dale would be cross with you when you came home. I told him not to worry, that a finer horsewoman didn't exist, but he was ever determined to worry for you."

Emily froze. "He really worried?"

"Of course he did."

Emily placed the tip of one finger between her teeth and mumbled around it. "I thought he was just angry because he'd failed to have his way."

She ripped the finger from her lips and paced to the bed. Be that as it may. She might not be able to control whether Dale admitted he loved her, she might have given herself to a man with whom she had no chance of a lasting commitment, but she'd be damned if anyone would talk her out of going through with the race. If she lost she would not only give her share of Castle Winters to Gerald, but . . .

The rest of her insane wager didn't bear thinking about. But she had never failed to follow through on a wager or agreement in her life and she wasn't about to start her life in Australia with the reputation of a welcher.

She stripped out of her riding clothes and climbed into the tub of warmish water.

"You understand why I must compete in the race with the horrid Mr. Brown, don't you, Ruth?" Emily leaned back in the tub, supporting herself with her arms on the edges, and tilted her head back.

Ruth poured a pitcher of water over her hair. "Mm-hmm."

Emily suspected her old friend didn't understand any more than the men did. She sighed and lathered her hair. She ducked beneath the surface before lathering her hair a second time and then her arms, torso, and legs. Exhausted from her lengthy ride, her argument with Dale and then Paul, she finally climbed out of the tub and allowed Ruth to wrap her in a thick, cotton towel.

After she brushed her hair free of tangles, she grabbed her nightdress from the foot of the bed. With arms that seemed to weigh more than her entire frame, she slipped the gown over her head and smoothed the soft, billowing folds.

"I've been thinking, Ruth, and I don't think you understa—Ow!" She winced and grasped her hip, spinning to examine the soft folds of her gown. A tiny black spider that resembled a miniature Black Widow fell to the shining floorboards. It scurried beneath the bed.

Panic seized her throat in an instant of fear. Her palms broke into a clammy sweat and she wiped them on her gown before pulling the trembling fabric above her hip. No, the fabric wasn't trembling. Her fingers were.

White-hot streaks of pain lanced her flesh and the tense muscles beneath before she managed to expose her hip to the lantern's yellow flame. She squinted in the dim light and focused on the dot where the pain had begun. A tiny red circle with a blanched center, no larger than a half a pea, marred her otherwise smooth skin.

"Are you all right, Miss Emily?"

"I . . . I don't know."

"You don't look very well. What's happened?"

"I think I've just been bitten by a . . . by a spider . . ." A queasy unease tumbled about her stomach and she sat on the edge of the bed. She wasn't ill, exactly, but the thought of one of a thousand deadly insects in Australia having bitten her . . .

She rested the flat of one hand on her belly and swallowed her panic. She was fine. There were plenty of non-lethal insects in Australia as well. She was simply allowing Dale's frightening descriptions of his homeland to run rampant in circles of paranoia. It was silly.

Still, Ruth rushed to her side and knelt on the floor nearest her hip. "Where? Just here?"

Emily could only nod, her own concern mirrored in her maid's wide eyes.

Ruth brushed the tip of her finger over the small red welt. "Does it hurt?"

A lump formed in the back of Emily's throat and she forced it down. "Some. More of a sting, really." She shook off a tremor. "I'm sure it's nothing to be concerned about. Not much more than a mosquito." She tossed Ruth's hands away gently and lowered her gown. "Lord, whatever you do, don't mention this to Dale or Paul. They'll only worry themselves over nothing."

But it didn't feel like nothing. She bit her lip to keep herself from wincing. The pain expanded to envelop her entire hip and shifted down her leg like a drop of rain on a windowpane. Ruth looked less than convinced when she rose and tapped one foot in a measured display of impatience.

"I think we should tell him right away! You might need a doctor."

Emily stood to test her weight on the affected leg. "A doctor? Where the devil do you think we're going to find a doctor here in the middle of God's nowhere? We're not in Arizona any more, Ruthie. There is no doct—" A cry tore from her lips in a voice she didn't even recognize.

"Emily!"

Ruth caught her just before she tumbled off the bed. With hands as gentle as a mother's, she helped Emily lie down and then bent to lift her leg onto the smooth, cool sheet.

"Thank you. I don't know what's come over . . . me." She almost shrieked but managed to quell the sound before she alarmed her maid any further.

"I don't care what you say. I'm going to find Dale and tell him about this."

"Don't you dare!"

"Posh. I'd like to see you try to stop me in your condition. This is serious, Emily Elizabeth Castle, and you've never been one to know what's good for you and what isn't. Now hush yourself and wait right there!" Ruth all but ran to the door, tossed it open and disappeared into the hall.

Emily frowned and forced herself upright in the bed. It was difficult, and by the time she swung her legs to the floor, she had forced the knuckles of her left hand between her teeth. Tears burned behind her eyes and the fiery agony in her hip had traveled past her knee.

She couldn't let Dale see her like this. Not with the race so close! She had to ride and there wasn't anything anyone could do to stop her. Certainly not some insect bite. By the time race day arrived, she'd be fit as a fiddle. Right as rain.

If she could only make herself stand up and walk across the room.

Holding her breath, she forced herself to rise. She stretched one arm to the bedpost and gripped it with as much strength as she could muster. Which wasn't much if the weakness in her limbs meant anything. When she slid her foot forward, the pain in her leg doubled and she tightened her life-hold on the bedpost.

Walk, damn it.

She bit her bottom lip until she tasted blood, compelled herself to stand straight and let go of the bed.

Her bedroom door crashed open, slamming into the wall like a brilliant thunderclap before Dale charged into the room with Paul only a second behind. Both of them wore masks of concern and doubt, but it was the fear in Dale's eyes that made her wince. The last thing she ever wanted to do was cause him more worry—more strain. "I'll be fine. Really, I will."

A heartbeat later, she lay in a heap on the floor unable to stem the flow of heated tears.

✦ 🐎 ✦

"Emily!"

The floor disappeared from beneath Dale's feet as he flew to her side. Her sun-kissed cheeks were pale—void of the sweet color that made her look as if she always blushed. Tears filled her violet eyes and made them almost black before they spilled over in glistening streams. He collapsed on the floor next to her, tucked her head against his chest and cradled her legs beneath his forearm.

The cry that escaped Emily's throat sounded like something from an animal—deep and guttural. Pure pain, it pierced his heart like nothing ever had. Not his parent's death, not Charles's. Not even Joel's.

He shoved the torture of that realization to the back of his mind and laid her gently on the bed. She stared up at him as if she begged him for help but was afraid to ask. How he hated that look in her eyes. She should never fear anything from him.

"It hurts!" Emily gritted her teeth and squeezed his arm so tightly he was sure a bruise would appear by morning.

"What did the spider look like? Can you describe it?" Dale pried her fingers from around his forearm and raised her gown to expose her hip.

"I know . . . it was black. It looked something . . . ow." She paused and caught her breath. "Something like a Black Widow. I don't suppose you know what a Black Widow is, do you? But it was much smaller, so I don't think that's what it was. Besides, Black Widows have a red mark on their belly, not their back." Her voice reached a high-pitched squeak before she sucked in a gulp of air and squeezed his arm again.

"Did you say it had a red stripe? Down it's back? You're sure?"

Emily bit her bottom lip and nodded.

Dale stared at her hip. In the center, a red welt with a pale, too-white dot in the middle, had already formed to the size of his palm. He frowned and cast a glance at Paul who craned his neck to see the mark.

Paul met his gaze and his brows drew together. He shook his head as he stood upright and rushed to the door.

"I'll go for help."

Ruth grabbed his arm as when passed. "Go for help? What do you mean? Is it that serious?"

Dale lowered Emily's gown and held her hand. "She's been bitten by a Redback."

"A what?" Emily tried to force herself to a sitting position, but fell back against her pillow with a gasp.

"A Redback." He lowered his voice. "The pain has only just begun, I'm afraid. It'll get worse over the next few hours and if you're like some people, you'll be quite ill by tomorrow." He turned away from her widened eyes. He couldn't stand to see her fear. She looked at him exactly the same way Joel had looked at him that final day in Palestine—as if he could fix anything.

But he couldn't fix this. They needed a doctor.

"There is no need to hurry for help." Blue stood in the doorway but didn't come into the room.

"Not now, Blue. The last thing we need is your mystic bulldust." Dale growled but he didn't care. He didn't want to hear what the old man had to say. His dream visions were always right, and based on Blue's sullen features Dale didn't want to hear anything. "We're not giving up without a fight."

"Fight all you like, the results will be the same. It has been written before now."

"Close your bloody pie-hole! Better yet, get out! You don't know everything, damn it! Take your magic and leave." Anger spawned from worry and desperation was evident in his voice. He couldn't think. Hell, he could barely breathe. He couldn't lose her now. "Paul?"

"Yeah, mate."

"How fast can you ride to Marble Bar and send a telegram to the doc in Port Hedland?"

"Bother that. I'll fly to Port Hedland and bring the old bastard back myself." Paul ran out of the room. Blue followed him down the hall.

"Am I going to die?"

Dale's heart shattered into razor-sharp pieces. He turned back to the bed where Emily put on a brave face as she tried not to writhe in what must be unbearable agony. He had nothing to give her for it. No laudanum. Not even any whiskey to dull the pain. He knelt beside the bed and brushed strands of hair off her forehead. "Why would you say something like that?"

Because it was as real a possibility as the sun rising in the morning.

He shook off the morbid image and stroked her hand.

"Something Blue said earlier. He said—"

"Hush. You can't go around believing everything that old bastard says. He's cracked, you know. Not a sane bone in his body."

"He's always right," Emily whimpered. "He said I was going to die."

The next time he saw Blue, the old man better disappear into the damned Bush and never come back. How could he say something like that to her? To anyone? What gave him the bloody right to muck with people's lives as if they were pawns in his sick, cryptic games? When the hell would he learn to keep his mouth shut? It wasn't good to know too much about one's bleeding path!

Besides, this time Blue was wrong.

She wasn't going to die because Dale wasn't going to let her. That's all there was to it. He'd rather sell his soul and spend eternity in the fires of hell than see her suffer for one minute. "Don't you listen to that rubbish. Everything will be fine, love."

He didn't know where the words came from or what made him want to make promises to her. He only knew that she must survive, even though many victims of the Redback didn't. She would. She had to. She was the only thing in the world that kept him grounded, the only reason he found for living each day. Without her, he'd still be a shell of a man, flesh and bone with no soul.

From outside the window, the lonely, mysterious chirps and barks of a *didgeridoo* cut the night like a knife. Emily squeezed her eyes closed. When she opened them again, a tear escaped and trailed a pink line down her cheek.

He wiped it away with his free hand and kissed her temple. "Please, don't leave me," he whispered.

A weak sob caught in her throat. Though it must have been agonizingly painful, she lifted one hand to palm his cheek. "I'll never leave you. I've loved you from the first time we met, a lifetime ago."

He closed his eyes and gently pulled her close. The

pulse in her neck beat an erratic rhythm against his flesh. What was wrong with him? Why couldn't he allow himself this one pleasure, the happiness and gratification that would come of her love? The absolute ecstasy of sharing something so wondrous with the only woman he'd ever known who would return it just as strongly.

He raised his head and her eyes had closed. He shook her. "Emily?"

No! He shook her again and still nothing. Not even a tremor in response. He studied her chest and when it rose, ever so slightly, he'd never experienced a euphoria so pristine or commanding in his tortured life. She was still alive. He closed his eyes in silent prayer and begged God to take him instead.

"She's fainted from the pain, I think," Ruth whispered.

He'd forgotten she was in the room. He faced her where she stood on the far side of the bed. "She's all I have left."

"I know. We'll see her through this, you and I. What do you say to that?"

"Aye. We'll see her through."

But a part of him denied it. Everyone he loved died. Everyone he treasured beyond his own life lost theirs. He never should have loved her; he never should have come home.

⚞ 🐎 ⚟

Blue sat on the top of Tower Rock and gazed down on the roof of the house where Emily slumbered and Dale worried. He brought the *kurmer* to his lips again and blew through the hollow sapling. If the earth could still speak, its voice would be the *kurmer* with its guttural, plaintive cry. The ancient sound brought healing with it, though it would be better if he played over Emily in person. Perhaps later, when Dale had finally seen that his path and Emily's were the same.

His vision had been unclear, as visions often were. He saw pain and death in Emily's future, but he also saw a line of descendants too numerous to count. It made little sense. He drew a breath and blew it out through the mouthend of the *kurmer*. Rolling his tongue he created the clicking sounds of the crickets behind haunting strains that seemed to flow from time itself. The vibrations in the air carried over the landscape and into the very rocks of the desert floor.

Below, the light in Emily's bedroom window shifted and a shadow passed behind the gauze covered glass. After a few moments, Blue pulled his lips away and smacked them together. He was getting old and he no longer possessed the stamina that he once had. In his youth, he played for his clan during many celebrations and the people would dance into the late hours. His wife had been drawn to the chirping sounds of his kookaburra song the night they'd met, so many, many years ago.

The weight of a thousand "if onlys" was a difficult burden. A thousand prophecies. A thousand visions.

He'd never once seen anything of his own life, his own purpose. But his path had led him here, to the world of the whitefella with his doubtful, ever despondent dreams. The road had been long and winding, but soon this particular journey would end. At least for Dale. He had only to be patient and have faith.

But those two qualities had been difficult for Dale, even when he was a small boy, running barefoot through the pasture. He had no choice, however, but to rely on them now.

Blue moistened his lips and raised the instrument again. He filled his cheeks with air and released a long, mournful cry into the darkness.

Nothing Dale would do would change his or Emily's path. Nothing he would do could change what was to come.

Chapter Fifteen

The night wore on in endless darkness. Emily's bedroom was filled with eerie shadows and the constant flicker of the lamp. Huge, shifting images danced on the walls every time the flame sputtered. It looked like angels of death sent to collect her soul, and more than once they seemed too real. Dale moved the lamp to dispel them. If only the world's real demons were as easily banished.

Dale stood and crossed to the window. He folded his arms over his chest and studied the few stars peeking through the blackened canopy of clouds. The sky had promised rain for more than a few days, but refused to make good. The air hung limp and heavy around him.

A small squeak came from behind him and he turned. Ruth, asleep on the floor, stretched and turned over. She'd made her makeshift bed after she refused to leave her friend. But, having carried dozens of buckets of water from the tub down the stairs and into the garden, then fretting about cleaning the room, she had finally allowed herself a respite.

After a glance at Emily's pale, drawn expression, he turned back to the window. Emily slept in fitful spurts, waking only when the pain grew so severe she couldn't sleep through it. The last time she'd awakened, she'd complained that her stomach hurt and the pain had spread to her entire leg. It was only a matter of time before it consumed her entire body.

As the poison traveled through her, she'd grow weaker. If she wasn't strong enough to sustain . . . He ran a hand over his face and choked back a groan.

And here he was, as worthless as ever. There was nothing he could do. Except wait for Paul to bring the doctor back with the proper medicines. But Dale was no fool. The doctor would bring something for the pain and nothing more.

"Dale," Emily groaned.

He spun and hurried back to the bed. Beads of sweat had formed on her forehead and her eyes were glazed in unfocused confusion.

"I'm here." He laid his hand on her forehead and winced. She burned, almost too hot to touch.

"I . . ." Her voice trailed away in a spasm and her eyes grew wide. Tendrils of hair, black as the night outside the window, clung to her temples and forehead with damp fingers.

"Hush, now. Don't try to talk. Everything will be fine in the morning." He prayed he didn't lie, but unless God provided them with some miracle, he did lie.

"I'm dizzy. Make the room stop. Please?" She squeezed her eyes closed as a shiver raced over her arms and legs. "So thirsty."

Dale lifted her head and pressed a glass to her lips. She parted them, but didn't drink. God, she no longer had the strength. He allowed several drops to pour into her mouth before she pushed the glass away in an attack of coughing that lasted more than a minute.

When she finished, her cheeks burned red before the color drained away to a sickening shade of alabaster. A moment later she fell asleep again.

Unable to maintain his own weight, he fell into the chair beside the bed. He held her hand and pressed his lips to the scorching surface.

"I don't know what to do." He glanced at the ceiling. "I don't know how to help her, God. All I can do is beg. If You have any mercy, please, don't take her. She has all the spirit I've never had. She deserves to be happy, to die surrounded by her children and their children. She deserves peace and love. If You take her now, You rob the world of one of Your most precious gifts." A sob stole his voice and he laid his forehead on the bed next to her, still holding her limp fingers in his hands. Hands that had killed in more ways than he could imagine. He didn't deserve to live, but bloody hell, she did!

"Take me!" He raised his head again and gritted his teeth. "If You have any love, if justice exists, Dear God,

You'll take me instead!"

"It doesn't work that way, Dale." Blue shuffled into the room and moved a chair from the far wall to place it next to Dale.

The old man's eyes held so much wisdom—more knowledge than any one man should possess. Flaxen light leapt into those eyes and reflected off his black skin.

"Tell me how it works, Blue. Tell me how to save her."

"There is nothing you can do."

Dale jumped to his feet, kicked the chair out from behind him and stormed across the room. "Don't tell me that. There must be something. I can't just let her die. Say something. Speak your magic and make her well."

"I am not your god."

"Then what the bloody hell are you?" He ran a quivering hand through his hair and held the back of his head. "What are you?" he repeated in a whisper.

"I am a man, just like you."

Dale scoffed. "Not from what I've seen. She said you told her she was going to die."

"No, I didn't."

"She wouldn't make it up, for Christ's sake."

"I told her not to fear."

"Don't think it's working, mate." The irony of Blue's warnings, lessons, whatever he preferred to call them, ate at Dale's soul. More than twenty years ago, Blue had told him about Joel. And he'd been right. That day on the rock when Dale had been only four years old had been etched in Dale's memory. From the color of the sunset, to the expression on Blue's face when Dale had accused him of telling the future. On that day he'd foretold of a new life; a new, wonderful, amazing life in his brother Joel.

And now he foretold of the loss of the only woman Dale had ever loved. It wasn't fair! He should have been given another chance to make her happy, to tell her all of the wonderful and insane things she did to him whenever she walked into a room.

Instead, he'd used her and cast her aside as if she meant nothing. All because of a self-imposed sentence of misery. How stupid had he been all this time? He'd had the opportunity to save her and he'd failed her.

Just like he'd failed everyone else in his life. He closed his eyes, gritted his teeth, and tilted his head back, waiting for the bolt of lightning that would trade his life for Emily's.

It didn't come.

For the remainder of the night, Blue sat in stoic silence next the bed. Dale found himself unable to stay in one place for long and moved from the bed, to the window, and back again until his back ached and his head pounded.

As morning approached, Dale stood by the window again staring into the night as if it held the answers he sought. Finally, the horizon turned to a golden light and, one by one, the stars winked and then vanished. He'd given up praying for a miracle and asked only that he be given the chance to tell Emily how much he loved her before it was too late. She should know at least that much before . . .

He choked on the thought.

Instead, he returned to the bed and checked Emily's temperature with the back of his hand. If anything, her fever had increased.

The house shook beneath the resounding roar of a plane engine. Dale raced to the window just as Paul's bright yellow airplane banked and turned toward his makeshift landing strip.

"Watch her, Blue."

Dale raced out of the house and met the plane when it rolled to a stop amid several hundred bleating sheep. He squinted into the dawn and cursed.

Paul jumped out of the contraption and ran in his direction carrying a small package.

"Where's the bloody doctor?"

"He wouldn't come, the old bastard." Paul handed the package to Dale. "He sent this instead. It's laudanum and should help with the pain, which was all he said he'd be able to do anyway. He also suggested a cool bath if she has a fever. Does she have a fever?"

"Aye. A bloody bad one, too. The tub is still in her room." Dale led Paul to the house. "Have you slept, mate?"

"Nah. Who needs sleep? I'm right as rain. You take the laudanum upstairs and I'll get the *Jackaroos* started on bringing cold water up from the Coongan."

What had he ever done to deserve a friend like Paul Campbell? He couldn't fathom it when everything else in his life teemed with his own deadly version of the Midas Touch. "Thank you."

By the time Dale hurried through the house and back into Emily's bedroom, she was awake again. She looked like hell and probably felt worse. But her eyes were clearer than they'd been the night before. Maybe her fever had broken, after all.

Ruth spun to face him with an obvious question in her eyes.

"He's not coming. But he sent something for the pain." Dale ripped open the package, withdrew a bottle the color of wet, desert mud and pulled out the cork. "Here, love, take a swallow of this."

Emily turned her head slowly, as if even that slight movement brought her more pain than any person should endure. "What is it?"

"Laudanum."

"No, I don't want it. It's little more than whiskey."

"If I had any whiskey, I'd make you drink that as well. But somebody poured all of my booze out." He smiled.

Emily returned a slight grin and then winced. "I still don't want any. It's not so bad, really."

"Liar." Dale sat in the chair he'd vacated dozens of times during the long night. "You always tell the truth, don't you? So don't start lying now. Drink it."

He hated the way her expression relented with so little fight, but it was for the best. She reached for the bottle, but her hand dropped before she grasped it. Dale put it to her lips and she managed a small sip.

"You'll need more than that. Try again."

After four attempts, she'd managed what amounted to a decent draught of the medicine. As Dale replaced the stopper, a line of *Jackaroos* filed into the room and dumped buckets of water into the copper tub. It took several trips, but soon the tub was close to overflowing.

Emily had fallen asleep in the meantime, which was probably a blessing. If she stayed asleep when he submerged her in the tub, it would be a miracle.

"Ruth, you might want to wait outside."

"Pardon?" Ruth straightened from laying out fresh linens in preparation for redressing the bed once Emily was in the tub.

"This isn't going to be easy and you might want to go downstairs with the men."

"But you might need my help. What if she fights you?" He raised an eyebrow and Ruth sighed. "I suppose you're right. I'll be right downstairs if you need me for anything. Anything at all."

Once the room was empty, Dale stiffened his back. She wasn't going to like this one little bit, there wasn't a question about that. But he didn't know how much longer she could withstand a fever of this magnitude and, after all, the doctor had suggested a cool bath. He cursed himself for not having thought of it himself.

He stripped away her nightgown and shuddered when she lay naked on the bed. It had been only two nights ago when they'd made love. Then, her body had been like a stick of wet dynamite ready to explode at the slightest touch. She'd given herself to him with more trust and passion than anyone he'd ever been with and he'd loved her for it. Not for sharing her body, but for sharing her soul. And now . . .

Now she lay dormant and her skin had taken on a pale, almost gray hue that made his soul weep.

He lifted her as gently as he could in deference to the pain in her leg and the infection that attacked her from within. She stirred, but did not awaken. When he shifted her weight so that her arm draped over his shoulder, she tucked her head against his chest as if she knew he was there—as if she needed him—even in sleep.

His heart almost stopped.

He carried her to the tub and dipped her feet below the surface. Immediately, her grip on his neck tightened and her eyes flew open. "No!"

"Hush, love. We have to bring down your fever."

"No, it hurts. Please, no." She sobbed and her chest heaved with each wrenching sound. Tears filled her eyes and she tucked her face into his neck. If she noticed she was naked, she made no indication of it.

"We have to. I know it's cold. The boys carried it straight from the river, just for you. Because they all love you so much. You don't want to let them down, do you?"

She sniffled. "It's so cold. It hurts."

Dale sat in the chair beside the tub, cradled her on his

lap and toed off his boots. He stood, held firmly to Emily's legs and back and stepped into the water.

Crikey, it was cold as ice. He could only imagine how much colder it must feel to a body raging like a bloody bushfire. As quickly as he could, he lowered them both into the frigid water. She roused again and screamed. But he held fast and brought her beneath the surface, resting her on the planes of his own body while water spilled over the rounded edges of the tub.

She cried like a child, softly and quietly, into his neck. He used his free hand to cup water to pour over her shoulders. She shivered and tensed. "I'm sorry, Emily. God knows I never want to bring you pain. I never wanted to hurt you."

*　＊　＊*

Dale's voice hovered somewhere on the edge of reality, in that place that exists between dreams and daylight. He whispered into Emily's ear and the words he spoke warmed her soul even though her body varied from sudden, severe chills to heated tempest. If only she could make out the words through the fog in her mind. She was vaguely aware of the icy water chilling her skin and even more aware that Dale's strong arms embraced her—protected her.

That's all he'd ever wanted to do. From that first day, he'd gone out of his way to make sure she was safe. And she'd been less than cooperative. Her conscience experienced a pang of remorse. She could have been nicer to him. She should've been.

The voice in her ear grew stronger, clearer. Finally, the words made sense even though, when she opened her eyes, the room spun in lazy, not-unpleasant circles around the tub.

She sat in a tub. A freezing tub. With Dale!

Emily struggled against the iron cage of his arms. "What-t are y-you do-doing to me?" Her teeth chattered and her head ached anew.

"It's all right, love. We're almost finished. Another few minutes and I think we can climb out of the pool."

"It-its not a p-p-pool."

"Right you are. Aye, I think you've had about enough. Up you go."

As if she weighed nothing at all and he wasn't soaked to the skin, he lifted her, stepped over the edge of the tub and laid her like a flower's petal on the bed. In all of the dreams she'd had of a life with Dale, never had she imagined anything so tender, so magical. With a single touch, he could make her feel as if she soared higher than the mountains that surrounded her Arizona home. With a heated glance, he stole her pain and replaced it with gentle yearning.

He covered her with a thin linen sheet and stared down at her with something in his eyes she'd never seen before.

Acceptance. Trust. Maybe even . . .

No, she wouldn't think of that now. Not when the pain finally ebbed beneath a snowy field of white and her limbs hummed with some unknown energy. The room turned a few undulating circles again and she smile. Just knowing he wanted her was enough. If he never loved her, she would drench herself in the part of him he was willing to share and love him enough for them both.

His gaze darkened and his eyes roamed over curves barely hidden beneath the sheet. "I like it when you look at me like that."

He chuckled. "Like what?"

"Like you could eat me for dessert." She wanted to laugh, but it would have taken too much energy and she wanted to sleep.

"That's the laudanum talking, I'd wager. The effects should last another few hours." His smile vanished behind a frown that possessed not only his lips, but his eyes as well. "If the fever doesn't break soon, we'll need to take another bath, but for now, just rest."

Why was he looking at her like that? Oh, yes. A spider bite. After all the months—no, the years—she'd loved Dale, he'd finally begun to feel something for her, and now she was going to die. It hardly seemed fair. And it was even worse that it would steal what little happiness Dale had allowed himself. He needed to smile more often. He should smile every day for the rest of his life.

"Aye," she mimicked his adorable accent full of 'I's and 'R's. "I'll rest now. And I'll dream of you."

And she did. Lustful, passionate dreams filled with entwined bodies, slick with moisture in the oppressive

Pilbara heat. And bothersome, frustrating dreams in which Dale sank further and further into a black void of despair and she could do nothing to bring him back. In one of the dreams, Dale sank below the surface of a deep, black pool. She pushed her arms into the murky, opaque water but she couldn't find him. She dove in and the water sucked at her soul until she couldn't breathe—couldn't feel. She broke through the surface and gulped the frigid air, still surrounded by nothing but black. It was pure emptiness, loneliness. Not even night existed in the darkness . . . just nothing. And Dale was gone. She'd failed him. He'd trusted her to bring him back and she'd promised she would save him. But he was gone and there was nothing she could do. She'd let him go. Something inside her heart splintered and cut her.

Crying his name where no one could hear, she dove below the surface again. This time, her guilt weighted her to the depths of the abyss. Her lungs burned and her throat ached. Still, she only wanted to exist in the dark until she forgot who she was and what she'd done.

Hear me, Emily. You did save me. Because of you, I can love again.

Dale's voice cut through the depths to echo in her heart. The water seemed somehow less cold, less murky. "Dale? Dale, where are you?"

I'm here. Take my hand.

"Dale, don't leave me." The water cleared her lungs and she tasted the fresh, fragrant air. The darkness pulled away like a canopy caught in the wind. Finally, something light.

"Emily, open your eyes."

Her lids fluttered. Her head hurt and her stomach growled.

"Open your eyes, love."

She obeyed and for a moment only blurred colors danced in front of her. Then she focused and found Dale leaning over her with a frown. His light eyes teemed a shade darker than she remembered.

"You were dreaming."

Her flesh prickled with sinister shades of distant memory. She *had* been dreaming. "Oh, Dale, I'm so sorry."

His frown deepened and he stroked her cheek. "What could you possibly have done to be sorry for, love?"

A sob struggled to make its way free of her throat, burning against her tongue, stealing her voice and replacing it with something coarse and broken. "I didn't understand, but I do now. I know what you must have been feeling all these months. The loss you've endured. The guilt."

Eyes suddenly lighter searched hers, and then she saw it—the glint that came with understanding and acceptance. "No, love. You were right all along."

"I was too hard on you. I made everything so much worse."

"You made me love again. How can that ever be worse?"

Dale gathered Emily in his arms and cradled her head against his chest. His embrace sent tremors up her spine that swirled in her mind before cascading over her entire body. "I only wanted to love you forever."

"You have, Emily. You have and I've been stupid and stubborn. But not anymore. Why didn't I see it before . . .?"

Emily's heart swelled and her stomach flipped on itself. Her cheek tingled where it brushed against his chest. His words disappeared behind a misty cloud, but it didn't matter. He'd forgiven her for being an obstinate, insensitive prig all these weeks. It was enough. As long as he didn't hate her, she could die in peace.

✟ 🐎 ✟

Dale laid Emily's head back on her pillow then rested his forehead in his palms. She'd fallen asleep before he's said the words. *She hadn't heard him.* Crikey, he was no good at this. Hour after hour he watched and waited for some sign that she was getting better. The medication only masked the damage the venom wrought in her system. Her fever still raged and even in those few moments of lucidity, she'd spoken in fragmented riddles.

Still, he'd believed her when she'd said she understood him. Something had happened to let her know the heart of his anguish—was that the miracle he'd prayed for?

No, the miracle came in the healing of his heart. And like most miracles, it came at a price. It might very well have come in exchange for Emily's life. The cost was too high.

Blue and Ruth came into the room and Ruth placed

a hand on his shoulder. "You haven't slept in more than a day. Why don't you let us watch her for a while and get some sleep?"

"I can't leave her."

Blue urged him to his feet. "You must. You are no value to her right now. She sleeps, and if she wakes we'll find you."

Maybe he should at least stretch his legs. The constant quiet and steady rhythm of Emily's breathing had lulled him into semi-consciousness more than once in the past few hours. He should walk around the garden and increase the flow of blood to his limbs. And his mind.

There must be something more he could do to help her.

"All right. I'll go. But only for a few minutes."

He left the room rubbing a cramp in the small of his back. With no particular direction in mind, he left the house by the front door and walked down the creaking wooden stairs. Within a few minutes he was in the stable, feeding sugar cubes to Jezebel.

Funny, how he always ended up in the barn. Without even meaning to, he invariably made his way to Jezebel and, more recently, Apache. It was as if his feet had their own course in mind. Or maybe it was the path Blue had spoken of.

But that didn't make sense. Finding his heart and risking the pain of loss to let Emily in didn't change his mind about riding again. He still owed Joel that much, at least. Crikey, he must be more tired than he thought. He was actually trying to make sense out of something that Blue had told him in one of his enigmatic lessons.

"What do I do now, Jez?"

Jezebel nudged his hand until it landed on her velvety nose. He rested his forehead against her long, hard face and closed his eyes. No matter how much he tried, *he* couldn't save Emily. It was in God's hands, not his. And if she did survive, that bloody stubborn streak wouldn't allow her to withdraw from the race with Gerald Brown. In her condition, she'd be lucky if she survived.

He had to give her credit. She was the most rugged woman he'd ever met, like steel wrapped in satin. But the desert through which she'd be forced to ride for two solid, body-wrenching, mind-numbing, excruciatingly hot days was more than a match for most *men*, much less a woman. Fifty miles each day through the most barren and unforgiving land in the world. The Bush had killed before and it would kill again. It was a certainty.

She couldn't possibly do it in her condition.

Apache neighed and stamped his foot against the lowest board in his stall door. The wood cracked like a sudden thunderclap and split into two jagged pieces. Dale knelt and pried the broken boards away from the adjoining rails.

He stared up at Apache and the massive black lowered his head to within inches of Dale's face. He blew a quick, impatient breath and backed up a step. "You trying to tell me something, boy?"

The horse nodded.

Dale landed on his arse on the dirt floor, scooted back on his elbows and quickly found his feet. *Horses do not nod*. He was overtired, that was all. He hadn't slept and his mind played tricks on him. Apache whinnied and stamped the ground then blew a loud, frustrated breath. He stretched his long, black neck over the top rail and tried to bite the edge of the broken board.

Dale frowned. Horses do not . . .

"All right then, I'll bite." He stepped up to the stall, stacked the broken pieces on the top rail and held them in place with his forearms. "What do you think I should do?"

Apache stamped again and nudged the board with enough force to knock Dale back several inches. "What? You want me to look at the boards?"

He lined the uneven edges against one another and frowned. The board's center fit together perfectly. Both of them broken, but when placed next to one another, joined. The break all but vanished. They were a perfect fit, as if they'd been cut instead of torn.

Just like he and Emily.

He didn't believe in signs, paths, or magic anymore, did he? Of course, that was before Emily had done the impossible and healed his heart. Maybe someone was trying to tell him something—either God, Blue, or the bloody horse.

But what? That he and Emily were two separate halves of the same heart. The same soul. He had no doubt that she'd lay down her life for him. She already might have laid it down *because* of him. There was nothing he could do, but lay down his soul for her. He knew exactly what he needed to do and the thought turned his stomach. "Jesus," he groaned. "I can't."

Jezebel and Sally joined Apache in a restless dance in their stalls. The barn filled with heavy dust and Dale reached over the railing to calm Apache. Once the animals had settled, he leaned against the top rail again and cleared his lungs with a deep, life-giving sigh.

"Joel, I don't know if you can hear me. I've never given heaven much thought before I lost you. I hope it's there and I hope you've found peace, but . . . I can't be a part of that anymore.

"When I promised Mum I'd watch over you, I didn't understand exactly what that meant. I realize it now. You grew into the man I wish I'd been. Damn, you made us all so bloody proud. And you did what you had to do, even though it got your arse killed." Tears pricked his eyes and he wiped them away. "And when I promised you I'd never live again . . . well, that was pretty damned stupid, too.

"Crikey, I can't help it. I've fallen in love with the most wonderful woman I've ever known. I think you'd like her, I really do, and that's why I need to ask you a favor."

❋ 🐎 ❋

When Emily opened her eyes, the sun had moved to the

far side of the house and only dim light shone through her bedroom window. Her leg ached, but not as badly as the day before and her stomach no longer shifted in place like a child's toy in a bathtub.

Bathtub?

With effort, she focused her eyes and leveled her gaze on the copper tub in the corner of the room. Then she ran her hands over herself beneath a light sheet and found . . .

Nothing. She was completely naked. Her hand rushed to her head. Damp. "Did I take a bath?"

"Emily?" Dale stood at the window but crossed to the bed as if he could fly. His warm fingers skimmed her forehead and he seemed to study her eyes for more than a moment. Then he released a breath as if he'd held it. "Thank God." He sat on the edge of the bed, gathered her in his embrace and buried his forehead in her neck. "Thank God."

Emily combed her fingers through his hair and cradled him like a child. "I'm fine . . . I think. Please, don't worry."

"I thought I'd lost you."

Emily wanted to reassure him, but she couldn't. Vague flashes of her own death strobed through her subconscious. A part of her had believed she would die. "Blue was wrong," she whispered.

"Was he?"

"I'm still here, aren't I? And I'm not going anywhere. Ever."

"Look who's awake!" Paul appeared behind Dale and

inclined his head as he smiled down at her with bright blue eyes. He tossed away an errant blond lock that had landed on his forehead. "You had us worried for a spell, but it looks like you'll be right in another few days."

"Another few days?"

Ruth knelt beside the bed and touched Emily's cheek. "No fever at all. Thank God." She made the sign of the cross over her breast and smiled so widely both of her dimples cut patches in her full cheeks. "You've been sleeping on and off, thanks to the medicine Paul brought back from Port Hedland, for about four days."

"Four days?" She tried to sit but Dale's hands on her shoulders stopped her. "Let me go, I have to get up. I can't have been here for . . . dear Lord . . . four days?" Emily pushed his hands away and forced herself upright. The room tilted, but returned to normal almost at once. She held the sheet to her breast and scanned the worried expressions around her.

"Your fever finally broke last night, a little after midnight." Dale shifted to a chair beside the bed. "Almost six hours ago. Does your leg still hurt?"

"A bit. Not terribly, though."

"Good. Doc says you need to stay in bed for another week or so, then you should be right as rain again. Ready to take on the world." As if he couldn't stop himself, he caressed her cheek again.

"I am not sitting in this bed for a whole week. I have a race to run . . . when is the race again?" She rubbed the pads of her fingers over the creases in her forehead. Everything was so fuzzy and askew. "What day is it?"

Paul frowned. "It's Thursday. The race is set for the day after tomorrow, but I, for one, haven't thought much about that rot. We've had more important things to worry over."

"Two days . . ." Emily bit her lip and tested her leg by moving it beneath the sheet. It still hurt, but she stifled the wince. "It's a good thing I woke up then, isn't it?"

Ruth's fists landed on her hips. "You can't seriously consider riding."

"No. Not considering it. I'm racing."

Dale shot to his feet. "The hell you are."

"Just try to stop me!"

"I'll do more than stop you. I'll tie you to that bed if you as much as try to stand up."

"You wouldn't dare." Would he? Emily studied the firm line of his brow and the determined spark in his eyes. Maybe he would. "Please, Dale. I can't forfeit now. You know I can't."

The hard lines of Dale's face softened and he tossed a glance at Paul. "You won't forfeit. You just won't ride."

"What are you talking about? I don't understand."

"I'm going to ride into Marble Bar today, find Brown and suggest it's in his best interest to call it off."

"He won't do that. You know that as well as I do."

"I have a plan for that, too."

Paul laughed. "You're not going to kill him, are you, mate?"

"Nothing that dramatic, I'm afraid." Dale traced a line over Emily's cheek with the tip of one finger. "Just know that you're not riding anywhere for quite some time." He turned to Paul. "Make sure she stays in bed."

Paul nodded and Dale tossed one more hooded gaze at Emily before he left the room.

"What was he talking about?"

With a Cheshire cat grin, Paul took up a position by the door. "I think he was talking about just how much he loves you."

"Right. I'm sure that was it." Emily rolled her eyes and refocused on Paul. "He's going to pick a fight with Gerald, isn't he?" Damn that man for his stubborn pride! "If you'll excuse me, please?"

"I'm not going anywhere."

"I can't very well dress with you sitting there."

"Exactly." His smiled widened and he crossed his arms over his chest.

Emily narrowed her eyes and considered dressing in front of him. But that would never do. Instead she leaned against the headboard and threw imaginary daggers at him with her eyes. "You'll have to leave sometime."

"If you set one foot off that bed, I'll tie you to it myself."

"Be reasonable, Paul. If Dale rides into town today, he could be hurt!"

"He can take care of himself. You're not getting out of that bed, much less riding through the bleeding desert for hours on end. The race is off."

"But I'll be fine by tomorrow, certainly by Saturday. I'm feeling so much better already."

"No." Paul leaned against the doorframe as if he had nowhere in the world to go, nothing to do—as if he had all the time in the world.

✶ 🐎 ✶

Dale pushed open the door to the public room at the Ironclad Hotel and strode inside. He waited a moment for his eyes to adjust to the dim interior then scanned the room in search of one man. He found Gerald Brown at the bar with his fist wrapped around a mug of beer. On either side of him his mates gathered like tykes to their hero. Dumb bastards. Gerald Brown was on the way down and they'd hitched their wagons to the wrong star.

With slow, measured steps, he approached the bar, Brown, and the group of low-life, good-for-nothing bushrangers who surrounded him. Just before he reached them, Brown turned and leaned his elbows on the bar. He narrowed his tiny black eyes and raked a glare over Dale that sent shivers of disgust down Dale's spine. What a whanker, this one was.

"What brings you away from home, Dale? In the mood for the company of real men, are you?"

"The race is off. Just wanted you know."

"The hell it is." Brown pushed himself off the bar and gained his feet. "Day after tomorrow at sunup. I'll be there and if Emily backs off, I win."

"Think about it for a second. What if you lose? To a woman? Are you really willing to risk that? Think of the humiliation, mate." Dale clicked his teeth, shaking his head slowly.

"Small chance of that." Gerald laughed. His cohorts joined him.

"All right then, since you won't listen to reason, here are the facts. She's ill and she can't ride—"

"Blimey! Well, there's some luck." Gerald slinked forward until he stood only an arm's reach from Dale. His greasy smile opened to reveal several missing teeth and those that remained were stained from tobacco and poor care. "I win, then, don't I? Hear that, mates? Winters and I are business partners."

"Shut up, Brown. I wasn't finished. You haven't won anything yet. I'm going to see to it that you don't."

"Right, what are *you* going to do about it?"

"You thought you had it won, didn't you? I mean, even before you knew she couldn't ride. You assumed you could beat a woman with no worries. I don't believe you were right about that, personally. I think Emily would have wiped the desert floor with your arse."

Brown's back straightened and he bristled like an angry cat. Dale ignored him and continued. "The game has changed. You're not racing against Emily; you're racing me."

Brown's jaw fell slack a second before he snapped it

shut. His hands formed angry fists at his sides. "No, mate. That wasn't the wager. Besides, everyone knows you don't ride anymore. Some promise you made to that spoiled rotten brother of yours."

Like bright red mercury filling a thermometer, Dale's body filled with rage. "Don't let your mouth get you hurt, mate. You're better served to leave that one alone."

"What? You killed your brother and now you want we should just forget about it?"

He hadn't killed Joel. Hearing this sack of rubbish say the words solidified that single fact in Dale's mind and relieved what tiny inklings of guilt he might have still possessed. His chest swelled and he braced his feet apart. The floorboards creaked beneath his weight. "If you insist on continuing with this ridiculous wager, you'll race me, and that's all there is to it."

"All right, but I still get Emily if I win."

As much as the fact pained him, as much as he wanted to tell Gerald to rack off, he knew Emily wouldn't appreciate the gesture. Instead, he swallowed his jealous rage. "That would be up to the lady, wouldn't it?"

Brown snorted. "A wager is a wager. But if the rider has changed, so should the stakes. I want more, mate."

Of course, he did—greedy little range pig. "What would that be?"

"Since you're doing the riding, the stakes aren't quite as certain, as you've pointed out."

"Get on with it."

"If you win, you get my station, just like before. But if I win . . . oh, now, if I win . . . I get your whole outfit. The land, that nice house your dad built for your mum, the livestock, everything. Everything from your woman to your horse. You got it?"

Dale weighed his options. Gerald was within his rights to cry forfeit and just take what Emily had offered in the original wager. Nothing forced him to accept the new terms except greed and pride. Dale hadn't sat a horse in more than a year. Jezebel might be in racing shape, but he was far from it.

Still, he'd never lost a race in the Pilbara. Never.

And Emily's future was at stake. Dale crossed his arms over his chest. "Agreed."

⚡ 🐎 ⚡

"You can't be serious." Emily tossed the sheet off her legs, gathered the skirt of her nightgown in her fist and forced her legs over the side of the bed.

Dale grabbed her shoulders and eased her gently back to the pillows. "Don't overexert yourself. You still need to rest."

"But your vow . . . I don't want to be the reason you break it." The pillow met her back and she collapsed against it. Even that small amount of movement had proven her weaker than she'd thought. And now Dale would sacrifice his own peace of mind because of her. Because of an insipid little insect that had decided she might taste good. She wanted to scream.

"What do you mean?" He almost laughed, but the sound held a measure of solemnity that reflected in his eyes. "You've been trying to make me change my mind about that since practically the day we met."

"Yes, but that was before. Now I understand how much it means to you. I understand the reasons, and while I want to you to come to this conclusion, certainly, I don't want you to be forced into it because of me."

"Ah, love. But you see, I had to be forced. Left to my own devices I would have wallowed in self-pity for the rest of my life."

"I doubt that very much."

"Paul, Blue, and most especially you, made me see that my whole life is out there. Waiting for me. And the first thing I want to do in this new life is make things right."

"I'm confused again, I'm afraid."

"You put yourself at risk for me. This insane wager with Brown, and it is insane," he added when she scoffed, "is only the beginning."

"You're sure? You're willing to do this?"

"I've never been more sure about anything in my life." When he smiled, his face lit up like a rainbow after a summer storm, bright and full of hope. "Except, perhaps . . ."

Emily's heart almost stopped beneath his gaze. How exciting—that feeling in her belly when he looked at her with such desire. "Except what?"

He strode to the bed and sat on the edge. One large, finely muscled hand cupped her cheek and she turned her head into the warmth he offered. His eyes dashed for one moment to her lips and she suddenly longed to taste him. Her pulse quickened in her neck in just the spot where she longed for his kiss.

"Except for how much I love you."

In the space of a few simple words, spoken with such sincerity, her heart shuddered and then exploded with more love and hope than she'd ever believed possible. How many years had she loved him? How many years had she prayed for his love in return, even before she'd met him, before she'd risked everything to come here and find him? And now, her prayers, her hopes and her dreams all met in the love shining in a pair of translucent blue eyes.

"Well, don't cry about it." He laughed.

Until he mentioned it, she hadn't realized her eyes had misted and a tear spun down her cheek. She wiped one cheek dry while he used the pad of his thumb to dry the other.

"I rather thought you'd be happy to hear it."

"Oh, I am happy. Those are the most wonderful words I've ever heard." She threw herself into the circle of his arms.

"You know, I've tried to tell you for days, but each time I tried, you fell asleep. I was beginning to take it personally."

"I'm sorry," she answered when she released him just enough to look into his face. He winked and she smiled. "You're teasing me, aren't you?"

"Aye. I never thought I'd tease anyone again. And then I found you."

The light left his eyes and he frowned as he settled her back on the pillow.

"What's wrong?"

He forced a smile. "Nothing."

"You're worried, aren't you?"

"About what? The race? Not a bit. I can take Gerald Brown. Could beat him with my eyes closed."

"What if he cheats?"

"Even if he cheats."

Chapter Sixteen

Every hour, it seemed, Dale wondered what he'd ever done to deserve the love of such a beautiful woman as Emily Castle. Even if she hadn't returned his confession, he sensed she loved him in the way she looked at him— almost caressing him with her eyes. He wanted nothing more than to drop into the bed beside her and make love to her for what remained of the afternoon and most of the night. But she was still too weak and despite her courage and strength, the pain hadn't left her completely. He could see it in her eyes.

"So, have you ridden yet?"

He shook his head, stood and crossed to the window. The sun wouldn't set for another hour or more. Jezebel, Sally, and several other horses raced along the pasture fence, their manes flowing behind their arched necks and their tails held high. He had time for a short ride if he wanted to go. That would mean leaving Emily and he wasn't sure he wanted to do that. In fact, he was quite sure he didn't. But if he stayed with her, she was in danger of his making love to her no matter what her condition. "I think I'll take her out for a bit now."

"You should."

"You're not going to try to keep me here?"

A mischievous smile formed on lips made for kissing. "No, I'm not."

"I think I'm offended."

"Don't be. It's a simple matter of scientific law."

"Scientific law?"

"Yes. The laws of attraction. You see, if you stay here, I'm going to have to insist that you climb into this bed and I don't think that's a very good idea for someone in my condition."

He laughed. From the very bottom of his soul and the overflowing depths of his heart. And it felt good. Not as good as burying himself in her lush curves, but good nonetheless. "I was just thinking that very thing."

He placed a kiss on her cheek in a gesture so comfortable it surprised him. Amazing how only a year ago he'd believed his world had ended, that nothing could ever make him want to come back to the shelter of his home. And yet, the only thing to make him truly at ease was a woman from another world. "I'll be home in a short while."

"I'll be here," she sighed.

He kissed the tip of her nose and went to the stable. He collected his old saddle from its rack on the wall and ran his hand over the dusty leather. It wasn't as dirty as he would have thought and the leather was still in fairly good condition. Someone must have cared for it while he'd been away. Charles, more than likely. He smiled.

Charles had never married, never had a family of his own. Even before Dale's parents had been killed, Charles had doted on him and his brother as if they'd been his own. He could imagine Charles caring for their saddles with loving strokes, just waiting for the time when Dale and Joel would return home and use them again.

He cleaned the saddle and carried it out into the pasture. The horses had finished their game of chase and stood grazing in the center of the field. When he whistled for Jezebel, she lifted her ears and looked at him. A moment later, she lunged forward and trotted to the barn.

He brought her outside the fenced pasture and saddled her. The movements felt foreign, as if he watched someone else's hands align the blanket, tighten the cinch, back strap and breast collar. He bridled her with that same distance between them. If he had to put a name on it, he would call it fear. Fear he'd lost the subtle, almost clairvoyant relationship he'd once had with Jezebel. Fear he'd be unable to live up to his responsibilities both on the station and with Emily.

Emily. Was there a better woman in the world? Somehow, he doubted it. Patient and more beautiful than any creature he'd ever seen, she embodied exactly what he'd needed to find himself again. To find that place where happy memories of his parents, Joel, and Charles met and flourished. Without Emily, he would never have found it.

With Jezebel saddled and ready to go, Dale held he reins in his left hand and ran his other hand over her glossy flanks. She looked at him with one huge, black eye.

It's now or never. He pulled himself up, tucked his foot in the stirrup and threw his opposite leg over the saddle. The fear disappeared. The whole past year of guilt and regret moved to somewhere in the pit of his stomach before it dissipated in the impatient prance beneath him. He patted Jezebel's neck and kicked her forward.

Slow at first, he gradually increased their gait until they galloped along the outside of the fence. Farther and faster, they moved as if they were parts of the same body. God, how he'd missed this. More than even he had realized. The euphoria that came with a powerful animal at a full run between his thighs was like a beacon of light in the midst of a storm.

He pushed her even faster when they reached the road beside the Coongan River. The wind in his ears and the steady, even thud of Jezebel's hoofs on the red dirt matched his heartbeat. Frantic. Excited.

His cheeks ached from the smile plastered on his face. He probably looked like an idiot while he rode on and on over the road, then the sheep pasture. Thousands of sheep bleated and scattered as he rode through them. They parted in a wide corridor, like a sea of clouds.

They might as well have been clouds since he felt like he was flying over them. Two *Jackaroos* sat atop their horses on the far side of the herd. They waved and he nodded in return, blowing past them at full speed. He cut a wide arc and climbed to the top of a rocky hill. There, he stopped and surveyed the whole of the Castle Winters Station. From the vantage point, millions of acres stretched in front of him. Red earth beneath the muted green of native plants glowed in the setting sun. The horizon turned all the colors of the rainbow and the sun cast those brilliant pinks, orange and reddish hues onto the smattering of clouds. The first stars winked. Somewhere below, a dingo cried.

He no longer felt the need to beg Joel for forgiveness. It was as if his brother had played a part in creating the gorgeous vista painted on the earth and sky. Instead of guilt, Dale had finally found peace. Instead of pain, his heart soared with nothing but love and hope.

In only a matter of days, he would put the last obstacle behind him. He would defeat Gerald Brown at his own game and Dale and Emily could begin their life together. And if she'd have him, he meant to make her his wife, and God help anyone who tried to get in their way again.

🐎

"What are you doing?" Dale hustled up the steps leading to the front porch and tossed his hat on the chair next to Emily.

"I wanted to see you ride." That's why she'd made the

arduous journey from her bedroom to the front porch. That's why she'd grimaced with every painful step and fought the vertigo which threatened to send her tumbling down the staircase. And that's the only reason she smiled through the twinges and spasms that plagued her hip every few seconds as if they could read a clock. "You looked wonderful."

Dale's brow creased into a worried frown, but even his obvious concern for her couldn't dampen the light in his eyes. For the first time since she'd known him, he looked truly happy. As if he'd read her thoughts, the lines in his forehead disappeared and he smiled. "It felt wonderful." He leaned against the railing and folded his arms over his chest. "I thought I'd feel guilty to a certain extent, but I didn't. I don't even feel guilty that I didn't feel guilty," he added with a laugh. "And there's only one reason for it."

"What's that?"

"You."

Heat crept up her neck and settled in her cheeks. His gaze deepened and something new and exciting fed the blue in his eyes. When he looked at her like that, she couldn't help but revel in the love in her heart. It wrapped her like a blanket. Not just in her heart, but in her entire being. Every bone, every muscle lived for Dale. Her heart beat for him, her lungs breathed for him, and her soul laughed for him.

His expression sobered and he pushed himself away from the railing. "Does your leg still hurt?"

"A little. But not so badly I need to stay in bed, if that's what you're thinking." She threw him a sidelong glance, daring him to argue the point.

"Oh, I'm thinking about bed, all right, but not the way you think I am." He levered his hands on the arms of the chair and dipped his face to within inches of hers. The rich scent of spice and leather encompassed her.

"Oh, really?"

"I was thinking of taking you back upstairs, slipping you out of that nightgown and into my arms. What would you say to that?"

"I'd say, that's the most pleasant thing I've heard all day."

The tip of Dale's tongue darted to wet his lips and a tremor shuddered up Emily's spine. She'd missed his touch. Even when she'd been barely lucid, she'd been aware of his caress—as if some part of her had been born to be a part of him; as if they were opposite halves of the same whole.

Breezy pieces of memory floated through her. Dale's hands on her body, keeping her still, holding her against the icy chill of her baths. Dale's lips on her neck when he held her in the night and whispered prayers for her life, offering his in her place.

No one had ever loved her so much.

"Can you walk?"

"Some."

Dale shook his head, lifted her from the chair and cradled her against his chest. The scent of leather and man enveloped her and made her stomach clench. He had spun in place and pointed them to the door when Blue shouted from the stable yard, "Riders coming!"

Dale glanced over his shoulder and groaned.

"What is it?" Emily craned her neck but couldn't see past Dale's wide shoulder.

"We have company, it seems."

He released her legs and guided her down the front of his hard torso until her feet met the worn floorboards. She turned within his embrace, his hands on her shoulders as if he protected her from something. She squinted into the distance where three men on horseback rode just in front of a large red dust cloud. "Gerald Brown."

"Aye." Dale stepped in front of her and tucked her half-way behind him. "Wait here."

"You don't have to do this, Dale."

He studied her over his shoulder. "Yes, I do."

The horses cantered into the garden, their hooves tearing at the lush grass. Emily cringed. Weeks of painstaking watering had created a smooth carpet of lawn and in only a few seconds, Gerald Brown and his fiendish cohorts had slaughtered her efforts.

"Brown." Dale nodded and walked to the edge of the porch.

"Winters," Gerald replied. "Are you ready to forfeit? Give me the girl now and we can call this whole thing off." He spun in his saddle and pointed to a parcel of land on the far side of the horse pasture, by the river. "I think I'll build my house right over there."

"Rack off. The race isn't for two more days, and when it's over you can build your house wherever you please. So long as it's nowhere near this station."

"Oh, if we run the race as planned, I'll do more than live on this station. I'll live in this bloody house."

Emily joined Dale at the top of the steps. "Gerald, you can't be serious. You know I'm unable to ride through no fault of my own, so why not be a good sport about the whole thing and just call it off?"

Gerald's eyes seemed to touch every part of her with greasy fingers. Her hand darted to her throat and she realized she wore only her thin nightgown. She gathered the open neck and pulled it tight under her chin.

"Don't the two of you make a cozy little picture."

"Mind yourself, Brown," Dale warned.

You know," Gerald sneered, "I don't know what I want more. Your station . . . or your sheila."

Dale's frame tensed like an animal ready to pounce. His thick forearm guided her behind him. "Emily's out of it. This is between you and me. No matter what happens, you have no claim to the woman."

"That's a load of Aussie bulldust, mate, and you know it. I have witnesses. She said if I win the race, she'd come with me. And I mean to see to it that I win." Gerald kicked his horse at the same time he turned the animal's head around and all three galloped away from the house.

Dale watched them go until they disappeared into a stretch of low hills. Even after they'd vanished, he stood on the porch and stared after them.

"What did he mean, he wants the station? The wager is for half ownership of the station."

"That's what he meant, then, I'm sure."

"You're worried, aren't you?"

He looked at her and frowned. "I've met my share of whankers in my day, but that one is about the worst of the lot. Watch yourself. Now that we know he's here, I don't want you wandering off alone."

Emily scoffed. "I can barely make my way down the stairs. I don't think I'll be taking any long walks in the near future."

Dale grasped her shoulders and gave her a small shake. "Listen to me, Emily. You go nowhere alone, do you understand me? He can't enforce that part of the wager and he knows it, which makes him very dangerous right now. If he wants you badly enough, when he loses, he'll take you."

The intensity of his gaze reminded her of a stormy sky. His eyes pleaded with her and she nodded. "I understand."

When he pulled her into his embrace, she wrapped her arms around his back and held to him as if she were afraid he might disappear. He held on to her with the same urgency.

"I've only just learned to love again, Emily. I can't survive if I lost you, too."

"Dale, you're scaring me."

"Don't be frightened, Emily. Just be careful."

Dale pulled his head back and his eyes fell on her lips. With the pad of his thumb, he traced the line of her jaw and sent tingles of anticipation to her limbs. His head descended slowly and when his lips met hers the world ceased to exist. There was no Gerald Brown, no illness, no bloody race. While his lips moved across hers in an ancient dance, her heart soared to the highest peaks where only love and happiness resided. So long as she had Dale Winters, she could face any challenge, any risk, and win. "Make love to me, Dale."

"With pleasure, love. With pleasure."

🕺 🐕 🕺

Emily walked through the small tent-city in the pasture beside her home with a barely noticeable limp. In the two days since Gerald Brown had arrived, it seemed as if the entire town of Marble Bar had come to Castle Winters to witness the first race since the Great War had stolen most of the territory's men. The citizens had needed a party, apparently, and this had proved as good an excuse as any to throw one.

The gardens were filled with people who laughed and ate their barbecued lamb and steak with the fervor of children. Several local musicians played guitar on the porch while their neighbors danced and clapped along.

Overhead, the night sky twinkled with a million stars and the moon shone bright and full over Tower Rock. It was still hot, but a gentle breeze made the temperature bearable. The only reason a beaded sweat broke out on

Emily's forehead was the lingering pain in her hip and the effort she'd put into walking with as little limp as she could manage.

"Here, love. Lean on me for a while." Dale appeared, seemingly out of nowhere, and wrapped his arm around her waist. "You should still be in bed."

His eyes rivaled the stars with their brilliance and a mischievous smile curled his full, soft lips. "You'd like that very much, wouldn't you, Dale Winters? You've kept me in that bed for quite enough hours, I think."

"I admit it. I'd rather have you in bed than anywhere, but that doesn't change the fact that you're not yet healed. Even the doctor said you needed several more days' rest."

"I didn't want to miss the party," she sighed. When his hand touched her just below her ribs, a delightful tingle shot from his fingertips to land with a jolt in the region of her heart. "It looks like everyone in the territory came."

"You're worse than Lizzy." His grin stole the sting of his words. "I suppose I'll have to take you to bed myself to keep you there."

She smiled. Dale had shown her the myriad benefits of taking one's time in the act of love over the last day or so. "Well, when you put it that way . . ."

Emily allowed Dale to lead her back through the milling crowd. She exchanged waves with several people she'd met over the course of her long weeks caring for her uncle, people she hadn't seen since before Dale had come home. By the time they reached the house, a cold sweat had beaded on her forehead and upper lip. She wiped it away.

Perhaps Dale and the doctor were right after all. She hated to admit it, but she really wasn't her old self. Yet. She would regain her strength, but for now she had to admit that without Dale's willingness to ride in her place tomorrow, she would have been in a world of trouble.

Once Dale opened the front door, he swept her into his arms and carried her the rest of the way to her room. Under normal circumstances, she would have hated that as well. Her entire life had been spent standing up for herself, taking care of herself. She'd never needed anyone more than they needed her and she'd liked it that way. She was the one who solved problems for other people. She helped them. No one needed to help her. She was the strong one.

Yet, when Dale took care of her it somehow felt right. It didn't make her feel like a burden he might want to be rid of. It made her feel loved.

And he had loved her well over the course of the past two days. If she hadn't been sleeping, she'd been in the throes of passionate abandon. He'd touched her in places she never dreamed possible and taken her to places she hadn't known existed. His hands on her body . . .

They had made love slowly, carefully, in deference to her aching hip. She'd urged him to take her furiously, but he'd refused, showing her instead the heights of controlled passion. Her stomach clenched when they reached her room.

Dale laid her on the bed and fetched her nightdress from the wardrobe. He handed it to her, turned and headed for the door. "I mean it this time. Stay in bed."

✦ 🐎 ✦

Blue sat on top of Tower Rock and studied the field below. The sun still slept and only the light of nearby campfires revealed the crowd. Dozens of whitefellas, maybe as many as two hundred, gathered around the horse pasture where Dale saddled Jezebel. When he finished, he attached a pair of haversacks to the back of his saddle. Blue had helped him pack them the night before. They contained water, a small amount of food, few handfulls of grain for the horse, and a blanket to ward away the chill of the desert night. Mostly, the horse would feed on the ironweed and grasses growing in the red earth of the desert. It would keep her fit enough to bring Dale home.

He turned to face the desert several miles to the east. Beyond the blackness, a harsh and unforgiving landscape of canyons, massive stretches of flatlands, and unpredictable winds waited for Dale. The Ancestors had created a place for men to die.

After all these years, he finally understood the meaning of the vision The Ancestors had shared with him when Dale had been no taller than a wallaby. It wasn't only Joel who would face death in the desert. It was Dale, too. At first, he'd thought the message obscure and twisted. A part of Dale *had* died in the desert with his brother—the part that made him a man capable of love and hope.

But more than that, Dale would face his own trials. It must be so, because this new vision had come after Dale had accepted Emily's love and forgiven himself for what he perceived to be his own failings.

Sometimes Blue hated the Ancestors for giving him the ability to see into the dreaming. He didn't want to know things yet to come; he had grown tired of interpreting the dreams for others. It had taken Emily days before she could look at him without pain in her eyes. She'd accused him of lying to her, making her believe she would die. Because of his words, she'd almost given up her fight to survive. If it hadn't been for Dale, she might have. Perhaps, he shouldn't have tried to reassure her.

Then again, perhaps this is what the Ancestors had intended all along.

He tossed a pebble off the edge of the rock and wiped his brow. He was old now, and tired. Enough was enough.

He wasn't going to tell Emily or Dale anything of his latest visions. Let them discover the path for themselves, without his help. If the Ancestors willed them to be together, they'd find their way through.

✳ 🐎 ✳

Emily hugged herself against a chill that shouldn't exist, even in the early dawn. The morning of the race arrived bright against the velvet night sky. The sun hadn't yet risen above the distant horizon and already the day threatened inhuman heat. Standing in the pasture, his slouch hat casting dark shadows over his rugged features, Dale held Jezebel's reins in one hand and rested the other over her shoulders.

All around them, the people of the Pilbara wished him good luck and cheered him to a sound victory. All they needed now was his opponent. "Maybe he won't show up."

Dale squeezed her shoulder. "He'll show."

Paul appeared out of the crowd and checked Dale's saddle and pack. "Are you sure about this, mate? We can still call it off, you know."

Dale scoffed. "Your confidence is reassuring. Honestly."

"You know that's not what I meant." Paul cast his eyes to the grass-covered earth and settled his hands on narrow hips. When he raised his face again, he stared into Dale's eyes with a determined, profound glare. "You're out of practice. It's been a long time since you've spent any serious time in the saddle."

"Too right. But the time I spent was more than any endurance race Gerald has ever seen. Do you think that blighter could have taken his horse three days across the *Sai-nai* without so much as a thimble of water? Not in his lifetime, I'll tell you."

"You've got a point there. Then again, it's not something I would have chosen given half a bleedin' chance. You did pack enough water, didn't you?"

Dale laughed. "I did."

A soft rumble moved across the spectators and a passage formed in their center. Surrounded by five of his friends and mounted on his dapple-gray gelding, Gerald Brown cut an imposing figure riding in their direction. But in a hundred lifetimes, he could never match Dale for strength—in character or stamina.

When Gerald came within several feet of them, he drew his mount to a halt and tipped his hat back on his forehead. "You still want to go through with it, then?" He nodded at Jezebel.

"Obviously," Dale answered at the same time he gathered his reins to mount.

"This is your last chance to back out. Forfeit now and I'll take Emily's half of the station and call it even. I'll take Emily in payments."

Dale's back stiffened and a muscle in his jaw jumped. Rage poured out of him like a tangible thing, so frightening it tempted her to step back. Instead, she slid closer and ran her hand over his shoulder.

"Rack off, Gerald!" Emily shouted. "You're racing for half ownership of this station and that's all you're racing for."

Dale glanced into Emily's eyes with a mixture of pride and something she couldn't identify.

"So, you haven't told her the new arrangement? Oh, this is rich." Gerald sneered. "Go on, tell her. Tell her what you're willing to trade for her."

Emily narrowed her eyes on Dale. "What in the world is he talking about, Dale?"

"I meant to tell you, but I didn't want you to worry about it. It's nothing, really."

"Nothing?" Gerald feigned a gasp. "If it's nothing, then sign the bloody thing over to me and we'll forego all this race business."

"Be quiet, you bastard," Paul announced. To Dale, he whispered, "Go on, mate. Tell her. It's not going to make a bit of difference anyway."

Emily dropped her hand and waited. The crowd had fallen into a hush. Only the cry of an eagle somewhere overhead and the rush of the nearby river pierced the silence. "Tell me what?"

Dale's eyes caressed her face a moment before he palmed her cheek. "We re-negotiated the wager a bit."

"I gathered that." Emily stared into Dale's eyes and read love and risk in the abyss. "Oh, no. Tell me you didn't."

"I—"

"You wagered the entire station?" Emily twisted out of his reach and buried her forehead in her hands. Her mind spun in circles. She dropped her tightly fisted hands to her side and stared at Dale. "Why? What would possess you to do such a thing? If you lost half, you would still keep your home and your land. Now you risk . . . everything!"

"Not everything, love." He closed the distance between them with one long stride and captured her. "I couldn't risk you. If I lose, so what? We'll leave. We'll move to America and race your horses. As long as we're together, I haven't lost anything." The truth shone in his eyes, making her heart swell.

"I love you, Dale Winters, but sometimes, you drive me completely mad!"

"I hate to break up this tender moment, but have either of you considered you might actually win the damned race?" Paul clapped Dale on the back and clicked his teeth. "However, in order to save the bloody day, you have to get on your horse."

Dale pressed a fast, forceful kiss to Emily's lips, winked, and leapt on Jezebel as if he were a boy on holidays. "Let's get started then. Gerald?"

"About bleedin' time." Gerald led the way to the starting point, just outside the pasture.

Dale joined him there while Matt climbed onto the bed of a wagon and raised his hands over his head. The crowd gathered in a wide arc behind the riders and watched with rapt attention.

Matt cleared his throat and his meaty jowls shook. "Welcome, friends. Now, about this race. It's been a while since we've had a race of this magnitude, so I want to remind everyone what, exactly, should happen. We start and end here. The course will take the riders twenty miles into the Great Sandy Desert where they will circle Flat Rock and return sometime tomorrow afternoon.

"To verify the parties reach the rock, we sent Old Man Kincaid out there last night. He'll be watching. Other than that, there is only the matter of the prize. At stake is the Castle Winters Sheep Station—some of the most prime sheep grazing land in the Pilbara. Are the riders ready?"

Matt drew a pistol and held it over his head.

Dale sat his horse as if he owned the world. His proud shoulders were relaxed and strong against the early morning light. He wiped a hand over his face then scratched his chin. As if he sensed her eyes on him, he turned. A smile parted his lips and he tossed her a wink. When he turned back to Matt, he shouted, "I'm ready."

Gerald echoed the comment and shifted in his saddle.

A sudden wave of dizziness washed over Emily. She swayed, only to find Paul directly behind her when his hands gently grasped her arms. "Will he be all right, Paul?"

"Aye. He will now."

A gunshot rang out like thunder from God.

Chapter Seventeen

Sweat poured over Dale's heated skin. It drenched his shirt and rivulets cascaded from his face like the great falls in the Chidester Range. The sun scorched the barren landscape in what could only be an imitation of Hell itself. All around him, the desert stretched in an endless sea of sparse, pale grass and red soil. The wind, what there was of it, only served to shift the oven-like temperatures around his baking flesh. Even the glare of the sun burned his eyes beneath the brim of his hat. In the distance, a willy-willy, the highly turbulent concentration of circulating air, tore across the plain in a cyclone that reached higher and higher into the bright blue sky.

In another few hours, the sun would seek its own shelter from the heat and he could rest. But for the time being, he pushed onward, eastward, searching the desert he once knew like his own hand for any sign of Flat Rock. A man could get lost in the Great Sandy Desert and despite the deeply rooted flora that managed to eke life out of the dry, unforgiving terrain, death hovered only inches away. Watching. Waiting.

A ragged, yellow dingo darted from behind a bush and bolted to the west, leaving behind a low stream of rose-hued dust.

Dale stopped Jezebel and dismounted. He glanced behind him for any sign of Gerald.

When they'd started, Gerald had kept pace with him for few miles. But as the sun had climbed to its zenith, his competition had failed to account for the severe rise in temperature. While Dale slowed his pace and conserved his horse's energy with frequent, short rests for water, Gerald had maintained an even trot.

Five hours later, Dale had passed Gerald and his gray without comment.

Gerald would have recovered by now, however, and could be making up his lost time. If he was, Dale couldn't see it. The only thing moving in the expanse of world behind him was the swirling heat.

With no sign of Gerald, Dale took off his hat, hung it on his saddle and wiped his forehead with his sleeve. He pulled a canteen of water out of his pack and shook it. Almost empty. A sneer formed on his lips while he unstopped the canister and put it to his mouth. The leather saddlebags in which he carried more than a dozen identical canteens had prevented the metal rim from absorbing the sun and burning his lips, but the water inside was distinctly warm. It would replenish his body, but did little to refresh it. He rinsed his mouth and spat the water out. He pulled on the canteen again and, this time, forced himself to swallow.

Jezebel whinnied and swung her head around to glare at him.

"You're thirsty as well, aren't you, girl?" Dale retrieved his hat, poured the rest of the water into it and held it beneath her muzzle. "There you go."

A few quick swallows and the hat was empty. Dale slapped it back in place and gathered the reins. "We'll have another go in an hour or so, Jez. You just keep up the good work."

He climbed back into the saddle and studied the horizon. He would continue east for another few miles then, when he reached the dry river bed where he and Joel had camped the summer before he'd left for the academy, he'd turn north. He should reach Flat Rock by nightfall, no sweat.

⚘ 🦒 ⚘

Emily stared at the moon as if she could reach out and touch it. She wished she could, considering it was the only link she had to Dale. Somewhere out in the desert—alone—Dale might be looking up at the same moon. Thinking of her with the same powerful love with which she thought of him.

Or he could be hurt.

Or ill from massive dehydration.

"Oh, I hate this. I really do." She hugged herself and rubbed her upper arms with quick, impatient strokes. "I want him home."

Paul rocked back and forth in one of the porch chairs, his boots on the railing and the front two legs of the chair several precarious inches off the floor. "He's fine, love. Don't you worry about a thing. The desert around these parts might be hot, but they've got nothing on the *Sai-nai.*"

Emily allowed her hands to drop to her sides and forced herself to sit in the chair beside Paul. "Was it truly terrible?"

"Oh, it was terrible all right. Probably worse on the mounts than us, though."

She smiled. Like Dale, Paul would think of the horses before himself. "I've seen photographs of the desert in Palestine and Egypt. They aren't like here, are they?"

"No, ma'am. We're a tropical paradise in comparison. When we made our way to Beersheba, we spent more than a few days crossing nothing but empty sand. The sun on our backs like a branding iron most of the day and in our faces the rest. And barely any water to speak of, so we gave what we had to our horses."

"That was nice of you." She did her best to suppress a chuckle.

"Like hell it was. If the horses gave out, we'd all have died. At least this way, they could've carried out our dead."

Any hint of mirth filtered out of her like tiny streams of water over river rocks. "How awful."

"Aye. But we made it through, and just in time, too. We took Beersheba the next day." He winked. "Then we had all the water we needed."

"And Joel was killed."

Paul let the chair drop to the floor, leaned forward and rested his elbows on his knees. "Joel led the charge. He was so bleedin' cracked when it came to that war. He was born to be a hero and he lived up to the task. He was injured in the fighting, but would have lived."

"I know. Charles told me about the bomb."

Silence fell over the porch. It simply didn't seem right to speak anymore and Emily settled back into the chair. After a moment, she allowed a weak smile. "So, what you're telling me is that Dale is fine in the Great Sandy Desert and I'm worrying over nothing."

Paul laughed. "Too right. He knows this land like he knows his own name. And if I know him, he's sitting at Flat Rock, gabbing with Old Man Kincaid and having the time of his life."

"I hope you're right."

In the pastures around the house, their guests sat in front of white, rectangular tents and a distant murmur spoke of easy banter and good friendships. Every so often, someone laughed above the others or the sound of a clanging pot would rise above the constant murmur.

Everyone, to the man, woman and child, had cheered for Dale when Matt had started the race that morning. They'd all stayed to greet him when he returned. If Dale had had any doubt about his worth in the world before this morning, he shouldn't have a single one now.

Well, almost everyone. There were the five of Gerald's friends who had skulked around the station for most of the day. She hadn't seen any of them in a few hours, she suddenly realized. Of course, they'd camped further away from the house, which proved that even addle-brained twits could manage common sense every so often.

Still, she couldn't help but wonder what, if anything, they'd been up to all day.

"Paul? Have you seen any of those men who rode in with Gerald?" She threw Paul a glance and found him with his hat lowered over his eyes and his head tilted backward at an awkward angle. Just when she opened her mouth to repeat her question, a loud snore emanated from his partially opened mouth.

She nudged him awake and he started.

"What?"

"You fell asleep. Why don't you go up to your room? It's late."

Paul raised his fisted hands over his head in a long, loud stretch. "You should do the same."

"I can't sleep. I'm too worried. I think I'll go for a *limp* and make sure our little city has everything its citizens need."

"I should go with you, then. You remember what Dale said about leaving you alone."

"I remember. But Gerald isn't anywhere near here, and

his little band has disappeared for the night. I'll be fine."

"Be careful, just the same. I'll see you in the morning."

Paul went into the house while Emily negotiated the stairs leading to the front yard. At least she hadn't been dizzy in quite some time. Her leg still ached, but on the whole she mended well. After a quick check on the townspeople who camped in every available space on the grounds, she meandered to the barn. Once inside, she clucked and Apache spun in his stall. He leaned his long, black face over the rail and Emily pulled a few pieces of sugar from her pocket. "Do you miss your gal, 'Pach?"

He seemed to nod, but really only nosed about her hand for another treat.

"I miss them, too."

A shuffling sound from the back of the barn caught her attention and she frowned. "Who's there?"

Only the sudden, blowing breath from her horse answered her.

She followed the echo of the noise to the rear stall and glanced over the railing. One of Gerald's boys, Roger Mortimer, reclined against a mound of fresh hay and stared at her with hard, black eyes.

"What are you doing in here?" She threw open the stall and pointed to the door. "Out. I don't want you in here stinking up the pla—"

A rough, callused hand covered her mouth while a thick, heavy arm wrapped around her torso, pinning her arms to her sides. She struggled, but Roger withdrew a pistol from the waistband of his trousers and pointed it at her head.

"That'll be just enough of that, Emily. Be a good sheila and tell us how much you heard."

The dirty fingers lifted and she filled her lungs with enough air to scream. Instantly, the hand fell into place again.

"We won't be having none of that. You tell us quiet like what you heard and we'll let you go."

She twisted in the grasp, but it seemed the more she fought, the tighter the muscled band became. Finally, she froze. Her eyes felt as if they might fall right out of her skull and her limbs filled with jam.

"If Jacob here moves his hand, are you going to scream?"

She shook her head.

The man nodded, cocked his gun, and the hand disappeared a second time.

"I don't know what you're talking about."

"Sure you do. You came into the barn just as my partner here and I were discussing a matter of some importance. I'll ask you nice one more time. What did you hear?"

"Nothing, I swear it. I have no idea what you were talking about." *Please, let me go.*

The man placed the barrel of the gun to her forehead.

✦ 🐎 ✦

Night approached and the world turned dark. Dale reached

Flat Rock at dusk, his mind and body exhausted. Old Man Kincaid often claimed to have single-handedly tamed the great American West. The easy manner with which he stood beside a cookfire, his baggy strides half hanging off his narrow hips and his shirt unbuttoned to his navel, almost made Dale believe it. The stock of Kincaid's prized Colt Revolver peeked from the worn leather gun-belt and holster drawn around his thinning frame.

Dale smiled. Old Man Kincaid had been a miner in his youth. He'd forever lamented the fact he'd spent his fortunes on a woman in San Francisco. He wandered the desert and Australia's unnamed *Interior* looking for a new claim. His skin bore the craggy lines of a man who'd spent most of his life out of doors, but his eyes were wide, clear, and as blue as the summer sky. Wild gray hair swept around his hollow cheeks as the evening blast-furnace kicked on in the form of northward breeze.

Thunder rumbled in the distance and a colony of bats winged overhead.

"You're the first here, son. How're you doing?" Kincaid's rounded lips smacked over gums devoid of teeth.

"Not too bad. Have you found your gold yet?"

The older man's spindly legs shuffled on the soft, dusty ground and sent a small cloud of dust around his ankles. "I'm gettin' close. Don't you mind me, none. I made something to stick to your ribs. You could probably stand a swig of something besides water hot enough to brew tea in a London fancy-house, too."

He'd love a coldie, but no chance of that out here in the Bush. He settled for bedding Jezebel down where she could graze on the clumps of desert grass around Flat Rock—a huge expanse of sandstone large enough to park a dozen wagons. Kincaid had set up camp a good twenty feet from the rock, which collected the sun's heat all day and served as an oven most of the night. Unlike the *Sainai*, which could turn from a furnace to an icebox with the setting of the sun, the Great Sandy Desert retained most of its warmth all through the night.

After a tasty dinner of Dale-didn't-want-to-know-what, he reclined and laid the back of his head on his saddle. The night loomed over him like a great sheet of black velvet. A few stars peeked from behind the high clouds and streaks of lightning danced on the horizon as an approaching storm rumbled its way across the desert. Kincaid slept a few feet away, his loud, grating snore interspersed with muted ramblings.

He'd been in camp for almost three hours and still no sign of Gerald Brown. It was always possible he'd been injured or given up and turned back to Castle Winters, but based on the man's greed, Dale doubted it. He'd probably made his own camp somewhere among the scrub brush.

That was fine with Dale.

Overhead, the clouds parted and a brilliant, white moon shone through the black. Huge and full, he studied the variations in the surface. An image of Emily's face crossed it. Her hair wild and tangled around her cheeks, her head thrown back, and the lines of her neck exposed for the taking. His body hardened with desire.

The first thing he was going to do when he finally put this wager nonsense to bed was make love to her until neither of them could walk. A smile formed on his lips despite his weariness. He'd be surprised if either of them saw the outside of her bedroom for a month.

But first, he had to finish the bloody race.

He had to admit it felt good to be back on a horse. And, if he were completely honest with himself, he was thrilled Emily had forced his hand. What if he'd never encountered her? What if Charles had never written those letters and made a young girl, thousands of miles away, fall in love with a boy she'd never met? Whatever forces in the universe had fallen into place, he would do well to remember how close he'd come to walking through a living death for the next sixty years. And that's what his life would have been without Emily. A living death.

He owed more than that to Joel. He owed it to his brother to live his life for both of them.

All it had taken for him to realize it was the annoying persistence of a tiny woman with a huge heart.

He had no idea what the future would hold for them, but whatever it was, they'd face it together.

Dale allowed his eyes to drift closed. A rock jabbed his back. At least Emily was comfortable, and safe, in her wide, soft bed.

✶ 🐎 ✶

The putrid aroma of Jacob's hand over Emily's mouth stole what little air managed to slip past his fingers. They weren't really going to kill her. Not right here in the barn around which dozens of the neighbors slept.

Were they?

The crazed, frightened glint in Roger's eyes argued with her. He was desperate. He would do anything. But why? What had she failed to overhear that would make them take the giant leap from lazy and less-than-savory to lunatics bent on her murder?

"Scream and I swear to God I'll kill you quick."

Emily nodded.

Jacob removed his hand again and she suckled her bottom lip where he'd bruised it. The bitter taste of blood made her queasy, not to mention the foul taste he'd left behind. Instantly, she put as much distance between herself and Jacob as she could manage while her gaze traveled the barn. She searched for any weapon within arm's reach and found nothing. She was too far away from the wall where Dale hung the tack, and his work table, adorned with any number of sharpened tools, was all the way at the other end. Could she make a run for it? Would she reach the heavy door in time and manage to swing it open before they caught her?

She doubted it.

"What do you think we should do with her?" Roger

tipped his hat back with the barrel of his pistol.

Jacob stood behind her and shrugged. "We can't let her go. She'll find Campbell and tell him everything."

"No, no, I won't. I promise. I didn't hear anything to tell."

"Quiet, you," Roger spat. "You would say that, wouldn't you? But we can't risk believing you, now can we?" He seemed to search the great cavern of his mind for a moment before shaking his head in obvious disbelief. "We'll just have to take her back to camp with us and wait for Gerald."

Jacob slithered forward until his chest brushed against her back again. His hand stroked her hair and goosebumps jumped from her flesh. "That might not be a bad idea, mate. We could just *take* her with us."

The next moments rushed past her in a blur of arms, legs, and curses. Paul catapulted over the outside stall door and landed like a great cat behind Roger. He kicked Roger's legs from beneath him, shock and surprise evident in her assailant's wide eyes and half-opened mouth. When Roger regained his balance, he spun to the right, but Paul met the reaction with a solid blow to Roger's jaw, reinforced by the direction Roger had turned.

Jacob, already so close to Emily his stench choked her, wrapped both of his arms around her and pinned her to his chest. She lifted her knee and slammed her heel onto the top of Jacob's foot. He immediately released her and she turned to place a well-aimed kick to his groin. He joined his companion on the barn floor, writhing like a large, round snake.

"Are you hurt?" Paul grasped her shoulders and forced her to face him.

"I . . . No, I don't think so. But something is terribly wrong. They're up to something."

"First things first."

Paul gathered a few lengths of thin leather from the work table and with Emily's help tied Jacob's hands and feet. Roger, still unconscious, proved easier to bind, so Emily tied him herself while Paul struggled to position Jacob's massive, bloated body against the wall.

"They're planning something, Paul. Something wicked. They thought I overheard them and they were rather concerned about the whole thing."

Paul stood over Jacob with a wide stance, the gun in his belt and his arms folded over his chest. "Fess up, mate. You're caught like a dingo in a trap, so you might as well tell us what's going on."

"Bugger off." Jacob spat and glared at Paul with a greasy sneer.

With a slow shake of his head, Paul clicked his teeth. "Em? Do you have any honey?"

"Pardon?"

Jacob's eyes grew large and he managed to scoot closer to the wall despite his hands being tied behind his back.

"Honey. You know, honey? That stuff bees make?"

"I think so. Why?"

"I was just thinking about an ant colony about two miles south of here. So huge I could see it from the air the last time I flew over. Massive thing, really. Must be a couple of million ants. The big red ones with pinchers the size of your hand."

Jacob shuddered and inched down the wall on his bottom and the heels of his feet. "Now, you don't mean that, Paul. We're mates, you and me, right?"

"I don't know, Jake. Are we mates? It looked to me like you were going to be rather nasty to my friend, Emily. And I think you have something you need to tell me."

"Rack off. Gerald will have my arse if I tell you anything."

Paul crouched low and rested his elbows on his knees before finding a strand of straw and picking at it with his fingertips. He whispered in a voice so low Emily had to strain to hear, yet at the same time his words had the impact of an echo off the Alps. "You need to worry about what I'll do with your arse, Jake. Because if you don't tell me what I want to know, I'm going to strip you naked, cover your privates with honey and drop you in the middle of a giant anthill."

The blood drained from Jacob's face leaving behind a sickly gray pallor. His eyes bulged on either side of his meaty nose and his lips quivered. "It's . . . it's Gerald. He's planning to do Dale in during the race. He'll make it look like an accident, like Dale's horse spooked or something . . ."

Emily's heart leapt into her throat and threatened to choke her. She stared at Paul who seemed remarkably calm considering what he'd just heard. His stony expression never wavered, never faltered.

"Where? When?"

"I don't know and that's the God's honest truth. I swear it."

Paul gained his feet and wiped his hands on his trousers. "Emily, go rouse Matt Macomber and bring him here. These two gentlemen need an escort into Marble Bar—the sooner the better."

"What about Dale?" Emily's voice squeaked, but her shock was quickly giving way to fury and fear. "We have to find him. Dear God, he could already be—"

"No. I'm sure Gerald would wait until the second day, after Dale passed Flat Rock whole and hearty. Dale's not riding in the dark, so my money is on sometime tomorrow. Please, go find Matt and bring him here."

Emily tore from the barn and wound her way through the many tents and sleeping bags placed in a haphazard grid around the pasture. Matt's family had elected to stay in a tent as well, except for Rachel who slept in one of the guest rooms.

Dale could be dead! He could be injured, in pain. The thought strangled her. He could be lying in the desert, his fragile body exposed and helpless to any manner of nocturnal beasts. By the time she reached Matt's tent, tears dampened her cheeks and her throat had grown raw from holding them back. Her neck ached and burned.

"Matt. Matt, wake up!" She threw the tent flap aside, hurried to where the huge man slept and shook his exposed shoulder, covered in striped pajamas. "Wake up!"

With a snore and a grumble, he turned to his back, tossed one hand over his face and suddenly sat up. "What the devil is going on?"

"Matt, it's me. Emily. You must come quickly. Dale's in trouble."

Chapter Eighteen

"I'm going. I dare you to just try and stop me!" Emily marched to the front door only to find Paul had blocked her path. She looked from his stern expression back to Matt, who stood in the parlor with his wife and Doctor Morgan from Port Hedland.

Paul took her shoulders in large, firm, but gentle hands and led her back to the parlor before urging her into her recently vacated chair. She couldn't sit. Each time she did, her bones jostled in her limbs and her soul came crashing down around her. The sun had been up for more than an hour. Why weren't they out there? Why weren't they searching for Dale?

"You're not strong enough yet. Hell, if you were, wouldn't you have raced yourself?"

"That hardly matters now, Paul. This isn't some ridiculous race. This is Dale's life we're talking about. Not you, not anyone, is going to keep me from finding him and warning him."

"You can't just ride off into the *Tamani*. That desert has killed more men than smallpox and Gerald combined. Blue is packing Matt's horse, and when he's finished Matt will search for Dale."

"No!" She leapt from the chair again and paced from one corner of the room to the other. Everything in the room, from the leather-bound books on the shelves, to the sideboard covered in china and silver, to the intricate flooring was a blur. "I'm going, damn it. I'm perfectly fine!"

The doctor cleared his throat. "All in all, I don't see the harm, really. If she feels strong enough and her leg doesn't pain her too greatly, she can certainly ride if she wishes. I wouldn't recommend it, but then again, if she's going to place herself under this kind of duress being left behind . . ."

Paul glared at the doctor. "Thanks, doc. Appreciate that."

"Ha! You see? You just don't want me to go. Doctor Morgan says I can and you can bet your life I'm going!"

She stomped out of the house to prepare her horse and ran into Blue on the porch.

"Apache is ready to go when you are, Emily."

"But how did . . . never mind. Thank you, Blue. This saves us a great deal of time."

Paul, Matt, and the others filed onto the porch behind her. She didn't turn around for fear she might actually strangle Paul.

"All right. You can come along. But you stay with

Matt, do you understand?"

"Of course. I'm not stupid."

A few minutes later, Emily sat atop Apache, pulling the reins and trying to steady the anxious animal. Even he knew something wasn't right. Every time he pranced, liquid fire poured through her left hip. But that didn't matter. She certainly wasn't going to mention it to either of her search companions. She had to find Dale before it was too late.

Paul pulled on a leather cap which molded to his head like a second skin. "I'll fly overhead and if I see anything, I'll find you and waggle."

"Waggle?"

"Aye. I'll dip my wings back and forth a few times if I've found him and there's trouble. If I found him and he's fine, I'll fly a circle over you."

"You're sure you'll be able to find us?"

Apache finally settled and chewed on his bit.

"I'll find you. Other than a few bands of wild 'roos and the occasional feral camel, the two of you, Dale and Gerald should be the only things moving."

"All right then. We're going to follow the designated route and hopefully we'll be able to see their tracks. With any luck, we'll find Dale safe and sound on his way home."

Please, let me find him well.

She kicked Apache to a gallop and tore away from Castle Winters.

It seemed hours passed before she reached the edge of

the pasture lands and faced the Great Sandy Desert in all its deadly glory. Hours since Paul had flown overhead and disappeared into the white morning light.

Finally, Emily found a set of horse tracks and kept her eyes trained on them while Apache picked his way up the first of many dunes. Every few feet the tracks disappeared into a clump of grass or skirted a scrubby bush, but she managed to find them again on the other side. When she crested the dune, she stopped and raised one hand to block the sun. Matt arrived at her side and mimicked the gesture.

"Nothing," he stated flatly. "Not a bloody sign of him."

A huge dust cloud traveled across the desert floor to the north. *Kangaroos.*

But no sign of Dale. No sign of anyone.

Emily's heart raced. "I'm not giving up. We haven't been out here very long."

"Aye, but I'd hoped to see something. Anything."

"Come on. We have a lot of ground to cover."

Paul's plane roared in the distance. Searching the sky, she found him against a fluffy white cloud. One of the bright yellow wings dipped in their direction. She waved. Paul leveled the aircraft and a moment later he was little more than a black dot again.

For the next several hours, Emily and Matt painstakingly followed the trail. She only hoped Jezebel had made the tracks and not Gerald's gray. Of course, either way, she would find what she sought. Some way to save Dale.

The sun arced and the higher it climbed, the more

she burned. She was used to heat. Arizona wasn't much cooler, but there was something different about Australian heat. Something that sapped her strength and stole her balance. Or maybe she simply hadn't recovered enough from her illness. Maybe the poison in her blood affected her ability to focus. After a brief rest to consume a few mouthfuls of warm, tasteless water she pushed on.

Emily had lost count of how many dunes they'd crossed. They'd just reached the top of another one when Matt yanked on his reins. "There. To the northeast."

A slender cloud chased someone across the desert. Matt reached into his pack and withdrew a long, slender glass. He opened the telescoping device and raised it to his eye. Squinting with the other, he trailed it over the landscape until he stopped, backed up, and then focused on something. "That bloody bastard."

"What do you see?"

"Gerald Brown."

"Let me see," Emily demanded, her hand outstretched for the glass.

Matt handed it to her, but never took his eyes off the distant rider. "He's headed in this direction. Like a bat out of hell."

Emily found him through the lens and studied his pace. He rode with an urgent bent; a man on a mission. He wasn't just racing, he was targeting something.

Her hands trembling, Emily fought to keep the glass still. She anticipated Gerald's course, inched the glass forward until she found him. Although the distance was difficult to judge in such a huge expanse of nothing, it appeared as if Dale rode less than three miles ahead of Gerald. Jezebel cantered across the desert as if she had all the time in the world. At this rate, Gerald would catch up to Dale in a matter of minutes.

They couldn't warn him in time.

Matt's horse pranced in place and he patted her neck. His mount was durable and strong. It could never reach Dale before Gerald did, however.

But Apache . . .

Apache could close the distance much faster, especially once she leveled out on the desert floor where the dunes were farther apart and not nearly as high.

Something flashed near the horizon and the roar of Paul's engine vibrated in her spine. She closed her eyes and bit her bottom lip. She couldn't think.

Paul dipped once and then leveled off. He adjusted his direction until he flew directly at her. Straight and level. Of course, that was only because Gerald hadn't found Dale.

Yet.

⚔ 🐎 ⚔

Where the hell was Gerald Brown?

Dale had been in the saddle for more than seven hours. He basically backtracked his own trail, making his way home. He was anxious to return to Emily, but had decided not to tax his horse too much in the oppressive, mind-numbing heat. Not now that he'd won, for all intents and purposes. But he'd expected to find Gerald somewhere along the way. Some sign he'd come through, perhaps during the night. But only one set of hoof prints marred the desert's dry, crusty surface.

The closer he came to Marble Bar, the stronger his suspicions became concerning Gerald's disappearance. Had he been injured or run out of water, Dale would have found some indication by now. Unless the whanker hadn't moved from the shade of the termite mound under which he'd sheltered when Dale originally passed him. Dale wouldn't arrive at that point for at least another thirty minutes.

That was a possibility. He might have simply given up and gone home, as well.

No. Gerald was many things, few of them decent or kind, but he wasn't a quitter. He was out there. Somewhere.

Something caught his attention from the corner of his eye and he spun toward what had seemed like a dark shadow. Gerald Brown raced at him with his reins between his teeth and both hands lifted in front him like some kind of demon. Before Dale had a chance to react, Gerald spit out his reins and threw himself off his horse. He impacted Dale's chest with the force of an artillery round, knocking both of them to the ground and sending Jezebel screaming onto her side.

Dale landed on his back and his lungs emptied. Gasping for breath, he gathered Gerald's shirtfront in his fists and rolled them over. Just when Gerald's back made contact with the earth, Dale gulped the sweet, broiling desert air. Gerald lashed out with one hand and wrapped his long fingers around Dale's throat.

Dale knocked Gerald's hand away with one arm and struck him in the jaw with his right fist. Gerald's face shot to the left and blood spurted from his bottom lip.

"What the bloody hell are you doing?" Dale shouted. "Are you cracked?"

Instead of a reply, Dale earned a fist to his left cheek. He tumbled off of Gerald, who scrambled to his feet and immediately kicked him in the ribs. Dale rolled, choking on the impact of Gerald's foot and the rising dust.

He rolled two more full rotations farther than the force had sent him and staggered to his feet. The additional distance gave him enough time to prepare for the next blow. Crouched low, Dale reached for the knife tied to his right calf. It was gone.

He scanned the nearby saltbrush and found the blade glinting a few feet away.

Bloody hell.

Gerald charged again, his eyes blazing and his mouth set in a horrific grimace. He *was* insane. Dale had fought wild animals and enemy soldiers, but he'd never encountered anything as unpredictable as a crazed human. He swung his fist and sent Gerald flying backward to land on his ass in the center of a large scrub. Unwilling to give Gerald a chance to recover, Dale lunged. Once he'd pinned the bastard to the earth, he landed a series of well-placed punches to Gerald's jaw and cheek. Blood oozed from Gerald's nose and his left eye was swollen and blood-shot. "Have you had enough? Crikey!"

"Get off me, ya bastard!"

"Be still." Dale remained in place, straddling Gerald's ribs with his knees. The afternoon sun scorched his neck and boiled the sweat that had soaked his clothing. He wiped a few droplets from his eyes and the salt stung them.

He tested his lip and when he drew away his finger-tips, blood stained them. His side ached as well and he wouldn't be surprised if more than one rib had been broken in the skirmish. Finally, he stood and immediately reclaimed his knife. He held it in a loose grip, pointed it at Gerald and sneered. "Get up."

Gerald lumbered to his feet.

A distinctive roar thundered overhead. Paul's plane approached from the southwest and banked in the beginning of a slow circle. He'd never been so glad to see a plane in his life. He waved and the wings dipped.

Dale returned his attention to Gerald with the intention of herding him to his horse and tying him to the saddle for the long ride back to Marble Bar. Instead, he found himself standing in front of the barrel of a gun.

Not just any gun. A Colt Single Action Army Model 1873 with gold inlaid into the barrel. Old Man Kincaid's most prized possession.

"What did you do, Brown?" Dale's throat burned and

blood rushed through his ears with deafening clarity. "You son-of-a-bitch!"

"That old man was dying more every day anyway." He drew back the hammer.

Each click of the meticulously cared-for revolving cylinder reverberated somewhere between Dale's soul and the weight of the heat on his shoulders. "Put the gun down. You don't want to do this."

Gerald laughed and shook his head. "You think I don't, mate? I've wanted to do this for as long as I can remember. You and your brother, so bleedin' high and mighty, prancing around the territory as if you owned it."

"Just put the gun down. We can work this out. Where's the old man?"

"That bastard got what he deserved. Put him out of his misery, really."

Dale's heart sank into what could only be the very fires of hell. Rage fed the flames. He still had his knife and he tightened his grip.

"You can't believe you'll get away with any of this, can you, mate? You've done murder now."

"I had some time to think about that while I caught up to you. You see, I had originally planned to break your bloody neck and make it look like you fell off your horse. Hell, everyone knows you don't hardly ride anymore. But then Kincaid got in my way and I had to shoot him. So I had to come up with another plan." Gerald sighed, licked his lips where tiny white flecks collected in the corner, and his eyes doubled in size. "Imagine my surprise when I arrived at Flat Rock to find you . . . standing over Old Man Kincaid with his gun in your hand and him dead." Gerald raised the barrel of the gun even with Dale's chest, and his trigger finger trembled. "I'm only doing my civic duty, you understand."

With a flick of his wrist, Dale sent the knife flying through the seemingly endless distance between himself and Gerald. It stuck just below Gerald's ribs on his left side at the exact moment the gun fired. Gerald dropped the Colt and his hand gripped the exposed hilt.

Dale's leg exploded with a burst of light and white-hot agony. He stifled a scream. It was as if someone had imbedded a branding iron beneath the skin. And then twisted it. He collapsed under his own weight.

Gerald pulled the knife from his torso with his free hand. Blood dripped from the blade even as it stained his shirt in an ever-widening circle, turning the collected dust to an obscene kind of mud. "Would you look at that?" He chuckled.

Dale gritted his teeth. The man had a knife hole in his chest and he laughed. Dale was as good as dead at this rate. He had to get his hands on that gun. Only one force drove him; he would live to see Emily.

No, he would live to love her.

Gerald collapsed to one knee, balancing himself with a blood-covered hand on the ground beside his boot. The gun shone brightly only inches from his fingertips.

A fierce cry erupted from his chest—a howl born of some power he hadn't known he possessed. Ignoring the injury, the blood pouring from his leg, he surged forward.

The world seemed to hover on the edge of some great cliff—watching, waiting. Finally, his hands wrapped around the gun, slick with a mixture of his blood and Gerald's. Gerald tackled him and they fell to the ground in a heap of twisted limbs. Overhead, an eagle cried.

The gun fired again.

✦ 🐎 ✦

Emily crouched low over Apache's neck while he flew over the rough desert landscape. She'd left Matt far behind and his voice had long since been lost in the rush of wind past her ears. Paul had circled the area twice and finally descended from the expanse of sky in an attempt to land among the scrub brush. Eyes trained on Dale and Gerald, she squinted against the sting of the reflected light and wind.

With each thundering hoofbeat, the two struggling men grew closer; larger. Less than a half-mile or so separated her from the melee.

Finally, she could make out the haggard, worn expressions on their faces. Closer. Only a little bit . . . closer!

A third gunshot rang. Apache halted and reared. She gripped the saddle horn with both hands and squeezed her knees into the hard leather of her saddle. When he landed, her body screamed in protest at the jolt.

She ignored the cry and focused her attention on the two perfectly still forms lying in a tangled heap only a stone's throw away.

Fear strangled her. She swallowed hard against it and threw herself off Apache's back. She raced to Dale's side on legs that seemed to have disappeared from beneath her. She fell to her knees and wrestled Gerald's frame off of him. On his back, he lay with eyes closed, his long black lashes spiking against his sculpted cheeks. What seemed like a great deal of blood soaked his trouser leg and she reached for it to rip away the fabric. Her fingers curled and hovered over the existing, ragged tear and the even more terrifying wound beneath. A wound that wasn't bleeding anymore.

Had he already bled to death? Was she too late? Tears clogged her throat and she choked back a sob. She refocused her attention on his face. "Dale? Can you hear me?"

Nothing. Not so much as a flutter of his eyelids.

She shook his shoulders. "Dale! Please, Dale. Wake up!"

He didn't move.

She released all of the worry and fear, love and obsession that had been her constant companions for as long as she could remember. It poured out of her in screams and cries to the expanse of endless heaven around her. When she finished, her body was drained and only one emotion remained. Her love for Dale. She had never faltered, never given up hope. She laid her head on his chest.

Something brushed at Emily's hair. She swept it away with the back of her hand only to have whatever it was move through the strands again. It was probably a desert mouse, but she didn't care. She would lie here until the earth took them back to the dust from where they'd come. She wouldn't leave him. How could she? He owned her heart.

"Emily?"

Her ears caught the faint whisper and she jerked upright. "Dale? Oh, God, Dale!"

His lashes fluttered and he opened his eyes. Beautiful, clear blue eyes. She laughed through her tears and wiped her eyes.

"It's me. I'm here."

"Help me up."

"No, we should wait for the others."

"Like bloody hell. I want to go home." He raised himself on his elbows and lifted his left hand. A gun glinted in the waning light.

Suddenly, her eyes fell on Gerald's lifeless body. When she'd shoved him away from Dale, he'd rolled to his back. His chest was still and a large, reddish brown circle of blood covered most of his shirtfront. "Is he . . . dead?"

"I certainly hope so." Dale groaned and attempted to gain his feet.

Emily grasped his waist and helped him to his horse. "Stay here. Paul and Matt should be here soon." She turned away to cover Gerald's frame with a blanket she pulled from behind Dale's saddle, but Dale held her in a firm, gentle grip.

"Not so fast." He pulled her against him and her head tilted back.

His lips found hers in a gentle kiss and his fingers grazed her jaw. When he raised his mouth, he wrapped his arms around her back and pressed her against his chest. Tiny shards of light bounced around her veins and she waited for her heart to explode with more joy than she'd ever believed possible.

She could easily spend the rest of her life in his arms. Just like this.

"Emily Castle!" Paul's voice tore through the heat like a whip. "I told you to stay with Matt! What the bloody hell were you thinking, riding into a bleedin' gunfight like some kind of cracked Annie Oakley?"

By the time Paul reached them, Dale had shifted his position and draped one arm over Jezebel's saddle and the other over Emily's shoulders. "Leave off, mate. All's well that end's well, right?"

Paul sighed and nodded in the direction of Dale's injured leg. "You call that well? It looks a bit less than that to me."

"Aye. But I'll heal."

Matt trotted alongside Paul, whipped his hat off his head and wiped his forehead with the back of his sleeve. "Can we go home now?"

✸ 🐎 ✸

Dale lay in his bed, his injured leg above the thin cotton sheet on a stack of feather pillows. A large, white bandage covered most of his thigh. Dale had been lucky. Though it had looked bad, the doctor had said it was only flesh wound. If a bullet of that caliber had found his belly, he would have been killed. Had it found his chest, he would have died instantly.

He turned Kincaid's gun over in his fingers and ran a soft cloth over the shining gold inlays. The whole town had turned out for the old man's funeral. It had been Matt's idea for Dale to keep the gun. *The old man wouldn't have wanted someone young to have it.*

He set the gun aside and picked up a watch and chain. The battered timepiece was made of gold with an intricate design engraved on the dingy outer surface. He clicked the lever and the front snapped open. Inside, the hands were pointed to twenty minutes past four, as they had been ever since Matt had given it to him. Opposite the face was a photograph, wedged inside the casing. A woman with light hair and dark eyes stood next to a man dressed in elegant finery, from the tip of his stove-pipe hat to the shine of his polished boots. The niceties couldn't hide the wild look in the man's eyes, however, and Old Man Kincaid stared back from the picture, his face smooth and his shoulders squared.

The door creaked open and Emily slid into the room with a tray between her hands. His body stirred. Those hands had spent the last four days exploring his body in ways he'd never imagined. Well, he had imagined them, but had been pleasantly surprised with the realization that Emily's imagination was equally as creative. He smiled, but the haunting image of Kincaid and his only love stole some of the curve from his lips.

"What are you thinking about?" She inclined her head and slid him a sidelong glance while she put the tray down on the table beside the bed.

"You, of course."

"You must be terribly bored, then."

"Not hardly. Unlike *some* patients, I'm perfectly content to lie here and heal. I have the best-looking nurse in the entire territory, after all."

If he lived for eternity he could never grow tired of her blush. It stained her neck and cheeks a perfect shade of pink and made her already kissable lips that much more tempting.

She sat on the edge of the bed and pointed to the tray. "Your soup is getting cold."

He laughed. "Good." He paused as a sudden flash of her voice calling him from the darkness echoed somewhere in the back of his mind. "Promise me you'll never leave."

"What?" She studied his lips and he had trouble concentrating on his words.

"I don't want to be alone anymore. Promise me you'll never leave and keep that promise forever."

Her gaze fell to her fingers, knotted in her lap. "I've loved you since I was a little girl. You're the boy who tames dragons. I will never stop loving you, Dale. Never."

His opened his arms. She fell into him and kissed his bare chest. Her fingertips played across him like a wildfire. "I promise I'll love you forever."

He'd finally made a promise he could keep.

Epilogue

Chaos reigned. But it was a controlled chaos and one that was familiar to Blue as he strode into the shearing shed. Outside the long, wooden structure, thousands of sheep waited their turn at the shears. Inside, Dale, Henry Albert, Paul and several others stooped at awkward angles over their current projects in a race to see who would finish their task the fastest.

Each man had fastened himself to the wall behind him with a wide strap that helped to relieve the tension on his lower back, but not by much. At the end of the two weeks dedicated to harvesting the station's wool crop, the men would be more than a little sore. As would those assigned to turn the hand cranks that powered the cutters.

The sheep barely struggled against the seemingly rough treatment they received. Their docile attitudes made the shearers' jobs that much easier, but it was still rough, sweaty work. After he'd drawn the cutters the length of his assigned sheep for the last time, Dale drew himself upright and held his shears above his head. A grin spread over his mouth and life danced in his eyes. Tossing damp, blond strands off his forehead, he released booming laughter. "Top that, mates! What was that, something like two minutes?"

"Rack off!" called Paul from the end of the line, finishing his own sheep. "Closer to five, I reckon."

A chorus of moans, mixed with cheers and several hisses, followed as the shed-hands collected the smooth single pieces of fleece from the shearing boards and spread them on the classing table.

Blue watched the good-natured competition from the shearing shed's open door. At last, everything was as it should be. Over the past few months, Dale had regained that part of himself he'd thought he'd lost forever. His soul had healed and learned to love again.

Emily hurried through the door at the opposite end of the shed. At least, she tried to hurry. Such swift movements seemed difficult for a woman in her condition. It wouldn't be long before she and her husband welcomed their son.

"They're here." She beamed a smile at Dale and waved him forward. "Stop your bragging and get out here!"

"I wasn't bragging."

She scoffed. "Of course you were. Now hurry up!"

Smiling to himself, Blue watched Dale unhook the harness from around his chest before he dodged the long row of shearing boards and classing tables to join Emily.

His expression reminded Blue of a much younger Dale full of hope and anticipation. Dale led his wife outside with one arm draped around her shoulders.

Rather than face the full brunt of the shed's stifling heat, Blue chose to meander around the outside of the building. By the time he reached the stable yard, a small crowd of *Jackaroos* had formed a half-circle around Dale, Emily, and two slick-coated thoroughbreds. One of the horses, an impressive sorrel whose hide shimmered red in the coming sunset, lowered its head and blew against the dust on Dale's boots. The other, a roan, flattened its ears and released a short whinny before backing away from the crowd. Emily struggled against the taut lead while it slipped from her fingers. Obviously concerned that the nervous horse might injure his wife, Dale snatched the lead. Blue grinned when Dale led the animal a few paces to the side—for a good talking to, more than likely. A few softly spoken murmurs, too low to hear, and a gentle stroke of Dale's confident hands on the glossy coat soothed the horse almost at once. Dale glanced at Emily over his shoulder with the gleaming eyes of a child. "You were right, love. They're perfect."

Blue skirted the dispersing throng, stepping out of the path of the groom who led the sorrel to the pasture gate. He leaned against the fence while Emily lumbered her way to Dale and the roan. "I told you," she replied when she reached them. "These horses come from the best lines in Churchill Downs. When we breed them with your Whalers, we're going to create some of the best horses in Australia."

"How could we go wrong?" Dale took Emily's hand and raised it to his lips.

"Oh!" Emily exclaimed, launching forward into Dale's chest.

"What is it? Is something wrong?" He immediately fell to his knees and placed his free hand on her rounded belly.

Blue shook his head and chuckled at the sight. Dale may have overcome many things, but he hadn't been able to free himself from protecting those he loved. It was a wonder he'd even allowed Emily to leave her bed after she'd shared the news of her condition.

She laughed and scooted Dale's hat high on his forehead before she gazed into his eyes. "I'm fine, silly. He kicked, that's all." Guiding his hand, she moved it lower until he cupped her beneath her navel on the left side. "Right there."

Blue watched while Dale's eyes grew wide. Even the horse seemed to sense something amazing and perked its ears. A smile spread across his young friend's mouth and he stared up at his wife with unmistakable awe. "That's bloody fascinating." After a moment, Dale gained his full height and held Emily as close as their child would allow.

To feel the blessed miracle of one's own immortality was indeed fascinating. It was a confirmation and a rare privilege. If anyone would appreciate the gift, Dale would. Blue knew it. He could read it in Dale's eyes every time he looked at his wife or spoke of his child's impending birth.

He would appreciate it as much Blue had, so many seasons ago.

Only Dale would be able to appreciate it longer. Happiness awaited the young family. That much was certain and written in the desert sand.

Sudden sadness gripped Blue's heart like an eagle's talons on a wombat. It ached and festered, even now. Blue's child had died at birth and his wife had joined their daughter within a few days. She'd slept too deeply for even dreams to reach her, and finally, on the fourth day, awakened long enough to say goodbye before the gods took her.

But Blue still remembered, after all these years, what it had felt like to be a father. To wait and plan. To live for another.

Would he ever live like that again? He'd spent the last three days on Tower Rock. The Dreaming had shown him things he couldn't explain—even to himself. For the first time, the Ancestors had spoken of Blue instead of those whose lives he'd been a part of. He had been given secrets regarding his friends, of course, which he would keep to himself. Little snippets that brought joy and pride about Dale's sons and the adventures they would share. He suspected they had been revealed to him for his own peace of mind, however. But it was the images of his own future that made his blood flow a little quicker in his veins. What, exactly, lay ahead for him? The Ancestors had only revealed enough to make wonder and hope exist where none had been.

Regardless, it was time. Whatever the gods had in store for him, Blue knew he wouldn't find it at Castle Winters. Not any longer.

He shoved away from the railing and scanned the station. The house was a home again, and soon it would be filled with laughing children. The sheep operation promised continued success. The horse pasture had been expanded to include pens for the newest American breeding stock.

Dale and Emily stood with their backs to Blue, having already placed the studs in their new homes. Now they visited with Jezebel who leaned against the fence, apparently hoping for a treat. She wasn't disappointed when Emily fed her a cube of sugar while Dale patted her strong back.

Blue turned to the setting sun and walked in the direction the Ancestors had shown him. Miles spread before him in open sky and dust-covered roadways. His land had changed much during his lifetime. But the life forces in the rocks, trees, and rivers remained the same. To his left, the newly sheared sheep bleated and three lambs chased each other through trampled grass. On the other side of the road, a group of horses thudded past him with their long manes flowing like standards. He heard the voice just above the thunder of their hooves, stopped, turned, and waited for Dale to catch up with him.

When Dale reached him, he didn't say anything for a moment. Instead, he glanced at the ground with his arms folded over his chest. Finally, he raised eyes lined with worry and the sun's caress. "You're leaving, aren't you?"

Blue answered him with a smile before he faced the sun again. Silently, he walked toward the future. His own.

CHAPTER ONE
England – Spring, 1243

"There it sits, milord. Just waiting for ye." Ian Douglas sat atop his horse, inspecting the man beside him through half-lidded eyes. A sly grin etched his dirty, bearded face. "We've nae been ridin' hard for five days and nights to just look at it. Ravenstone's done this to his own, and ye should no' feel guilty about takin' what's yers."

"Do you think I don't know that?" Morven Barnett Douglas, Laird of Clan Douglas, snarled in reply.

Ian stared, eyes glazed with greed, toward the thick walls of Morven's former home. The tall, black walls made for an impressive profile against the gray sky. Sitting precariously on the edge of a cliff, the castle looked as if it would fall into the raging sea beyond. But he knew it wouldn't. He spat on the muddy earth. Nearly impenetrable, the castle boasted only one entrance: a guarded portcullis.

Convincing the Douglas to raid the castle had been simple enough in the end. Ian had spent many months designing this raid and its certain effects on his own people. The death of Morven's father had been a catalyst he hadn't expected, but he'd used it well to his own ends. With the old earl dead, Morven had appeared more than eager to pay his homeland a visit they would not forget.

He hid a smirk as he adjusted his saddle in preparation for the attack. Devlin Barnett had taken his knights on campaign, foolishly leaving his home unprotected. Nay. Should he live a thousand years, there would never be a better day for this raid.

Finally, Morven stood in his stirrups and raised his sword above his head, releasing a fierce battle cry from deep in his throat. The column of horses and riders raced with breakneck speed toward the walls of the castle.

As Ian approached the solid walls, the sentry at the portcullis sounded an alarm. The gate creaked free of its restraints. Before it closed Ian jumped inside the outer defenses. Swiping his sword with practiced ease, he let the blade down on the single guard's shoulder. Instinctively, he closed his eyes. His blade found its mark. The warmth of blood on his cheeks soothed him. When he opened his eyes, the guard lay on the ground, his own sword only partly removed from its casing. He spat on the lifeless body. Gripping the heavy ropes attached to the gate, he pulled, clearing the way for his clansmen to follow him into the bailey. His attention shifted to his laird.

Morven rode like a man possessed. His face twisted with rage. His eyes reflected a wrath that could only be borne of hatred. The charger he rode matched his master's fury, stamping wildly at any unfortunate who crossed his path.

Ian smiled. Morven knew where to go, having been raised inside these bloody, English walls. Ian watched as Morven rode his destrier up the chapel steps and through the large doors.

Ian secured the gate open before turning his mount and following his laird.

His laird. He cursed to himself. He should be Laird of Clan Douglas. He would be Laird of Clan Douglas this very night.

"Ye!" Ian pointed his sword to one of his clansmen. "Find the Lady Ravenstone and bring her to me!"

He ignored the frightened pleas of the scurrying crowd. His clansmen herded them into a circle in the center of the bailey, as he made his way through the screaming women and old men toward the chapel.

Ian dismounted, dropping his leather rein. His blood seethed as he entered the dimly lit chamber, the sweet taste of victory hovering on his lips.

The jeweled sword.

It sat atop the altar, on display and unguarded. Like none he had ever seen, the hilt, made of gold and encrusted with gems from every part of the world, winked in the filtered sunlight pouring through the stained glass windows. Pearls, rubies, and diamonds were set into the hilt and scabbard and even in the belt. It was worth a king's ransom, and Ian's mouth watered even as his fingers twitched to grasp it.

But more than gold and jewels, it held the power to slice through the heart of his enemies.

Morven, still seated upon his horse at the foot of the altar, stared at the sword as if he'd never seen it before. Ian grimaced. He'd never believed Morven worthy of such a prize. He believed it less now. The man oozed weakness.

Morven's anger and thirst for vengeance were a boon only to Ian. But Ian harnessed the emotions. He breathed them in until his entire being thrummed with power. That very power cascaded through him now as he spoke.

"Take it," he growled.

Morven's body tensed, as if startled by the words. "Is all well without?"

"Aye. Now take the bloody thing."

Almost hesitantly, Morven reached for the golden hilt. When his hand clasped around it, his eyes fell shut. "When I was a boy, my father told me this sword was a gift from the Giants of the Northland for his bravery in battle."

" 'Tis only gold and steel."

Morven seemed not to hear him as he continued. "Then later, when the time for boyish fantasies passed, and I knew it had been a gift from the King, a human king, but king nonetheless, I loved him even more."

"Aye. And he betrayed ye. Denied ye."

Morven examined the blade carefully and then turned in his saddle to face Ian. "He loved Devlin more."

" 'Tis not true, my son." Lady Ravenstone gasped. Ian spun sharply at the plaintive voice.

" 'Tis true," Ian called toward her, approaching her with long, predatory strides. The heels of his boots echoed in the stone chamber like the bells of hell.

Ian watched the color drain from her face as she eyed the blade of his sword. Still covered with blood, it hung easily from his grip. He squeezed the hilt and raised it toward her face, twisting it so the light from the doorway reflected off the still-wet, life's blood of one of her own.

"Morven?" She whimpered.

"Enough, Ian."

4

Morven turned his anxious horse and approached them. His voice sounded tired. Good.

"We have what we came for. Gather the men."

"Why, Morven? Why have you hated us these many years?"

Ian grimaced at the weakness in the old woman's voice.

Finally, Ian witnessed the hate and anger he had spent years breeding inside Morven bubble to the surface. Morven's face twisted as he held the jeweled sword before his stepmother. " 'Tis what bastards do, Mother. The day ye and my father tossed me aside was the day I vowed to hate ye forever."

"We never 'tossed you aside,' my son. You chose to leave, after . . ."

"After I was named a bastard instead of heir." Morven laughed, the sound hollow and without humor. "Aye, I left. And even the welcome I received by my true mother's people little quelled my fury."

Morven's mount stomped on the stone floor. A small shower of sparks shot out from the shod hoofs. "Once I married Elspeth, I believed 'twas enough to be accepted by the Douglas. But 'twas no'. The past still haunts me."

Once more, Ian hid a smile. He had never allowed Morven to forget the betrayal by his family. He fed the weeds of hate daily, as together they trained the men, making them as fierce as possible.

For this day.

For the day when their loyalty to Morven would give Ian the power he needed for this raid.

Morven, looking as if, were he pricked, regret would pour from him instead of blood, stiffened his spine and stopped the animal's nervous pacing. "I came for what

5

should have been mine. 'Twas no' given to me, so I take it. Devlin can have the manor, but I will take this sword."

He placed the prize in a bag hanging from his saddle and urged his mount forward. Once his head cleared the framework, he and his horse leapt as one from the doorway, over the stone steps and into the bailey.

Lady Ravenstone turned to follow. Ian grasped her shoulder, forcing her to face him. A shiver of pleasure raced through him at the fear reflected in her tearful eyes. He longed to take her life, but refrained. He remained focused instead on his final goal. Killing Morven would have to be enough. He pushed her small frame out of his way and hurried to his own mount.

A cry from Morven's twisted lips told the clansmen the task was done and to make for the portcullis. Ian knew most of his clansmen had already fled, as he'd instructed them even before leaving Scotland. Those who remained fled the minute they heard their laird's cry of retreat.

Leaping into his saddle, Ian followed Morven out of the bailey. He laughed when one of the women behind him raised a hue and cry. The bulk of the Douglas's forces were well out of sight already. Ian and Morven rode side by side, their horses lathered and breathless from their exertion. Ian glanced back, the castle nearly a mile behind them now, and then shifted his narrowed eyes to his laird. Without warning, he lifted his sword and swung it down upon Morven's right shoulder.

Morven reacted instantly, blocking the blow with his own sword. Taken off guard, he was unhorsed after only a few, quick thrusts. Morven's arm bled where Ian's sword had found a gap in his armor. Ian absorbed the fear in his laird's expression as Morven scrambled backward, trying to avoid the next blow.

Ian made a move to dismount, then cursed. Shouts of alarm reached him through the early leaves on the trees. Several men, torn from their spring planting, had answered the hue and cry. He made them out through the branches, their faces set in determined lines. One or two opponents he could best, but there were too many. He cursed. He would be unable to finish what he had set out to do. Taking Morven's horse by the reins, he plunged into the forest.

At least he had the jeweled sword.

✝ ✝ ✝

"Yer father's been captured!" Ian stormed into the solar, jerking Meghan's attention from the tapestry she'd been nervously stitching as she waited for her father to return.

"What?" She could feel the blood drain from her face just as the tapestry fell from her trembling fingertips to land silently at her feet. Mattie, her maid and closest friend, rushed to her side, placing her hand reassuringly on Meghan's arm.

"Ravenstone's men took him," Ian answered simply, as if that explained everything.

"And ye left him there?" The accusation was plain in her voice as her blue eyes narrowed toward her father's second-in-command.

"What would ye have me do, storm the keep alone? The others had fled. Nay, I'll no' take that risk when I promised yer Da I'd watch over ye."

The lustful gleam in his eyes made her shiver in disgust. Thank God, Mattie stood with her. She refused to think what might happen if she were ever alone in a room with Ian.

7

"I'll never marry ye, Ian." She stood and met his hollow glare through sheer force of will, her heart racing in anticipation of his reaction. This topic of conversation never went well. "My father has no' decreed it, and as long as he is laird here, he will no'."

The furious outburst she had been expecting never came. Instead, Ian turned his massive back to her and moved with deliberate strides to the door. Without turning, he replied, "Yer father is no' here."

The door shut behind him, and Meghan felt her knees wobbling before Mattie lowered her back into her chair by the fire. "Dear God, he's right."

" 'Tis only a matter of time before Ian declares himself Laird of Clan Douglas." Mattie's voice, filled with fear, stated exactly what Meghan had been thinking. Ian and her grandfather were cousins, after all, and he was next in line.

Meghan patted Mattie's hand. She didn't know what she would do without Mattie for her friend. She relied on her for so much more than the services of a maid.

Mattie continued, "And he grows more forceful in his pursuit of ye, as well."

Meghan closed her eyes against the truth.

"He fails to understand ye do no' want him. Ye'd think after so many years, he'd learn it well."

"Aye," Meghan replied, pushing Ian's insinuations from her mind. "But I'm more concerned for Da. He's changed over the years since Mother died."

" 'Tis Ian's doing, milady."

Meghan stood and walked to the hearth, letting the heat from the fire warm her chilled bones.

"And now Da is held prisoner by that vile man."

"The Lord Ravenstone is that, milady. A monster from

8

all I've heard."

Meghan released a quiet snort. "Ian is a monster. His hatred of my father's family is borne from a hatred of anything English." She paced away from the hearth to the window overlooking the tiltyard. "I'm no' naïve. I ken terrible things happen on both sides of the border. But for so long, Mattie, we'd lived in peace. Before Mother died." She wanted to stamp her foot. "I wish Ian had never convinced Da to go after that horrid sword."

Mattie approached her, wrapping her arms around her in a comforting embrace. "Do ye suppose we can get yer father back? Before 'tis too late?"

She shuddered at her next thought. 'Twas only a matter of time before Ian achieved his goal and became laird. He would try to rule her as well.

Worse, her father's unreasonable pride and Ian's unquenchable greed had placed them all in danger. From what she knew of her uncle, the Lord of Ravenstone, he would not take the news of this raid easily.

" 'Tis more than likely already too late, Mattie. If the stories we've heard of Lord Ravenstone hold even a feather's weight of truth, he already plans his revenge."

Meghan closed her eyes. Her father was held captive. Her life and the lives of her people were in peril. Ian's intentions for her were more than clear. It had been a very long time since Meghan had cried, and she hated the acidic bitterness rising in her throat.

† † †

"We were wont to put the man in the dungeon, but your Lady Mother insisted we keep him locked in his chamber, my lord, ever since the day of the attack. I am afraid his band escaped with your father's sword and scabbard." Oswald, the bailiff of Ravenstone Castle, followed Devlin through the feasting hall.

"I don't think he's listening, Oswald."

Will was wrong. Devlin had heard everything. He'd heard everything since he'd returned home, less than an hour before, to learn of Morven's raid. He heard the cries of his people as they mourned the dead. He heard the accusations in their voices when they greeted him upon his return. And he heard the guilt beating in the hollow of his chest.

Clenching his fists, which ached to destroy, he made his way toward the stone steps rising along the far wall. Morven reclined in one of the rooms above.

Fat as he pleases.

Devlin felt his face twist in disgust as he mounted the first step.

"Whoa, there." Will put a hand on Devlin's shoulder, with just enough force to spin him on the step.

Devlin did not speak. Instead, he looked at his cousin's hand, then raised his eyes to glare directly at Will's face. Only two years Devlin's junior, Will was nearly his twin in all aspects save one.

Temper.

"I don't think it wise for you to see Morven as yet. Take a few moments and put the events in perspective."

Devlin descended the step, placed his feet well apart, and folded his arms over his chest. "Three of my people lay dead."

And my family's greatest treasure has been stolen. As much as that bothered him, 'twas just a sword. Killing his people took matters too far.

10

"And what do you intend to do about it?"

Devlin's expression did not change. Will's comment, designed to make him think before he reacted, was well timed. Ever the cautious one, whether it be his emotions, battle, or selecting the right field to plant, Will acted now as Devlin's conscience.

"I'm going to kill Morven," Devlin responded plainly, shrugging.

"And this will solve what? You would enter into a border war over this?"

"Aye." He nodded, turning on the landing and mounting the steps again. The rage sweeping through him racked him to his core.

"And the sword?" Will's voice lowered at the mention of Devlin's father's prize.

"Make no mistake, Will. I will get it back."

Will sighed. "Well then. I suppose I'll have to go with you. You'll just get yourself killed if I don't."

When Devlin reached the door of his traitorous brother's chamber, Will only a step behind, he turned the key in the lock.

"Easy, Cousin. You don't really want to kill him."

"Aye, I do."

But heeding Will's advice, he took several deep breaths and ran his fingers through his hair before pushing the heavy wood away from him. "You wait out here."

He ignored Will's heavy sigh.

"Brother?" The deep voice came from the farthest corner of the room. Devlin turned to the sound and found Morven sitting in a cushioned chair before a well-tended fire.

Devlin did not answer, except to close the door behind

him and stride across the room, his temper barely checked. Morven shifted in his seat to follow Devlin's movements. Pity he hadn't been killed during the madness instead of suffering what had amounted to a mere scratch when compared with the deaths of his people, according to Oswald.

"What have ye to say, Devlin? Nothing? That's no' like ye. I would think ye would be railing by now."

"You have made a grave mistake, Morven, harming these people. They have naught to do with our quarrel. These people have done nothing to you."

"Ye mean yer people!" Morven rose to his feet, raising one trembling hand to point at Devlin. "Say what ye mean without honey for my sake. They should be my people. Instead I choked on lies fed to me with a golden spoon and was cast aside like a hunting hound, too weak for the chase!"

" 'Cast aside?' You chose to return to your mother's people. At no time were you ever promised the title or the lands. You assumed too much. But Father never treated you like a bastard, and Mother treated you like her own despite her knowledge otherwise. Did you think the decision easy for her? Taking in her husband's by-blow? Yet you were always welcome here, and you knew that. Nay, you chose to stay away for nothing more substantial than wounded pride. And then you do this. Father barely in the ground, and you make war? A coward's war at that. 'Tis obvious I should have expected no less from you."

Morven's face contorted with rage, and he crossed the room in two long strides, throwing himself at Devlin's head. Morven swung his uninjured arm furiously, landing a powerful blow against Devlin's jaw.

Devlin reacted instantly, his movements honed by

12

years on the battlefield, and knocked Morven to the floor with one neatly placed fist in his stomach. His blood boiled in his veins, and he dived onto Morven. He released his fury on his brother for another full minute before he heard a scream from the doorway, and several pairs of hands pulled him free.

"Now see, Cousin. I told you not to come up here. I told you to wait, but do you heed my word? Nay." Will stepped in front of Devlin, his equal height and weight making an effective shield for Morven.

Devlin's temper ached for release. His eyes darted from Will to Morven, standing offensively behind one of the guards, to his mother, who he hadn't realized stood in the doorway.

Lowering his head for a moment, he steadied himself with a deep breath. When he spoke, the unquestionable authority of his title filled the chamber. "This man is not my brother and deserves no quarter from anyone here. Take him to the dungeon." Leveling a glare toward Will, he silently dared him to argue. Will didn't. The release of a heavy sigh spoke well enough to indicate Will's disagreement. "And prepare a garrison to ride. We leave at dawn for Scotland."

ISBN#1932815066
US $6.99 / CDN $9.99
Jewel Imprint: Sapphire
Historical
Available Now